For my father and mother

God For A Day

The Further Adventures of Adam & Eve

NEIL COLE

INGLEWOOD PRESS

Toronto

INGLEWOOD PRESS
www.inglewoodpress.ca

Unfinished Business

If at First You Don't Succeed

❧ "HOWEVER PROBLEMATICAL for all concerned," God sighed, "I'm beginning to suspect I may just be getting a little too old for this line of work."

"Holy shit!" This certainly was not the judicious reply expected from a senior archangel, but it came (albeit *sotto voce*) as an understandably stunned response to a divine revelation unlike any other.

As this sudden spiritual thunderbolt sizzled across Heaven, angels of every size, shape and technical specialty braked in mid-flight, haloes spinning wildly. God gazed at them all sadly.

"Be honest. Do I really look as tired, bored and frustrated as I feel?"

For the Archangel of All Archangels, best and literally brightest of a host of celestial advisors, it was rapidly becoming the most unsettling moment of a uniquely challenging career.

While Heaven's chief operating officer might have a multitude of sterling qualifications for the job, the greatest was his ability to discern God's ever-changing presence as revealed in the ceaseless mirror of Creation. Nevertheless, there were still moments when even he was left speechless by the Boss's uncanny knack of asking the most disturbingly unexpected questions. Undoubtedly it had something to do with God being not only omnipotent, omniscient and omnipresent, but also, of course, having an unparalleled advantage as the original and seemingly permanent occupant of the archetypal executive suite.

Glancing carefully around, the senior angel nodded warily.

"And in your well-considered professional opinion...." There was a thoughtful pause, held just long enough to set even the most seasoned seraphim on edge. "How's My one and only universe making out?"

Chaotic though the cosmos might often seem, the Archangel-in-Chief reflected, it remained for him the most fascinating imaginable, if also the most demanding.

For starters, it was difficult to get the attention of all those residents of the now countless galaxies. They went merrily about their lives, their current mood reflecting a mixture of local weather conditions, the daily horoscope, ready cash and their own fluctuating levels of insight. Given the universe's size, creatures on billions of planets had little or no communication with their closest neighbouring constellations.

Occasionally, they would stare upward to the enticing infinity of far-off glittering stars, taking a moment or two to wonder how everyone else in the universe might live; and how they passed their own fast-disappearing days, and where they spent their summer vacations, and what they might possibly know of such timeless conundrums as life, love and the meaning of everything.

Most days, however, the majority of cosmic residents were content to struggle, as best they could, with pressing everyday problems in their own small self-preoccupied corners of Time and Space. Heaven (if and when most thought about it at all) was widely believed to exist somewhere 'out there'.

In God's understandably biased opinion, however, the celestial realm was both inward gift and outward goal. For those with eyes to see beyond the seen, Heaven was always and everywhere at hand – journey and destination paradoxically one. Enjoyed in the afterlife, to be sure, but just as secretly present in every atom and encounter of this one. In the words of one ancient, still admirably epicurean sage, "Why wait for eternity when you can enjoy it fresh today!"

Regrettably, however, this limitless, luminous achievement – the capacity to live simultaneously in Heaven and Earth, to find Heaven within oneself – proved throughout the cosmos to be a frustratingly slow and problematic work-in-progress.

Accordingly (and as an interim measure only) an all-purpose, three-dimensional prototype of Heaven had been constructed specially in a strategically undisclosed location at the exact centre of the universe. Complete with the requisite shimmering towers, incomparable celestial vistas and delightfully numinous staff, this 'still point of the turning cosmos' served as both a tangible incentive to those who preferred their ultimate spiritual destination be concrete, and also the much-needed administrative headquarters for an ever-evolving cosmic enterprise with a correspondingly huge workload.

If God needed to build a new prototype for Heaven, another new prototype at the opposite end of the continuum was also needed. As the universe expanded, the range of intergalactic misdemeanours grew steadily greater, and their perpetrators all the more numerous and cunning. It had become clear to the hot-tempered, twin-horned beings (who just happened to be the angels' karmic cousins) that, as a matter of satanic necessity and professional pride, the introduction of entirely new, technologically advanced techniques of temptation and retribution was long overdue.

It was not very surprising, therefore, that at their most recent general meeting, the august and totally scary members of the Intergalactic Senior Devils' Association (their motto – Speak softly, but carry a really big pitchfork) should unanimously have chosen an impressively debonair rogue by the name of Big D to lead them. His deceptive powers refined on a series of progressively more disorderly planets, he was someone clearly destined for greater things. With him in charge, his associates agreed, a turn for the worse could only be for the better.

Lost in contemplation of his ancient twin brother's very different temperament and talents, the Archangel of All Archangels suppressed a fleeting, almost envious smile. Angels should never be underestimated, especially the supposedly fallen ones.

᪲

"Perhaps I might rephrase My question." The tone was now even more Olympian and insistent. "On a scale of one to ten, how is the universe really doing?"

Heaven's second-in-command resurfaced hastily from his reverie. "Six," he admitted reluctantly. "Six-and-a-half on a good day."

If he heard correctly, the first 'Harrumph!' in celestial history came instantly in reply. Obviously Someone had gotten up on the wrong side of infinity this morning. The next query followed swiftly.

"We've come a long way together since that first little archetypal diaspora called the Big Bang. Remind Me again: how many galaxies are your staff looking after? At last count?"

There was no need to consult the Celestial Monitoring Centre for its latest, up-to-the-nanosecond summary of cosmic complexity. "A hundred and one billion," came the quick, proud reply. "More or less." However unimaginable a figure, it seemed as nothing when compared to the sum total of subsidiary stars and planets requiring constant adult supervision.

"And how many seers, saints and sages have I so generously made available, over how many millions of millennia, to all those gazillions of consistently inattentive worlds?"

Perfect memory notwithstanding, the Archangel of All Archangels knew when no reply was needed. Or sought.

Again the brief pause was all too short.

"More importantly right now, how many of My cosmic offspring secretly suspect that – given half a chance – they themselves could probably do a much better job of running what several of your more irreverent subordinates persist in calling 'The Whole Sacred Shebang'?"

If the Archangel-in-Chief had wisely declined to answer the first question, he certainly wasn't about to touch the second.

Chin resting pensively on an equally invisible fist, God carefully weighed the universe's accomplishments to date against the far greater promise of its sadly still unrealized future. And sighed. Given the current cosmic stasis quo, it was clearly time to shake up the joint. But how?

Suspending the laws of gravity – without warning – would most definitely get everyone's attention alright. Dramatic, certainly; counter-productive, no question.

In a flash, God simultaneously surveyed every nook and secret cranny of the cosmos. And came to a sudden halt.

As angels of every rank and responsibility glanced at one another apprehensively, some senior staff found themselves wondering whether their literally peerless leader might finally be showing the effects of so many aeons in office.

However unthinkable, was it possible that God was edging just the tiniest bit past an invisible Heavenly best-by date? Or, more heretically still, becoming an anachronism now ready for the celestial equivalent of rocker, cardigan and fleece-lined slippers? If so, it shouldn't be totally surprising. After all, the still largely secret source of everything (including themselves) had been at it, under countless names and in myriad guises, for far longer than probably even God could remember.

Just when the Archangel-in-Chief was debating whether to start polishing his resumé, a boundless, exultant laughter flowed throughout Heaven, sending even the heaviest of angels bobbing up and down in its wake. A moment later, a divine *joie de vivre* miraculously, if mysteriously, restored, the universe's greatest magician began whispering softly.

Heaven's second-in-command blinked. Then blinked again, as he saw what had taken God's attention.

In the dining room of a luxurious, little-known retirement home in an unpublicized constellation of the Milky Way, an aging, still impressive couple called Adam and Eve glanced at the well-worn menu.

"How long has it been," the hauntingly lovely woman asked softly, "since we've done anything even remotely exciting?" Her equally striking escort, his nearly full head of hair greying suavely at the temples, gazed thoughtfully at the other couples ringing the room, like them passing listless hours in their own repetitive conversations. Reaching out, he placed his hand over hers. "If you ask me, I've always thought it's such a waste of truly original talents!"

෪

Though he had last seen their faces a very long time ago, the Archangel of All Archangels had no difficulty in recalling two memorably independent subcontractors; an unusually promising couple who, almost without warning, had suddenly, recklessly upped stakes and left, turning their backs on what everyone agreed had been a perfectly good garden. Not to mention condemning quite a few of his already busy staff to long hours of frustration-filled overtime ever since.

The Archangel-in-Chief sighed. Undeniably charming though Earth's primal pair of *persona non grata* may have been, they undoubtedly still remained no less wholly unpredictable.

"OK. If You say so." He took a deep breath. "But may I ask one small question?"

"As big as you'd like."

"With so many galaxies to choose from, why them?"

The near-invisible grin grew all the greater. "Because if that obstinate little blue-and-white ball of perennial conflict, confusion and roller-coaster credit ratings can finally get it right … anybody can!"

Seconds later, rejoicing in the pleasure of an existential purpose now magically renewed, God coalesced into that radiant whirling sphere of light which was both a favourite form of celestial self-expression and also the most intergalactically recognizable.

"All things considered," Heaven's pre-eminent host declared, "it's time for … Plan B!"

This announcement, the Archangel-in-Chief was doubly delighted to see, was instantly followed by the most enigmatic smile in an already illustriously eventful career.

The two luminous figures stared solemnly at one another, eye to transcendent eye. Then, crossing their fingers at the exact same moment, they both began to grin. Heaven was back in business!

Under the circumstances, God couldn't resist. "It's … show-time!!"

The Archangel-in-Chief chuckled affectionately. "A perfectly accurate description, I agree; but, if You'll pardon me saying so, isn't that already something of an intergalactic cliché?"

"Not on the scale I've got in mind!"

Make Me an Offer

🕊 SCHEHERAZADE AWOKE from her dream to the sight of a small white-and-gold bird hovering purposefully by her bedroom window. The early edition of the Milky Way Daily Herald lay open on the bedside table, a glass of water resting on her horoscope for the week: "Today is the perfect day to begin something truly extraordinary."

"A very good morning to you," the feathered new arrival announced, bobbing its head gallantly in greeting. "My apologies for interrupting you, but I was wondering if I might have a word? Regarding a somewhat delicate matter of – how shall I say – unfinished planetary business?"

Scheherazade's serene green eyes widened in surprise, then in characterstically gracious welcome. "By all means. After all, it's not every day...."

"That the saying 'a little bird told me' might turn out to be more than just a picturesque figure of speech," the cheerful little ambassador agreed. Waiting, eyes courteously averted until Scheherazade had put on a handy pale silk gown, the bird hopped across the bed to lean comfortably against her pillow, cocking its head and studying her carefully.

How heartening it was, the tiny messenger thought, to have one's deepest instincts so satisfyingly confirmed.

The poised, lithe, effortlessly entrancing woman now seated before it was everything exhaustive research had reported her to be: an arrestingly talented transgalactic trouble-shooter, an adventuress *extraordinaire* of legendary diplomacy and daring combined. Some women are born to individual greatness, some, adept at bringing out the best in those they meet. A rare few are unerringly capable of both.

The most beautiful secret agent in the universe, (her time-tested motto – An open mind, a watchful and discerning heart) returned her unlikely guest's gaze with a curiosity as much personal as professional, already receptive to anything the bird might propose.

"Any pressing engagements for the next month or two?" the little bird asked offhandedly, better aware of her pending schedule than she was.

The challenges of a heroine-for-hire had lately been both frustratingly repetitive and seasonally slow. Whatever this new assignment might be, it couldn't have come at a better moment. "Make me an offer – impossibly demanding yet even more tempting," Scheherazade answered, the words echoing her visitor's own private thoughts. "The one invitation I can't possibly refuse."

"My very great pleasure." A small throat cleared softly, a tiny eyelid raised in anticipation. "Care to assist a certain over-confident, under-achieving and potentially self-destructive little planet by the name of Earth rediscover its way to Paradise?"

Scheherazade blinked. Then blinked again.

&

Well-travelled and just as well-read, Scheherazade was certainly familiar with melancholy tales of magnificent, long-lost gardens at the beginning of Time, even if, to be honest, she had yet to encounter even the smallest fragment of their ruins in her far-flung journeys.

"Paradise!" she repeated softly, suddenly finding herself falling once more under a vanished Eden's lingering spell. "That fabled long-gone, long-sought home of perfect harmony, grace and love, where all remains fully and forever well…."

"The very same," the small bird confirmed quietly.

Scheherazade sought to recall scattered news reports on that increasingly crowded little blue-and-white sphere which had been but an infrequent stop-over in her travels. The lingering image of an abandoned oasis of infinite delights continued to exert its own nostalgic appeal; a chimerical idyll still able to evoke a bittersweet yearning for a bygone yet better world.

Not that such fitful longings seemed to have made any difference in the way Earth's inhabitants currently went about managing their own problematic affairs; or facing up to the many dangers they much preferred to evade or avoid.

"Based on my very brief visits, I would guess that Earth still remains a long way from Paradise."

"So I'm given to understand." Small eyes glistened watchfully. "A very long way, indeed."

As Scheherazade mused on all the reverberations of ancient choice, of roads not only not taken but now lost, her visitor hopped over to sip unconcernedly from the glass of water beside her bed, quite content to wait.

"According to certain ancient yet usually reliable sources," she began at last, "it's whispered that after Adam and Eve turned their backs on that first fully-furnished, rent-free residence, an all-knowing Providence deftly moved Paradise into the future." Her voice grew even softer, more reflective.

"Where, supposedly, it still waits in secret, until their descendants are not only ready but also finally worthy of it once again."

"I recollect hearing the same story," the little white-and-gold bird nodded affably. "Rather touching and possibly true, I suppose," it paused, "although no one seems to know quite where such an ultimate reward might be found, or even what it may look like."

"Which means…."

"All the more fun for you, I suspect," the tiny envoy observed, a mischievous twinkle arising in its far-seeing eyes.

Scheherazade felt a sudden, sharp surge of exhilaration.

On the one hand, so completely unexpected a request – to help an outwardly ordinary and (on the evidence) not especially talented or reliable little planet find its way to braver tomorrows – was definitely not a challenge to be taken on lightly. On the other, the prospect of an open-ended search for a second Eden – mysterious, timeless, it's whereabouts completely undefined – promised to be her greatest adventure so far.

Moments passed as she contemplated her little visitor with even greater curiosity, and a growing sense of professional admiration. It was, she had to admit, the most perfectly timed, perfectly suited and even more perfectly irresistible invitation.

⸙

Despite never having negotiated with a bird before, Scheherazade found the interplay surprisingly smooth.

"No limits?"

"None whatsoever."

"Go anywhere, consult with anyone?"

"Absolutely – Past, Present or Future." There was a delicate pause.

"Especially the last." The bird continued, "Heaven only knows how helpful that might prove to be!"

For some reason, Scheherazade suddenly had a very good idea that the enigmatic ambassador already had an even better one of how things might eventually turn out.

"Enlist the services of all and sundry?"

"Definitely. Take your pick of allies old and new. And, of course, make the most of a boundless budget."

Given past encounters with unconventional, secretive transgalactic philanthropists, Scheherazade couldn't help but wonder as to the identity of her new patron.

Reading her thoughts, her small guest shook its head. "For now at least, I'm afraid that information must be considered classified."

"Wouldn't be the first time I've begun without knowing the ending." After all, the most entertaining puzzles often came with their best parts missing. There was a cautious pause. "If you don't mind my asking, Earth's uncharacteristic gratitude aside, what's in it for me?"

The little bird cocked its head, studying her with the oldest, wisest eyes in the universe. "What, or who?" it replied calmly, gaze fixed on a woman so evidently destined not only for greatness but also supreme delight. A worthy match – and an equally hypnotic challenge.

Blushing without knowing why, Scheherazade found she no longer had a choice. Nor did she want one. With a deep breath, she leapt into the unknown, and said, "Yes!"

As so often in life, it was the only word needed.

"Wonderful!"

The little white-and-gold bird dipped its head in salute, then hopped up to the open window, preparing to return to its mysterious home. It paused, one wing raised in appreciation and farewell.

"If I may suggest, a good place to start might be: whatever became of Adam and Eve?"

Have Cloud, Will Travel

❧ AS A COSMIC HEROINE, Scheherazade long ago discovered, being open to the universe was both professional duty and personal delight. Much of her success as a spy for the divine, a secret agent for the mysterious and mystical, came from an instinctive largeness of heart and mind, a natural spaciousness of soul.

It also helped to have truly supernatural friends. In particular, in this case, a certain wise old gentleman celebrated not only for his deft touch with a magic wand but also for his eco-friendly transgalactic transportation.

To those who knew him, Abracadabra was an unduly modest wizard. While lesser sorcerers might show up on scene in a flash of ostentatious lightning and an exaggerated flourish of overly loud thunder, he was more than happy to drift in unannounced on his own little white cloud, steering it apparently absent-mindedly with one hand.

His timing, however, was always impeccable, his abiding curiosity unsurpassed.

"Something of a minor challenge, I gather," the old wizard ventured, favourite elixir in hand, an ancient, undiminished sparkle in his eyes. A moment later, he raised his trademark magic wand, darkening the surrounding sky and bringing the small, far-off blue-and-white enigma into sharp and sudden focus.

As the two watched in silence, the unsuspecting little planet spun on its axis, its multitudes hurrying onwards, time zone after crowded time zone, in their separate, all-important lives; each one chasing his or her own all-too-transitory thoughts, each one dreaming dreams of possibilities too soon forgotten as the sun rose and set and they yawned and sighed and fell asleep.

On and on, round and round, from snowscapes to tropics, tidal pools to desert sands, hovels to high-rises, and beyond....

Under the sun, the moon and the stars, Scheherazade wondered, what was that small planet ultimately seeking? What did it fear? What did it secretly hope might one day come to pass?

The old wizard's voice interrupted her reverie. "If it took immense courage to leave that first Paradise, how much more will it take to find and inhabit the second?"

Nodding pensively, Abracadabra tucked his magic wand back into his robe, carefully propping his feet on the edge of the little white cloud as if wishing to sleep on so weighty a matter. A moment later, he abruptly opened one eye.

"Early days yet, but I'm beginning to get a certain strangely exalted premonition about this particular adventure."

Scheherazade raised an affectionate eyebrow, returning her old friend's gaze. "I suppose I could ask what you already know that I don't?"

"You could." The master of everything from alchemy to algorithms smiled. "But I suspect the real question is: what might Adam and Eve still secretly know, that Earth seems largely to have forgotten?"

Sunset Villas

"THE FOUNTAIN of Eternal Youth Retirement Home! Who knew!" Abracadabra deftly spun the small steering wheel as yet another asteroid in too much of a hurry went whizzing by. The little white cloud soared onward, star after star nudging one another as it passed. Farther off, distant galaxies glowed restlessly in the darkness.

"Be assured, this humble little interstellar seniors' haven – long and justly famous for its distinguished clientele – is a treasured secret among discerning oracles. You'll enjoy Adam and Eve," he continued. "Hundreds of thousands of years old – and yet, despite the inevitable wear and tear, they're still the perfect couple!"

Scheherazade tried hard to picture those final, irrevocable moments in Eden: a young man and woman, naked, ashamed, trembling on the threshold of a fiery gateway guarded by silent, sorrowing angels. Adam, Eve, a wily tempter and a fateful apple *extraordinaire*.

That, at least, was the authorized version.

At the news of Scheherazade and Abracadabra's arrival, Earth's first couple had quickly excused themselves from the afternoon's enter-tainment of long-familiar sports reruns. Tea was arranged at a private table, flowering gardens sheltering the four of them from the curious gaze of other timeless couples.

"May we offer you anything? Tea? Cake? Some fruit, perhaps?" Adam asked, bemused curiosity in his dark and watchful eyes.

It was, in truth, exceptionally rare that the residents of this unique getaway – specially designed for original founding pairs from planets across the Milky Way and beyond – enjoyed the bittersweet pleasure of unexpected guests. In almost every case their children's children seemed completely unaware of their ancestors' continuing existence, let alone willing to make an effort to visit on birthdays, holidays or anniversaries.

It was a situation all the more regrettable, Scheherazade decided, as Earth's most notorious, and yet least known woman quickly proved everything the old wizard had foretold. And more. Astutely tender, as she'd guessed. Quietly tough, as she'd hoped. And, most enjoyable of all, tantalizingly open and unconstrained.

As Abracadabra watched with ancient satisfaction, the two women took to one another instantly, recognizing across the ages an instinctive kinship of large powers and larger hearts.

For his part, Adam, his eyes twinkling approvingly, still seemed the same affable, even-tempered yet indomitable gentleman the old magician had met very briefly long, long ago; a good friend to have by your side in a dark alley, or an even darker time.

"Not much has changed over the millennia," said Eve, catching Abracadabra's gaze and pretending to study her consort intently. "As you can see, he's as gallant and handsome as ever."

"And she's still as beautiful and beguiling as on that very first day we met," her one true love responded just as proudly.

Fresh though their new acquaintance might be, Scheherazade quickly found herself asking – woman to woman – the one question increasingly in her thoughts ever since a certain little white-and-gold visitor had flown through her welcoming window.

"What was Paradise really like?"

The eyes of Earth's first, oldest and still most alluring adventuress came alive, dancing with light and shadow.

"Strange to say, not quite all it's later been cracked up to be. Incredibly lovely at first; and then, all too quickly, disappointingly repetitive! Day after sunlit day, we awoke to the same scenes: wondrous vistas of jungles, rivers and plains, birds and animals playing endless games together, exquisite food that appeared on time from nowhere, hidden groves with piped-in music, charming little cottages that appeared at dusk wherever we happened to be, dark chocolates on the pillow, towels and linen changed daily, mesmerizing sunsets – all you could ask for, really.

"We were – as you may have heard – totally, blissfully drawn to each other. Perfectly suited, in fact. It wasn't so much a matter of making love as often as possible (although of course we did) as it was discovering every moment together interwoven in a kind of seamless intimacy. Nothing was hidden. Nothing needed to be."

Not unnoticed by her host and hostess, Scheherazade suppressed the quietest of sighs.

"But…." Adam paused.

Eve continued: "The trouble was that, after a while, we found we had nothing to talk about. Absolutely nothing. Everything came and went in its own perfect rhythm in its own perfect way. Day in, day out.

"In theory, it was supposed to be idyllic: gazing adoringly, moment by endlessly blissful moment, into one another's equally unrivalled eyes." Eve paused, frowned. "Ultimately, however, it turned out to be always and forever about us. And only us. Adam and Eve, Eve and Adam – and nobody, absolutely nobody else. Nothing to get dressed up for and go out to; no other people or places to come home from, gratefully or not; no others to share with; and nothing more to strive for."

"All passion," Adam declared in summary. "No pillow talk."

"So, to what do we owe the honour of your visit?" Eve asked after almost too long, carefully pouring more tea while Adam studied their guests over the rim of his cup. The arrival of two very unexpected guests had awakened hundreds of thousands of years of silent yearning.

Scheherazade stared upwards into the clear azure afternoon sky, instinctively seeking that unseen, far-off point in space where a wayward little blue-and-white globe revolved all unawares.

"And so, that's the assignment," Scheherazade concluded as Adam and Eve listened intently, hand in well-worn, well-known hand. "To help the citizens of your first and former home find their way to an all new and improved Paradise."

There was a long silence. "I hate to be what you might call a spiritual spoilsport," Eve said finally, "but I rather doubt you'll find it easy."

"Knowing our descendants," Adam added laconically.

From their expressions, it was obvious that while Earth might be unaware of its original inhabitants' continuing existence, the latter were clearly familiar with the little blue-and-white planet's subsequent achievements, or lack thereof.

As Scheherazade and Abracadabra waited in silence, Earth's first couple studied the earliest, faint stars in the evening sky, sharing thoughts known only to themselves. At last, of one accord, they nodded quietly. More detailed explanations seemed necessary – especially given how far their visitors had come, and why.

"The truth is, it was our decision to leave Paradise," Eve cautiously began. "Ours alone. Later accounts notwithstanding, we actually were not fired. We quit!"

There was a brief, reflective pause. "Or, in the diplomatic wording of the subsequent celestial press release, 'left of their own accord to pursue other, more suitable opportunities elsewhere'. That was true enough. We had the greatest of good intentions," Eve affirmed. "In place of a cosy, pre-paid but wholly uneventful garden, we wanted to leave our descendants so much, much more – the boundless inheritance of an entire universe."

Eve's voice softened with the memory of those first confused steps beyond Eden, the two of them simultaneously exhilarated and lost in a primordially uncharted world. "Of course, we've often regretted that, somehow or other, we didn't find a way to stay on Earth forever, the better to help our offspring make sense of it all."

"Then again, we never wanted to interfere." Adam frowned. "After all, given that little – how shall I say – contractual misunderstanding at the outset, it seemed wiser, for our descendants' own sakes, if they were left to live their own lives in turn."

How unfortunate it was, Scheherazade reflected, that there had been no reassuringly helpful guide strategically pre-positioned at the exit from Paradise; someone suitably far-seeing to give Earth's pioneering couple all the timely info needed (plus, of course, a ready supply of cash) to help both them and their descendants on the interminable, ever-winding journey ahead.

As if reading her new friend's thoughts, Eve gestured toward other aging couples drifting toward the dining room, their sometimes stooped figures silhouetted against the setting sun, clearly a long way from their last memorable knees-up.

"I gather the dilemma's not just Earth's alone. Apparently more than a few planets, both in our galaxy and beyond, share much the same problem."

"Always tough to be caught between a hard rock and infinite space,"

Abracadabra murmured with the wry empathy of a truly senior sorcerer. "Growing up, even for the luckiest of star-systems, nearly always turns out to be far more difficult than it looks."

ʂ✦

Not wanting to impose any further, Abracadabra and Scheherazade declined an invitation to dinner. Preparing to say goodbye beside the little white cloud, Scheherazade hesitated, then voiced, as gently as she could, the still unconfirmed legend at the very heart of her quest.

"One version of the Fall has it that soon after you both left Eden, God removed it all – lock, stock and benefits – and placed it somewhere in the Future."

Earth's first couple exchanged quick glances.

"We've heard that rumour before," Adam said finally. "In fact, it seems to be repeated on other planets as well, both in the Milky Way and beyond." He paused, eyes on Eve's. "At least, that's the word from some of the other residents here; founding couples who, like us, chose to make a midnight dash from one celestially-designed five-star or another."

"Unfortunately, however, God hasn't been in touch directly ever since." Eve's expression changed, suddenly more than a little wistful. "No doubt for reasons we can quite appreciate."

Oftentimes, Abracadabra mused quietly, there were advantages to a deity who had the longest memory in the universe. On other occasions, however....

"And so," Adam continued, staring up at a resolutely silent sky, "I'm sorry to say that, for now at least, we have no idea exactly where such a second Paradise might be found. Or what it might look like."

As Earth's first parents linked hands, seemingly resigned to rejoining their companion retirees over yet another predictable meal, Eve suddenly turned, the glint in her eyes like a flame leaping from the embers.

"That's not to say, of course, that we haven't wondered!"

Delighted to Meet You

❧ AS A VENERABLE SAGE long dedicated to the unpredictable and unknown, Abracadabra found it all the more satisfying that some things seemed never to change. In this case, both the shellfish and service at a little out-of-the-way seafood restaurant just two constellations over provided consolation for what seemed a largely unsuccessful trip.

Scheherazade raised the last of her wine, studying its crimson lustre in the flickering candlelight.

A part of the tale, at least, had now been told, but much more still remained unrevealed. Although Adam and Eve had been helpful, nary a word had been said about the third, most pivotally-fateful member of Eden's infernal triangle, let alone what that supposedly-irresistible gentleman might actually have done. Or undone. Or even where the devil might the Devil be now (other than up to no good, of course).

"To Adam and Eve," she said pensively.

Abracadabra clinked glasses. "Wondering what happens next?"

His dinner guest paused, thinking back to her first sight of Eve, welcoming, watchful, her quiet strength the more impressive for being so graceful and unforced.

"Yes." Scheherazade looked the ancient wizard in his simultaneously far-away, ever-present eye. "And I suspect she is too."

❧

Back at the helm of his little white cloud, Abracadabra suddenly began searching the many hidden pockets of his custom-tailored robe.

Retrieving a weathered almanac, he skimmed its pages before settling on a single highlighted entry.

"Mind if I follow a hunch? Especially since we've come so far."

Only moments later, the two went skidding between the most enormous mountains Scheherazade had ever seen, their violet peaks shimmering under seven small suns.

The old wizard chuckled. "Our next stop, sad to say, is guaranteed to be much less inspiring." He double-checked his battered almanac. "Then again, if we're lucky, there's a charmingly impressive couple, fatefully still unknown to one another, whom I suspect you will definitely need to meet!"

&

"This way! This way!" A thousand and one ferocious exhortations grew louder still. "Not that way. *This* way!" As the little white cloud touched down, the shrill cries seem to increase in volume: "For the sake of your immortal soul, and an even better night's sleep...."

"Welcome to the very latest in transgalactic spiritual trade shows," Abracadabra announced dryly. "Here you have the deafening display of chaos and incipient spiritual gridlock known as 'Gods R Us'!"

Small stands lined both sides of the many broad walkways, each staffed by excited figures of every origin and theological conviction.

"Beware of all false substitutes!" "Our way is the only way!" "Repent – and be saved!" "What's right for me is undeniably right for you." "Convert – or be damned!" "Submit – or be sacrificed!" "We know – you don't!"

Scheherazade shook her head (not that it helped). True believers, one and all, desperately defending themselves from their own inner doubts.

"It gets worse every year." Muttering darkly, Abracadabra gestured to the opposing rows of fiery-eyed prophets of this or that perfect solution, all of them trying their loudest to be heard above everyone else. "Everyone here is equally certain he or she alone grasps the ultimate cosmic truth."

He paused as two particularly strident spiritual snake-oil salesmen leaned out from their respective stalls, each doing his best to whack the other over the head with the nearest object of ill-designed, over-priced and proudly parochial veneration.

"While, in reality, every one of these increasingly dangerous relics only glimpses a narrow and all too transitory part of the whole. If that!" His frustrated analysis complete, the ancient wizard proceeded, with two satisfyingly ungentlemanly thumps of his magic wand, to reduce both evangelists to an infinitely more congenial silence.

Beneath the strident exhortations, Scherezade began to sense a deeper shared unease, both secretive and sad, a hidden yearning for something still far from fully understood. For every evolving star-system, it appeared, the story was not what it seemed. "However minor a planet Earth may be, it's clearly not the only one with problems."

"Eventually, they all get stuck," Abracadabra responded cheerfully, clearly feeling the better for his recent exercise. As he spoke, the old sorcerer discreetly rechecked both pocket watch and schedule.

"Right now, in fact, quite a few of them look like they could use a drink."

"Allow me," replied Scheherazade, suddenly quite thirsty herself and happy to take the hint.

&

Strange there doesn't seem to be anyone here from that congenitally opinionated little planet called Earth, Scheherazade thought to herself. Retrieving her order from the bartender, she glanced around the crowded café, which was doing a brisk business in favourite regional aperitifs from the farthest reaches of the Milky Way.

"Scotch, please," said a deep, unhurried voice behind her.

The tall, ruggedly dignified figure best known as the World's Greatest Gravedigger deftly shifted a gleaming silver shovel from one broad shoulder to the other, the better to reach for his glass with a suitably decisive hand.

"Single malt. No ice."

&

"Hi there, Gravedigger. Enjoying the show?" the old wizard asked, gesturing toward the surrounding unholy hullabaloo.

"If everyone in the Milky Way Galaxy remembered that his or her life story actually unfolds in an endless, unfinished graveyard…." Eternity's favourite undertaker inhaled the deep peaty undertones of his chosen

Highlands solace, took a long, restorative sip, then shrugged. "Then again, they ain't called burial *plots* for nothing!"

The deceptively soft-spoken guy now at Abracadabra's side had lent a firm but gentle final hand to high and low across more than a few centuries, cemeteries and solar systems. Affable by nature, solitary by profession, the World's Greatest Gravedigger was a disconcerting reminder, to all those seeking daily to forget, that the same ground which opens to reveal the flowers of each new spring, just as easily receives back every one and every thing on the last day of his or her own final winter.

Spinning his shining emblem of office in the air, he caught the shovel easily with the same calloused hand, surveying the loud, crowded scene once more.

"One thing's for sure. Given these ungodly goings-on here, everyone who now enjoys the larger vantage point of the grave is desperately hoping…."

A light, clear voice spoke swiftly beside him, effortlessly continuing the thought.

"That all these unconvincing true believers may some day, preferably very soon, come to see themselves and one another with infinitely wider, wiser eyes!"

The new arrival's finely-drawn, sensitive face and bright golden hair shone with ethereal light, her sky-blue summer dress flashing with a hundred stars. Under one slender arm she held a well-worn volume of astronomical calculations, and a small but boundless telescope.

"Hello to the World's Most Beautiful Astronomer," Abracadabra announced gallantly, pleased to find his earlier hunch as to the pending encounter of time, four people and fate so charmingly confirmed.

"I don't believe you've met my colleague, Scheherazade," he went on, introducing them both. "She's currently involved with a small but not unimportant interstellar research project," he added cryptically.

The two women smiled at the same moment, certain at first glance there was much to appreciate in the other.

"I don't know whether you've already met this equally distinguished gentleman," the old sorcerer continued off-handily, turning to the silent figure on his left. "Like you, an eminent yet under-appreciated outlier of a perennially distracted little blue-and-white world."

The far-seeing eyes of the buried past met the equally prophetic ones of the hidden future. The World's Greatest Gravedigger's shining silver spade trembled imperceptibly. For a brief moment, the World's Most Beautiful Astronomer's own smaller telescope made involuntary little reciprocal arcs of its own.

There was a delicate silence while Abracadabra enjoyed watching the stalwart champion of Earth's yesterdays and the graceful herald of its tomorrows enjoying watching each other, cautiously, carefully, and conclusively.

"You spoke of a new vision," Scheherazade said encouragingly.

The World's Most Beautiful Astronomer gazed skywards, as if seeking an answer from among the many encoded transmissions of light reaching them from far beyond and far ahead.

"Whatever the reason, there have lately been strange portents on a hundred horizons, persistent rumours from unexpectedly restless and unruly stars. Even now, observatories throughout the Milky Way are tracking spectacular new meteor showers, unprecedented in their beauty, size and speed."

Her voice dropped, its tone profoundly wistful. "Enigmatic overtures, perhaps, from far-flung worlds forever longing for us to see them for ourselves."

While this latest news, if accurate, would surely complicate her own assignment, secretly Scheherazade was not concerned. On the contrary, she'd been hoping for just such interstellar invitations for longer than she could remember.

"I would enjoy hearing more," she ventured quietly.

Even as she spoke, the two latest arrivals exchanged their own quick, more covert glances. The World's Greatest Gravedigger found himself thinking it might be a good idea if he too were to give his newly-met counterpart a call.

"Perhaps it might be helpful if we all swapped business cards," Abracadabra suggested. As even the most junior oracle learns in the first year of synchronicity training, it is always wise to reinforce initial success, no matter how promising.

Signs and Portents

❧ ONE OF THE MORE tangible rewards of being a much sought-after adventuress, Scheherazade found, was that she was able to afford an ever-changing variety of temporary second homes on a series of scenic, if frequently unsteady, planets.

In this instance, her new, charmingly secluded seaside *pied-à-terre* on Earth combined semi-tropical simplicity with the very latest in imported technological expertise. To her delight, these included unseen domestic powers which had already restocked her refrigerator, turned down her bed, made just the right drinks for both herself and her well-aged guest and, without a word, adjusted the clear blue swimming pool's temperature to perfection.

As she and Abracadabra relaxed on the deck, watching a resplendent sunset and considerably less radiant news broadcasts from all corners of planet Earth, it quickly became clear that little had changed. The mass of men and women, it seemed, continued to live lives of increasingly noisy exasperation.

His gaze turning away from the doleful reports, the old wizard sighed. It was never easy for individuals, let alone planets, to risk possibilities still unseen, to grasp the prospect of larger, far lovelier vistas to come.

"The residents of Earth seem to have considerable difficulty coping with reality in only three fairly simple dimensions," Abracadabra muttered to himself. "Makes one wonder what might happen if they suddenly found themselves having to compete in those far more intricate worlds of five, ten or even twenty-nine!"

There was, Scheherazade reflected, something deeply endearing about the old sorcerer in his all too evident professional frustration, paradoxically at his most admirable when most irascible. Then again, wasn't so much of a true magician's real work a matter of forever reminding his audience that what was often most vital, was also often most invisible?

"Earth's citizenry may yet one day find their way to Paradise," Abracadabra announced, his tone suggesting that he was unlikely to make even the smallest bet on their present chances.

An instant later, an impulsive search of his robe was followed by a triumphant smile as he hoisted in the air a well-worn, enviably arcane address book. All the best projects, as his great great-grandfather (also in the occult trade) used to say, were usually the better for being shared.

Whatever lay ahead, instinct suggested it might be prudent to make contact with some resourceful, highly-placed associates, who, whether or not they might be of immediate help, would undoubtedly be more than happy to see him again. Preferably over lunch.

As the old saying goes, mystery loves company.

ֆֆ

"Are things as bad as they seem?" Eve inquired suddenly over her morning coffee in their small private suite in the Fountain of Eternal Youth Retirement Home.

Adam raised an eyebrow above the morning edition of the Milky Way Daily Herald. From all reports, their native planet had just enjoyed an unusually bad day.

"Reading between the lines, I'd say potentially much worse."

ֆֆ

Though they might not have seen each other for countless aeons, the Archangel of All Archangels and his long lost brother Big D, proudly the blackest sheep of the celestially separatist flock and current Chairman of the Intergalactic Senior Devils' Association, remained very much alike in many ways.

Brilliant chief operating officers of their respective divisions of Universe Inc., each bore his unique responsibilities with uncommon grace and skill. Hard of hide and harder of heart (or so both would wish it believed), the two looked after their respective administrations of Heaven and Hell with a dedication continually inspiring to their equally devoted, formidably industrious staff.

In both locations, however, recent developments had left their respective long-range surveillance teams more than a little concerned. The World's Most Beautiful Astronomer had not been wrong. From across a broad spectrum of constellations there continued to come reports of growing unease so widespread as to trouble even the most imperturbable observers.

For their part, the keenest of keen-eyed angels, returning home from their routine reconnaissance missions, all confirmed signs of new, highly contagious strains of impatience and irritability at work among the stars.

For the middle managers and staff of both 'Upstairs' and 'Downstairs', however, it was the inexplicably sanguine response of their respective senior executives that proved even more disconcerting.

Instead of sending out, as was customary in difficult times, a newly reinforced selection of spiritual emissaries and advisors, the Archangel of All Archangels was much more interested in less pressing matters closer to home: including, in particular, a wholly unexplained programme of celestial renovation, refurbishment and expansion.

To their surprise, senior angelic assistants normally responsible for a wide range of day-to-day Heavenly operations abruptly discovered themselves the beneficiaries of totally unexpected increases in both budgets and staff, along with extensive lists of suggested departmental upgrades. Long-serving celestial professionals, disoriented as their reassuringly daily routines of caring for the universe were replaced by countless new construction projects, found their ethereal blood pressure going up while their equanimity went south.

The problem, most agreed, was that while 'Plan B' appeared to be firmly under way, all those required to help carry it out still had absolutely no idea what it was!

It was highly unfortunate, not a few whispered, that divine providence seemed congenitally predisposed to operate strictly on a need-to-know basis.

It certainly didn't help to end speculation when two enigmatic, globe-shaped seraphim – widely respected for their string of successes in that demanding field best known as clandestine spiritual discombobulations – were observed in animated discussion with the Archangel-in-Chief.

For their part, the two seraphim (the Angel of Unprecedented Opportunities and his companionable look-alike *confrère*, the Angel of Hidden Agendas) kept an otherwise unbreakable silence.

Elsewhere, in those vast underworld havens where an aromatic stew of the seven deadly sins was forever simmering on countless satanic stoves, devils of every degree seemed equally perplexed at their own boss's apparent reluctance to make the most of what might be called a Heaven-sent opportunity. Rather than sending out teams of devils to those galaxies now seemingly teetering opportunely on the very brink of catastrophe, Big D appeared happier instead to keep his specialist squads of red-eyed *agents provocateurs* closer to home.

To his associates' surprise, a programme of courses in advanced temptation techniques, illusory yet irresistible special effects, and ever more subtle interrogation skills was introduced at the demonic colleges throughout the universe.

"Never hurts to brush up on satanic fundamentals," Big D announced.

"I suppose so." His very large and very crimson second-in command frowned in disappointment, running a giant hand through his bright red hair, then scratching his head mournfully. "From all reports, however, an unprecedented number of cosmic no-goods are starting to plot and plan as never before." His eyes narrowed aggressively. "Lots of potentially delicious disorder out there for us to take advantage of."

"Or, perhaps, just as judiciously arranged to take advantage of us?" Big D raised a philosophic eyebrow. "Especially if we act too hastily."

"You think maybe God knows something we don't?"

The new Chairman of the Intergalactic Senior Devils' Association chuckled wryly. "Sure wouldn't be the first time."

Reinforcements

❧ SCHEHERAZADE AWOKE to an encouragingly sunny day, her first, inconclusive flight on a little white cloud now only a memory.

A tall glass of grapefruit, mango and orange juice, freshly squeezed by the latest in automated kitchen attendants, awaited on her bedside table. The small adjacent monitor showed daily temperatures, trends and weather forecasts around the world; and, as anticipated, confirmation that both her retainer and first advance on expenses had been anonymously deposited, as a little white-and-gold bird had promised, into her private off-planet bank account.

With an auspiciously cheerful, "See you soon, I suspect," Abracadabra had whirled off home, leaving Scheherazade alone with one of life's more unrelenting questions: what next?

Her little feathered visitor's confidence notwithstanding, this new assignment was proving less and less easy. For now, neither Past nor Present appeared particularly helpful. If Adam and Eve were content to offer only an understandably circumspect response, their descendants, in contrast, seemed to be arguing longer, louder and more inconclusively about anything and everything.

Shaking her head, Scheherazade sighed, stretched languorously, then reached for bikini and beach towel. Ocean or pool, pool or ocean?

Sometimes deep waters were their own reward.

Slipping between the sun-lit waves, she had a momentary sense of being suspended equally in water and in time – a fleeting, contemplative speck floating among six continents, adrift in the midst of ancestral seas swirling endlessly back and forth, sloshing forever up and down to the moody enticements of the moon. Turning on her back, she stared up at the azure sky, its steadily warming light effortlessly hiding billions of unknown starry worlds beyond. Motionless between waves, she sought to become one with the timeless blue, that infinite sky above forever offering and yet concealing its silent answers to questions she hadn't even fully begun to ask.

What might so many other unvisited realms know that Earth did not? And – perhaps even more important – what would this little blue-and-white planet do, if and when it finally found out?

White-tipped waves lapping over her, she gazed heavenwards, buoyed up under an endlessly changing sky as the whole planet itself, wheeling on its axis, carried her and all its citizens – past, passing and yet to come – inexorably forward in time and eternity.

If humanity was to have a future, it was likely only to come in the eventual realization that all boundaries were temporary, all identities contextual, and whoever they had yet to become lay ever farther beyond who they currently were, or thought they were. In being able to see, in other words, the far scarier yet richer worlds of infinite wonder and possibility that lay ahead; to discover, in short, a future … with a future!

With that thought, Time itself seemed to open in a flash, beckoning irresistibly.

If she wanted to find the way forward, Scheherazade saw suddenly, might not the best course be to go ask those who were, even now, already there?

It was an idea, she realized, that a certain mysterious little white-and-gold emissary appeared already to have had very much in mind.

Laughing aloud with relief, now sure what she needed to do, she flipped over in the sparkling blue water and struck out fast for shore.

Latest model interstellar cell-phone in hand, eternity's well-chosen *femme inspiratrice* began the first of a series of successful invitations.

When they heard Scheherazade on the line, one by one, Marina, Leila, Qingling, Yazmina, Tatiana and Sybilla each listened intently. In every case, the initial, surprised response of "Why Earth?" swiftly became a unanimously enthusiastic, "Why not!" Within hours, all six stylishly eclectic adventurers were en route throughout the Milky Way, united by the appeal of six separate reconnaissance missions ahead, all instinctively open to the most unlikely of encounters in however many dimensions.

As her guests took their places on hastily arranged lounge chairs facing the sea, ready for explorations both sacred and profane, Scheherazade had a fleeting sense their select gathering remained incomplete.

If there was one thing Earth's greatest grandmother had not lost, she suspected, it was a uniquely disconcerting sense of adventure.

✇

"And so it seems," Scheherazade concluded, "our next best move is to go ask the Future just where it thinks Paradise might be hiding."

Heroines do not hesitate.

"Lucky, lucky Tomorrowland," Tatiana declared, amber eyes sparkling in anticipation.

As a relieved Scheherazade laughed with the others, a voice spoke softly from the far side of the pool. For Sybilla, mercurial queen of the still unknown and yet to come, proud possessor of deep turquoise eyes and the equally bewitching gift of second sight, the day-to-day world was but a transparent illusion; a theatre rich with all the ever-changing chimeras of time, forever hiding deeper unities it sought just as urgently to reveal.

Firstly, she began, there already appeared to be more than enough fantastic adventures to go around. Secondly, the devils lying in wait (of whom there were intriguingly quite a few) asked only that the seven women be both worthy of them and unafraid. And finally and most importantly, she added, the countless angels also in their path sincerely hoped that they would not to have to do all the work.

An instant later, a meteor shower streaked across a momentarily darkened sky, followed immediately by the faintest, fleeting rumble of distant thunder: the first, errant, quickly muffled practice notes from an ethereal orchestra whose newly-written, planet-shaking symphony wasn't yet quite ready for public performance.

Melodies and Moonbeams

🖎 JUST AS SCHEHERAZADE started to speed-dial the best garage in seventy-seven solar systems, its chief mechanic rang through. Promised highest-tech tune-up complete, her very own personal time-and-space-craft was even now, as he put it enviously, "just a-ready and a-rarin' to go." In however many dimensions its owner had the courage to explore.

Over a long and celebrated career, the eminently sleek and reliable S.S. Serendipity had already taken its owner to stranger places than most could imagine. Thanks to the overnight flurry of custom upgrades and subtle body shop modifications, it might now go absolutely anywhere!

Since it was impossible to foretell the latest in future fashion, all seven ladies chose to travel light, the better to pick up whatever they might need wherever each might eventually arrive. As they shared a pre-departure dinner, the sun sank slowly beneath a darkening sea.

Earth spun a few more degrees on its axis, the invisible hands of twilight slipping the veils from star after star, releasing them to shine ever more brightly in the deepening indigo sky. Each passed its flame to still others unseen, until at last the heavens sparkled with fire from horizon to horizon.

"So many equally wonderful choices." Yazmina leaned even further back in her chair, twirling her long dark hair thoughtfully, savouring the far-off mysteries twinkling silently overhead. "It's almost impossible to know where to begin."

"I've already put in an advance call to the Future." Scheherazade's eyes sparkled with anticipation. "If all goes according to plan, we'll be met on arrival by literally the most illuminating concierge anywhere!"

At her words, a rising crescent moon gently turned its head and stared.

Over millions of years the moon had enjoyed all the mixed blessings of a dramatic co-dependency. Ancient object of worship and wonder, changeful inspiration for lovers and all those longing to love and be loved, it forever danced the same luminous steps in a constant duet with a distant sun. Waxing and waning, ebbing and flowing, rising and falling. And then waxing and waning all over again. Which, while it certainly guaranteed enviably steady employment, could also become just a bit boring.

Wouldn't it be lovely, it had often thought, if it too could travel miraculously through the stars, rejoicing in the ever-changing light of unknown worlds. Gazing down on Scheherazade and her friends, the slender outline of SS Serendipity gleaming whitely off to one side, the moon trembled with sudden yearning. Wherever these seven women were bound, it fervently wished that it too could be going.

Now waning (according to its own hitherto unchanging calendar), in an instant it reversed itself on its axis and began to glow. Then, despite feeling slightly giddy at the effort, it just as resolutely became full.

"Good luck!" it whispered softly, even though sure no one could hear.

A moment later, reverting from unscheduled orb to a timely, less demonstrative crescent, it shot off, returning to its proper location a little further along in the sky.

※

It had been a long day, with the promise of still longer ones ahead. Having said their mutual good-nights, Tomorrowland's explorers retired to make their final preparations, think their private thoughts and try to get some sleep before the dawn.

Scheherazade drifted off immediately, her dream, when it finally came, appearing at the darkest hour of night. Countless stars, their time now come, arose magically out of nowhere to take their places on a vast celestial stage. Earth itself slid silently above the horizon of her sleep, a little blue-and-white orb making its tremulous way across the sky.

There was a sudden crash of cymbals, an endless celestial drum roll. Deep within, the planet's magnetic core now pulsed and reverberated, as if itself awakening from a dream within a dream. The little blue-and-white world split open and from its centre, across unimaginable distances, came an unknown yet hauntingly familiar music.

A wild sweet song of birth and joy, death and sorrow, defeat and victory, courage and love. Requiem and overture at the same time, it wound ceaselessly, rhythmically back on itself, both grateful farewell and glad new beginning conjoined. From the planet's heart poured singers from every land and time, their voices blending in a fierce yet magical refrain.

"Be worthy! Make us proud!"

&.

In their ancient bed in the stillness of the Fountain of Eternal Youth Retirement Home, Eve turned restlessly, breasts to chest, against the comfort of Adam's deeply familiar body. The image of a small precious blue-and-white world arose of its own accord above the horizon of her sleep. From its now-open depths, she began to hear a fleeting, far-off music, a yearning, a poignant human cry reaching out to her over thousands and thousands of years.

"Be worthy! Make us proud! Be worthy! Make us proud!"

No Time Like the Future

"FIRST, SYNCHRONIZE YOUR WATCHES. THEN, THROW
THEM AWAY."

— *A Sightseer's Guide to Eternity*

A Thousand Welcomes

❧ SS SERENDIPITY SOARED upward through the void, leaving Earth's constraining calendars far behind. Historical time had disappeared. Fragments of antique and modern watches sailed past the windows. Small comets of clocks darted into view only to sweep away, their ticking trails vanishing just as swiftly. Silence and stillness embraced. Everywhere was another horizon, and beyond every horizon lay mysteries beyond number.

"The Future is so much bigger than the Past," Marina whispered in awe as the seven women skimmed onwards over the vast surfaces of Time Yet To Come.

"It sure better be!" Qingling laughed, expressing not just the hopes of all on board but quite likely, she suspected, the entire universe as well.

Ahead, an enormous searchlight pierced the air.

As SS Serendipity drew closer, however, what first seemed a single welcoming beacon gradually revealed itself to be the combined radiance of many smaller lights, together forming the increasingly cheerful gaze of a very large gentleman clearly delighted by their safe arrival.

"Welcome to The Future Everyone Wonders About, But Usually Doesn't Quite Know Where to Find," declared the aptly named The Man With a Thousand Eyes, glancing surreptitiously at the largest of all possible wristwatches. "Or, as we prescient locals like to call it, The Great Beyond beyond the Beyond!"

As he spoke, he beamed fondly in a thousand different directions simultaneously, carefully illuminating just as many yet unexplored possibilities ahead.

"Take it from me, you've definitely come to the right place. We've got futures in time, futures in space, futures retrieved unused from the past, and futures that won't come to pass until a million other preparatory tomorrows have long since come and gone. We can supply futures in three dimensions and futures in thirty; futures that can happen to anyone and others meant only for the fewest of the few."

Just as Scheherazade was about to ask their unusual host where he might suggest they begin, a faint whirring grew steadily louder in the distance. A moment later, destiny's imperturbable doorman shone his high-intensity smile on a familiar-looking little white cloud gliding in on its final approach.

"Just in time," said The Man With a Thousand Eyes.

"Just as ever!" whispered Scheherazade, beginning to laugh.

"My apologies for startling you like this," Abracadabra announced, removing his flying goggles, "but every last one of my latest prognostications suggested it was in every one's best interest (mine included) to meet all of you exactly here and precisely now." The sprightly old sorcerer beamed. "Then too, as a chivalrous old rogue, I couldn't very well pass up this opportunity to wish so many lovely ladies well in your escapades yet to come."

"Most thoughtful of you," Scheherazade replied cautiously. Abracadabra might be a very old and very dear friend but, first and foremost, he was an even more canny wizard.

"One tries to be of service," the latter replied, bowing modestly. With one merry eye on his luminous host, the other firmly on Scheherazade and her friends, he drew from behind his back a huge, shimmering bowl.

"Behold!"

On the bowl's gleaming surface, a pair of phoenix gazed calmly and proudly at one another over a set of white-and-gold dice, moments before their next return to the same shared renascent flame. Abracadabra watched, calculating time's ever-changing odds, then smiled with quiet satisfaction.

"Somehow or other, I seem to be the chosen custodian of certain esoteric means to help you find the next step in your journey. Or, should I say, journeys!"

Eyes twinkling ever more brightly, the ancient sorcerer gently shook the giant bowl, its interior rustling loudly in response to the papery sounds of ten thousand folded-up possibilities. Raising his magic wand in blessing, he whispered his favourite, most potent spell of protection and power.

"Ladies, this is where so many picaresque adventures all begin. Pick your fortune; pick your future; pick your fate. May the divine luck of the draw lead you onward!"

One by one, each of Scheherazade's associates thrust a resolute hand into the shimmering bowl, rejecting all but the one path in The Great Beyond beyond the Beyond that was exactly right for her (and, ultimately, for the little blue-and-white planet soon to be dragged, screaming and kicking, in directions secretly relished but just as long resisted).

One by one, each drew a folded piece of paper out from under the watchful eyes of the two phoenix, now interrupting their non-stop roll of the cosmic dice to discover the outcome of this far larger, more fascinating game of celestial hide-and-go-peek. One by one, each woman stepped back, secret destination in hand.

"Till we meet again," Leila affirmed, already conjecturing on adventures unknown.

"Paradise – or bust!" Yazmina replied to approving laughter. The outcome was never in doubt. The fun lay in getting there.

A moment later, in tune to a well-timed wave of Abracadabra's magic wand, Marina, Leila, Qingling, Yazmina, Tatiana and Sybilla all vanished from view, each on their separate way to pre-ordained encounters with some very esoteric beings even more impatient to meet them.

❦

As Scheherazade watched in silence, Abracadabra's little white cloud whirled to its master's side, a small white-and-gold chest opening instantly to his words. As calmly as possible, given the circumstances, the little old wizard drew out the sole existing copy of a map only recently entrusted to his care, together with an accompanying set of similarly sealed flying instructions embossed with gold lettering and marked 'Scheherazade – For Her Eyes Only'.

Handing them over, he angled his magic wand skywards in a deft, imperceptible salute.

"A little something from a charming, if rather circumspect presence called The Angel of Celestial Invitations."

As she prepared to break the seals, Scheherazade found herself trembling unprofessionally. Given that her apparent destination must be Heaven, it now seemed a wise precaution to have long been (mostly) on the side of the angels.

After all, when invited to one's very first up-close-and-personal encounter with the head of the universe's biggest, most dynamic spiritual enterprise, a favourable word on one's behalf from its trusted, long-serving staff could be considered both a strategic and tactical imperative.

❧

Waving goodbye as SS Serendipity became a glowing speck on the horizon, Abracadabra checked his robes once more, then proffered a flask of his favourite bubbly to The Future's clearly satisfied host. Together they raised a toast in turn to all seven ladies, each even now soaring somewhere out in The Great Beyond beyond the Beyond, each on her own special rendezvous.

"Always exciting," the old wizard declared.

"Truly," replied the now gently shimmering Man With a Thousand Eyes. "No matter how many visitors arrive, I never get tired of helping them onward."

"We share a noble calling," said Abracadabra as modestly as he could. There was a long, contented silence while the two ancient gentlemen contemplated their selfless service to the universe.

Marina and Leila

❧ IT'S ONE THING to take on the world, quite another that boundless future best known as The Great Beyond beyond the Beyond.

"Welcome to the fabled Interplanetary Centre for Joy," an ever-insouciant Dr. Professor O'Bliss exclaimed, eyeing the elegantly *sportif* woman studying him with matching pleasure in return.

Even as he spoke, a flourish of bright neon musicians ambled past, three sets of arms playing three different instruments in nonchalant harmony, their three heads bouncing in tune. Around them, lovers of every age and origin fell impetuously into one another's arms, each pair more uninhibited with every swoon. Nearby, a small group of rabbits, eagles and lobsters played a leisurely game of bridge while a handsome polar bear poured a convivial toucan a stiff drink. The once-pressing troubles of a small far-off planet disappeared, replaced by an overwhelming sense of unending ease.

"What an unusual place," Marina said approvingly. The renowned interstellar fact-finder-at-large took a second look and then several more. "Absolutely enchanting!"

"And so it should be," her host responded, cheerfully leading the first of Scheherazade's co-explorers to a pre-arranged table in the garden café. "In fact, it's the original prototype of a hundred and one similar intergalactic research institutes dedicated to celebrating the universe's inimitable, all-pervading *joie de vivre*."

Everywhere, the scene confirmed his words. Trees giggled, brooks laughed, rocks chuckled quietly, seventy-seven multi-coloured suns in the sky chortled back and forth as they vanished then reappeared behind beaming clouds. Laughter exploded from the wide-open windows of a thousand terraced workshops and playrooms.

Dr. Professor O'Bliss appeared profoundly pleased, not just with himself but for the universe at large. "While some say effort leads eventually to happiness, our studies here confirm exactly the reverse. Whatsoever you do, do with delight – and the seeds of all you hope for will usually reveal themselves to be already present!"

If women tend to find a gentleman's genial confidence in himself greatly appealing, how much more so if he shows a similarly relaxed faith in the entire cosmos!

"I should warn you: I've come here looking for Paradise," Marina allowed. There are moments when an adventuress knows instinctively that the challenges ahead, both personal and professional, are precisely those she can't wait to enjoy. "In as many dimensions as possible."

"Aren't we all?" her host's unfeigned laughter was an irresistible balance of both professional approval and personal anticipation. "Shall we retire to the laboratory?"

"Earth should be so lucky," Marina thought to herself.

"Time will soon tell," Dr. Professor O'Bliss replied enigmatically, offering his arm and leading them both where each most wished to go.

One of the most under-publicized rewards of exploration is the pleasure of being discovered in return.

❧

Slipping between weathered limestone columns, Leila, Scheherazade's favourite galactic historian, pressed the gleaming brass doorbell of a long-forgotten Museum of Interstellar Culs-de-Sac.

"Good morning, good morning, a very good morning," a small yellow monkey exclaimed, swinging open the huge enamelled door with one deft paw while juggling a bundle of guidebooks in the other. "Do please come in. It's so very exciting to have a visitor!"

The unusual little custodian peered up at Leila through beguiling purple eyes. "An authorized handbook, perhaps? Very helpful, if overly academic." She looked round hopefully. "Or perhaps, if you prefer, I could give you an unofficial summary? The inside scoop, as it were!"

Everywhere she looked, Leila made out rows of dusty cabinets holding the detritus of dynasties long gone, their contents intriguingly obscure. "I'd be delighted," she replied, glad of the offer and not wanting to disappoint someone so obviously thrilled to have company.

With a grateful nod, the little monkey drew herself up as high as she could, then launched into a clearly much-rehearsed introduction.

"Once upon a time, a number of very distinguished intergalactic entrepreneurs began comparing notes on their respective careers. To their surprise and delight, all found themselves proudest, not of their celebrated achievements, but rather the many more embarrassingly youthful errors which, in hindsight, had proven so vital to later success."

The little monkey paused, a fleetingly wistful look on her small earnest face.

"Very soon, these same heroically open-minded ladies and gentlemen found themselves speculating on similarly essential faults and foibles over the entire course of cosmic history. Millions of years of seemingly time-consuming wrong turns and disappointingly unproductive ideas. And all of them totally unappreciated. Until now!"

At those words, Leila's small guide couldn't resist an especially irresistible grin.

"Eureka! And so it was," she hurried on, "that these remarkably far-seeing, fortunately well-heeled folk decided to finance the very first institution dedicated entirely to Highly Instructive Failures and False Paths in the Still Unfolding Story of the Universe, otherwise known as The Museum of Interstellar Culs-de-Sac."

It made complete sense, Leila concurred. While the past might be full of mistakes, the best of these offered their own edifying lessons in return.

"You betcha!" The small yellow monkey bounced up and down, purple eyes beaming with curatorial pride. "And a very fine and unusual place it is. All over the universe, there are monuments to achievement, temples to triumph, and shrines to success.

"This museum, on the other hand, *my* museum," the little monkey continued breathlessly, "is the only one dedicated specifically to the exact opposite! To showing roads not taken, paths that went nowhere, experiments that failed, evolutions that didn't evolve, concepts and construction projects that totally collapsed, big bangs that went bust, and a million bright shining prospects and possibilities that just plain petered out.

"A truly exceptional place, where, as our ad campaign puts it so well, others may benefit from our complete lack of positive example.

"It's all so exciting," the little monkey continued, tugging on Leila's pant-leg in her enthusiasm. "And so profoundly useful! I mean, how can you fully appreciate what really works…."

"If you don't know what doesn't – or didn't, in this case," Leila replied, finishing her new friend's thought. Given what little she knew of an earthly paradise inadvertently gone belly-up, this highly unlikely landfall in The Great Beyond beyond the Beyond was beginning to seem a wondrously inspired choice.

"I can see you do understand," the small yellow monkey said fervently, tilting her head to one side. "Sensitive, and quite lovely too. What's your name?"

"Leila," said Leila.

"And I'm Aurora," the little guardian of first attempts responded, adjusting her guidebooks and offering a slim graceful paw. "Where are you from?"

"Earth," Leila said simply, pointing generally north east and, for the moment, many thousands of years back in time.

"Never heard of it."

Leila looked deeper into the vast awaiting rotunda of the Museum of Historical Culs-de-Sac, with its still shadowy outlines of the beat-up bric-a-brac of bygone worlds. "Under the circumstances, that's probably not such a bad thing. Reassuring, actually."

The little yellow monkey laughed, then turned up the museum's lights, illuminating a bewildering multiplicity of display-cased corridors. "So, where would you like to begin?"

Leila studied her small new friend. "It's all totally fascinating," she answered as reassuringly as possible; then, following a sudden hunch, added, "but where would you suggest we start first?"

With a mischievous smile, Aurora held out the museum's guest registry where Leila's name had already been entered light years before, together with today's date. And a brief, indecipherable note.

"Tell me, if you please – if you know yet why you're really here." The little guardian of the one and only intergalactic Museum of Historical Culs-de-Sac peered up eagerly. "And what do you know about an opening-night gala?"

The Plot Thickens

❧ EVERY UNION, however strong, has its inevitable silences. It was, accordingly, not so very surprising that two people who'd managed to stay together for a hundred thousand years should welcome a little time apart once in a while.

All the same, Adam reflected, his one-and-only seemed to be spending an unusual number of afternoons by herself lately, lost in thought over what she liked to call 'our extended-family albums'. And what might Adam be thinking, Eve wondered in turn, on those long evening walks he'd begun soon after the lovely Scheherazade's brief but unsettling visit.

One thing was certain. Comfortable through the Fountain of Eternal Youth Retirement Home might be, its twice-weekly bingo games were fast losing their already marginal appeal.

Each decided it was time for the other to talk.

❧

Big D did not get where he was by being a celestial pushover.

Even the angels who had stood in awed silence at his earlier abrupt departure from Heaven in search of more temperamentally suitable career prospects, had to confess they would miss his truly masterful management skills. Indeed, as subsequent celestial intelligence reports confirmed, all that had once made him so good in Heaven, made him truly great in Hell.

Tired of scanning even the most outwardly uneventful of galaxies for clues, Big D turned to the Satanic Weather Office's chief climatologist and repeated his now routine *question de jour*. "Any change?"

At the same increasingly frustrating answer, the incoming Chairman of the Senior Intergalactic Devils' Association shook his impressive head. "Don't worry. There will be."

Turning away, he considered the merits of action. (God helps those, etc.) One or two exploratory provocations, perhaps? Or, more discreetly, an unexpected press release? "In a recent exclusive interview, the Devil is quoted as viewing current cosmic developments with grave moral concern."

Accurate, certainly. But probably premature. And (given his present reputation) unlikely to be widely believed.

Big D shook his head a second time. Deviltry might offer its own rewards, but it seldom gets the appreciation it deserves.

⁊⦁

Although being God was inevitably a full-time job, there were moments when the seemingly eternal incumbent was all too aware of its infinitely delicate exigencies. Long experience had shown that just as there were times it was best to push, so there were others when it was even better (sacramentally speaking) to pull. While the ultimate intent might be always the same, the individual direction and degree of force involved varied enormously.

And then there were those times, such as now, when it was best simply to be patient.

Reaching across a crowded desk, God pressed the button on the white-and-gold intercom to his 24/7 operations staff. "I'd greatly appreciate it if you'd increase the regular flights of the angelic reconnaissance squadrons. Let's say, double them, to start with."

"OK, Boss," came the quick reply. "Already under way, actually," the Archangel-in-Chief added. "Thought You wouldn't mind if I took the liberty. Never hurts to be sure." There was a long, slow, affectionate chuckle. "And besides, the suspense was getting to me, too!"

Not for the first time, God reflected on what a wise decision it had been not to take on the universe alone. More to keep track of, perhaps, but also infinitely more interesting. After a word of sincere appreciation, the founder of the cosmos leaned back, content once more to admire the ever-changing view. And wait.

Qingling and Yazmina

&. AS A MATTER of professional courtesy Qingling carefully flipped herself upside down before slowing deftly to a stop at her unorthodox destination. Ahead, a small crowd of similarly inverted people, standing easily on their heads, welcomed her with fluttering hands. As she returned their greeting, a pair of identical close-cropped silver top-knots on a single body detached themselves from the others and pressed quickly forward, emerald-green eyes peering approvingly into hers.

"Welcome to the justly famous Intergalactic Recreation and Repair Centre," Chief Inspector Go-Go said ceremoniously.

"Very auspicious timing," Chief Inspector Stop added. "Neither a moment too soon…."

"Nor an instant too late," his inseparable *confrère* confirmed.

Nodding in unison, the two-headed greeting committee led the way to a series of clinics nestled among wooded groves and winding streams. Furnished with the latest in medico-recreational technology, all were gratefully occupied by patients from a hundred star-systems enjoying the ultimate in comprehensive health coverage.

"Virtually all our major reconstructive work goes on here," Chief Inspector Go-Go explained. "Nowadays, as you may have heard, the average life span between total overhauls is now approximately two thousand years. No matter their constellation or credit limit, however, anyone who lives past a thousand usually ends up needing more than the usual routine maintenance. Not to mention emergency repair."

"Intergalactically, in fact," Chief Inspector Stop beamed, "we're proud recipients of award after award for almost five thousand years."

"Most notably for our simultaneous second opinions," the two topsy-turvy twins exclaimed as one, puffing out their shared and single chest.

"It's all most impressive," Qingling agreed diplomatically, quietly re-examining the surrounding, similarly double-headed attendants, all with inverted emerald-eyed smiles. As her hosts prepared to lead the way to her pre-assigned guest room, she could wait no longer. "Pardon my curiosity, but," sooner or later the question had to be asked, "why are all of you going about your duties upside down?"

"Makes our job easier, of course!" Chief Inspector Stop exclaimed.

"No matter the galaxy, there are essentially only three basic maladies," Chief Inspector Go-Go hastened to elaborate. "Things are either upside-down, back-to-front, or, much less frequently but considerably worse, inside-out."

"And so, by taking an upside-down position ourselves," his associate continued, "we find it gives us a much better understanding of what should obviously be right-side-up."

"And so on and so forth," Chief Inspector Go-Go concluded.

"Hmmmnn." Qingling tried her best to grasp the intricate, if somewhat contrarian premises involved, her thoughts quickly straying to a certain little blue-and-white world's own faltering, unfinished journey toward whatever it hoped might offer a happier, healthier future.

If there were such an extraordinary thing as planetary lab tests, she wondered, what might Earth's latest results show?

Chief Inspectors Stop and Go-Go exchanged glances, then tried to be as gentle as possible.

"It's never too soon to put one's affairs in order," Chief Inspector Stop observed.

"The ECG readings, in particular, really don't look all that great," Chief Inspector Go-Go confirmed.

The pleasures of Paradise regained, it seemed, might have to be put off till another day. If, that is, there were one.

❦

"Who are you?" the tall wiry skeleton asked, barring Yazmina's path and opening their conversation with one of life's abiding challenges.

"And what are you doing here?" added the second skeleton, shorter and, for a collection of skull and bones, somewhat burly.

Yazmina smiled as charmingly as possible given her disguise. "Like both of you, I assume, I'm here for the annual Dark Energy, Bright Secrets Conference." Though long adept at choosing the perfect camouflage for any occasion, she had never before appeared as a skeleton. One with a poised and contemplative air, to be sure; but a skeleton nonetheless.

"She looks like a spy." The first ivory figure smiled approvingly. "There's a certain cool allure."

"She certainly smells like a spy," said the second, sniffing the air.

"Actually, she smells rather lovely." The tall skeleton leaned a little closer, the better to catch an eloquently under-stated fragrance.

"Thank you," Yazmina replied, smile deepening in amused satisfacion. For a lady, perfume can be a favourite, even lethal, disguise.

As they took their seats near the front of the crowded auditorium, the master of ceremonies, an authoritative, silver-haired gentleman with ruby eyes, a scythe in one hand and a glowing lamp in the other, moved purposefully to centre stage, his arrival greeted with prolonged applause.

"Thank you. Thank you all so very much," the Spectre of Carefully Concealed Eternities commenced. Raising the lamp in his right hand, he directed its glow out over his hushed audience.

"Welcome to tonight's opening session. A superbly arcane astrophysisist and spymaster, our distinguished colleague will now share with us the hitherto elusive answer to one of life-after-life's greatest mysteries: namely, in an ever-changing universe of planets big and small, where do the best-behaved rocks really go when they've finished every assignment, cashed their last pay cheque and finally packed it all in?"

With that the huge, shiny, black-and-yellow skeleton ambled with casual gravitas to centre stage. A multi-tasker from birth, his words came simultaneously from sixteen concentric skulls, accompanied by the clapping of sixty-four equally harmonious hands.

"Contrary to popular belief, the so-called death of a conscientious, hard-working planet is actually an illusion. In reality, the ghost it gives up soon sneaks happily away to other, less-publicized realms, there to enjoy its well-earned reward for millions of years of unselfish service."

The guest speaker paused, all sixteen skulls aglow with admiration.

"Once arrived at these celestial resorts, some planets (more exhausted than others) are inclined simply to hang out with one another, watch unfolding news stories from their own former solar systems and catch up on the latest gossip from more exotic spheres. Others take up hobbies.

"Still others, however, more adventurous by nature, go off to explore galaxies unknown to them until now, often visiting distant stellar relatives en route." Thirty-two eyebrows suddenly lifted in emphasis, sixty-four hands gently underscored the main point about to come.

"A celebrated few, however, sign up for special rest and recreation centres. Their cores recharged, their selfless dedication renewed, they re-emerge to play a larger role elsewhere."

Sixty-hour hands now joining in thirty-two simultaneous gestures of appreciation and benediction, the very large shiny black-and-yellow skeleton bowed to his audience.

"All in all," he concluded, "a wondrous example of unconditional cosmic altruism. And a very timely lesson to any planet hoping to take short cuts and rest on laurels unearned!"

❧

It is an impressive sight to see over a thousand burnished ivory figures leap to their feet as one, clattering their hands together in a fierce skeletal ovation.

The tall gentleman on Yazmina's left nudged her with a bony arm.

"Not sure if Earth quite fits that description, eh?"

"Notwithstanding your current assignment, so hush-hush, rush-rush," the second skeleton followed up breezily.

If it takes a spy to catch a spy, it takes a great one to admit when her cover is well and truly blown. "Time will tell," Yazmina demurred, since, for now, *she* certainly couldn't.

"Be sure to call us if you need more info," the tall slender skeleton said, smiling expansively.

"Or assistance." The two bony gentlemen exchanged a perfectly matched pair of meaningful looks. "Especially assistance."

"Any hour," the shorter, burly one added, patting the air where his pocket would have been, searching for an ethereal business card. "Business is slow right now."

They grinned at each other. "Most days we're free to do out-calls."

The Plot Thickens Some More

❧ IT IS AN OLD cosmic truth that rapidly growing planets with rapidly growing populations tend to have even more rapidly growing problems. Unfortunately, however, it is equally true that they're unlikely to find perfectly matching solutions at anything like the same speed.

Leaning against Heaven's balcony, God reached for another after-dinner mint and contemplated the unfolding scene. One eye on eternity, the other on the unfinished workings of Time, the secret source of both carefully reread the draft schedule which had occupied the better part of an afternoon, and nodded approvingly.

After all, this wouldn't be the first time that the primal puzzle-maker *extraordinaire* had quietly rearranged a few key pieces; or, in this case, not so quietly.

It was not that the universe's intermittently good and faithful citizens were wholly unwilling to learn. The real challenge lay in getting – and keeping – their attention, preferably before the potentially combustible became the conclusively catastrophic.

"So, what do you think of my homeopathic pre-emptive remedy," God inquired, one meticulous professional to another.

The venerable angelic engineer in charge of Intergalactic Special Effects and Cosmic Sensory Overload ran his eyes once again over the huge master plan, re-examining it cautiously in all its precise, inspired scope and scale.

"Incredible!" he exclaimed at last. "Unbelievably believable in every way." It was an expression of the highest praise from one senior scientist to the very best in the business. "You could have fooled even me."

"I sincerely hope so," God replied, offering the last of the remaining mints. "Any problem in bringing it off?"

"Shouldn't be. Not with all the technical expertise we've got lounging around this place. What a total blast!!"

"Let's hope everybody thinks so," God agreed.

❧

Invisible antennae quivering as rarely before, Big D awoke from daydreams of a thousand galaxies suddenly gone kaboom.

There were definite professional benefits in being able to sense, long before the event, much of what only later appeared predestined to occur. "Probably an inherited skill," he acknowledged ruefully.

"What's up, Boss?" one of his more promising junior assistants inquired, poking his head round the well-padded door.

"I smell smoke," the newly elected Chairman of the Intergalactic Senior Devils' Association declared. "Figuratively speaking, at least. And where there's smoke...."

"There's usually a professional opportunity," his youthful associate chortled, rubbing his hands together in cheerful anticipation.

If the devil closes one trap door, he opens a thousand others.

Unconsciously checking for the nearest temperature gauge, Big D smiled the beginnings of a long-suppressed smile.

"In this case, if we're lucky, one greatly overdue!"

❧

"Pardon my curiosity," one of Eve's sister retirees asked unexpectedly, "but are you feeling slightly out of sorts these days?"

There was an awkward silence.

"No more than usual," Eve replied at last, as honestly as she could. "Must be the weather, or the cooking here lately."

"Hmmmnn," said her friend, looking her up and down.

Tatiana and Sybilla

❧ FLAME-HAIRED, amber-eyed Tatiana, uninhibited adventuress *par excellence*, was rarely surprised by Creation's irrepressible eroticism, everywhere offering opportunities for amorous enlightenment.

As she rocketed on through ten successive dimensions, each opening in turn to reveal ever more entrancing vistas, the air became brighter, a far-off music louder, an enchanting but unknown fragrance stronger, and her own excitement, progressively greater.

"Welcome to the celebrated Wondrous Winding Gardens of Desire!" The graceful woman with violet eyes leaned forward, pouring lavender tea into matching golden cups. "I'm Valentina."

As Tatiana stared about her, nearly every imaginable combination of lovers (and then some) quietly materialized around her. Beings with only seven heads strolled companionably with partners having twenty.

Gentlemen, all the wiser for centuries of sensuous experimentation, did their best to live up to the expectations of ladies enjoying at least twice that number. Elsewhere, pairs of inseparable amatory pioneers drew inspiration from a highly charged celibacy interrupted only once every hundred thousand years. But what a long weekend!

"What an extraordinary place," Tatiana exclaimed, long having wanted to visit this interstellar tribute to all those unafraid to live, laugh and, above all, love in the moment; all those forever rejoicing in their own sweet ephemerality, confronting time and decay with a brave, epicurean abandon.

"Truly astonishing," Valentina agreed. The Garden's designer-in-chief inclined her head as an elegant quartet, with the bodies of giraffes and the heads of suitably small elephants, paraded by hand in hand.

"But surely not all that surprising, given so exuberantly inventive a universe."

Taking Tatiana's arm, her hostess led her swiftly through a maze of succeeding paths, each arrangement of flowers brighter and more colourful than before. Ahead, lovers of every shape and shade swayed suggestively to music outlawed in more than a few places over more than a few aeons.

Red spherical cylinders seemingly without heads, but with six provocative eyes in the centre of their waists, set the pace for their partners' glowing tan-and-cream boxes with a shapely red mouth on each of all four sides. A trio of mauve star-forms kept steady company with five appreciative orange-coloured admirers whose accordion-like bodies flexed up and down to the music while adding exotic tonal embellishments of their own.

"When the intergalactic hedonists decide it's time to party...!"

"They do it exceedingly well," Valentina agreed proudly.

Seconds later, with perfect timing and grace, the leader of a group of slender, peacock-blue gentlemen disengaged himself from his dancing companions. The very elegant Unofficial Ambassador (Plenipotentiary) of Cosmic Hedonism approaching Tatiana drew from the air an exquisite bouquet of white roses flecked with gold.

"I look forward to seeing you again soon," he declared with the most confident of winks. "At training camp, perhaps?"

❧

When it came to multi-dimensional divination, Sybilla had won more trophies than many a palm-and-planet-reader a hundred times her age. As a result, when she found herself needing more than a few answers in less than a few days, she already had a good idea where to go.

The elegant yellow door to the Interstellar Oracle Training Centre (and Psychic Spa) opened automatically, its seven successive antechambers leading the way to this exclusive club's hidden core. Sybilla strolled unchallenged through them all, her inimitable turquoise eyes flashing an enigmatic, encrypted look confirming her permanent, out-of-town associate-membership status.

The vast exercise hall remained, in its restrained white and cream, as quietly dignified as ever: a suitably subtle setting for suitably subtle work. As Sybilla entered, a score of veteran soothsayers paused in coordinated greeting, third-eyes blinking in unison before they returned to their individual self-improvement regimes.

"What took you so long?" a deep voice observed quietly, neither seeking nor needing an answer.

As Sybilla spun round, a tall, athletic figure just finishing his own psychic workout sauntered forward, thoughtfully polishing his distinctive head in the form of a gleaming cut-glass ball. Glimpsing her own suddenly flushed reflection in its surface, she was not surprised to find two other companion oracles approaching from either side.

"Very pleased to meet you," the mid-sized figure on her right announced, gracefully bending a large translucent cube.

"Likewise," said the shorter presence to her left, his own tilted top consisting of a similarly transparent pyramid.

Under the circumstances, mutual introductions were brief. "If I'm not mistaken," Sybilla ventured, "you can only be…."

"The Three Crystals!" the trio confirmed, speaking in turn. "Distant cousins on our mother's side." They beamed through dark, medium and light coral eyes respectively. "Gives us a certain edge in occult triathlons."

"I tend to look after everything that goes around and around: constellations, eternal verities, stuff like that," the tallest seer confided.

"While I handle most everything going up, down and sideways," the second explained, his shining cube bobbing in every direction.

"And I seem to be astonishingly good at angular themes. Anything temperamentally predisposed to the oblique," the shortest continued, gently tilting his pyramid by way of illustration. "I also sideline in psychic ricochets," he added proudly.

Sybilla eyed the three shining seers carefully. "Don't suppose you'd be open to doing a little cosmic charity work? A few not-too-demanding prognostications, perhaps?"

"On behalf of…?" they responded politely, if unnecessarily.

"A little place called Earth, of course."

"Told you it was going to be an interesting few months," the cube-headed sage exclaimed.

"Somehow I knew you'd all be delighted to take on the task," Sybilla beamed. "And, of course, I'll buy lunch."

As might be expected, the first and original Interstellar Oracle Training Centre (and Psychic Spa) was renowned among the *cognoscenti* for its superb yet unpretentious restaurant, its menu featuring only the finest seasonal produce from neighbouring galaxies, all tele-transported fresh hourly.

Similarly inclined to the simple but very best, all four seers settled on the day's special (starfish soup, asteroid-raised spring lamb, triple-lunar greens and *crème caramba* for dessert) plus a shared economy-size bottle of *Chateau Miraculosa*. Over double espressos, they reminisced on truly stunning performances by some of the great fortune tellers of the past.

Swivelling comfortably in her chair, Sybilla cast a speculative eye on the Three Crystals.

"Given what you already suspect," the littlest, pyramid-headed sage ventured softly, "I'll make our synopsis short and bittersweet. Some fine, not-too-far-off day, a certain excessively self-absorbed little blue-and-white planet is going to wake up to find itself face to face with Destiny!"

Whether it likes it or not, Sybilla thought, her hunch confirmed.

&a.

One of the benefits of a professional sixth sense (as the Centre's famous hot tub, if not sworn to secrecy, could reveal in enviable detail) is that seers subtly attracted to one another have similarly delicate and often profoundly delightful ways of finding each other out.

As the other two sages slipped diplomatically away, their elegant, sphere-headed cousin turned to his waiting guest. "I've often wondered," he began carefully, "if and when one superbly talented foreteller of fabulous fortunes, finally meets his equally gifted match...."

"What happens," Sybilla interjected, "if and when, inevitably and just as irresistibly, she too reads his mind?"

"Yes."

"Try me."

Sometimes, in searching for Paradise, one finds oneself already savouring it en route.

Chez God

"PERSONALLY, I'VE ALWAYS HOPED THERE'S A REALLY
FABULOUS SHOE STORE."

— Aurora, Curator-in-Chief, Museum of Cultural
Culs-de-Sac

Welcome to Heaven!

✍ "OF COURSE, I don't really exist," God exclaimed, hastening past the Angelic Doorkeeper of the Ultimate Entrance to open the golden gate for Scheherazade. "At least, not as so often still portrayed; that archaic, frustratingly inadequate image of Me as taciturn, touchy and always, always aloof. Hard to find, and then even harder of hearing." A pair of incomparably broad, albeit metaphorical shoulders shrugged cheerfully.

"For better or worse, My celestial lot seems to be, how shall I say, forever beguilingly undefined, always just a little beyond the grasp of the imagination."

Endless flight over, amazed to find herself here, Scheherazade bowed the most respectful, heartfelt bow of her long career.

"Whoever You are, and however many tantalizing forms You choose to take, I'm profoundly honoured to meet You!"

"Of course you are. Everyone is, sooner or later!"

En route, Scheherazade had wondered whether it might be difficult to carry on a conversation with a seemingly unseen power able to anticipate one's every fleeting thought and word.

She was delighted, instead, to find how swiftly God put her at ease, eternal light courteously taking whatever intensity the moment required.

"Before we get down to business, perhaps you might enjoy a small, informal tour?"

To Scheherazade's fascination, her introduction to Heaven began with a companionable stroll through the Eternal Celestial Records Office. As she gazed around in wonder, angels of every professional predisposition were busily winging to and fro, effortlessly keeping track of the names, dates, duties and destinies of everyone who had ever lived, was now living or might ever hope to do so.

As they approached God's office, Scheherazade looked about, catching a first sight of the universe as seen from its innermost core, galaxy after luminous galaxy unfolding around her on every side. There's nothing quite like seeing the cosmos from its Founder's point of view, she thought wryly, to put everything in a whole new light.

For most individuals, life's day-to-day demands were more than enough. Perpetual accountability, clearly, was something else again.

"Must be difficult at times, having Creation at so many ages and stages," she observed.

"It's true. I do have to remember to be patient," the words reaching out to embrace a vast array of surrounding galaxies, all pulsating at their own speeds. "And yet while I'm grateful for everything they've done…," there was a pause of infinite tenderness, "I treasure far more all they have yet to become."

A moment later, Scheherazade felt herself moving, gently drawn closer to the open window.

The scene before them began to shift, rotating around them as galaxy after galaxy flashed into sight, each with its own distinctive constellations twinkling against a backdrop of still more stars.

"Quite the view, isn't it?"

"Heavenly," Scheherazade exclaimed. There was no other word.

God made a small attempt to bite an appropriately invisible tongue, only to be unable to resist.

"You know the old slogan: location, location, location!"

❦

Pleasantries complete, God cut to the celestial chase: "Which brings Me to…."

"The question of what it is that brings me here?" responded Scheherazade.

"Exactly." A quiet smile flickered in the air. "I don't suppose you'd find it excessively miraculous if I confess I already know the reason for your visit."

"I'd only be surprised if You didn't!" Scheherazade acknowledged.

"To be honest, I don't envy you your assignment. With so many galaxies competing for My attention these days, it's hard to say exactly where one rather minor little planet's supposed second Paradise might be found." There was a pause, another smile. "Then too, My memory doesn't seem what it used to be."

When God decides to change the subject, it's usually considered wise to go with the heavenly flow. Diplomatic though Scheherazade might normally be, however, a fleeting memory of Adam and Eve waving farewell seemed to leave her no choice.

Reaching across time and space, she conjured up the image of a small blue-and-white planet rotating on its axis, circling a mid-sized sun in the company of a few, far-distant planets it had yet to visit and which themselves, in turn, had so far never bothered to say hello.

"I suspect I don't need to tell You much about Earth," Scheherazade said, handing its very own designer-in-chief a holographic replica of this one among so many, many worlds.

"Tell me, instead, what you think it needs," God responded, cradling the little translucent globe in the gentlest of upturned, unseen hands.

Scheherazade closed her eyes, seeking an answer from the wisest, strongest and yet most vulnerable part of herself. After all, where better place to pray than, literally as well as figuratively, in the presence of God.

"For Earth, going around and around every twenty-four repetitive hours is no longer enough. All those same circular conversations on the same circular subjects daily become even less rewarding. Even at its best, something's truly missing!"

God waited in silence.

"If Earth is ever to find the Paradise it lost or, given its current population, an even larger one…."

Scheherazade hesitated, as if drawing inspiration from Heaven itself. Moments later the words came in a rush, as if of their own accord.

"It needs to change – and be changed. To transcend its old ways and even older fears. To see the universe with far humbler, bolder eyes. And, most importantly, to become worthy of all it has yet to discover, to celebrate and to share! Earth owes it to itself. And…."

Scheherazade paused, eyes fixed on the luminous source of past, passing and yet to come; including, however unexpectedly, this present electric encounter.

"And, ultimately, to You!"

In the silence that followed, Scheherazade felt herself the subject of a gaze more profound than any known before.

"To put the matter bluntly, you're firmly convinced it's time your little adopted planet did something truly heroic?"

"More than time!" (Crossing one's fingers in the presence of the deity, she decided, was probably frowned upon in the handbook of celestial guest etiquette.)

"A truly ambitious goal, under the circumstances. Any suggestions as to how?"

"Not yet," Scheherazade confessed. "But then I've a feeling You've been doing this kind of upgrade-and-development work quite a bit longer. than I have."

"Keeps Me fit!" A barely visible grin hovered in the air. "Every time is different. Every transition from an old world to a newer one, however inevitable and overdue, is always a challenge."

God turned, gazing outward upon so many whirling stars, lost in studying darkness forever becoming light. All the while, the little blue-and-white globe spun slowly in the same unseen hands.

"Seems like something of a long shot." A pause. "Especially given the latest news reports." There was another, much longer pause. "But I'm sure something will come to mind."

§

When a mysterious little bird had flown in through Scheherazade's open window, its visit had not been inspired by her beauty, courage or enterprise alone. Indeed, it was her subtle, limitless empathy that was the most admired, and often also the most timely.

Standing at God's side, she studied the invisible presence carefully. Sometimes the simplest question was the best.

"What's up?" she asked softly.

The Boss of All Celestial Bosses began to laugh. "When My advisors assured Me you were good at your work, they didn't say just how good."

"For some reason, I thought You looked the littlest bit … overtired perhaps?" she replied.

God stretched, sighed quietly, gazing all the while over trillions of starry worlds. "I'm not complaining of course – after all, I somehow seem to have been born for the role – but this particular universe-in-progress is unquestionably a very large enterprise to look after."

"More than a few galaxies, if I remember correctly," Scheherazade replied in a considerable understatement.

"With most having erotically charged inhabitants even now doing their usually literally level best to beget ever more descendants. And each of them, in turn, having unique yet kindred hopes and fears and all- too-poignant aspirations."

The distinguished head of Universe Inc. sighed once more, a long, slow exhalation older than time itself.

"Under such circumstances, it's really not surprising that every one of them, sooner or later, should find themselves turning to whatever happens to be their current local version of Me. Not just to know them and care for them in all their secret contradictions, but also to guide each of them toward that more abundant future, long desired yet still so indistinctly seen, which will surely prove their ultimate destination and reward!"

"Somehow I doubt anyone else could do Your job," Scheherazade said reassuringly "I greatly doubt anyone else knows how!"

God paused, frowning, as if deliberating how much to reveal.

"Yes?" she ventured.

"Since you asked…." God smiled wryly. "Truth is, the older I get, the more a short break in My so admirably never-ending routine begins to seem all too welcome."

God's sudden yawn was followed by an equally eloquent grimace. "Some mornings lately, in fact, I find Myself yearning to go back to sleep." The celestial frown deepened. "Probably not the best response when the cosmos is still expanding, still greatly in need of hands-on attention and care."

Scheherazade gazed out Heaven's open window. A wholly improbable idea, a seemingly-impossible possibility slowly began to take form in her mind. She took a deep breath. And a very big leap.

"Have You ever considered the possible overall health benefits of … taking a day off?"

"Only twenty-four hours?"

There was a long silence. "Hmmmmmnnn."

Advance Warning

☙ A SMALL BELL chimed ceremoniously.

"Please excuse me, but there's a delegation of spiritual leaders from the Galaxy of Indefinable Grace whom I previously agreed to see. Something about preserving the sacred unpredictability of their agenda for the next five million years."

The small bell chimed again, though now twice in succession. Then it began a small tinkling refrain which, as God listened attentively, was repeated ever more urgently.

"And it also appears that one of My more promising, if still rather excitable young star systems, is facing its very first major theological emergency. Seems a little reassurance and a broader, less catastrophic perspective are in order."

God smiled benevolently. "Around here, somebody's forever needing something. I'll be right back. In the meantime, make yourself at home."

☙

With growing fascination, Scheherazade wandered slowly through a series of celestial reception rooms furnished with ritual images and sacred objects from a million faiths, each seeking to express the same unseen power which sustained, affirmed and ultimately understood them all infinitely better than they did themselves.

"I always knew you'd get here eventually," said a quiet voice by the door. "Care for a little something for the celestial road?"

Pale chartreuse eyes beaming with pleasure, the Angel of Uncanny

Encouragement slipped into the room, a crowded tray balanced on one shapely wing. "How long has it been since last we met?"

Sharing a cup of tea, Scheherazade and one of her earliest angelic acquaintances reminisced over parallel professions, recalling moments in which they found exactly the right answers, or new and even better questions for clients ready at last to benefit from them. As the two stood before Heaven's open windows, taking in the starlit vistas, one of the wisest angels in the business contemplated her visiting ally thoughtfully.

"While I'm delighted you're finally here, there's something you should know." The Angel of Uncanny Encouragement paused, reflecting on how much to tell. "While invisibility may be the chosen default disguise, it doesn't mean God is entirely unreadable."

Scheherazade nodded, clearly having experienced this herself only moments before.

"Just between ourselves," her old friend continued, "the Boss seems unusually preoccupied lately. With the fate of universe in general, and...." There was the most diplomatic of hesitations. "And one rather dramatically underperforming planet in particular."

"Not entirely without reason," Scheherazade responded dryly.

"Point taken," the Angel of Uncanny Encouragement replied, her expression suggesting she too might be readying herself for emergencies better forestalled.

"Quarrels in the sandboxes of time so often end in tears. After a moment or two, however, all is usually forgiven, forgotten and a new game begins." The angel's lyrical voice darkened. "These days, however, more and more *enfants* increasingly *terribles* have the means to do each other in once and for all."

"A very big bang can be a very big temptation," Scheherazade agreed. "Eventually, ever-more-metastasizing defence spending can become totally self-defeating."

"Trust me; this is not one of those times where Heaven wants to have to pick up the pieces afterwards."

If there are any, that is, thought Scheherazade!

❧

"The sight of a blazing, lifeless, little black ball in space," God said, soundlessly re-entering the room, "is hardly the sort of pre-breakfast spectacle likely to make My day." The invisible founder of the cosmos gazed thoughtfully through all Heaven's windows. "Nor, for that matter, the preferred legacy of so many equally disappointed spiritual guides and guardians over time."

As Scheherazade listened, it was clear that the proverbial road to Hell might not be the only one paved with frequently frustrated intentions. Even God, it appeared, sometimes needed a little moral support.

"However ironic in hindsight," she ventured softly, "it almost seems as if such well-meant spiritual *largesse* is itself part of the problem. When Earth's citizenry are not busily laying claim to their little corner of the cosmos, they're likely squabbling over who has the most compellingly correct interpretation of You!" Scheherazade paused, then tact made way for truth. "Or, most probably, doing both at once with blind conviction."

"A huge dilemma," God agreed, the measured voice deepening under the double weight of cosmic responsibilities and companion regrets.

"Sad to say, I've seen this happen again and again. Temporarily, world after world after world mistakes the self-serving for the sacred, the momentary for the eternal. They forever confuse the all-too-evanescent parts with the quintessentially timeless whole."

"And the solution?"

God looked away, appraising so many watching, waiting, starlit worlds.

"Do you remember, when you first arrived, I confessed that I did not exist? At least, not in that painfully restrictive way in which far too many still continue to see Me; as an ultimately unknowable Someone or Something out there, forever problematically apart.

"Well, the equally good news is that they don't really exist either!"

There was a pause, a wry smile, and a long nod of appreciation to the Angel of Uncanny Encouragement.

"If the truth be told, more than half the efforts of My tirelessly selfless staff are spent reminding the Universe that outward appearances are finally both fleeting and false, and that no matter how isolated and alone every individual may sometimes feel, in reality not one among them stops where their temporary, illusory bodies seem to end.

"Everything is connected," God declared expansively, an invisible eyebrow lifting in quiet satisfaction. "Wherever you go, it's impossible to leave Home!"

In the distance, stars seemed to pause in their journeying.

"Personal evolution, it seems, is a long waking-up to soul. And the work of the soul is a long waking-up to all the worlds that lie beyond and await within; and to all the other, seemingly-separate souls and worlds from which it is at once both temporarily estranged and permanently indivisible."

The air filled with a fond, infinitely patient, all-encompassing laughter. "It's so simple, really: I can never belong to anyone, because … I am Everyone!"

As if in subtle harmony with the divine, Scheherazade's thoughts ebbed and flowed with all the possibilities of cosmic fate and cosmic folly, of freedom, faith and fortune intertwined. Around her, the vast celestial scene seemed suddenly, ever so subtly to shift, the air filling with the most hauntingly rapturous of sounds.

"Look," said God, "and listen."

Suddenly it seemed as if every circling planet, visible and invisible, and every star and star-cluster near and far, somehow shared in the same secret music: each one offering up in the surrounding darkness its own uniquely brave and poignant song, and yet all playing faithfully together in a greater symphony.

God's gifts may come in God's good time, but Scheherazade's gratitude, expressed in soundless tears of joy, was immediate, immense and profound.

"You're most, most welcome," God said softly.

Still transfigured by her vision of the great ethereal starry concert that was the universe resounding in its own delight, Scheherazade could only nod.

"All God's children…," the Angel of Uncanny Encouragement began to whisper.

"Are One with Me." There was a pause, then a widening smile, now infinitely more contented than before. "Trust me. I know this stuff. By heart."

꙳

The small celestial bell chimed softly once more. Scheherazade, taking her cue, rose to her feet. "Thank You," she said softly, grateful for all that had been said, aware that so much more remained unspoken.

"My pleasure. And, of course, just doing My job." God scrutinized

Heaven's latest visitor carefully. "I hope your stay here has been instructive."

"Profoundly so. Though I suspect it may take a while to come to terms with this particular experience."

"Oddly enough, almost all My guests feel that way."

Scheherazade turned, taking her angelic old friend's hand. "And thank you again as well. You've given me, and Earth, much to ponder."

"May it ponder happily away – but not for too long." The white-winged figure winked. "Remember, there's a widespread saying in these parts: God helps those...."

"Who help themselves," Scheherazade concluded. "Don't worry; I'll try my best to remind them."

She took a last sip of celestial tea, fortifying herself for the return journey. "And on Earth, I believe, there's an equally brief, if all-too-often forgotten prayer," she continued, looking directly into God's eyes. "Help us that we may help You."

"Never fear," God replied with a suddenly bemused smile. "One way or another, Earth still has a special place on My to-do list, its local cast of singularly irrepressible sins and sinners notwithstanding."

Taking Scheherazade's arm, her host led the way toward a gleaming SS Serendipity, waiting patiently to return her to those lesser, more fractious, all-too-human dimensions of reality.

"*Au revoir*, as we say around here," God whispered. "No matter what happens next...." There was a brief pause as a bevy of high-tech angels swept by at even higher speed to destinations and duties unrevealed. "Or, perhaps I should say, only seems to happen. I'm sure we'll meet again soon."

Clearly, thought Scheherazade, there were times when the universe could be a very small place. Especially if you happened to be God.

Just as she rechecked her flight instruments a last time, there was a sudden tap on the still half open canopy.

"Please give My best wishes to Eve. If, that is, you should chance to be in her neighbourhood again." There was a quick, aeon-encompassing smile. "Tell both her and Adam I said hello."

Scheherazade blinked. "I most certainly will – and I'm sure they'll be delighted." She looked up warily. "No hard feelings?"

"*Au contraire*," God chuckled. "To tell the truth, I've been secretly rather fond of that particular pair, however unexpectedly precocious and contract-averse they turned out to be." There was a brief pause. "Funny how things work out: no sooner had I created them than they both decided to hop the garden wall and tear off in a totally different direction, thereby sending some very embarrassed guardian angels hurriedly back to training school!"

Scheherazade joined in the laughter, shaking her head as she gazed around Heaven one final time.

"Strange, isn't it? From this vantage point, everything has a way of seeming somehow part of a larger plan!"

"Divine inspiration, perhaps?" God replied.

Kismet

"QUE SERA, SERA!"

— Dante and The Infernos

Classic Symptoms

❧ IT IS NOT UNUSUAL, if one has unexpectedly found oneself in the far distant future – or even in Heaven itself – to depart those fabled realms somewhat reluctantly. It was, accordingly, not so very surprising that as SS Serendipity rocketed back toward Earth, successfully picking up Scheherazade's associates en route, its passengers should find themselves progressively more contemplative.

From all reports, something sizeable seemed soon to occur, but what that something was remained a mystery.

Once safely returned to *terra* supposedly *firma*, there would be time enough to exchange tales, compare thoughts, and, in general, do their best to decipher their recent, so-varied encounters. For the moment, however, as increasingly familiar galaxies faded swiftly behind, all seven women were content to savour the rich, reflective silence of eternity.

From past exploits, each knew that conclusions need not be forced, nor decisions prematurely made. If they gave themselves time, Time itself would ultimately give them answers in return.

Ahead, a tiny globe flickered invitingly in the darkness of space, gradually growing larger to reveal shadowy oceans and vast, crowded cities of light, their hopes and fears still unseen.

A moment later, all aboard SS Serendipity shared a deep, involuntary breath. Directly in front of them, the outline of Earth seemed to flash briefly in the darkness, the premonition vanishing as quickly as it came.

Welcome home ... but to what?

❧

Returning to Scheherazade's villa, their first wish had been for sleep, preferably by the pool. It had been a long trip and even the most resilient of heroines was the better for a little judicious pampering. And yet....

Around them, rising winds surged unseasonably through the palms. Flowers murmured among themselves, then hurriedly closed. On every horizon, the sky darkened with flocks of birds suddenly hoping to migrate to any other planet than this.

All, certainly, did not appear for the best. At least, not today. And, if first impressions were correct, tomorrow didn't look all that promising, either.

"Can't leave this place unsupervised," Tatiana muttered, "even for a week."

Scheherazade declared, "This feels like one of those planetary medical emergencies where I'd welcome a second opinion. Maybe even a third."

⁊❧

In matters of great significance, the cosmos seems temperamentally inclined to the view that while simple solutions may be best, unexpected ones are far more fun. So it was that, only moments after making her request, Scheherazade was not surprised to find three figures come sailing over the horizon.

"Abracadabra sends his apologies," a small marble statue exclaimed, cheerfully tethering his own personal little white cloud to a neighbouring palm tree. "A rather pressing occult emergency elsewhere, I gather."

His two passengers still fashionably incognito beneath matching hooded sky-blue cloaks, the small marble figure swept off his own frayed straw hat, bowing to Scheherazade and her six friends with gallant, if slightly arthritic, panache.

"Permit me to introduce myself. I am, even to my own occasional surprise, the widely-renowned if seldom seen, creakingly well-preserved Truly Ancient Oracle of the Not Completely Indecipherable Past."

"Your reputation precedes you," Scheherazade replied just as courteously, fragments of the jaunty little statue's astonishing exploits springing unbidden to mind.

Chuckling modestly, the new arrival expanded on his distinctive expertise for the benefit of the women and his own evident pleasure.

"As you well know, the universe is already jam-packed with the sage of this, and the seer of that, and so on and so forth. One or two of whom, I must admit, are astonishingly good at guessing at a respectable percentage of developments yet to come.

"Whereas I, on the other hand, have a talent infinitely more subtle and rare: namely, the uncanny ability to predict what happened yesterday, and all the yesterdays before that." Aged marble eyes flashed with pride. "Not just weather, sports and stock market results, but – infinitely more important – the normally well-hidden truth of what really, really happened!"

Near-inevitable answer notwithstanding, Scheherazade sensed she still had to ask what had gone on – or, more accurately, gone wrong – while they were away.

❦

"Would you like the whole, entire, detailed and documented ex-planation?" Abracadabra's antique stand-in asked hopefully.

"It comes complete with charts, calculations, analogies, and reference notes. Terrifically impressive stuff." There was a reluctant pause. "The only drawback, however, is that fully to do justice to all the disturbing developments of the past week might itself take roughly the previous fifty thousand years. More or less."

"Is there, perhaps, a slightly abbreviated version?" Scheherazade inquired gently.

"Indubitably!" The new arrival drew himself up, his expression suddenly as grim and inarguable as a tombstone.

"What really happened while you were away is that every last one of Earth's long unacknowledged debts, deferrals and self-deceptions finally got understandably furious, ganged up and, metaphorically speaking, rode into town guns a-blazin'!"

"Oops," Scheherazade murmured. There clearly wasn't much else to say.

"Tarnation!" Tatiana echoed. "There go our pedicures!"

❦

"Probably had to happen," declared the taller of the two hooded figures now stepping together, hand in hand, from the little white cloud.

In the next moment, he threw back his sky-blue cowl to reveal the World's Greatest Gravedigger.

"Predictably, the response so far has been more of the same." His companion's matching cape slipped aside in turn, showing the equally troubled face of the World's Most Beautiful Astronomer. "Planetary denial and plea bargaining to the max."

"And it's not working?" Scheherazade ventured, already sure of the answer.

"Hell's bells a-clanging over the joint," the World's Greatest Gravedigger confirmed. "Not that anyone's going to admit it, of course."

There was an awkward silence.

"Sometimes a little objectivity and clear-eyed repentance can go a long way in helping sort things out," Marina suggested, her optimism less than total.

"In theory, perhaps." Leila frowned. "Judging by its record, however, Earth seems far from ready for the restorative benefits of silence, self-examination and contrition, let alone developing an enduring taste for same."

There was a brief pause while everyone present tried to imagine a crowded little blue-and-white planet resting uncomfortably on its knees, whispering in the ear of an understanding, no-nonsense spiritual advisor its many and manifold departures from all its best intentions for itself and toward others.

"Do entire planets ever freely and fully confess their inevitable failings?" Qingling asked.

"Some are said to have been so inclined. Surprisingly successfully at times." The little marble statue gave a diffident shrug. "Then again, from the look of so many galaxies these days, they're probably just rumours."

The World's Most Beautiful Astronomer glanced at her companion, his arms crossed over the handle of his heraldic spade. Current planetary difficulties notwithstanding, their eyes shone with a mutual delight all the deeper for having been so long denied.

"The more common pattern," the Truly Ancient Oracle continued, "seems to be that most eventually do something catastrophic to both themselves and others. And then (and only then) become supremely scared out of their wits and orbits as a result.

"Immediately, of course, they promise solemnly never ever to do it again, whatever that particular 'it' might be. Until, of course, enough time has passed that, unfortunately, their lessons are unlearned again."

The World's Greatest Gravedigger stared upwards, searching for answers as urgent as they were still unknown, his face bearing the look of one who in his time had seen both an infinity of smiles and the fadings of smiles.

"Earth's beginning to look not so much like a recipe for disaster," he grunted, "as damn near the entire cookbook!"

The hand of the World's Most Beautiful Astronomer reached out to cover his.

Pastoral paradise Earth might once have been; garden of earthly delights it now clearly wasn't.

Foremost among Scheherazade's qualities (as a certain nonchalant little gold-and-white bird would have readily agreed) was her ability effortlessly to conceal decisiveness beneath calm detachment. Until, that is, the suddenly opportune moment came....

There might, or might not, be a short-cut to a second Eden. But, for now, Scheherazade was content to know the current whereabouts of a certain, still well-preserved pair who'd once been on intimate terms with the first.

"I hope you won't mind, but I'd like to borrow your little white go-getter for a few days." Having watched Abracadabra earlier, she felt sure she could manage both accelerator and brakes. If worst came to worst, there appeared to be a small but mighty horn.

With a swift, chivalrous bow, the venerable marble intermediary held out a spare set of ignition keys, his pale stone eyes twinkling with a potent mix of insight and surmise.

"Let me guess," he announced, suddenly rejuvenated and impish beyond his years.

Scheherazade put a discreet finger to her lips.

Solemnly nodding his long-ago reattached head, the Truly Ancient Oracle held an alabaster forefinger firmly against his own sealed lips.

"Mum's the word!"

Girl Talk

&⚹ SCHEHERAZADE LAY BACK, watching as constellation after bright constellation flew by, each shepherding its familiar stars, and from time to time gently nudging errant or absent-minded ones back to their pre-assigned places.

Dozing off, she was confident her six time-travelling friends would make the most of a few well-deserved days of R & R. As for the World's Greatest Gravedigger and its Most Beautiful Astronomer, she sincerely hoped that uniquely impressive pair would find her secluded villa exactly the right place for the extended *tête-à-tête* so decidedly deserved.

Still in their prime, each possessed an enviable, if very different, professional expertise, together with a hard-won and deeply compatible sense of personal and cosmic proportion. There were much worse things, she well knew, on which to build even the most undefined and unrestricted of relationships.

Happy at the prospect, if not also perhaps just the slightest bit envious, Scheherazade fell soundly asleep.

&⚹

"She looks even lovelier when she's dreaming," Eve whispered, polishing her spectacles and peering even more closely.

"Almost as beautiful as you," Adam responded, gallant and prudent at the same time. He edged closer. "Seems a shame to wake her."

The little white cloud had done exactly as Abracadabra would have wished, bringing its passenger safely to her destination, setting her down on the well-kept grounds of the Fountain of Eternal Youth Retirement Home without sound or bump.

As Scheherazade's unbidden dream came to an end, the last of a line of shadowy crimson spectres capered confidently off into the mist, waving as they went. "See you soon," they seemed to say. Her eyelids fluttered.

"I told you today was going to be different," Adam exclaimed.

Eve nodded, attention fixed on their guest. "Hello again, my dear."

"Hello to you both," Scheherazade answered warmly, relieved to see Earth's first couple still looking reassuringly alert, still willing to make the most of their present world, however shrunken it might now seem. Even if, the better to do so, they both discreetly turned up their hearing aids, their welcoming smiles radiating over understandably well-lined faces.

"I wasn't sure we'd ever see you again," said Adam.

"I, on the other hand, simply wondered when." Eyes narrowed, concealing yet searching at the same time. She studied their repeat visitor carefully.

"What's going on? Or should I say, what's gone wrong?"

Over drinks on the patio of their small suite, Scheherazade brought Earth's two most senior citizens up to date; describing, to their increasing distress, how their descendants now seemed dangerously close to losing not only their way but also (and far more disturbingly) the ability to find it ever again.

"Alas, Earth now seems unconsciously more intent on disaster than deliverance," she concluded.

"Progress there has never been easy." Adam shook his head, reliving the long hard slog beyond Eden. "The most extraordinary stamina is needed. Sometimes you just have to keep on going on – and then on and on some more. A matter of faith, almost."

"Speaking of which…," Scheherazade hesitated, unsure how to convey the unexpected message entrusted to her care. "God says hello. In fact, I was expressly asked to convey the warmest of greetings to you both."

"How is our erstwhile Landlord?" Eve asked cautiously, cheeks flushing despite herself.

"From what little I saw, extraordinarily busy these days," Scheherazade answered diplomatically. She paused, wondering how much to reveal. "But I did get the impression that, crowded cosmic calendar notwithstanding, God somehow still manages to keep a fairly steady eye on Earth."

At the words, a little blue-and-white planet's earliest ancestors reached reassuringly for one another's hand.

"Glad to hear it," Adam declared, looking both impossibly young and as old as Time.

"All the same," said Eve, her smile both rueful and proud, "I wish there were something we could do! Once a mother, always a mother...."

❧

After a pleasant but unremarkable evening meal, Adam had taken out his dentures and gone to lie down for a nap. Arm in arm, the two women set out together for a companionable stroll in the softening twilight. Birds flitted through the evening sky, flowers tilted their heads toward sleep and the first stars from surrounding constellations began to echo one another in an ascending chorus of light.

Eve paused, the setting sun and rising stars together illuminating an increasingly thoughtful face. "It all seems so long, long ago," she mused, then turning quietly toward Scheherazade, already deciding how much of a secret to share.

"Let me guess," Scheherazade ventured tenderly, opening the way. "The truth is you're...."

"Bored stiff!" Eve confirmed, before adding even more emphatically, "Absolutely, definitively, totally bored! Though it's not as if I'm ungrateful for what we now have," she added, shaking her head. "This unlikely little retirement community is an anonymous, genteel haven discreetly tucked inside one of the most uneventful constellations of the galaxy, offering a full range of commendably lethargic virtues: theme parties every month, and seasonal celebrations for every faith under a hundred thousand suns.

"Requisite appreciation notwithstanding, I'm finding myself mightily disenchanted. And I'm more than certain Adam feels the same way. After all, this seems hardly the place for two once such notoriously fractious pioneers to spend the rest of eternity!"

Scheherazade, expression half-hidden in the dusk, could only agree.

"You should have seen me in Eden!" Eve whispered at last.

"There was no one around to compare me to, of course," she continued, eyes coming alive with a sudden joyous fire. "But I was so, so beautiful. Not just because I was a young woman, quickening for the first time like the earliest blush on the budded rose ... but because all of Eden was reflected in me. And I reflected it back.

"Paradise was ... *paradise!* I was there, but it was not me alone. At one with everything, I shared at once the light and love of all Creation."

She glanced sideways at Scheherazade before confiding archly, "Adam didn't stand a chance!"

"How could he!"

The two women burst out laughing, the sound startling a few elderly couples taking their after-dinner brandies on the retirement home's darkening veranda.

Eve lowered her voice and leaned closer. "In fact, if truth be told, neither did the Devil!"

Scheherazade's eyes widened. She now felt even more certain that Eve's version of what she and the Serpent had been up to in that famously contentious Garden, would prove dramatically different from so many later, misogynist interpretations.

"What really happened is that our roles were actually reversed. The Devil didn't tempt *me*." Eve smiled, her eyes half-closing as she replayed a swift, solitary struggle and subsequent triumph so long, long ago.

"Truth is ... I tempted *him!*" As she spoke, Time itself seemed to open in a radiant flash.

In this small, stooped but still proud woman now standing beside her, Scheherazade suddenly saw all the incomparable, sadly long-forgotten bravery of an irresistible, invincible young girl. Alone in all Creation and in her choice. Determined to take upon herself that first, fateful responsibility for all the joys and sorrows of generations yet to come.

"As I told you when first we met, Adam and I could have stayed in Eden – gone nowhere, done nothing. But if we had ... then nothing more would ever have happened! No Fall, and so no consequent attempt to arise and go forward. No suffering, and so no victory beyond. No selfless, primal communion lost, and so no subsequent search for ever deeper, greater understandings still."

Eve's face darkened.

"The Devil's true job, all subsequent reports to the contrary, was forever to deny us Eden's greatest treasure; that so tantalizingly-forbidden fruit which contained within itself, like the explosion hidden within the first atom God ever made, the seeds of all things yet to come.

"His real task was not to lure us to go; it was to sweet-talk us to stay. But somehow, in the face of my beauty, and my determination…," she paused, searching hard to find words for powers she still couldn't quite express or explain, "Satan himself seemed strangely powerless to resist."

"And so?" Scheherazade asked softly.

"And so together Adam and I ate from the Tree of Knowledge," Eve said simply, "and the apple proved only an appetizer!"

&

"The Devil must have been rather disappointed you got away with it," Scheherazade ventured.

"Maybe yes. And maybe no. I've sometimes wondered if he gave in almost too quickly. On reflection, I think he might secretly have been just as curious as we were about how everything would turn out." Eve gave a bewitchingly renegade smile. "Then, too, given our grandchildren's undeniably checkered history, that first, so fateful choice certainly seems to have given both him and his crimson associates more than enough work to do!"

There was a long silence while Scheherazade contemplated all she knew of the unending inventiveness of Satan & Company over time, their many elaborate stratagems expressly designed to make even the best of worlds all the worse.

Or so it might seem. And yet….

Overhead, on this night so much like other nights, star after star continued to appear, glittering in their shared dedication to whatever might be the universe's still unfolding purpose.

Eve looked closely at Scheherazade, still lost in thoughts of worlds within worlds, and worlds beyond.

"You were thinking…?" Earth's first woman inquired gently.

"Even though I've never met him, I've sometimes wondered whether the Devil himself – like most everyone and everything else – might be somehow playing a part, secretly or not, in a far larger, grander game."

"It's been a very long time since I last saw him," Eve's voice took on a new tone of affectionate reminiscence, "but chances are you could be right. And what's more, I suspect he, too, occasionally wonders – his own earlier exile notwithstanding – whether he might ultimately still be working for somebody else."

"Sort of an unwritten, unspoken celestial subcontract," Scheherazade mused aloud.

"Something like that. For all his faults, he's an exceptionally engaging, unusually well-informed gentleman." Eyes gleaming mischievously, Eve stopped in mid-stride. "If you'd really like some answers to the questions that brought you here, why don't you go and ask him? After all," Eve continued, breaking into a conspiratorial smile, "it might be simplest to find out what the devil's wrong with Earth…."

"By going directly to the source!"

"Exactly! In fact, if only I can remember where I put it, I still have his business card somewhere. Just in case," she added with a wink.

'Never say never,' Scheherazade thought before wondering what God might be thinking.

€

One standing on aging tiptoe, the other bending gratefully down to kiss a weathered cheek, Earth's oldest, greatest-grandmother and her new, long-awaited friend hugged one another tightly.

"Call it a hunch, but somehow I'm certain my ancient adversary will more than welcome your visit." Eve smiled a quiet private smile, the most ancient knowing smile in the world. "As well as the challenge…."

Scheherazade blushed.

"Don't worry. You'll do fine," Eve added. "From the look of you, you've definitely got my genes."

Welcome to Hell

❦ MUCH TO HIS endless amusement, His Most Satanic Majesty remains an undisputed master of professional disguise.

Like his better-behaved, but far less newsworthy celestial brethren, he is capable not only of changing shape at will, but also of being everywhere and in the company of everyone (whether they like it or not). Such omnipresent versatility is, understandably, a source of great power and pride, the former all the more effective for being so deceptively unseen.

Being rather careful about just whom he reveals himself to directly – given thousands of years' experience with some exceptionally shady characters with equally-long memories – the Devil rarely agrees to unexpected, unvetted business meetings on the spur of the moment. Not surprisingly, he much prefers to be the one who sets the terms of encounter.

In Scheherazade's case, however, forearmed with the benefit of a memorable but regrettably unrecorded phone call which Eve secretly made on Scheherazade's behalf – an unprecedented personal interview was swiftly arranged. Providing, of course, that she could successfully negotiate Demonic Security.

❦

Conventionally, the Devil's realm is to be found at the end of an increasingly slippery slope, metaphorical or otherwise, disappearing down into the ever hotter, more shadowy depths at the centre of every planetary core. In the interests of time, however, Scheherazade and her friends chose to take one of the new top-secret, ultra-high-speed elevators only very recently installed as Earth's population began exponentially to increase, and the requisite devilish duties correspondingly to expand.

"Welcome to Hell," proclaimed a deep-voiced, red-haired giant with flashing orange eyes, extending his huge hand in turn to Scheherazade and each of her friends.

"Must take some getting used to," Scheherazade replied with no little empathy. Adam and Eve, it was clear, were not the only ones in the universe to have found themselves unexpectedly sending out change-of-address cards. She peered past the crimson-robed reception committee of associate demons, and on to a selection of seemingly empty cells available for both short and extended stays. The ultra-large furnace at the centre conveniently provided both less light and more heat than most would normally prefer.

"More of an extreme climate, you might say," the chief of Demonic Security observed. "After a while, though, you may find it becoming surprisingly comfortable."

"It's very different than I anticipated," Leila observed. "All so neat and tidy."

"Of course it is," the red-haired giant replied, his large orange eyes beaming. "We've modernized!" Obviously proud of recent developments, he continued on just as cheerfully. "We've become more market-oriented.

"That said, we continue to focus on the same basic themes: temptation, of course, along with punishment (a house speciality, as ever). Not to mention the very latest in new and improved variations on The Old Seven Deadlies, as we like to call them. Then there are all the many wonderful secondary opportunities for anyone and everyone to turn away from the straight and narrow. Or, if we're lucky, to fall or be enticed from grace." He puffed out his not inconsiderable crimson chest. "All in all, we've built up quite a distinguished reputation over countless generations of sins and sinners: a proudly infamous tradition of being the very best in the cosmos in our ability to seduce, beguile and deceive!"

"In which case, where are all the sad-faced souls in torment we've come to expect and shudder at?" Marina glanced about carefully once more. "All those woebegone sinners who, repenting too late, now drag themselves round with anguished cries and pointless lamentations, forever condemned (in over-sized, over-stuffed classical paintings at least) to interminable torments?"

"They've all been out-placed, of course," the giant responded with a hugely satisfied grin.

"Fortunately for us," he went on, "all the latest research studies show that sinners are better punished (some might even say improved) by coming inwardly to understand the true nature of their own misdeeds. Given enough time and the invisible workings of an uneasy conscience, this inevitable awakening leads, sooner or later, to repentance; which leads to compassion (for themselves and others); which leads to redemption; which leads to...."

"In other words, you let the sinner live with his or her sin and all its consequences – hidden and otherwise – before, during and even after what passes for death, until he or she figures it out," Scheherazade said, summarizing the process.

"Yup. Either all by themselves, or with the help of as much kindly satanic assistance as is needed. It's a much less crowded, more cost-effective way to run this place, believe me," the senior demonic vice-president declared proudly. "Far better to let the guilty do most of the work," he chuckled. "We find it helps build character."

"Besides," he shrugged winningly, offering up a small confession of his own, "I'm sure you've heard the old expression, 'lazy devil.'"

❧

More able than most to follow the faint, elusive pathways of cosmic justice wherever they might lead, Sybilla could not avoid asking a harsher, darker question.

"But what about all those self-obsessed psychopaths of history? All those who, century after blood-stained century, see every virtue – honour, bravery, beauty, love – as nothing more than offerings to their own insatiable hunger, as just another course in evil's endless, gluttonous feast, and everyone else as merely their well-deserved appetizers?"

The red-haired giant stared grimly at his red-robed associates, then rubbed his large hands together in slow satisfaction. "Let's just say that, when and where it's really necessary, we demons haven't lost our historic touch!"

"No skills like the 'olde' skills," piped up one of the more grizzled figures in the all-crimson crowd, to a burst of devilish laughter.

The red-haired giant devil examined Scheherazade and her friends carefully. "Appearances to the contrary, in the long run no one ever really gets away with anything! Absolutely everyone we 'interview' eventually comes to see the error of their ways. After all," he added fearsomely, "there's that not so little matter of our professional demonic integrity to consider!"

A moment later, realizing that, thanks to the power of all seven ladies' distracting charms, he had nearly forgotten the most important part of Hell's standardized pre-screening procedure, the red-haired giant's hitherto largely hospitable expression changed. Looking deep into Scheherazade's eyes, his appraising, interrogatory stare was that of a senior devil who had successfully exposed quite an impressive list of ultimately inadequate would-be heroes and heroines in his long subterranean career.

Scheherazade, however, returned his gaze with a bemused, unblinking smile, until at last the crimson giant looked away. He sighed, his secret suspicions confirmed.

"Somehow I suspect it's already too late to ask you to sign our standard non-disclosure form."

Enter, Big D

❦ MUCH TO THE Underworld's satisfaction, a host of nifty, new hi-tech features had been added during its recent renovation. The sudden obligatory cloud of multi-coloured, sulphurous smoke from which the Devil now emerged, while already a bit of a theatrical cliché, still never failed to impress and delight the younger demons.

Scheherazade and her friends appeared equally enthralled. Not least perhaps because, as the smoke cleared, the imperturbable figure now standing before them, happily asserting pride of place in an elegant three-piece imported wool-and-cashmere suit, red silk tie and perfectly matching rose in his lapel, was only twelve inches high.

"Welcome to my kingdom," the Demon-in-Chief said courteously. "We're fairly informal around here. You can call me 'Big D'."

❦

About to introduce herself and her friends, Scheherazade stopped.

"Do you always look like that?" she inquired softly.

Grateful for a question he appeared even to have been secretly awaiting, Big D snapped his fingers. Instantly disappearing into a second enormous fiery cloud, he re-emerged now fully sixty feet tall, resplendent in shining black armour, looking suitably daunting and beaming down.

"So, what do you think of this version?" he asked cheerfully. A six-foot, bright red plume swirled above the helmet tucked carelessly under his left arm.

"Even more elegant and dramatic, and highly useful on festive occasions,

I'm sure," Scheherazade replied honestly, not unappreciative of the benefits, both personal and professional, of a suitably versatile wardrobe.

With a snap of demonic fingers, another well-executed cloud of multi-coloured smoke came and went as the heraldic black colossus faded swiftly away – to be replaced in turn by the smiling, now human-sized figure of the Devil himself, updated and undisguised, in all his casual, laid-back, contemporary glory.

Perennially youthful-looking, tall, dark-haired with traces of silver and gold, he was irresistibly handsome, comfortably yet fashionably dressed in designer jeans with a turquoise-and-silver belt buckle, a pale-yellow linen shirt with sleeves rolled part way up his sinewy forearms, a subtly restrained, pre-owned imported gold watch (won in a bet) and a pair of expensive, well-worn hiking boots.

"Yes, just in case you're wondering, this is it: the real me," Big D admitted, his suitably hooded eyes twinkling softly. "For the moment, at least. Just a plain, ordinary workin' man."

Marina, Leila, Qingling, Yazmina, Tatiana and Sybilla all looked at Scheherazade. Then at a quietly smiling Big D. Then back to her. Six remarkably experienced ladies exchanged slow glances and fast thoughts.

There was no denying that devilishly good-looking men had ways of getting a woman into a world of trouble, welcome or otherwise. Or that exceptionally beautiful heroines, left to their own devices, could just as readily lead even the most seductive of silver-tongued devils into unexpected worlds of wonders, and mazes from which they, too, might find themselves surprisingly unable, or unwilling, to escape.

To their delight, Scheherazade, as if already well on the way to confirming their suspicions, said absolutely nothing.

*

"As you so rightly guessed, those first apparitions, however much fun they may be, are but minor parts of a necessarily extensive repertoire." The most hypnotic eyes this side of Heaven lingered on Scheherazade. "I'm delighted, although not surprised, that you saw through our little test so quickly."

"I didn't really expect you to show up with horns, fangs, barbed tail and well-polished antique pitchfork," Scheherazade answered, one eyebrow raised in lingering amusement.

"These days, unfortunately, we reserve our traditional attire for ceremonial occasions – formal dinners, parades and such like." Big D gave a sudden sigh. "Hot and heavy though they may be, I must admit I sometimes rather miss our ancient regalia."

To her surprise, Scheherazade was finding it increasingly easy to follow her host's extraordinary thoughts. "I would imagine one of the benefits must have been that anyone meeting you in the good old days, as it were, would be in absolutely no doubt whom they were dealing with."

"None whatsoever," Big D agreed, clearly pleased to be so readily understood. "Our famously scarlet uniform had a way of getting and keeping our guests' attention from the very start, offering far less room for confusion or belated excuses.

"Times change, however. Nowadays we find it's better if we blend in." He smiled a small sly, ironic smile. "Let's just say, we adapt!"

❦

Introductions complete, the Devil fell silent, lost in an uneasy reverie.

"A mutual friend phoned to say you might be coming," he confided at last. "An all too brief call, quite out of the blue."

Scheherazade wasn't sure, but he seemed to stifle a sigh. Given Eve's parting words, she suddenly found herself studying her host with the most exquisite, even strangely tender sensitivity.

"When I last saw her," she began, "Eve asked me to convey her warmest wishes, and to say that, ancient disagreements notwithstanding, she still remembers you quite fondly." She paused at the last word, recalling the recent, shared confidences of two open-hearted women on an evening stroll. "In fact, to quote her exactly, she said you were an exceptionally fascinating, unusually well-informed gentleman."

At those so evidently appreciated words, the Devil began to glow, albeit discreetly.

"If only you had been able to see Eve in those earliest days!" His eyes flashed with a memory clearly still poignant and never far away. "So young, so radiant! It was as if she taught the sun to shine! Breathtakingly beautiful, heart-breakingly joyful, so astonishingly wise beyond her years…."

Big D stopped, his expression suddenly unreadable. "And also, unfortunately or not, totally unpredictable! On the one hand, I still think of her as the one that got away. On the other, I'm strangely glad she did!"

He shook his head, as if he, too, was trying once more to free himself from memories of a hauntingly long-lost world. "I'm not quite sure why, but I expected great things from her even then."

❧

"I expect you'd enjoy the grand tour?"

Scheherazade beckoned to her friends, all of them now happily busy making the stimulating acquaintance of a range of demons of various talents and predispositions frowned on in polite society.

Leaning against the largest of a series of dark red reception desks, Big D began a relaxed commentary.

"As you can see, this recently refurbished, ultra-secret facility is the operational headquarters for our regrettably under-appreciated global enterprise. In addition to offering all the latest demonic amenities, technological upgrades help make our work ever more efficient and effective. It's a strategic necessity, of course, given current trends; day after day, year after year, Earth is busily producing more and more planetary citizens, as they like to think of themselves; or sinners-in-training, as we prefer to call them."

"What an amazing organization," Scheherazade exclaimed, raising an ironic eyebrow. "It seems you benefit at both ends: first, by encouraging people to sin, and then being rewarded with even more work when they do!"

"It's a dynamic, sophisticated business," Big D agreed with a craggy executive grin. "Highly integrated, as energy-efficient as possible, and with an enviable record of productivity improvements. We've had to make some adjustments over the millennia, of course. But even from the very beginning I've always liked the synergy.

"One way or another, we somehow manage to get the best of the worst of both worlds."

❧

"Pardon my curiosity, but what's it like being Satan?" Leila asked, fearlessly. "What do you actually do here, personally speaking? Totally off the record, of course."

"You mean, something along the lines of 'A day in the life of a Chief Executive Devil'?" Big D inquired teasingly. "I guess you could say my primary job is strategic demonic planning. And occasionally, as the subterranean spirit moves me, ultra -subtle operations."

Their host shifted position, now leaning even further back against the reception desk, thumbs in his belt, one smoothly booted foot crossed casually over the other.

"Given so unique an enterprise, the biggest challenge – beyond keeping the staff happy and as much in line as is temperamentally possible – is to maintain a sufficiently philosophic overview.

"In terms of daily duties, there's the standard, early-morning review of all our major ongoing accounts – evil empires, tyrants, dictators, mass-murderers, wars, wars and more wars, etc. Second, making sure we're up to date on current new subversive ventures. And, finally, our all-important planning for even more successful business development and product-line diversification in the future."

The Devil paused, turning in unsolicited tribute to his crimson co-workers. "A future which, I'm glad to say, looks to offer us truly tremendous opportunities for continued growth and dynamic devilish expansion." He smiled a proud, wry smile. "Our in-house ad agency, for example, is currently finishing a range of promos for an increasingly volatile, and even, if we're really lucky, totally anarchic age."

Scheherazade shook her head in amusement.

"While the final choice hasn't been made," Big D continued, "our current favourite tag line is still: Demon Inc., your ultimate collection agency."

"We've almost finished the accompanying jingle." The red-haired giant beamed. "And we're set to shoot the first videos early next month."

There was a long silence while Scheherazade and her friends all looked at one another. Even for seven so well-travelled ladies, there still appeared much to learn.

"It sounds like you definitely enjoy your work," Yazmina ventured, quick dark eyes holding the Devil's deep blue ones. "But it also seems an exceptionally demanding business. Non-stop action, as it were."

"Always something to do," Big D agreed, at the same time quietly admiring her oblique interrogative style. In his spare time he taught introductory humility, along with other artfully beguiling skills, in the technical training programme for young apprentice demons.

"How does your staff cope with the ever-increasing workload?" asked Marina.

"So far, so good," came the reply, accompanied by fingers crossed. "We're lucky to have seasoned, highly-skilled departmental managers who've been here almost from the beginning. And while we always try to promote from within, we also keep an eye open for those rare, exceptionally imaginative individuals who are just plain instinctively good at being bad.

"After all, we take very great pride in our ability to provide what some might call a truly essential service. People depend on us to follow through." Big D paused, savouring long millennia of satisfying accomplishment, then began to smile, his rugged features just as suddenly all the more irresistible.

"Whatever are you thinking of?" Qingling asked, eyes already twinkling in response, her curiosity, as usual, overcoming caution.

"Trade secrets," Big D replied teasingly. "Ones I probably shouldn't expose," he added, quite obviously wanting to.

There was the briefest of feigned hesitations.

"As all of you know, sin is a highly individual matter. People are normally drawn only to those sins which, consciously or otherwise, have for them deep personal relevance and appeal; sins for which they have not only long prepared, but are also uniquely suited. Highly specific sins, in fact, from which, if lucky, they can actually learn a great deal."

"Everybody sins, but everybody does it differently. From our admittedly prejudiced perspective, it's rather like looking down – or up, in our case – at an infinite series of intersecting individual learning curves."

All seven women blinked, momentarily imagining a very, very crowded map of all the seemingly wrong paths rightly taken over time.

"Unfortunately, however," Big D continued, "a few years ago, we somehow slipped up. A brand new shipment of experimental temptations arrived here during rushhour, was wrongly sorted and labelled, and then delivered by mistake to people all over the world wholly unsuited, by virtue of age, temperament or inclination, to make the most of them. For a few weeks, needless to say, it was all unbelievably confusing."

He began chuckling all over again at the memory.

"There were old men roaring around in stolen sports coupés, raging with teenage lust but completely unable to figure out why; certified engineers unable to resist sudden yearnings to blow things up; and hitherto dedicated anarchists trying desperately to construct the state-liest of monuments for the ages."

"Sounds exciting," Tatiana exclaimed. "And so?"

"Once we understood what had happened, of course, everything was set right. The Temptations Department quality-control manager was quietly reassigned. Ever since we've made triply sure that, in every aspect of the demonic, we continue to be completely, utterly meticulous.

"Although for a while, to tell the truth – when everything that was normally supposed to be going wrong, was itself going wrong – it was actually tremendous fun to watch. A wonderfully unexpected break in our usual routine."

Devilish Secrets

WITH THE CRIMSON-CLOAKED giant leading the way, various lesser demons escorted Scheherazade's friends to the guest quarters of Hell, the better to relax and freshen up before dinner.

"We certainly hope you enjoy your stay. The head chef always seems more inventive whenever we have company. And Saturday night is usually movie night: reruns of some of the great debacles of history, where good only appears to be triumphant and, at the very last moment, the devils arrive to save the world for evil. Tremendously exciting, always inspiring footage!"

As he and the others left, Marina shook her head. "Well, at least he enjoys his work."

"Amazing, isn't it," Sybilla observed, "just how much misplaced dedication a universe can handle and still survive."

Alone together in the luxury of his private retreat by an appropriately bubbling scarlet lake, Big D handed Scheherazade a fashiionably dry martini. "*A votre sant*é," he toasted formally in one of his countless official languages.

"And to yours." She lifted her glass. "And to absent friends."

Big D appraised his guest warily. While she might have an admirably wide range of acquaintances, one or two happened to serve in very high and potentially still quite problematical places indeed.

Scheherazade was content that, for a time at least, some things had no less power for remaining unspoken. As for the rest, she decided to get right to the point.

"I assume you've been following events on Earth?"

"Not much I can do about it – at the moment." Her host shrugged, his features now more harsh than handsome. "Unfortunately, it's a near-cataclysmic pattern I've seen repeated again and again. And certainly not just on one small planet that doesn't like itself very much. There are times, intergalactically-speaking, when self-defeating behaviour seems almost like an epidemic."

Far from being delighted at the prospect, Big D seemed not only frustrated, but also even slightly sad.

"You were thinking?"

"That while such chaos inevitably creates new opportunities for me and my associates…."

"The personal cost on the planet concerned seems often all too great?"

Big D nodded. "Over and over, even the best don't listen, let alone learn. Blowing themselves up, figuratively speaking, they keep at it until, one suddenly-foreshortened day, they finally manage to do so literally!"

He paused, face averted, lost in thought. When he finally spoke, it was almost as if to the universe at large. "Time and again, they forget what they came from, who they are, and where they truly need to be going."

"For one whose reputation depends on hellfire and damnation," Scheherazade observed quietly, "you seem strangely sympathetic."

Spirits lifting at the compliment, Big D let slip an ironic smile. "Maybe, but please don't tell anyone." He reached out to pour them both another martini. "Then again, perhaps it's that I just can't help it. If, that is, one considers my own earlier, understandably exalted beginnings."

"It's always difficult to forget whoever gave you your first big break." A moment later, an invisible nudge prompted into words her thought so far unspoken. "Ever consider reapplying to the old firm?"

"Who says I ever really left?" A hitherto hidden delight shone suddenly in Big D's eyes.

Comes the hour, comes the revelation.

"On secret assignment?" Scheherazade ventured, already guessing at the answer. "Underworld … undercover?" She waited a beat. "Nothing in writing, of course."

"Something like that." Big D gave a mock ferocious grimace, delighted to be so perfectly understood. Not everyone did.

"God and I may have had our differences, it's true; but if you look closely, it seems we still somehow manage to work in surprisingly complementary ways, our respective wonders to perform."

Silence, thought Scheherazade again, seemed the best reply.

"One way or another, my old Boss and I might even be considered parts of a uniquely qualified duet. A timely transcendental twosome, which, in my more grandiose moments, I sometimes like to call Cosmic Spiritual Incentives Inc."

"And, in less high-fallutin' words?"

"Push ... and ... pull!"

Scheherazade took a long, slow breath. It was especially encouraging when one's faith was proven justified all along.

"It's not surprising so many are fond of you, despite yourself. Fallen angel or not, Mr. Devil Incarnate, you're still an exceptionally good bad man!"

"Everybody needs a reason to get up and go to work in the morning," Big D replied cavalierly. "For the present, all these sinners are mine. After all, somebody has to look after them."

"In both senses of the phrase, I assume."

༄

"So, what about Earth?" Scheherazade asked once more. "What's the probable outcome? Given, that is, your engagingly unorthodox view of good, bad and everything in between."

"Don't really know. Can't really say." Big D pointed skywards. "In fact, throughout most nearby galaxies all the usually reliable sources suddenly seem to be drying up."

He studied Scheherazade thoughtfully. "Don't suppose, by any chance, you've ever heard of a free-spirited little interstellar outfit called ISDA?"

Over the aeons, Scheherazade had encountered many fascinating individuals, organizations and acronyms, but definitely not this one. She shook her head.

"That's good. Because its stands for the Intergalactic Senior Devils' Association: an informal circle of my peers together making up what is, as you might expect, a fairly exclusive little subterranean supper club."

Big D paused, sipping the last of his martini contemplatively.

"Every decade or so – or sooner if there's a local emergency or spectacular karmic opportunity – eminent devils from star-systems all over the universe get together to share experiences, exchange information and let off a little steam.

"It's a highly effective network that keeps us up to date, especially given the astonishing wealth of constellations throughout the cosmos, all of them being at different stages of evolution, and needing different degrees of demonic intervention."

He hesitated, gathering his thoughts.

"This time, however, it was different. Under the surface, where it mattered, none of us was truly paying attention. It was if we were all waiting, even secretly preparing for something else, something extraordinary, huge, profoundly important, that had already begun without our being asked."

Scheherazade gazed quietly at the devil-in-chief, no less powerfully attractive for being at that moment so strangely vulnerable, adrift in his own thoughts.

"And?"

"And yet, despite all our admirably long experience and rightfully senior role in what we like to call the great demonic scheme of things, we had absolutely no idea what it might be."

An instant later, with suitably melodramatic timing, came the first drumroll of distant thunder.

ε

Finishing her drink, Scheherazade took Big D's offered arm to join her friends and various lesser devils of every rank at dinner. Tired from a long day, she ate lightly, then excused herself from the entertainment to follow, ready for bed in the finest of Hell's many guest rooms and very much looking forward to a long, uninterrupted sleep.

She was already brushing her hair when there was a soft knock at the door. It opened at her call and the giant, crimson-cloaked senior demon leaned through.

"Sorry to disturb you, Ma'am; but Big D sent me to tell you he's just had word from one of his oldest, most reliable sources 'Up There.'"

"Yes?"

"Apparently, there's some sort of strange buzz going around Heaven, to the effect that God may not be feeling well." His huge forehead furrowed in disbelief, as if he couldn't quite grasp the news himself. "And may even need to take time off!"

There are some situations for which only one response will do.

"Hmmmnn."

"It's still only a rumour, of course." The senior demon began to chuckle quietly. "But, if it's true, it could mean that, for a while at least … absolutely nobody will be in charge!"

The giant was already closing the door when he stuck his head in once more.

"I almost forgot. The Boss said he hoped you'd sleep well nonetheless. Also to tell you that he wished you sweet dreams."

Paradise Postponed

"LIGHT FUSE. STAND WELL BACK."

— Fireworks 101

Pre-emptive Strike

❧ "I MUST ADMIT, when You finally make up Your mind to do something…," the Archangel of all Archangels snorted.

"Ever heard the expression, 'timing is everything'?"

"Easy for You to say," the Archangel drawled in exaggerated reply.

"Do not bet on it." God tried (successfully as usual) to look both incomparably humble and casually omnipotent at the same time. "This job's a whole lot harder than it looks."

"So You keep telling me."

The two most exalted celestial co-conspirators in Creation stared at one another impassively. Then both began to laugh.

"We shall soon see!"

❧

Earthly tasks are frequently daunting: heavenly ones, however, can occasionally be nerve-wracking in the extreme.

The manager of Operation Preventive Medicine (more cheerfully known as Grim Reapercussions) went around the crowded control room three times in succession, checking with every section chief in turn: once to verify technical and tactical readiness, twice to confirm artistic finishing touches and ultimate believability and, last but not least, one final time for good luck, which, under the circumstances, might well be needed.

Time-tested celestial expertise notwithstanding, none of the assembled angelic staff had ever before attempted an apparition of such a size and scale. Just when the Senior Engineering Angel for Intergalactic Special Effects and Total Sensory Overload felt his wings fluttering erratically between complete confidence and absolute doubt, an unseen hand touched his shoulder.

"Trust Me. It's all going to be fine." On the surrounding screens, God surveyed the vast pyrotechnical plans soon to be set in motion. "Even though, if you'll pardon the expression, it sure as Hell won't seem like it for a while!"

Courage renewed, the senior engineering angel began to smile. "Desperate times...."

"Call for equally breathtaking countermeasures." Knowing not only what lay ahead, but also all that lay still further beyond what lay ahead, God couldn't stop grinning.

"Let the flames begin!"

As cosmic historians would later confirm, it was at that exact moment – precisely when a wobbly little blue-and-white planet finally managed, all by itself, to reach its own long anticipated tipping point of cataclysmic mistrust, fear, animosity and despair – that God reached out a firm and not so gentle unseen hand to help it cheerfully over the edge.

Feu d'Esprit

OF ALL POSSIBLE nightmares, those in Hell are universally considered the worst.

Exhausted though she might be, Scheherazade could not fall asleep. Behind her eyes a macabre slideshow of sinners condemned for a future without foreseeable end, went around and around the treadmills of their past. When she tried counting sheep, those woolly little white phantoms transformed into bright red devils capering merrily around pots of boiling oil, sticking out their shiny forked tongues with sulphurous glee.

'Sweet dreams' indeed.

As she finally began to doze off, it was with a suitably malicious wish that, wherever he was, Big D himself was equally sleepless and wide-eyed.

Suddenly, in her dream that was not a dream, Scheherazade awoke to an unimaginable crash of thunder, louder than any before, a sudden, unending roar that reverberated from the Earth's surface throughout the whole of the Devil's kingdom.

As she started up, it was to find her bed ringed by spectral figures, their faces fierce with sorrow. Hooded and silent, taking her unresisting hand, they led her upward through the bitter fumes of a dying world. With every step, the ground shook as the planet staggered on its axis. Sun and moon had disappeared, the blackened sky splintered by an endless unnatural lightning.

What happened next was completely surreal, for Scheherezade and for every inhabitant of planet Earth. Although no one felt personally harmed, around them appeared total devastation. A relentless firestorm swept over countries and continents. Huge metropolises disappeared in a flash, biochemical second strikes completing whatever their nuclear counterparts had left undone.

Everything confirmed that the long-feared threat of self-destruction had finally been realized. Old and young were indistinguishable in their common fate. The now-final generations of an irrecoverably broken world swirled upwards as dust and ash, an incinerated Earth's last testament rising toward the stars as ragged, acrid mushroom clouds.

❧

When the air cleared, Scheherazade found herself standing on a small uneven asteroid that, only moments before, nonchalantly en route from one great galaxy to another, had halted horrified in its path. In the distance, what had once been the bright blue-and-white globe of Earth, glistening in the sunlight, was now only a small black smouldering ball in space.

"Not an especially pretty sight, is it?" a low, familiar voice said evenly. Big D stood staring across space at his home planet's shattered remains, his eyes dark with rage and regret.

Scheherazade, even in this worst of nightmares, strangely found she could still read hearts as easily as minds, or at least this particular one.

She waited in the silence.

"If you had put as much time into that little bundle of self-centred contradictions as I have," Big D said at last, "you'd be furious, too! After so many painstaking centuries, so much dedicated effort since I first lent an all-important hand in that inaugural little fenced-off Garden of Glowing Possibilities...."

His eyes blazed. "Do you have any idea just how much carefully-timed temptation and instructive torment it takes to get a mid-sized planet in anything like conscientious working order? Let alone making progress?"

Big D shook his head. "Just when I was starting to be proud of Earth's inhabitants, struggling to overcome the instructive obstacles I put in their way, they proceed to go totally off the rails and do themselves in!"

The bitter eulogy came of its own accord. "Here lies Planet Earth. RIP – resting in pieces. Died from fear, hate, greed, cynicism and sheer impenetrable stupidity." Earth's most notorious renegade spread his hands in satanic disbelief.

"That perennially contentious little place also just so happened to be my home as well. It now seems, no thanks to them, that I'll have to start looking for other work!"

Overhead, a faint glow heralded the arrival of one of the late planet's earliest friends. One hand over its eyes, an inconsolable moon peeked out at what remained of its old travelling companion.

"Seems like I'm out of a job, too," it exclaimed, in sudden unbearable loneliness. "Nobody there to care whether I light up their nights, or what particular shape I'm in, or even whether I'm still worth exploring."

Personal grief gave way to greater sorrow as the moon recalled all those it had watched over throughout so many millions of years: all who had been born, lived and loved in their turn under the abiding reassurance of its rhythmic silver spell. Unable to speak, it turned forlornly away, spinning slowly on its own axis in sadness and loss, revealing to Earth for the first time its own dark side, blasted and pitted by meteors and time, its ravaged face now a mirror image of its ancient, savaged friend.

❦

Big D ran his eyes slowly over Scheherazade. It was as if, already in mourning for Earth, she too was becoming a ghost as well. "Are you alright?" he asked softly, his voice hesitant and tender.

Scheherazade stared at the doubly darkened sky. Around them, all the constellations had come to a standstill. Frozen in their orbits, they gazed down on one of their own, now transformed into a flickering, macabre funeral pyre of vanished lives and vanished loves.

It was all too true, Scheherazade reminded herself, that Earth's history had been a bittersweet tale of joys and sorrows intertwined. The eye that sparkles with delight can quickly shine with tears. Tears for oneself or others; and tears sometimes, in moments of breathtaking clarity, for everyone and everything with whom we share the same inescapable fate.

If Earth's first Eden was but a distant memory, any possible future paradise now seemed even more tragically lost as well.

"Heartsick," Scheherazade answered. "I feel heartsick beyond words."

The two sat in silence, numb to the passing of time.

"At least your companions should be fine," Big D observed at last. "Say what you may about Hell, one of its more convenient features is that it's virtually indestructible!"

Ever the gentleman, he withdrew from his pocket the smartest of demonic smartphones giving video access to his subterranean world, including its guest accommodations. One by one, as Scheherazade looked on over his shoulder, he keyed in six separate room numbers in turn.

In every case, each carefully turned-down bed stood untouched and empty.

"Hmmmnn!"

Scheherazade took a deep breath, a first hint of colour returning to her face. What was it God had said in a sudden provocative aside, earlier and very much elsewhere, regarding a little blue-and-white world's all too possible self-extinction? "Hardly the sort of pre-breakfast spectacle likely to make My day."

Smoking wreckage notwithstanding, Scheherazade thought, all might not be as it appeared. What was the meaning of God's carefully chosen parting words? Was this disaster divine intervention, perhaps?

"Ever wondered what six resourceful super-sleuths might get up to in an Earth-shattering spiritual emergency?" Big D asked, more relieved than he was prepared to let on to see Scheherazade returning to her instinctive, confident self.

"Under such circumstances, I'd say just about anything is possible," Scheherazade laughed, already making a reassuringly accurate guess as to where her lady friends' inimitable get-up-and-go was likely to get them.

෴

Like Scheherazade, her companions had found it difficult to get to sleep.

Particularly when, in every case, stylish off-duty demons tapped softly on their individual doors, selflessly inviting them to make the most of so fortuitous an opportunity to improve relations between the upper and lower realms. Having in the course of earlier adventures, however, already encountered a variety of highly instructive entreaties from a wide range of charming young devils, actual or self-styled, all six ladies graciously but firmly declined.

So it was that, when Earth's final moments so abruptly began, all of Scheherazade's friends were unwinding in Hell's most luxurious guest lounge, not quite ready for bed and reminiscing on travels either solo or shared. It seemed an entirely relaxed, if also (given the excessively scarlet surroundings) somewhat unorthodox evening.

Without warning, the first images of a charred and broken planet began to play on the giant video screen, the room itself shuddering from fierce, seemingly fatal explosions on the surface far above.

"If this is a movie," said Yazmina, "somebody just blew the budget."

"And damn near everything else, as well," Qingling added to the accompanying echo of the loudest of all possible crashes.

As all six women continued to stare at the giant screen, new images of a now-devastated world appeared. As for Scheherazade, Qingling reported, their leader seemed to have completely disappeared, her whereabouts unknown.

Comes the hour, comes the heroine. Or, in this case, six. With a single glance, half a dozen very different women reached the same conclusion.

If, as it seemed, the Present was well on its way to ruins and mute ash, then perhaps only their unorthodox, far-seeing new friends in The Great Beyond beyond the Beyond could tell them what was going on.

Or, if present appearances weren't deceptive, then help with the only task now remaining, the final draft of a once promising little blue-and-white planet's sadly abbreviated obituary.

❦

Time, even in the most fantastic of cosmic dreams (or, as in this case, nightmares) inevitably wanders on. The little asteroid on which Big D and Scheherazade were standing began bouncing gently up and down, as if signalling a readiness to be on its own predestined way.

"Under the circumstances, I think I might just go look for my friends," Scheherazade announced, already certain where to begin.

Big D gazed up into the frozen heavens, lost in thoughts she could not begin to divine: vast, private meditations going back nearly as far as the universe's birth pains, and forwards to perhaps only he knew where.

"And I, in turn, should probably go look for mine." There was a brief pause. "I have a distinct feeling they're all wondering what comes next!"

If the run-of-the-satanic-mill devil is happy finding work for a small but respectable number of idle hands, the grand masters of the demonic order are only satisfied when doing so on a truly universal scale.

Gone (Perhaps), but Not Forgotten

&. SOMETIMES THE MOST terrifying dreams prove ultimately the most beneficial, particularly when they help prevent far more horrific nightmares from actually happening.

As God had more than once observed (most recently during the senior angelic staff's latest professional development weekend): "Remember. If you want to get anywhere in this business, you've got to be really, really convincing!"

United in carnage and grief, and yet each now unutterably alone, everyone on Planet Earth shared the same stark conviction: that their entire world, including everyone they had known and loved, and who had known and loved them in return, was now catastrophically, irretrievably gone.

Simultaneously, in galaxy after galaxy, beings beyond number turned to stare as a once-promising little blue-and-white world seemed to have become a vast flaming crematorium in space. The entire cosmos shared a quick, sharp sadness beyond time.

For one small, planetary experiment at least, the hopes and fears of billions of years seemed only to have ended in tears. No planet is an island. Each one's premature passing diminishes the whole, especially when, throughout the universe, the music of the spheres suddenly stops in mid-note, and everything everywhere comes to an utter, unprecedented standstill.

Guidance from Beyond

❧ AT MOMENTS OF supreme crisis, Time becomes infinitely elastic and obliging, Present and Future opening to one another at truly impossible speeds. In an instant, Scheherazade's six co-adventurers found themselves back in The Great Beyond beyond the Beyond, their return already awaited with mischievous anticipation.

❧

Trees giggled, brooks laughed, rocks chuckled softly as before, and the same seven small suns in the sky still skipped cheerfully back and forth among wide-eyed clouds. Most important of all, a still-just-as-enticing Dr. Professor O'Bliss waited expectantly beside the Interplanetary Centre for Joy's newly remodelled entrance.

"More than delighted to see you again," he exclaimed during a satisfyingly prolonged welcome. "Although I was, of course, deeply sorry to learn of so premature an end to your ambitious little project."

Marina waited.

"Then again, it could be one of those moments when it's simply much too soon to tell!" There was a delicate pause. Then an even more delicate wink. "After all, who knows what Earth could make of itself? Given time ... and a really great advisory board!"

❧

"Hello again," said Aurora, opening a now familiar door leading to the long dusty passageways of the Museum of Historical Culs-de-Sac. "When I heard the news, I guessed you might be coming back." The small yellow monkey's face grew suitably sombre. "It's never easy when big things don't work out."

Bending down, Leila kissed the little museum tour guide on the cheek. Empathy, she was touched to rediscover, can come in the unlikeliest of forms.

"From your professional vantage point," she asked carefully, "do you have any idea what could have caused Earth to blow itself up, down and so dramatically sideways?"

Lifting a tiny eyebrow, Aurora studied her return guest carefully. "Maybe – and maybe not." Then, despite herself, she began to giggle. After all, if the most promising of the museum's many retroactive prophecies were true, then a certain little tour guide with beguiling purple eyes might soon be in line for a change in career: or, at the very least, her first really big vacation in thousands and thousands of years.

"It is all really straight-forward," Chief Inspector Stop and Chief Inspector Go-Go exclaimed, looking up at Qingling while standing on their heads in their effortlessly contrarian way. "It's just a matter of everything in the cosmos being temporarily upside down!" they declared. It was obviously a pleasure to provide so reassuring an explanation.

"Are you both absolutely certain?" their concerned guest inquired.

The two distinguished chairmen of the Intergalactic Recreation and Repair Centre (North Quadrant) pretended to look questioningly at one another, then nodded. Flipping themselves over, and tilting their heads every which way, they inspected the scene from what was for them a completely inverted position.

A moment later, their expressions seemed to grow even more fascinated. "Whichever way we look, everything now seems totally back-to-front as well," Chief Inspector Go-Go observed quietly. "Not to mention seriously inside out."

The two stared at one another solemnly, the better to orchestrate their mutually-agreed, now definitive professional opinion, one already arrived at long, long ago.

"Yippee!"

Yazmina's two new effervescently-ivory acquaintances were not surprised to find her knocking firmly at the door of their ultra-secret surveillance centre.

"I'm very sorry to hear about your tragic loss," the tall wiry skeleton exclaimed merrily.

"Seems some things are just meant to be. Or, in the case of your blue-and-white planet, maybe not to be!" his shorter burly associate added.

"Somehow you just don't sound desperately sympathetic," Yazmina responded, intrigued by such oddly-cavalier equanimity.

The taller skeleton did a little jig, snapping his bony fingers and singing softly to himself. "Planets come, and planets go; sometimes fast, and sometimes slow." He contemplated their visitor soberly. "Sad to say, it was probably a very good thing that Earth expired when it did."

"We've already done an initial remote autopsy." The shorter skeleton gestured to one corner of the adjoining laboratory, where miniature holograms of dozens of rather battered and bust-up moons, planets and asteroids were scattered about on ultra-high-tech examining tables.

"We'll do more detailed studies as soon as our power systems are restored – for some reason, they seem temporarily interrupted. But as far as we can make out right now, that little blue-and-white planet's passing was completely unavoidable. Beneath so many good intentions and repeated altruistic protestations, Earth unfortunately turned out to be almost totally sclerotic and diseased. Blood-pressure readings off the chart. Not to mention all sorts of nasty internal feuds, virulent suspicions, toxic resentments and so forth."

"A decidedly contagious state," the tall wiry skeleton confirmed, shaking his head dolefully. "All too busily killing time … while time was quietly returning the favour. If it had continued to carry on in that way, sooner or later Earth would undoubtedly have gone looking for new planets to play with and then unavoidably infected them as well!"

"Couldn't have let that happen," his shorter, burlier friend confirmed. "Somebody would have had to intervene." He smiled amiably. "As it was, Earth appears to have spared us that choice, if not, it seems, itself."

Yazmina's eyes darted back and forth between the two skeletons, both of whom remained unusually unperturbed. "So this sort of thing has happened before?"

"Every planet has a self-destruct button somewhere or other, and all the implosive impulses to go with it," said the tall wiry skeleton with a shrug.

"The tricky part is figuring out how to keep their hot little hands off it," his burly associate added, as sternly and convincingly as he could, while simultaneously failing to stifle a beatific, telltale smile.

Suspicions confirmed by that smile, Yazmina breathed a sigh of relief.

For whatever reason, her assignment – together with Earth's (whatever that particular planetary task might turn out to be) – wasn't over yet.

Not by a skeletal long shot.

Tatiana arrived to find the Wondrous Winding Gardens of Desire's exuberant floral pathways deserted, all those earlier sharing explorations of interstellar delight now nowhere to be found.

A tall, familiar figure stood alone, serene violet eyes glowing softly in the mist. "As soon as they heard the news, everyone here – staff, guests and visitors alike – instantly agreed we should close for the day."

With the warmest of smiles, Valentina stepped forward, embracing her guest. "Ironically, this empathy seems one of these Gardens' more ambiguous rewards. Even as hearts open in pleasure and love, a disturbing sensitivity to everyone else's darker states and fates inevitably arises as well." Valentina's eyes darkened as she contemplated the now empty floral maze. "It's a truly startling emotion, this feeling of a limitless cosmic tenderness. Even across wildly different galaxies, certain exceptionally sensitive planets can somehow sense when all is not well with even their most distant, uncommunicative kin."

Trance and Circumstance

&. THE LITTLE ASTEROID soared single-mindedly through space, carrying Scheherazade on towards a future few others now seemed able to share.

Everywhere she looked, from the nearest galaxies to the farthest edges of the universe, Time itself remained frozen. All the once-reliable rhythms of the stars had vanished.

Whatever was going on, moreover, it appeared in no hurry to come to an end. It was almost as if whoever or whatever lay behind such sudden dramatic developments was secretly enjoying themselves. Even, perhaps, making the most of the occasion, if not, indeed, the occasion itself.

"Don't worry. I'm sure I know where I'm going," the small asteroid exclaimed, closing all six eyes and swerving just in time to avoid an unmapped fragment of an antique satellite.

"I have total confidence in you," Scheherazade replied, wondering if there might be a patron saint of space junk and, if so, how best to ask for immediate protection. Moments later, her unvoiced prayer was rewarded as a now familiar searchlight pierced the air.

"Hello again," said The Man With a Thousand Eyes, his deep bass voice resounding in characteristically imperturbable welcome. "Obviously, I don't have to ask what brings you back to The Great Beyond beyond the Beyond. But if, as I suspect, you were hoping for the very latest in all-inclusive explanations, I'm sorry to say it's a little too soon for that."

His thousand eyes all swivelled independently, sending rays outward in a thousand directions in time. Everywhere the light shone, everything was still. Even The Future, it seemed, was having an enforced rest.

"And yet somehow you don't seem terribly bothered," Scheherazade observed.

Her host's response was a long, slow, shimmering wink. "If you'll permit me...." Half his eyes remaining shut, the other five hundred became an unerring beam which, reaching over his guest's shoulder, illuminated an otherwise completely secret event taking place in a world now seemingly far, far behind.

"That's Big D!" Scheherazade exclaimed. "In ultra-crimson, ever-so-living colour."

Centuries of deeply satisfying independence notwithstanding, she had to admit she was becoming disturbingly drawn to the elegant rogue now in urgent discussion with a cluster of similarly striking devils. Illustrious members of the upper crust of the lower world, as it were, all were readily identifiable by the matching pairs of disguised antennae protruding from their heads like conventional demonic horns, and by the tapered, sharply-barbed tails flung so casually over their broad shoulders. Their individual uniforms, custom-tailored needless to say, were a suavely exuberant display of turquoise, aubergine, indigo, chartreuse and citrine, as well as the occasional, ever-fashionable, cinematic black.

"But who are all the others?"

"Can't remember all their names," The Man With a Thousand Eyes replied, watching thoughtfully all the while. "But, based on aeons of the most enjoyably classified experience, I can assure you each of these eminent outliers is a supremely distinguished demon from some of the finest, red-hot realms throughout the entire universe."

"And they're definitely plotting something," Scheherazade observed unnecessarily, torn between concern for their potential victims, so evidently outmatched, and admiration at their professional ease.

"Why not?" her host exclaimed merrily. "After all, they too have their job to do."

Scheherazade suppressed a sigh. Good men may be hard to find, but truly good bad ones are an interstellar rarity.

"Under the circumstances, I felt you'd like to know."

"Much appreciated," Scheherazade said softly. "In the case of this particular gentleman, however, I suspect being forewarned rarely, if ever guarantees being adequately forearmed!"

"And in the opposing corner," The Man With a Thousand Eyes continued melodramatically a moment later, "appearing straight from

Heaven itself, and still as resourceful and dependable as ever." Closing his first set of five hundred eyes, he simultaneously opened wide the second, illuminating a series of winged figures busy putting finishing touches on an ultra-secret, intergalactic public communications network. "The wondrous, worlds-famous, ever-awe-inspiring Angelic Forces For Good!"

Scheherazade scanned the assembled group slowly. She'd never seen any of this industrious crew of white-winged cosmonauts before.

"The highest of celestial high-tech staff," her high-voltage host interjected, reading her thoughts. "Special occasion, special requirements."

"Clearly. But to what purpose?"

"Let's just say it's probably the biggest surprise in history." The luminous gatekeeper of Everything Yet to Come began to chuckle.

A moment later, his face resumed the terrifying calm of one who routinely kept an unhurried, unblinking watch on billions of galazies.

❧

"What now?"

"As for you and me, I'm sure we'll see each other again one day." His contribution to the secret celestial scheme of things complete, The Great Beyond beyond the Beyond's master of ceremonies seemed content to bid farewell. "In the meantime, however, it's best if you and your friends (who, by the way, are all fine) return home a.s.a.p."

"To Earth? And then what?"

"And then you wait."

"For…?"

"For the Past to catch up to the Future, of course. And *vice versa*." A thousand eyes twinkled in tune. "Just to be on the safe side."

"And then…?"

It seemed that Earth, if still looking much the worse for wear, had narrowly avoided giving up the ghost. As for Scheherazade, near-apocalypses or not, she still had an assignment to complete, a retainer to earn and, quite unexpectedly, a devil of a dilemma to resolve. Or was it, more accurately, a dilemma of an unresolved devil?

"Let me put it this way." The reply came in a deep, no-nonsense growl. "Time for Earth to get a grip!"

The good thing about angels (even in disguise) is that, when necessary, they're all as tough as nails. Message conveyed, The Man With a Thousand Eyes bowed gracefully. "*Au revoir*, Milady. Your personal chauffeur awaits you."

"All aboard!" cried Abracadabra, reaching for the newly-acquired, gold-laced pilot's hat proclaiming him an officially certified intergalactic cargo carrier. Offering a welcoming hand to the seat by his side, he muttered several time-tested aeronautical spells, followed by a few more all-weather ones for good luck and extra speed.

"And away we go! Next stop … Earth. Or whatever's left of it!"

Still dreaming or not, Scheherazade was once more racing through time, the little white cloud bouncing through the fiercest of cross-currents and riptides.

"Never seen it this rough, even in the worst mirage," the old wizard said, making triply sure his magic wand was safely secured. "Must be another storm building."

As Scheherazade looked carefully, however, she sensed the nearest constellations inexplicably returning to their traditional orbits, happily no longer frozen, though still not quite whirling anywhere near as fast as they might have preferred.

"I'm so grateful you came to get me," she exclaimed, starry winds blowing through her hair.

"All in a day's work. Once I've dropped you off, I'll hotfoot it around other parts of Tomorrowland and pick up your friends. It's probably faster, and certainly much safer today if I give them a ride," the little old wizard observed, taking a firmer grip on the wheel. "Lots of room," he added proudly. "In fact, with some judicious crowding, this fluffy little dragon boat can seat up to twenty."

"You're such a thoughtful sorcerer," Scheherazade responded.

"Ain't I just!" Abracadabra agreed. "But then, of course, I do seem to have a weakness for the ladies."

Actually, the old wizard thought to himself, his appreciation of women's unbounded powers – their potential, however, as yet so seldom fulfilled – was one of his greatest strengths.

An Immodest Proposal

  THE SMALL WHITE cloud skidded left, then right, then half-left again and began to descend. Ahead, their little blue-and-white destination made slow juddering movements as it attempted, with renewed determination, to spin successfully on its axis once more.

Around the world, barely half the normal number of lights were on. But they were on. And the moon, circling overhead once more, was beginning to look not only greatly relieved, but also tremendously curious.

Given recent developments, it was doubly a relief for Scheherazade to find her now familiar villa awaiting her. Waving a grateful goodbye to Abracadabra, she was more than ready for a hot bath, soft music and a long uninterrupted sleep in her very own bed once more.

"What kept you?" a warm, deep voice asked from the shadows, followed by an unforgettably devilish smile as Big D stepped into the light.

Drinks in hand, a gentle breeze swirling through the trees, Scheherazade and the Devil himself sat quietly on the patio, appraising one another in an increasingly companionable silence; each sensing the other equally unsure whether, against all odds, this was one of those rare, seemingly brief encounters which could lead to an infinitely more uncommon and lasting one.

Since both Scheherazade and Big D, when they wished, could each be more patient and circumspect than the other, it was fortunate that Hell's happily-laid-back champion at last recollected that he had some rather pressing matters to discuss. And, perhaps, an even more important proposition to present – however provisional, if not wholly impossible.

Extraordinary times, however, were exactly made for extraordinary invitations.

"I've been thinking…."

"Yes?" Scheherazade said encouragingly.

"I hoped that might be your answer," Big D smiled.

"In which case, it might be best to ask me the question first."

The Devil stretched, stared up at the sky, then down through the core of the earth to his invisible kingdom. Nothing ventured, nothing gained, as every acolyte was reminded on day one of Junior Devil School. "Let's just suppose…."

"Mmmmnn."

"Let's just suppose – purely for argument's sake, of course – that this little foretaste of Earth's still possible fate might just be a very different kind of warning."

"Mmmmnn."

"A first, telltale indication, perhaps, that Divine Providence (not exactly a devil's favourite euphemism, by the way) isn't quite what it used to be."

Scheherazade's third "Mmmmnn" was even more guarded than her previous two.

God, it was true, had looked understandably tired when last they met. But it also seemed to her that any bet whatsoever on an unexpectedly early expiration of the Deity's uniquely-unrestricted cosmic driver's licence would probably be the longest of long shots in universal history.

She leaned back with a smile, enjoying Big D's indefatigable resilience and optimism. And his every move.

"Think about the possibility. The Boss has been at it since the very beginning, say fourteen billion years, and maybe long before that, some might argue. And, all things considered – given the extensive product line, competition from former employees and perennially hard-to-satisfy customers – has done surprisingly well."

"But even so!" Big D spread his hands in a gesture of limitless yet gentle stoicism so characteristic of a genuine celestial insider. "There's no question that running the cosmos is a job like no other. With little or no time off, and usually even less recognition.

"As God grows older then, surely it's not unreasonable to expect the occasional celestial lapse? Not quite a fall from grace, perhaps, but at least a momentary stumble. Wholly unintentional, of course," he added, giving his personal favourite among a range of convincingly broad-minded shrugs. "But probably unavoidable. Even inescapably progressive!"

"The onset of a sort of sacred senility, perhaps?" Scheherazade raised an ironic eyebrow. It was amazing how attractive the Devil could be, even when he was tryhing just a little too hard.

Something like that," Big D replied, raising a bemused eyebrow in return. Approaching his main argument, he paused, the better to prepare them both.

"So, given all that's at stake, wouldn't you agree it's likely wise to give some thought to that not so little matter of celestial succession planning? All in the universe's best interest, of course."

Big D and Eden had clearly been made for each other, the apple only the nearest, if also juiciest excuse. Try as she might, Scheherazade couldn't keep from laughing. "I don't suppose, by any chance, you just happen to have someone uniquely suited in mind?"

Impressively broad-shouldered, head tilted laconically to one side, Big D took a long tall breath. "Strangely enough, there does appear to be one near-perfect prospect: bold, imaginative, resourceful and – miracle of all miracles – extensive prior celestial experience."

"An admirably independent-minded gentleman, perhaps," said Scheherazade, effortlessly taking up the theme, "who continues to show unrivalled skill in what is, undoubtedly, an almost equally challenging executive hot seat."

"Couldn't have put it better myself!" Big D exclaimed. It was heartening to be so well understood. His eyes gazed even more thoughtfully into hers. "Someone with almost too many praiseworthy powers, in fact; and yet, so far, no one to share them with."

Comes the hour, comes the woman.

"Are you offering me a job?"

"Would you consider one?"

"As?"

"Take your pick: 'Senior Advisor', 'Second-in-Command', even 'Deputy Demonic Chairwoman' if, as I greatly doubt, you have hitherto un- confessed bureaucratic yearnings."

"For some reason or other, the term 'second-in-command' lacks a certain *je ne sais quoi*," Scheherazade smiled quietly. "And besides, I'm sure I can find ways to advise you informally anyhow, wherever I happen to be and whatever else I might be doing."

Big D studied the woman opposite, his inherited analytical abilities once more confirming that first, all-too-powerful attraction. "If it's too soon now, then perhaps…." To his surprise, he found himself playing his biggest card. "Maybe consort one day?"

The hottest lady in Hades?

Perhaps the real secret in succeeding with the Devil, Scheherazade decided, lay in being more tempting to him than his temptations were to you.

Still, as she admitted once again, he was, all in all, the consummate epitome of a charming rogue. Despite herself, she began wondering what he might be like with just a few discreet minor changes, a few selectively-redemptive alterations. Not too many, mind you. Just one or two she already found herself thinking of.

"Thank you for so flattering an offer," she replied at last. "I could ask if anyone ever told you that you sure know how to make a woman feel appreciated. But somehow I don't really think I need to."

Big D said nothing, patience being paramount among his many virtues, strategic and tactical. After all, it didn't take the collective wisdom of every angel and devil in the universe to know that a woman's initial hesitation, however temporarily disappointing, might be only the necessary prelude to a later, larger and much lovelier acceptance by far.

"I'll give you my answer when the moment's right." Scheherazade paused. "But first, I have my own timely test question for you. Let's just suppose," she continued softly, "that, only a few hours ago, when you had that sudden hush-hush, rush-rush meeting with so many other eminently senior demons from all over the universe, I just happened to be watching!"

Scheherazade's next words were to the point.

"So, care to tell me exactly what you all-too-prescient rogues, renegades and rascals were up to?"

Grand Opening

❧ "YOU SAW US?" Big D appeared more impressed than surprised.

Scheherazade's only response was a nod, and a quick silent thanks to The Man With A Thousand Eyes. When dealing with devils (one's own or others') it was generally a good idea to keep certain secrets secret. A little discretion might not only save a lot of trouble, but even prove unexpectedly helpful down the road.

"Whatever it was that you gentlemen were talking about, you seemed both confident, and yet even more profoundly unsure."

Big D shifted from one foot to the other, as if determining exactly how much to tell. Whatever had been the covert meeting's subject, it was obviously still very much on his mind. Scheherazade had only to wait.

"Have you ever heard of a massive, wholly unprecedented feat of celestial magic called, utterly inadequately, a truly total universal trance?"

She shook her head.

"Neither had I," Big D confessed, "although three senior devils from remote super-constellations swore they'd heard reports of some early, highly-classified trials. Psychic prototypes, so it was rumoured, for the scary interlude of all scary interludes."

Big D's eyes darkened with professional envy.

"Presto – Earth seems to blow itself up and in doing so, jams the celestial gears. Presto again – the universe instantly stalls, and everybody's stuck thinking long, dark thoughts. Then presto a third and final time – and it turns out that Earth, for now, is probably alright after all, and everything everywhere starts moving again."

Closing her eyes, Scheherazade recaptured that earlier image of a blackened, lifeless ball in space, its last offering to Heaven the acrid flames of its own self-immolation.

Seconds later, reopening them once more, she rejoiced anew in the quiet villa garden, its flowers bobbing and dancing in the wind, firmly rooted in the fertile earth of a fast-spinning, little blue-and-white globe which, as far she could make out, continued to hold its predetermined place among the stars.

She sighed in admiration. "A feat of mass hypnosis on a universal scale. A truly transstellar mirage."

"One such as might occur," Big D continued with undisguised delight, "if and when a certain congenitally-close-lipped Someone wanted it thought that a wholly irreversible planetary catastrophe was actually happening," he paused, his appreciation clearly no less personal than professional, "when, in fact, other, far greater developments are already secretly under way!"

Scheherazade tried hard, but just couldn't resist. God, she was sure, would understand. And maybe even approve.

"All in all," she ventured, "what some might be tempted to call a truly immaculate deception!"

When he finally stopped laughing, the Intergalactic Senior Devils' Association's newest Chairman shook his head one last time at the enormity of it all, not to mention the sheer celestial moxie. However old God might be, one thing was abundantly clear; more than a few unplayed aces remained all too handily hidden up those voluminous celestial sleeves.

Scheherazade took a thoughtful swallow of her drink, then an even longer glance at her companion. For a fleeting, unguarded moment, Big D's face had the simultaneously devoted yet fiercely independent glare of a favoured, rebellious son.

"I must confess, my old Boss still seems considerably more resourceful than we devils are temperamentally inclined to admit." His expression softened. Reaching for his glass, he raised it in a toast. "So many billions of years in office," Big D continued with undisguised pride, "and yet the subtle source of all still remains capable of the most unexpected surprises."

Taking Scheherazade's hand he gently turned it over, as if searching her palm for answers large and small, and as a way of gathering his own scattered thoughts. Their first, mutual tests so successfully, if flirtatiously passed, it was almost time to risk the truth. Or at least, all he could make of it so far.

He looked up into her calmly-waiting eyes.

"As you undoubtedly guessed, our hurried little senior devils' discussion was less about the origin, and more the potential implications of this recent fiery fantasia. Congenitally independent natures notwithstanding, we all found ourselves able to agree on at least one sure thing.

"Mmmmnn?"

"Whatever's going on behind the celestial scenes...."

"Mmmmnn?"

"It's definitely big!"

A moment later, as if on cue, the sky abruptly darkened, a sizzling bolt of lightning shooting suitably melodramatically from horizon to horizon, followed by a roll of perfectly-syncopated thunder.

"Ever get the feeling," Scheherazade ventured, "that someone might be listening?"

⁊

After her bath, Scheherazade began to prepare an early supper for Abracadabra and her assorted co-explorers yet to arrive back from the Future. Her guest, in the meantime, made several attempts to contact his giant red-haired deputy down below. Overhead, perfectly-executed lightning bolts crackled through the early evening sky at ever-briefer intervals.

"Whatever's happening, I can't seem to reach any of my associates," Big D muttered, reaching out deftly to skewer the marinating shish kebabs.

"I wonder what's still keeping the Sorcerer's Express?" Scheherazade glanced up from the makings of a very large salad as one particularly talented flash repeated itself a dozen times in succession before rocketing upwards out of sight. "I know Abracadabra's an all-seasons, all-weather magician, but...."

As if in rebuke to the slightest wavering of her absolute faith in the versatile little wizard, a small bright light bounced over the horizon, scooting between thunderclaps towards the haven of her welcoming villa. As the little white cloud whirred to a stop beside the pool, Abracadabra leapt nimbly over the side. Producing from nowhere a set of stairs, he offered a gentlemanly hand to each of the six ladies as, one by one, they stepped gracefully back to the welcoming solidity of Earth.

"What a ride!" Marina exclaimed. "Thunder and lightning crashing all over the star-systems, solar winds blasting every which way!"

"If it hadn't been for Abracadabra, we would probably have been stuck out somewhere for centuries!" Qingling confirmed.

"Nice to know I haven't completely lost my old celestial racing skills." The little old magician's eyes glowed. "Though I must admit it was touch-and-go a few times, especially as we rounded that last big rippling curve out near the Constellation of Discontented Arpeggios."

He bowed deeply to the Devil just now coming out of the kitchen, who returned the same courteous greeting between two proven, illustrious professionals.

All six ladies said a surprised hello to Big D, casting a covert glance at Scheherazade a split-second later.

"The good news," Abracadabra announced, "is that, apart from this rather distracting sound and light show, the universe seems to be working again. Stars, constellations, galaxies: they're all finally back in motion, gradually resettling into their preferred orbits.

"The bad news, however, is that this unseasonable little thunder storm appears to be getting worse." As Big D glanced thoughtfully at Scheherazade, the sky turned a brilliant white as thirty-six gigantic lightning bolts linked arms, dancing in unison across the sky while keeping perfect time to the loudest heavenly explosions so far.

Watching in silence, Abracadabra unconsciously took a firm, reas-suring grip on his magic wand.

An instant later, the sky went completely black.

❦

Before anyone anywhere had time to react, light exploded in the darkness, a swirl of rainbows arcing from horizon to farthest horizon. Moments later, as a haunting, ethereal music began to play, the rainbows themselves were drawn slowly aside.

As every resident of the universe gazed, awe-struck, a shimmering vision of the celestial realm's first-ever Heavenly Broadcast Studio rose magically out of nothingness.

Surrounded by flowers from a billion galactic gardens, hosts of seraphim stood serenely in an arc, wings freshly cleaned, starched and pressed, their eyes aglow with pride, purpose and divine mischief. Before them, rows of the most senior angels and archangels throughout the universe sat in perfect stillness, faces impassive, their many hard-won medals, decorations and embroidered insignia of office gleaming on alabaster robes. No one anywhere, all agreed, had ever before seen so many gleaming haloes in one place at one time.

At the raised dais at the very centre, a radiant, indistinct presence sat composed and assured behind a vast golden desk, piles of white-and-gold cosmic research files on either hand.

To one side, a tall, deceptively slender angel swung an enormous golden hammer, the crash as it met the huge adjacent gong reverberating instantly throughout all hundred and one billion galaxies.

"Now that I finally have your complete and undivided attention …. I believe there are one or two things all of you very much need to hear." There was a long, perfectly-timed pause while God's fingertips drummed on the great golden desk.

"And then I've got a proposition!"

Help Wanted

"WHY EXACLTY DID YOU CREATE THE UNIVERSE?"
"SEEMED LIKE A GOOD IDEA AT THE TIME."
"AND NOW?"
"JURY'S STILL OUT."
— NSA Intercept

Job Opportunity

❦ FROZEN IN WONDER, the citizens of every galaxy all heard God's hitherto unheard voice resounding in every language.

"In these last few dark and deafening hours, many of you were sure that the very worst had occurred, and that – as a result of their own misadventures and My presumably finite patience – a potentially sprightly little blue-and-white planet had come to an abrupt end."

There was a brief silence, then the flicker of a celestial smile. "Ill-founded rumours of My celebrated temper notwithstanding, let Me assure you I am not naturally inclined to something so terminally inconsiderate as a genuine Apocalypse simply in order to get people's attention, or, for that matter, My own way."

There was a quick, appreciative nod in the direction of the beaming angelic engineering manager in charge of special effects and cosmic sensory overloads. "Not when a divinely-inspired simulation of the real thing seems to work just fine!" The smile grew larger. "Frankly, it's amazing what can be achieved these days with a few celestial fireworks, a little smoke and some hypoallergenic ashes."

A miniature replica of a small blue-and-white planet, smoke still curling round its burned and blasted shores, suddenly popped into view, hovering self-consciously at God's side.

"Indeed, I'm delighted to report that this earlier, seemingly so shattering sound-and-lack-of-light show has accomplished exactly what I've been hoping for throughout our long, shared history; namely, for every cosmic citizen to stop in the middle of whatever seems so desperately important … and finally take a wider, larger look around!"

Across the universe, everyone watching suddenly felt the most momentous of shivers up and down their varied evolutionary spines. As most everyone knew from personal experience, God could be stunningly swift in getting to the point.

"After so many aeons in office, I've decided that a major, how shall I say, strategic change in the celestial realm may not only be overdue but even, perhaps, intriguingly opportune.

"Moment by moment, our combined experiment in Time and Space continues everywhere to expand. As it does, Earth's recent near disaster now seems, sad to say, no mere local exception. Similarly depressing instances of such chaos-in-the-making have lately been recorded in countless star-systems."

At God's side, the little model globe gagged on its last few puffs of smoke.

"Taken together, such incidents form a pattern of cosmic events understandably all too troubling." There was a brief pause.

"Especially if you happen to be in My position."

As a now increasingly uncertain cosmos waited, God's voice softened with that storied empathy which everyone listening hoped would forever remain one of the Deity's most dependable qualities. Particularly in their case.

"Then again, perhaps it's not so surprising that so many planets – ancient perhaps in geological time, but barely teenagers by My calendar – are becoming increasingly unruly as the years go by. They are more and more inclined to quarrel among themselves over all the inevitable duties and distractions of adulthood."

Pausing, God took an invisible sip from the crystal goblet positioned and filled with trembling hands only moments before by one of the youngest, littlest angels.

"Seen from a larger, more indulgent perspective, however, this wide-spread rambunctiousness may turn out to be not such a bad thing after all. Nothing more, perhaps, than an inevitable case of intergalactic growing pains, or so I most sincerely hope!"

Setting the blackened simulacrum of Earth gently to one side, invisible fingertips brushed across the carefully stacked piles of cosmic reports.

"If true, it may explain why more and more up-and-coming, cosmic go-getters now seem to believe that, given half a chance and the right weather conditions, they themselves might just do a better job of running the universe, or, at least, their own local corner of it. A much better job, perhaps, than an undeniably elusive, seemingly reclusive and now, just maybe, increasingly super-annuated Deity whose time has long since come and, just maybe ... gone?"

Throughout the universe, residents of countless star systems glanced nervously at one another. God was widely believed to have super-secret ways of listening in; but not, they'd always hoped, quite this accurately.

Leaning back, the first and seemingly permanent C.E.O. of Universe Inc. ran an unhurried, all-seeing eye over the hushed lines of bright-winged angels. Even the Archangel of All Archangels, justly famous for his imperturbability, now appeared more on edge than his celebrated patrician reserve could conceal.

"Well, maybe all you would-be holier-than-Thous could replace Me."

A sudden fascinated, simultaneously horrified murmur rippled throughout the universe.

"And then again, maybe not!

"In any event," God continued, the aura of deep philosophic concern giving way to a triumphant smile, "we're all soon going to find out!"

With that, the explosive source of the original big bang lit the fuse on a second, almost as large.

"In response to unspoken popular demand, therefore, I've decided it's time to let some lucky soul borrow the keys to the cosmos and – for better or worse – have his or her very first go at the celestial steering wheel."

God leaned forward, reaching out (courtesy of the newly-established Heavenly Broadcast Studio) to put the same unprecedented question to every incredulous viewer throughout a hundred and one billion now totally non-plussed galaxies.

"So, who wants to be God for a day?"

Aftershock

❧ WHAT WAS HEAVEN coming to! The celestial statisticians on duty later calculated that the sudden collective intake of breath which followed was the second-largest in the history of the universe.

The largest, record-setting cosmic gasp was the one after that, as the significance, and potentially limitless possibilities, of the offer began everywhere to sink in.

At Scheherazade's side, Big D appeared barely able to keep from raising one lightning-fast hand to become Earth's first and most deserving applicant. "After all," he confided, his calm, measured tones already reflecting so eminently suitable a professional upgrade, "I'm probably the greatest secret understudy around!"

As for Scheherazade, she was already speculating affectionately, if also slightly apprehensively, about all that this particular handsome extra-celestial candidate might bring to this particular job.

Looking away, she stared upward to the sky, delighting again in the vast, glowing, completely unforeseen spectacle of the Heavenly Broadcast Studio high above her.

The echo of her own words, resounding from an encounter not so very long ago, rang again in her ears: 'Have You ever considered ... taking a day off?'

❧

Marina, Leila, Qingling, Yazmina, Tatiana and Sybilla, for their part, found themselves uncharactistically close to speechless.

"This could be somewhat momentous," Qingling finally opined.

Abracadabra spun his magic wand through the air in a series of increasingly-intricate, high-speed arcs, trying unsuccessfully to calculate the incalculable number of potential candidates for the position. The old wizard quietly tucked his magic wand into his robe, only to begin scratching his head. While he'd long been one of God's greatest admirers, he couldn't help wondering whether, this time, Heaven really knew what it was up to.

A moment later he began chuckling, already sure of the answer.

Divine Prospectus

❧ AS EVERYONE THROUGHOUT the cosmos watched on the giant screens of their respective planetary skies, The Angel of the Golden Hammer and Gong swung a second mighty blow, its clang reverberating throughout all possible worlds.

From one darkened corner of the Heavenly Broadcast Studio, a radiant, globe-shaped advisor advanced purposefully into the light, then bowed to the Source of this spectacular moment.

Then, slowly unrolling the large golden scroll entrusted to his care, the Angel of Unprecedented Opportunities began to read his unprecedented invitation:

The One and Only,
Supreme Being *Extraordinaire,*
Aided and Abetted by Heaven's
Most Distinguished Angels, ,
Takes Literally Infinite Pride and Pleasure
In Announcing
Our Very First, Cosmos-wide
'God for a Day' Contest

Dispite countless secret rehearsals the Angel of Unprecedented Opportunities was not surprised to find himself trembling at his final words, glancing up in search of God's reassuring nod.

Heartened, he continued in the same clear voice to read the rules of the Contest:

Official Rules and Regulations

One

The quintessentially-worthy candidate selected will assume the role of Official Substitute Supreme Being for a period of twenty-four (24) hours (Celestial Standard Time), during which period he, she or it will enjoy and exercise (subject, of course, to certain obvious restrictions and safeguards) all the rights, powers and privileges of the original and abiding Creator and Preserver of the universe.

Two

Applicants are now solicited from every galaxy. Given the universe's extreme variety and complexity, it will be up to prospective candidates to decide whether their qualifications may be adequate.

Three

All candidates must submit, within seven (7) days, a completed application form, a brief resumé, three letters of reference, and a short essay on why they feel especially qualified for so singular an undertaking. A brief summary of everything they hope to achieve during their brief stay in office must also be included.

Four

An angelic sub-committee will screen all applications to determine one hundred (100) finalists from across the cosmos. If, in the sole opinion of these senior celestial advisors, no single applicant is found who completely meets all the desired requirements, a winner will be chosen from among the finalists by a random draw overseen by the Archangel of all Archangels.

Five

The Winner of the 'God for a Day' Contest will be announced at a universally-televised ceremony to be held in exactly fourteen (14) days' time.

Please note:

In all matters relating to the Contest (and much else besides), God's decision is final.

❧

From the tiniest planet with only twelve residents to the largest star-system making the most of over two trillion taxpayers, the same, sharp thought echoed simultaneously throughout countless galaxies. "Can God be serious?" So startling a question was instantly followed by a second, even more urgent one. "If so, then what's going to happen to us?"

One of the benefits of omniscience is the ability to read individual minds light years before they have been conceived. Literally infinite understanding – and synonymous compassion – come with the territory.

"Yes, definitely, I am serious, if that's the right word," God replied. A suspenseful moment passed. "But not, of course, that serious. Whatever you plan to do, please remember,all this can be fun!"

An instant later, as the haloes of every angel shone brighter in unison, a shower of celestial application forms in every colour of the rainbow began falling gracefully towards suddenly uplifted hands throughout the universe. Electronic advances notwithstanding, sometimes the old ways were best, or at least, more dramatic.

"Enjoy yourselves. And be sure to print legibly."

A judiciously non-denominational hymn entitled "Now What!" – especially composed for the occasion and sung by the newly formed Heavenly Broadcast Studio Choir – marked the close of this unique celestial transmission.

As the music faded, an imperturbable Deity disappeared once more into the radiance of Heaven, God's parting challenge lingering in the air.

"And for your own sakes – if not also Mine – I sincerely urge you all to make the most of this truly once-in-a-celestial-lifetime opportunity!"

Timely Twosome

❦ STANDING ON TIPTOE, Scheherazade reached out to a yellow celestial application form fluttering to rest in a tangle of white jasmine flowers. Big D, an appropriately crimson form in hand, remained lost in thoughts beyond words.

Scanning the golden-inked invitation, Marina, Leila, Qingling, Yazmina, Tatiana and Sybilla swiftly began conjecturing as to who across so many exceptional galaxies might even begin to think of applying. And from that unsurprisingly-limited number, the even more improbable few anywhere near qualified to do so.

"Ain't so easy being God," Abracadabra observed, drawing on the accumulated wisdom of millennia of successful divination. "For that, you need a really big, really magic wand, among other things."

It seemed clear, for now at least, that being the unassuming lord of a little white cloud and all it might survey was, for the humble old sorcerer, power and responsibility enough. He turned to his old underworld acquaintance, curious as to whatever it was that continued to keep the Devil's unspoken, unresolved thoughts circling round and round.

"Shouldn't be too hard for you to find three outstanding references," he ventured conversationally.

Big D looked up, still preoccupied.

"Yes?" Abracadabra inquired slowly.

"That globe-shaped advisor, the one who read the proclamation," Big D held out the application form. "It says here, in the list of participating officials, that he's the Angel of Unprecedented Opportunities. From the enthusiastic looks of him, a fairly recent promotion, I would guess." Big

D paused, the well-earned lines of his face growing deeper. "Whoever he is, I have the strangest feeling I've seen him before."

Abracadabra said nothing. Like the Devil, he'd come to know quite a number of angels in his time. In flight, at a distance, they could often look much the same.

Then again, he recalled – the image of a second globe-shaped figure springing merrily out of nowhere – there had been some talk of a set of exceptionally talented angelic twins. A pair of terrifically flexible celestial fast-trackers, currently being groomed for highly classified tasks.

Under the circumstances, Abracadabra decided, such information was best kept to himself, especially since the other brother's title was, if he remembered correctly, The Angel of Hidden Agendas.

Choices, Choices

❧ EVEN ON THE MOST seemingly uneventful day, the universe tends to be a very busy place.

Not surprisingly, as the potential implications of the 'God for a Day' Contest began to sink in, quite a few anxious galaxies found themselves with far too much to consider in far too little time, their social media swiftly reaching warp speed and beyond.

If the entire universe might (by some reports) have been built in just six days, discovering a replacement for its Creator in only fourteen proved almost as hard. If being God requires no small commitment, so too did even the simple act of applying for the position.

Almost everyone had an opinion on what was needed and, of course, almost every opinion differed.

Schoolchildren on widely separated star systems independently decided that, while individually they might not be quite old enough yet to be God, then, all the same, if it was okay, they and their classmates would like to apply for the position as a group.

Business leaders were quick to establish project teams to understand and adapt to the changing needs of the overall spiritual marketplace. The successful rebranding of Heaven was clearly the only way to go.

Countless politicians argued that they alone (more than their electorates, certainly) understood how to make the really important decisions. All promised that, if selected, they would immediately begin extensive polling to determine in what direction it seemed celestially least problematic and personally most beneficial to proceed.

Throughout a wide range of constellations, assorted dictators, despots and ne'er-do-good diehards expressed the conviction that, in the event of their promotion to the ultimate in grandeur (if not grandiosity) the universe would become an even better place, especially for them.

Quite a few hitherto happy theocrats found themselves distinctly out of sorts. Having long served that particular one-sided interpretation of the divine which, most conveniently, also best served them in return, they were firmly convinced that change of any kind had absolutely no appeal, whether God liked it or not.

More advanced spiritual luminaries across the cosmos sent letters suggesting it would be best simply to leave the position vacant for a day. If God was wisely taking a break, maybe everyone else should, too. No one they knew was remotely qualified for the job. What could God have been thinking! Yours reverently, obediently, etc.

෪

In the stillness of her villa garden, Big D kissed Scheherazade on the cheek.

"Sorry to be off so quickly," he announced, meaning it far more than he was prepared to let on. "An emergency planning meeting with some of my more impulsive associates."

A devilish new light shone in his eyes. "It's not fully decided yet, but me and the boys are thinking of making the most of our long tradition of down-home cooperation and applying as a transstellar team." He looked off in the distance, his face unreadable. "I was considering suggesting myself as Chairman…."

The difficulty, and delight, of the underworld's brightest sparks is that it's hard to tell when they are up to no good or something even better.

"Can't think of a finer Devil for the job," Scheherazade replied in all honesty. Who knew what might happen? It would certainly be a first.

As her lips brushed his cheek in return, Big D disappeared into thin air, his timing effortless yet perfect.

"I've always liked his style," Abracadabra muttered to himself.

Moments later, the old sorcerer himself said a fond farewell to all seven ladies, promising to return in two weeks, in time for the Heavenly Broadcast Studio's next fateful transmission. Whatever lay ahead, it would undoubtedly be best to meet the unknown well rested.

Wizards (as they knew all too well) were always on call.

Given her capacious heart, Scheherazade was not one to forget her friends. Especially when they appeared no longer all they might once have been. As the days of waiting passed, she found herself brooding over Earth's first couple in their forgotten retreat. They must have had news of the 'God for a Day' Contest. Given their past experience, she couldn't help wondering how they might be taking it.

The answer, she soon discovered, was troubling. While Adam appeared pleased by her thoughtful call, he was also sorry to say that, for reasons unknown, Eve no longer seemed quite herself. In fact, whatever the undiagnosed cause, she had recently taken to resting a lot. If it was alright, he went on, he would prefer to let her sleep.

Though disappointed not to speak with her aging friend, Scheherazade was quick to concur. While far too discreet to say so, she wondered momentarily whether perhaps so extraordinary a woman, her ancient powers flickering, might finally be drifting toward those sadly silenced landscapes of the old and infirm.

Quiet concern notwithstanding, Adam still seemed in fairly good spirits. The recently-announced divine contest, he reported, had been the subject of much discussion among the universe's most senior citizens, their increasingly strong opinions asserted over breakfast, lunch, tea, dinner and, despite some sideways glances and muttered rejoinders, the normally inviolate afternoon games of cards.

The overall consensus seemed to be that a candidate offering an unlikely combo of antique savvy and contemporary technosmarts would be ideal. Someone sufficiently complex for a universe which, to most of Adam's fellow retirees, was seeming excessively so.

Scheherazade laughed. "And what would be your guess?" she asked diplomatically. Adam circled the subject before confessing that, whoever the ultimate choice, he certainly hoped God's still-unknown stand-in might prove just a tad more indulgent and forbearing, this time.

For his part, he continued wistfully, he often wondered what might have happened if only he and Eve had done things a little differently and enjoyed a friendly sit-down, a little mutual give-and-take instead of so hasty an exodus. "It's just possible we could have made that quiet little beginner's kit of a Garden into something truly splendid.

"Oh well," he concluded soberly. "Woulda, coulda, shoulda…."

Given even the little she now knew of Eden, Scheherazade's reply was heart-felt. "All the same, I think both of you can be very proud!"

"Thank you," Adam answered softly. He coughed as if he, too, might be catching something. "That means a lot."

"Look after yourselves," Scheherazade replied in farewell, not wanting to discomfort him further. "When Eve wakes," she added, "please give her my love, and tell her we're all thinking of her."

❧

Thanks to a supremely dedicated celestial support staff, 'God for a Day' application forms and apps had been successfully conveyed to every being throughout Time, Space and grace.

Modesty removed quite a few potential candidates, caution even more. In the end, less than one percent of one percent of one percent of all application forms circulated throughout the universe were submitted for the Celestial Preliminary Review Committee's official consideration.

Of these, three-quarters were swiftly rejected because of a surfeit of enthusiasm over experience or excessively positive references. Such preliminary editing notwithstanding, the senior angelic subcommittee still found itself reviewing too many imperfect semi-finalists from too many imperfect galaxies. As the hours until The Great Day grew fewer, countless angels struggled ever harder to stay awake at their overladen celestial desks. It was not surprising that all drew renewed energy from the certainty that God knew exactly what God was doing. Or so, at least, they most fervently hoped.

For their part, as the last days before the contest approached, Scheherazade and her six friends all found themselves waking, again and again, from the same dream. In it, countless stars pulsed and flared overhead, a vast panorama everywhere sending swift, indecipherable signals to one another.

As the dream faded, every constellation in Creation transformed on cue, together becoming an unending series of shimmering question marks, each one alive with mute, yet infinite longing.

In Contention

᠍ FINALLY, THE SEEMINGLY endless night before The Great Day arrived. Everyone everywhere carefully set their alarm clocks, then kept waking up every half-hour to check the time. Eventually the entire cosmos got up early, settling in to wait through the last interminable minutes before the universe (and their own so brief but all-important lives) would be irreversibly transformed.

When it came to planning their second, cosmos-wide broadcast, the Angelic Coordinating Committee contest had no hesitation in tinkering with earlier success. What had worked so splendidly the first time was, as far as they were concerned, merely an artistic warm-up exercise. Not for them the easy route of simply adding a few more catchy show tunes, enlarging the cast and turning up the volume.

After all, a day like this hadn't happened since eternity itself had been only a twinkle in God's all-seeing eye.

᠍

To the faintest of celestial drum rolls, the skies of everywhere turned a pure brilliant white, and the air filled with billions of balloons, rising and falling to the first strains of a now familiar ethereal symphony. Each balloon had, in holographic form, an exact replica of one of the candidates who *didn't* make the finals. In perfect time to the music, every bubblicious hologram swivelled up, down and sideways, enjoying the company of all those who, although competitors in this contest, were, nonetheless, in the great unfinished scheme of things, their transgalactic colleagues. Filled with hot air, they began to chorus: "Hark, the envious angels sing, we really wish we coulda won this thing."

As the last bright balloons disappeared and the justly-deserved standing ovation faded away, a host of celestial technicians breathed a collective sigh of relief.

"What a performance!"

"What even better luck!" their team leader responded. "Do you know how hard it is to teach that many balloons to sing? In under two weeks!"

A second drum roll heralded the return of those exhibitionists whose sizzling performance had so wowed the crowd on their first appearance. Now, however, the Heavenly host of perfectly trained, exceptionally large lightning bolts were arrayed in every shade of the celestial spectrum. Flashing and crackling in a kaleidoscopic repeat performance, they linked arms, dancing in unison from horizon to horizon. Through the swirling rainbows left in their wake, every galaxy began to make out, once again, the incomparable vista of the Heavenly Broadcast Studio.

Centre-stage, visibly nervous and very well scrubbed finalists sat as still as possible on one hundred shining silver chairs surrounding the uniquely radiant Presence each hoped to replace.

Looking carefully at the candidates, veteran observers of Time and Space could make out quite a few regionally pre-eminent individuals from across the cosmos: time-tested teachers of the heart, doctors of trans-substantial serenities, intergalactic experts in exponential virtue, all invincible warriors in the unending battles for ever-greater interstellar understanding.

As the Heavenly Broadcast Studio cameras panned slowly over the scene, everyone everywhere felt the same rush of humility, wonder and pride. It is one thing to be part of an ongoing cosmic mystery, quite another suddenly to feel it in one's all-too-evanescent bones.

A moment later the Angel of the Golden Hammer and Gong, eager as ever, stepped forward anew, his now familiar clang reverberating throughout the universe. As the echoes died away, the globe-shaped Angel of Unprecedented Opportunities strode purposefully into the light.

"On behalf of all our extended celestial family, it is my pleasure to welcome every one of our viewers to this, the truly spectacular conclusion to the first-ever 'God for a Day' Contest! Given that trillions of worthy applications have been received, the task of arriving at a mere one hundred finalists, as you can appreciate, was exceptionally difficult."

The next words had clearly been just as carefully considered. "God has asked me to express Heaven's gratitude to all those who, however unfortunately, did not make it this far." There was a pause, then a long, slow smile. "And also to thank so many of you for your suggestions (frequently unsigned, generally diplomatic, sometimes wondrously irreverent) as to how God's earlier efforts might best be improved upon."

After a quick glance at the commanding presence at centre stage, the Angel of Unprecedented Opportunities turned back toward the rows of hushed candidates. "And now, without further ado, it is my extreme pleasure to present to you the one hundred carefully chosen deities-in-the-making in this great, grand and gloriously unparalleled competition!"

Unrolling the golden scroll with elaborate care, the globe-shaped angel proceeded to reveal to a uniformly rapt Creation the identities of those rare individuals from whom one, and only one, would soon be selected. Given their widely varying places of origin he did so not by generally unfamiliar individual name, but rather the slightly more recognizable planet and constellation of their birth.

With each announcement, ecstatic shouts rang out from widely scattered corners of the universe as, galaxy by equally elated galaxy, its citizens leapt to their feet at the news that one of their own had made the final cut.

Slightly more than two-thirds of the way through his recitation, the Angel of Unprecedented Opportunities brought a whirling little blue-and-white world to a stop so abrupt and unforeseen as to nearly send it into reverse.

"Number sixty-nine. From the Milky Way Galaxy, a contender from that hitherto unnoticed, yet recently so surprisingly newsworthy little planet best known as Earth!"

The terrestrial shouts and cries which followed easily drowned out the announcement of the next fifteen finalists.

As silence returned, the inhabitants of a suddenly subdued little sphere stared at one another with the most puzzled look its residents ever had the possibly great good fortune to share.

And the Winner Is

❦ WATCHING FROM THE comfort of Hell's largest boardroom, Big D leapt to his feet in a barely controlled blast of flame.

The effort of preparing his own application had proved far more demanding than he'd imagined. So much to make sure he put in, so much he couldn't very well leave out. A checkered career perhaps but, all in all, one displaying undeniable versatility. And, given the unforeseen change in climate, more than a little fortitude.

On the one hand, Big D acknowledged, he just happened to know Somebody. Quite closely, if the truth were told, which might still be a very good thing, even after so long. Then again, as a wily old devil in good standing, he was well aware that having influence could be a slightly tricky business. Sometimes the people you knew, knew more about you than you knew.

Whatever the odds, this truly Heaven-sent opportunity had appeared his best chance so far to win recognition – and a potential homecoming celebration – so regrettably long overdue.

In the last few days, however, the Master Demon had quietly begun to accept that a triumphant return to the celestial parade ground was likely not in the cards. At least not, perhaps, in this extraordinary way.

All in all, it was probably spiritually wiser (if not ultimately safer) to remain the Devil he knew, rather than the enigmatic Deity for whose role he had considerably less recent practice. As his associates began speculating excitedly, Big D himself couldn't help wondering who on Earth this wholly unforeseen finalist might turn out to be.

Watching intently by the villa pool, six equally astonished ladies all shot upright in their lounge chairs, wondering aloud as to the identity of so unexpected a candidate from a little planet seemingly far sneakier than any had realized.

For her part, Scheherazade found herself recalling a certain, recent, deep-voiced ultimatum from a well-informed gentleman with both a thousand eyes and a knack for knowing far more than he let on.

Was it possible, she wondered, both for Earth's sake and their own mutual delight that the World's Greatest Gravedigger and the World's Most Beautiful Astronomer had somehow jointly applied?

The more she thought about it, the more there seemed a very good case for a duo offering all the advantages of opposite sexes, strengths and perspectives, together with a kindred courage and well-intentioned equanimity. Not to mention, given their respective metaphysical vantage points, an inevitably droll sense of proportion.

Highly improbable, it was true, but not impossible. After all, being God was unquestionably a job most would find difficult to attempt alone.

Returning to the great drama continuing to unfold on the Heavenly Broadcast Studio stage, Scheherazade tried to make out the individual finalists now waiting in rising suspense on their silver chairs. So far, however, she could find no sign of the tall graceful woman with her ever-present telescope, nor the broad-shouldered gentleman with his trusty silver spade.

Nor, for that matter, any sign of Big D as well. Not for the first time since they parted, she wondered how he was doing, and whether, against all odds, his own undoubtedly persuasive application form might have found its way to the final round. While she still couldn't quite imagine him as the winning candidate, it certainly wouldn't be the first time in so subversive a career that Satan had chosen to show up in disguise.

After all, if one wished to be God (however briefly) it undoubtedly helped to have an extremely mature and finely tuned sense of humour.

࿗

As the Angel of Unprecedented Opportunities finished his recital of the last few contestants, the Heavenly Broadcast Studio Choir began a deeply moving anthem of celebration and thanksgiving. At its close the entire celestial staff bowed to the finalists in appreciation.

For every angel present, this was an utterly extraordinary day. Whatever the venture, change in management always brings mixed emotions. How much more so if it should occur at the highest level of what was the most colossal, longest-running outfit in the entire universe!

As trillions of stars looked on in wonder, God brushed away an invisible tear. Not for nothing is gratitude considered the noblest of virtues.

ॐ

Truly spiritual beings are instinctively disinclined to keep others in any more suspense than is strategically necessary. So it was, that when the Angel of Unprecedented Opportunities next spoke, it was to the final one hundred contenders themselves.

"On behalf of the Angelic Selection Committee, I would like to thank you all for everything you bring to this incomparable occasion. Indeed, we are convinced that any one of you would be a wise choice."

There was a dramatic pause. "And therein lies our problem."

At the great golden desk, God nodded imperceptibly.

"Unfortunately," the globe-shaped angel continued, "since all of you come from such widely dissimilar worlds, your individual achievements, while praiseworthy, are completely different." Another pause followed. "And so, try as we might, it seems impossible to determine which one among you is truly first among equals!

"That's the bad news." As the Angel of Unprecedented Opportunities carefully surveyed the scene, a hundred finalists unconsciously began edging to the front of one hundred increasingly unstable chairs.

"Now for the good. Since it seems impossible to choose the winner by comparative merit alone, we are therefore officially required, by the previously announced Contest Rules to leave the ultimate decision to what could best be called The Far-Seeing Hand of Fate.

"In other words," the globe-shaped angel continued, big round eyes growing merrier by the moment, "today's all-important outcome will now be determined by ... a very special draw!"

While the Heavenly Broadcast Studio Choir tried its best to provide a temporary distraction for a now highly-animated universe, the Angel of

Unprecedented Opportunities hastened off-stage to join his equally-agile twin in completing the last and most important step in the proceedings.

§a

Millions of galaxies away, alone at the helm of his little white cloud, Abracadabra began jumping up and down, suddenly youthful despite his years. "I knew it! I knew it! I knew it! Or at least I think I know part of it," he added, his smile getting larger by the second.

After considerable reflection over the past two weeks – on both the needs of the universe in general, and the rumoured talents of the Angel of Unprecedented Opportunities and the thus-far unseen Angel of Hidden Agendas, in particular – the old wizard had reached several conclusions. The most important of these was that, no matter how long or hard one stares at them, identical twins somehow manage always to look very much alike.

"I'll bet my very best magic wand," he began, "that we are witnessing the most spectacular teleological bait-and-switch in Heavenly history!"

In the next moment, in confirmation of Abracadabra's hypothesis, a most definitely globe-shaped angel reappeared on the Heavenly Broadcast Studio stage, pushing before him a large transparent globe filled with one hundred brilliantly-coloured envelopes, all firmly sealed.

If there was one thing he admired most about God, the old wizard decided, it was the sheer, inestimable panache.

§a

As viewers everywhere watched in fascination, the Archangel-in-Chief took his place beside the Angel of Hidden Agendas. With princely grace, Heaven's second-in-command lifted the cover from the large, envelope-filled globe. Try as they might to contain themselves, one hundred finalists from every corner of Creation trembled in their seats.

The glowing presence behind the golden desk gestured once more, quickly, discreetly and decisively. There were moments, God thought, when it was more than just standard operating procedure to work in mysterious ways.

Slowly, the Archangel of All Archangels reached in to the globe.

"The envelope, please."

As God stretched out an invisible hand, everyone in the entire universe took a deep collective breath. "Before announcing the result," God began at last, "I would like to thank all of you whose extraordinary qualifications ensured you a place in this so unlikely contest. I am as proud of every one of you as you should be of yourselves.

"To all those who are about to find yourselves celestial also-rans, as it were, I would normally be the first to wish you better luck next time." There was a subtle pause, then a wry smile. "Under the circumstances, however, I'm sure you'll understand if I say it's probably best to wait and see just how this particular little experiment works out first.

"And now...." Slowly, exquisitely slowly, God opened the single white-and-gold envelope. Then, at last, turned once more toward all the many breathless, waiting worlds.

"Esteemed candidates and all other beings throughout this vast splendiferous universe which is both home and inspiration to us all...."

God paused, whispering in the limitless overlap of Time and Eternity a simple heart-felt prayer; then, confidently yet irrevocably, committed the entire universe to an adventure alarmingly unknown.

"It is My profound pleasure to announce that the winner of Heaven's first-ever 'God for a Day' Contest is...."

As the Angel of the Golden Hammer and Gong set to once more, a brilliant array of celestial spotlights came together to focus on a single, slender figure, now suddenly unveiled.

At the very centre of the very back row of candidates, a poised, un-imaginably radiant young woman, eyes as ancient yet bright as diamonds, said her own small silent heartfelt prayer. Not for herself, but rather for all that she might yet do.

"Too late to turn back now," she added softly.

"What took Me so long!" the seemingly insoluble enigma of all enigmas echoed *sotto voce*.

"Eve!" God declared triumphantly. "Intrepid chatelaine of a long-lost Eden, and Planet Earth's very own once and future leading lady!"

Fan Reaction

৯ AS GAZILLIONS OF viewers across the universe finally exhaled, God mused contentedly on all the many intricacies of poetic justice.

Backstage, the Angel of Hidden Agendas shook the equally discreet palm of the Angel of Celestial Opportunities. Then, switching hands, they did it again. Just to be on the safe side.

Down under, Big D pretended to glare incredulously at his demonic friends and associates; then broke into a delightedfully devilish laugh.

"I *know* this woman," he exclaimed. "And I wouldn't underestimate her for even the smallest subdivided nanosecond. Trust me: this is where things start to get really interesting!"

Having shared, over the past half-hour, the exact same suspenseful rollercoaster, Marina, Leila, Qingling, Yazmina, Tatiana, Sybilla and Scheherazade exchanged similarly astonished looks. "So, the greatest of Earthly great-great-grandmothers wasn't in well-deserved retirement after all," Scheherazade mused aloud. "She was actually in training!"

৯

Less than an hour later, far away from the celebrations still taking place within the Heavenly Broadcast Studio, a proud, blushing gentleman by the name of Adam made his first terrestrial media appearance in quite a few millennia.

"Why am I not surprised?" he asked, one hand shading his eyes as journalists pressed in from every side behind jostling microphones and constantly flashing cameras.

There was a quiet smile. "Ever since the beginning of our eventful relationship, I've had the adventurous good fortune to be continually reminded of one of the universe's most enduring truths; namely, that every woman – even when most alone – contains within her at least two women, the one you see … and the one you don't.

"The lesson I continue daily to learn from Eve is complex but simple: always keep your eye on the woman you don't see!"

Change of Command

"I ALWAYS FELT SHE WASN'T REALLY INTO BINGO!"
— Concierge, The Fountain of Youth Retirement Home

Classy Reunion

❧ "AFTER ALL THIS TIME, may I say that it's truly a pleasure to see you once again. Not just in person but, more especially, *chez Moi*."

"Of all places," Eve responded with a matching grin. "Sorry about that little misunderstanding last time."

God's smile grew even larger. "Apology accepted, but unnecessary. After all, in many ways you really had no choice."

"Somehow I always felt that breaking our lease and leaving Paradise early was what, in Your heart of hearts, You secretly wanted us to do all along. An unstated hope that Adam and I, thoughtful and considerate as You made us to be, just couldn't resist taking the strain off so poignantly overburdened an apple tree and…."

"And, for better and worse entwined," God continued, "open the stage door to freedom and fortune, temporary pain and larger purpose, transient death and timeless destiny."

Eve couldn't resist. "What some might be tempted to call a 'fate *accompli*'!"

The resulting laughter echoed throughout the universe, causing residents of even the outermost planets to blink in sudden surprise.

"Always reassuring to find one's hunches confirmed," God announced, pouring more tea and offering a biscuit, entirely free of ulterior motive. "In fact, I'm delighted we now have this chance to work together again."

"Your humble servant," Eve replied, bobbing her fair head gracefully. "Well … more or less."

"Nervous?"

"And excited, and determined, and a thousand other emotions all inextricably entangled. So, yes," Eve replied, "nervous!"

"This job can definitely do that to you. I can remember more than a few sleepless nights before I finally settled in."

"Making up the universe out of absolutely nothing mustn't have been exactly easy. Especially when You had to do it entirely on Your own."

"From humble beginnings...," God declared affably. "Then again, everybody has to start somewhere."

Taking Eve by the arm, God led the way to the great bay windows of Heaven, constellation after shimmering constellation swirling by, each to its own inspiring music. Beyond, in every direction, galaxy after galaxy receded away toward endless horizons. As Eve grew lost in wonder, God watched in companionable stillness.

"It's so beautiful; infinitely more beautiful than Eden," she said at last. In the distance, millions of stars flickered in harmony. "And very much busier."

"Rarely a dull moment."

"From the looks of things, I'd guess You've been more than busy since last we met. What with all so many new interstellar subdivisions under construction, an unlimited supply of all-purpose angels must come in handy."

"Wouldn't be the same without them. Even so, it's always a juggling act – as you will undoubtedly soon discover." God took a quiet step forward, studying Heaven's pending replacement closely, even protectively.

"While I'm profoundly glad that you won, on behalf of the universe, I'm also obliged to ask: any second thoughts?"

As countless stars swirled by in turn, each momentarily stopping to stare, Eve recalled her brief, selfless prayer before rising from so many qualified contenders to become the one now standing at God's side.

"Somehow I have the oddest feeling I was meant to be here." Earth's first woman smiled a smile a hundred thousand years younger, the quiet smile of a young girl, apple in hand, gazing over a garden wall. "I'm just not completely sure why, at least not yet!"

Sooner or later, Eve knew, she would find an answer. She only hoped it proved the right one, and not just for herself alone. God, clearly, had far more at stake in this particular little once-in-a-celestial-lifetime experiment than anyone else. After all, if it failed, who else would be left to clean up the mess?

Sooner or later in every life, as Adam and Eve's descendants continue to rediscover, God can be counted on to ask the really tricky questions.

"So. The universe apart, what are you going to do about Earth?"

Pointed though the query might be, it did not catch Eve completely by surprise. Her native planet had troubled both her reveries and dreams, and all the more so since Scheherazade's first surprise visit.

"They're not the only ones, of course." God interjected, reading Eve's mind in a way she was beginning to find less disconcerting. "Every constellation, no matter how evolved, occasionally still finds itself wide of the mark, if not off the celestial beam entirely."

There was a sudden, aeons-old, almost apologetic frown.

"Yes?"

"I sometimes wonder whether, in arranging for all these planets to orbit about their own axis (even if, engineering-wise, it still seems the most elegant and economical solution) I inadvertently caused them to become figuratively self-centred as well."

"Quite possibly." Overly blunt reply or not, Eve guessed she probably hadn't been promoted for an underdeveloped skill in flattery.

"And then again, maybe it was simply inevitable," she continued. "What with each of them being so distinctly separate and, given the distances, communication all the more difficult."

She paused, then committed herself. "It's my guess that far too many of them think they might just as well be absolutely alone in the universe." She paused again, a sense of possibilities becoming clearer still. "And that, in itself, is likely more than half the problem."

God gazed at Eve, reading in the calm depths of her eyes a determination which might soon come from the heart of the universe as well. Time, and all that Eve might choose to do, would tell.

"Any suggestions?" God asked quietly.

Her body suddenly tingling, Eve experienced anew that first, fateful moment before Eden's gate; she and Adam standing side by side, alone yet unafraid. Now, gazing through Heaven's nearest window to where millions of nearby stars watched in silence, each in its own poignant solitude, she brushed away a tear.

Billions of galaxies, trillions of stars, trillions of planets, trillions of Gardens of Eden, trillions of Adams, trillions of Eves. A near-limitless cosmic cornucopia, a veritable Big Bang buffet. And a wealth of home teams beyond counting.

"Can You keep a secret?" she asked.

A moment later, she began whispering the outlines of an idea already beginning to take shape, she now realized, long before Scheherazade had first arrived.

"What if I said: gold, silver, bronze?"

If anyone could take a hint, Eve, figured, it would likely be God.

"Brilliant idea. Absolutely brilliant!" There was a judicious pause. "Only wish I'd thought of it Myself!"

Transition Planning

&. ONE OF THE PLEASURES of being God is the ability to know exactly how to assist with any possible plan. Considering the scope of Eve's proposition, something extra now seemed very much in order.

"In view of what you have in mind, perhaps you might like to borrow My personal Cosmic Address Book," the keeper of the universe's ultimate birthday card list suggested. "Specially revised and updated for your arrival." There was a delicate pause. "The more I think about it, the more I like your plot!"

"Early stages yet. And, besides, I'm beginning to suspect it could very well be Yours … with slight modifications, of course." Eve batted her eyes melodramatically. "What I prefer to think of as my feminine touch!"

An amused, if invisible eyebrow flickered momentarily. "It's nice to think that all those many years since you and Adam made that overly-hasty getaway haven't been entirely wasted."

"If at first You don't succeed…!"

A knock on the study door was followed by the entry of an extremely burdened Angel of Celestial Press Relations, widespread wings bearing summaries of the latest news reports, commentaries and social media exchanges from across the universe. To Eve's surprise and delight, a single glance brought complete understanding of the contents. It seemed the exquisitely-subtle transmission of divine powers had already begun.

"A record amount of well-meant, but impatient expectations," God observed, "however unrealistic sometimes." All-seeing eyes clouded over. "In fairness, I should warn you; being God is infinitely more difficult than it looks."

For an instant, Eve had a sudden involuntary image of the universe wreathed in smoke and flame, black ash rising from the bitter burnt-out shells of hundreds of thousands of sadly-self-important planets left to their own lethally-loveless devices.

God reached out, gently taking her own small hand. "You're right. It's not just a game."

"High stakes?"

"The very highest."

❧

As God and God's soon-to-be-official replacement strolled out into Heaven's gardens, the Angel of Unprecedented Opportunities made his own timely reappearance.

"Everything is arranged, exactly as You wished," he declared, bowing gracefully, studying Eve all the while.

He and his celestial twin, together with their closer angelic associates, had already made their own bets on what their new employer might, or might not, attempt in the short celestial day at her disposal. With so much in the universe to keep track of, it would easy for a newcomer to get distracted, which, they agreed, would be such a waste.

He stared fleetingly at Eve who, catching both his glance and his hesitation, winked instantly in reply. A reassuringly warm but equally authoritative wink.

Not this one, he reckoned. Whatever else she might be, undoubtedly this was one very determined lady. Extremely encouraging, he concluded, to have her on the side of the angels. He might just win his wager after all, if he could only figure out what she was up to.

"Perfect. And thank you," said God, turning back to Eve, savouring, as never before, her quiet, hypnotic radiance, and sharp, resourceful eyes.

"The show starts tomorrow at noon."

❧

"Given everything you have in mind, twenty-four hours is not a very long time."

"Absolutely not," Eve agreed, grateful to be returning to the subject.

"On the other hand, once you have My not inconsiderable powers," the Creator continued mischievously, "a day can just as easily be as short, or as long, as you want."

"Ahhaaa!"

"Exactly. As you'll soon find, this job comes with a truly phenomenal range of perks."

Eve and her heavenly counterpart shared a calm, half-invisible supper.

Given what lay ahead, the most resolutely adventurous woman from a little blue-and-white planet was determined to be, inwardly as much as outwardly, at her absolute best. An early night would allow sleep and dreams to work their magic, bringing her safely to the borders of a miraculous new day … and a profoundly new identity.

An early night, that is, after she first had a long-distance word with that wondrously open-hearted gentleman who remained, like her, so capable of breaking all sorts of lesser, more conventional rules, the better to observe the larger, more abiding ones.

At this moment in her life, on the edge of another, even greater unknown, the two of them would most assuredly go forward together once more.

Even if, once again, she just happened to be in the lead.

Eve's first sleep, in the most luxurious of Heaven's guest bedrooms, was deep, restorative and serene. In the early hours of morning, a half-expected dream still took her by surprise; leaving their traditional orbits far behind, taking their places excitedly one after another, every galaxy in Creation joined together in an endless, winding path of light; a vast, luminous procession flowing boldly onward toward cheering crowds even now awaiting them in the immense, overflowing heart of the universe itself.

Transfer of Power

&. MINUTES RACED BY, rolling up the last hours before noon (Heavenly Standard Time) and what media commentators across the universe were already calling, hopefully, "Our really big leap of faith"!

To the delight of so many, gathering since early morning throughout galaxies galore, the Heavenly Broadcast Studio had signed on early. Countless worlds had applauded as images of the universe's greatest saints, sages and spiritual heroes and heroines appeared on the starry screens above them. In the background, the newly formed Heavenly Broadcast Studio Orchestra played inspirational excerpts from a little-known blue-and-white planet's surprisingly diverse musical repertoire.

Throughout Heaven, greater and lesser angels carefully checked their individual to-do lists, and then adjusted their respective haloes one last time.

Eve, for her part, took her time dressing, declining a resplendent orb and sceptre in favour of the simple pair of pearl earrings Adam had given her on that serene, satiated morning after their first joyous night together, now so long ago.

While the divine may appear in countless ways and forms, in this case there came a soft tapping on the guest bedroom door. And a quiet, incontestable voice. "Ready or not...."

Eve bit her lip, searching in the mirror a last time.

"If you'd like a second opinion, may I say I most definitely like what I see?" As Eve began to tremble, God put an invisible, affectionately steadying hand on her shoulder. "And so should you."

The small antechamber's windows offered but the barest glimpse of a universe in waiting, the final few moments going by both all too slowly and far too quickly.

"Any last-minute suggestions?" Eve ventured.

God gestured towards all the worlds making up Creation. "If and when they become especially irritating, which, I can safely assure you, they most assuredly will, I've always found it helpful to focus on all they have yet to become, however difficult that exercise in celestial self-restraint may sometimes be!"

Eve found herself smiling easily in return, somehow inwardly already alive with a kindred compassion and resolve. "Under the circumstances, I may have some very special requests for some very special angels."

"Call on whomever you need. They're all exceptionally well-trained and, more to the point, eminently reliable in case of emergencies."

"What about You?"

"Mmmmnn." God stretched happily, so evidently delighted at a very first day off since Creation's all-too-distant rosy dawn. "Hard to say. I may just sleep in. Or go exploring. Or both!"

"You were always rather good at dreaming things up, as I recall!"

"Beginner's luck," God replied, looking invisibly but obviously pleased.

Side by side, two Supreme Beings, one so temporary, the other eternal, quietly contemplated the still unfinished mystery of those early days, and how the love of Creation itself became the unfolding creation of Love.

"If the need arises, how do I reach You?"

A divine eyebrow rose momentarily, a divine eye couldn't resist twinkling.

"Strangely enough, prayer usually works." A moment later, smiling gently, God handed Eve a little white-and-gold card. "But just in case, here's My private mobile number. I had it specially installed."

❦

As a more suitably traditional overture, golden hammer and gong had been replaced by the shrill yet stately Airborne Angels of the Shimmering Silver Trumpets.

The doors to the Heavenly Throne Room were flung open and, as viewers throughout every star system got their second glimpse of the woman about to become the guide to their suddenly-unreadable future, God and Eve entered together, arm in arm.

On an awe-struck little blue-and-white planet far, far away, a watching Scheherazade sighed with delight, thinking that her youthfully ancient friend had never looked more radiant, or more determined.

At Scheherazade's side, stalwartly keeping Earth's home fires burning whatever might come, Adam whispered a quiet prayer for his far-off beloved, never more proud or certain of her than now.

The entire universe held its breath.

"Any parting thoughts?" Eve whispered, as she looked up toward the huge, shimmering and now-so-clearly-empty throne.

"However tempting the possibilities might be, it's probably not a good idea to tinker with My personal chemistry set while I'm away."

"Wouldn't dare." Outwardly serene, Eve felt her heart beating faster. And faster still. "Anything else?"

"Think big!"

"How big?"

There was a silence as God relived so many long aeons past, reflected on the countless others still to come and then offered up the secret at the universe's heart.

"It is love, and only love, which guides us onward; our boundless, indomitable love for the cosmos and one another, ever open to all that awaits our awakening wonder!"

There was a long pause, a proud yet rueful smile. "It's a mystery so simple that even I don't fully appreciate it sometimes."

Even God, it seemed, Eve realized with a sharp, sudden pang, could still be surprised by all Time had wrought ... so far.

The silver trumpets sounded once more. As Eve reached the base of the iridescent stairs leading up to the Heavenly Throne, God kissed her gently on the cheek.

Then, letting go of her arm, disappeared in light.

§.

The very first woman on Earth took a deep breath, made a solemn promise to herself and all she was about to serve and started upward.

Moments later, ever so cautiously, she placed a trembling right foot on the very last step leading to the celestial throne, now instants away from becoming the universe's first-ever God for a Day.

So much for the ultimate glass ceiling.

As viewers throughout the cosmos watched in awed silence, and everyone on a little blue-and-white planet began wildly to cheer, Eve turned to face all those who, on so many, many far-flung worlds, were about to become her unfailing responsibility.

"That's one sublime step for a woman," she proclaimed, crossing her fingers and hoping she wouldn't trip.

"And one momentous leap ... for the entire universe!"

So Much to Do, So Little Time

"TOUJOURS L'AUDACE!"

— Celestial Horoscope for the Day (all signs)

New Job

۶ "I'M SORRY, but God is currently on vacation. May I direct you to one of Eve's executive assistants?"

While virtually every resident of the universe had seen the unprecedented Heavenly handover, those few somehow still unaware were greeted nonetheless with the same courteous response.

A number of cautiously anonymous calls came, as anticipated, from those seeking to confirm that the reports of an entirely new Supreme Being (however limited her term in office) were not simply some sort of celestial hoax.

Quite a few others, however, who felt for whatever reason that their earlier prayers had not been answered in quite the specific, abundant way they had so often requested, called in to try again; each certain that God's temporary replacement (being human) would be more understanding.

All such calls were deftly referred to the appropriate angelic department for action, inaction or deferral until the original Supreme Being returned from holiday.

All of which, as God had kindly foreseen, left Eve entirely free to do the work that was hers and hers alone. At her command, Heaven's hitherto-unruffled diplomatic relations staff excitedly began sending out a series of carefully crafted, equally carefully encoded invitations to a select group of seriously under-employed women throughout the entire universe.

"Lunch?"

۶

For her part, Eve's own first ultra long-distance call was, unsurprisingly, to a certain gentleman who had for so long shared – throughout the good, the bad and the occasionally worse – the same unfathomable destiny.

"So, how are you making out with your plans?" Adam asked.

"Do you remember those earliest days together? Naked beneath the sun, the moon … and so many, many stars?"

"Every moment new, every touch electrifying!"

"Ours alone – and yet not alone." Eve's voice was soft, reflective, her tone bringing a vanished garden back into flower. "Body to body, hand in hand, beneath a hundred million stars, wondering even then if there might be other founding couples in the universe."

"And, if so, whatever might lie in wait for us all."

In silence, the little blue-and-white planet's first man and woman, temporarily separate and yet never truly apart, contemplated the outcome of bygone choices and a paradise foresworn.

"Somehow I always knew this would be far more than just a one-woman show," Eve whispered, preparing them both for the next, so critical move. Extreme it might be … but it still felt right.

"I've decided to call a meeting of The Sorority!"

Adam needed no time to understand the allusion or the possible consequences. "Let's just hope God can still recognize the universe on return."

"As our esteemed celestial parole officer would have said, 'Have faith'!"

Eve followed this observation with a question. "By the way, how do you feel about doing a little extra-terrestrial male bonding?"

❦

"Great sages, if they persevere, shall one day be rewarded in Heaven!" Abracadabra re-read his long-range horoscope with increasing delight.

Moments later, he began rummaging around his little white cloud in search of an earlier, even more battered copy of his intergalactic address book, and some long-unused contact numbers for some suitably-skilled, far-seeing fly-by-nights.

Just in case.

❦

"What's our new deity-in-chief likely to do?" Tatiana asked, certain, like them all, that the real fun was yet to come.

Scheherazade fell silent, musing on the odds of an unprepared universe suddenly face to face with Eden's so obviously-still-agile escapee.

"From what I've seen, Eve has a truly uncanny sense of timing. And, given the number of her descendants, this is also a lady who really knows how to delegate!"

Wisdom of the Ageless

&. WHILE THE UNIVERSE waited and wondered, and paparazzi from galaxies beyond number lingered in frustration outside Heaven's walls, a hundred fearless women from across as many star systems came rocketing in unseen on a hundred separate, hastily-organized comets.

Though few of the women representing the Ancient and Honourable Sisterhood of the Interplanetary Dawns of Creation had met before, all recognized one another instantly; each one seeing in the others a shared origin in paradises lost and yet still bravely, if secretly sought in new, far greater forms. Once an interstellar Eve, always an interstellar Eve.

Quietly surveying so extraordinary a scene, Eve felt her own small terrestrial heart grow larger moment by increasingly grateful moment.

Behind every radiant, unyielding face lay vast planetary narratives of passions fulfilled and unfulfilled, of purposes and powers unfolding still, of poise and pride despite all odds and, throughout every individual tale, all the fierce, invincible tenderness of a cosmic mother's tenacious love.

"Thank you, everyone, for leaving your current homes and coming here on such short notice," Eve began. "Be assured that, as only one Eve among so many, I hold this position in trust for us all!"

As the standing ovation began to subside, an admiring, half-envious voice rose from the rear. "What's it feel like, being *'La Suprema?'*"

"Almost like returning to Eden." Eve waited a well-timed moment. "But as owner, not tenant!"

As the laughter faded, Eve's gaze returned to myriad star systems, each masking countless others still unseen; and all of them, she sensed, anxiously wondering what came next.

"As most of you know," she began, "I come from a relatively minor planet, a still spectacularly-beautiful place characterised by high ideals, great ambitions … and more unresolved problems than even the most indulgent of guardian angels would willingly admit."

There was a pause as Eve surveyed the room.

"And, in this, I believe I am not alone."

More than a few sister planetary founders nodded in response, their native worlds exhibiting their own fair share of large promise and poor performance. 'Not good enough,' all hundred carefully chosen ladies would have scribbled at the bottom of an imaginary report card. 'Definitely should be encouraged to do better.'

For all its remoteness, the Fountain of Eternal Youth Retirement Home had offered the latest in imported, wide-screen TVs, its intermittent sports telecasts providing some unexpectedly thrilling (if occasionally nostalgic) afternoons. Even as Eve was about to speak, fleeting scenes of the close contests, hard-won victories and equal, if not greater bravery in defeat flashed before her eyes; images of long-held records unexpectedly eclipsed, then shattered again within a single afternoon.

Behind her, in perfect harmony with her thoughts, the large screen began to flicker with carefully-chosen, increasingly-compelling scenes from a progression of summer and winter Olympics in cities around a far-off little blue-and-white globe.

Whispering her own small prayer, eyes on her sister Eves, Heaven's choice prepared to light a second, hopefully no less noble flame.

❧

The Archangel of All Archangels stole a glance at his senior colleagues. From their expressions, all shared the same slightly discomforting thought. Whatever God's interim replacement might have in mind, the illustrious members of the Association of Certified Professional Angels were about to become busier than they had been for many light years.

The Archangel-in-Chief brightened. If the truth be told, it had been far too long since his celestial associates enjoyed a challenge worthy of their tactfully underpublicized skills.

"So there you have it," Eve concluded, "the prospect of an electrifying set of cosmic games – with a splendiferously special twist – open to all galaxies, no matter their size or circumstances."

Her gaze embracing the room, she raised a fond, if mildly ironic eyebrow. "Just the sort of long overdue extended family event, in other words, as to make a bunch of planetary grannies proud!"

"Yes! Yes! YES!"

"From rude beginnings on a dusty plain beneath Olympus, to the potential glory of these Heavenly heights…".

Cheering, laughing, a hundred representatives of the Ancient and Honourable Sisterhood of the Interplanetary Dawns of Creation rose to their feet as one, their faces alight with all the dedication of those now distant days when, each on their own isolated worlds, the first couples of the cosmos had begun their shared search for ever greater meaning among the stars.

God, whether in abiding wisdom or an unimaginably rash moment of over-confidence and miscalculation, had chosen the leading lady of a little backwater in space to dare and to do. And so dare and do Eve and her long-separated sisters-in-arms most definitely would. While Operation Escape From Eden might now be but a distant memory, an even more heroic adventure was about to begin.

Love might have to work exceptionally hard just to make one little blue-and-white world go round. It would be interesting, to say the least, to see what would happen if and when it took on the entire cosmos.

Total fiasco – or the ultimate in transgalactic inspiration?

Task Force Angel

੪ GIVEN HIS RESPONSIBILITIES as a penultimate role model, the Archangel of All Archangels was fortunately able to maintain just enough of his official composure that the little jig he couldn't help dancing was both circumspect and brief.

As he moved swiftly to her side, Eve consulted a small golden notebook.

"By my calculations," she announced, "we're going to need nearly all your very best experts.: firstly, the Angels of Intergalactic Special Events, of Transstellar Transportation and of Truly Exceptional Scheduling and Officiating; and secondly, those currently in charge of Facilities, Grounds and Gardens and of Hospitality and Accommodation."

"Plus the head of Protocol and Visiting Dignitaries," the Archangel in Chief added helpfully. "Very diplomatic dude." He paused, remembering more than a few awkward conversations with unexpectedly early celestial arrivals. Or worse, those whose guardian angels had, in a moment of over-eagerness, prematurely directed them to the wrong address.

Eve tried hard not to think of the billions of things that had to go right, or of the trillions that could far more easily go wrong.

"I shall also need to speak to the current head of Multi-galaxy Media Relations and the Cosmic Marketing Angel." She checked God's briefing notes once more. "And, just in case, we'll need the Angel of Unanticipated Celestial Emergencies, the Angel of Divine Back-Up and – last but not least – the Angel of Truly Infinite Resources."

"I've already alerted the specialist managers you've requested," the Archangel-in-Chief replied, reassuringly confident of the resourcefulness of his multi-talented operations staff, "as well as a sterling up-and-comer to look after Medals, Flags, Bouquets and Podiums."

He made no attempt to hide the deepening gleam in his eye. "If I may respectfully suggest, you might also want to talk to my old friend, the Angel of Celestial Spectacles and Cosmic Fireworks." As masters of instructive encounters, archangels have a professional fondness for the brightest of bright lights and loudest of sudden bangs, as and when judiciously applied.

"Key questions," he continued, re-examining his own fast growing to-do list. "How much time do we have? When, exactly, do you want this cosmic extravaganza to begin?"

"Let's see. After the public announcement, we'll need to allow for initial reaction time, team selection, training, travel, opening ceremony rehearsals and…."

Eve pushed one of several buttons on her (borrowed) celestial wrist-watch showing the interconnected intricacies of local time on billions of galaxies. In less than a split nano-second, it rewarded her with the only possible conclusion.

"Exactly twenty-two and a half hours from now – Celestial Standard Time, of course," Eve replied, relieved at the wondrous freedom of Heavenly relativity. "For everyone else in the universe, however, that should give them two unbelievably-busy months in which to prepare."

"Encouragingly-tight schedule." The Archangel-in-Chief scanned the universe, skipping swiftly from star system to star system. "But, one way or another, they should all just about make it."

He turned, studying his new boss thoughtfully.

Blast from the Past

&. FOR THE VAST CROWDS assembled outside Heaven, an unusually high-speed flight of angels was the first sign their waiting might finally be coming to an end.

As before, the deaf-defying Angel of the Golden Hammer and Gong opened the day's proceedings, with a cherubic chorus of tambourines, bells and castanets adding a more rambunctious flourish to its deeper reverberations.

As the skies turned a pure light blue, a Heavenly host of the most exotic birds, beasts and flowers from vanished gardens of paradise all linked arms, kicking up their multi-coloured heels from horizon to awestruck horizon.

In their wake, ten thousand equally radiant reinforcements from the Ancient and Honourable Sisterhood of the Interplanetary Dawns of Creation pirouetted teasingly through the skies to their own mischievous refrain:

> There's life in the old dames yet,
> There's life in the old dames yet;
> Just remember, when you place your bet:
> There's a whole lotta life in the old dames yet!

As this tribute began to fade, and a now familiar celestial anthem rose on the freshly jasmine-scented air, every star system in Creation found itself entranced anew by the Heavenly Broadcast Studio's spell.

At the centre of its vast stage, a lovely young woman, encircled by a hundred other planetary Eves and flanked by the most senior angels this side of paradises-yet-to-come, held every watching eye with individual tenderness and welcome.

"Most of you are likely wondering, quite understandably, just what to expect from me." God's replacement waited a well-timed moment, then smiled. Gently, but alarmingly firmly. "Not to mention all that I might be tempted to hope for from you in return."

"Definitely the right choice for the job," the Angel of Unprecedented Opportunities whispered to his globe-shaped twin as the two exchanged discreet thumbs-up.

"Let me begin by reassuring everyone that I have absolutely no plans to meddle with long-standing celestial governance and routine," Eve continued, hands extended in a gesture of calm.

Throughout the universe, gazillions of galactic residents breathed half a sigh of collective relief.

"I have, instead, something else in mind...."

A hundred and one billion galaxies suddenly found themselves sitting as still and unreadable as possible.

"When I decided I had no choice but to apply for this job (however presumptuous the idea and impossible the odds) one thing quickly became clear. After so many aeons apart, it was more than time we widely-scattered sister Eves enjoyed a much-belated get-together, and some long overdue conversations regarding our collective offspring's progress." God's replacement paused, knowingly. "Or lack thereof!"

As one hundred planetary great-great-grandmothers glowered on cue, the entire universe sat even stiller still, now trying its very best to look as innocent, earnest and well-behaved as possible.

"While much has changed since those distant days when we each took leave of our respective Edens, all our inter-related descendants have much in common.

"First, whatever our respective planetary progeny may look like, or however many dimensions they currently inhabit, or however many light years they've amassed in overtime, all of them still tend to take both themselves and their local agendas far too seriously."

The encouraging warmth behind these words lessened the impact of an observation which, everyone agreed, was certainly true. Especially about everyone else.

"Second, while our universe may indeed be the most fascinating one around, it remains tragically under-travelled and unexplored. It would be in everyone's best interest, we agreed, if we could find ways to greet each other more often, however outwardly peculiar, even intimidating some of our more redoubtable cosmic cousins might initially seem."

Suddenly, viewers found themselves imagining destinations long dreamt of but never attempted; of supposedly fantabulous star systems, their exotic vistas so sadly unknown.

Eve paused, gazing out over all the starry landscapes receding away, strangely able to discern each and every one watching her even now; all those who, with all their individual histories and yearnings, their hopes and fears of countless years, together called this potent, fragile universe home.

Standing in silence, entrusted with Heaven's throne, Earth's first woman felt the eyes of a hundred planetary mothers narrowing in unison around her, silently adding their strength to hers.

Her voice took on a new, all-encompassing tenderness and resolve.

"Isn't it about time that we finally came out of our countless self-preoccupied and unsustaining exiles and discovered everything that might happen if we sought at last to love, not just our neighbours, but the entire universe as ourselves?"

Consider Yourselves Invited

❧ EVERYWHERE, friend turned to friend, planet to nearest planet, constellation to closest constellation, only to find reflected back the same half-thrilled, half-wary look. On the one hand, love could be exciting, even totally fantastic. On the other, it was also the scariest, most volatile explosive around. Who knows what might happen if all the unconstrained energy of love in the universe came together, in the same place, at the same time? The most magical shared radiance ever, or a totally cataclysmic Bang?

Every watching eye shifted nervously back to Eve, poised in perfect equanimity amid a hundred founding members of the Ancient and Honourable Sisterhood of the Interplanetary Dawns of Creation and a host of seriously impressive angels. Near and far, the same uncomfortable thought crossed every uneasy mind.

"Does God, by any chance, have any idea what this spiritually reckless replacement might be up to?"

An even more disturbing possibility followed an instant later. "And if so, then what?"

❧

"Somewhat weighty reflections, it's true," Eve agreed, taking a long, slow sip from the newly etched official water glass at her side. "On the other hand, I've recently rediscovered an old but timely celestial proverb: 'All work, and no cosmic play'...."

Shifting on the Heavenly throne, Earth's first and foremost exile beamed mischievously at her planetary peers, not a few already waving in the direction of their own far-distant homefolk. "Hands up, all those of you out there in favour of a cosmic homecoming celebration … complete with the most magnificent spiritual sporting event in the whole of Heavenly history!"

As the Angel of the Golden Hammer and Gong brought both together anew, causing a hundred and one billion already startled galaxies to jump even higher, Eve spread her arms in an all-encompassing invitation.

And challenge.

"By the powers entrusted to me as Divinity for a Day, I hereby invite each and every galaxy throughout the universe to your very own, first-ever strut-your-very-best-spiritual-stuff extravaganza."

Eve's voice echoed throughout every nook, cranny and congenitally reticent corner of the universe, effortlessly seeking all who sought unsuccessfully to hide.

"A cosmic block party, henceforth to be known as the one, the only….."

There was a perfectly-timed, exquisitely-suspenseful pause.

"Heavenly Games of Love! In all its many mysterious forms and even more exquisitely problematic combinations."

Eve glanced quickly at her sister Eves, all rising to their feet, applauding fiercely and, to her delight, grinning even more wickedly.

In the back row of planetary founding mothers, a small, stooped, highly wrinkled and even more highly satisfied lady somewhere around a billion years old gave, missing teeth notwithstanding, one of her largest smiles of satisfaction ever.

"I always figured she'd know what do," she exclaimed, thoughts already turning to which of a number of carefully preserved frocks she'd wear for the inevitable late-night intergalactic gala.

And then there was the ever-tricky question of shoes.

Hear Ye, Hear Ye!

❧ "AHHHHEM...."

The newly-appointed Grand Master of Celestial Ceremonies (also known as the Archangel-in-Chief) resettled his wings, inclined his noble head and began to read from an impressively-large golden scroll.

"The Preliminary Rules and Regulations are as follows.

"Each galaxy in the universe will be invited to choose for itself its own preferred team. Sporting events will proceed in the customary sequence of qualifying heats, finals and, however ultimately illusory, triumph and disappointment."

Smiling inwardly at the prospect of so many edifying rivalries to come, the Archangel-in-Chief went on with his introduction.

"Given the unconstrained enthusiasms and eccentricities of love (both sacred and so inaccurately called profane), it is suggested that preliminary categories of competition include: exploratory love (without restrictions); passionate and compassionate love; healing and revealing love; private, semi-private and embarrassingly public love; energetic and unmoving love; transitional and transformational love; natural, and (most definitely!) supernatural love; and, last but far from least, a limitless yet hard-to-define category best described as inventive, invulnerable and invincible love."

Otherwise known as winner-takes-all love, Abracadabra mused from afar.

❧

"Now we're finally getting somewhere," cackled one sprightly fifty-million-year-old matriarch, gleefully waving her sturdy blackthorn cane in the front row.. Her descendants, needless to say, were already good to go (especially if they remembered where they got their start!).

Inclining her head in appreciation, God's temporary replacement added her own words of encouragement. "Needless to say, an immense amount of local activity awaits you all. Over an unbelievably short time!"

Eve's gaze flickered throughout the Heavenly Broadcast Studio where a host of angels, already in express mode and clearly finding it hard to keep still, were sitting firmly on their wings.

"But there will also be, I can safely assure you, a surfeit of impeccably talented celestial advisors more than ready to put in triple overtime to help you with your individual plans."

A whole lot of planets in widely separated star systems suddenly found themselves taking similarly deep breaths as they realized that, when it came to the subject of love, each had a whole lot of catching up to do.

Contemplating the encircling stars beyond number, Eve could hear Adam's voice, rising on the morning breeze of a provisional paradise now long ago and far away.

"No guts, no grandeur!"

Heartening yet harsh, his words were no less true today. Though Earth might have a prior claim on her loyalty, this time it too had a job to do.

His little white cloud continuing to circle on autopilot, Abracadabra jumped up and down with the satisfaction first-rank conjurers only feel when the longest of long-shot hunches are confirmed.

Readjusting his excitement to 'mellow', the old sage settled back in his seat, quietly wondering whether the final rules might allow him to be as much competitor as coach. Not that he really needed to win yet another bright shiny medal for long-distance wizardry, of course.

All the same, he decided, a nice little grouping of first-ever celestial bling (preferably one of each: an undeniably well-deserved gold, a selfless silver and a suitably modest bronze) would make a quietly impressive addition to his best velvet robe at the next Intergalactic Senior Sorcerers Conference black tie affair.

Cosmic Complexities

"SATURDAY NIGHT'S SPAGHETTI NIGHT."
— God's *Comfort Food Cookbook*

"STEAK DIABLO, OF COURSE!"
— Big D

Busy, Busy, Busy

❧ A MERE TWO months ERC (Earth rotation calendar), a hundred and one billion galaxies all firmly agreed, provided nowhere near enough time to prepare.

"Much preferred life when the genuine original maker 'n' shaker was looking after things," one hyper-conservative constellation sniffed peevishly to another. "Life may have been less eventful, but at least then we had a routine. Planets could book their holidays in orderly succession, comets could be retired on schedule for regular maintenance checks, and people weren't rushing every which way with some new-fangled spiritual make-work project."

"Couldn't agree more. I've always said that love was too important to be left to amateurs."

"Who knows what might happen if it fell into the wrong hands?"

For their part, the senior angels of the Heavenly Games' Celestial Coordinating Committee appeared largely unconcerned, at least at this stage. Miracles being for them not only a well-proven part of their professional repertoire but also simple every-day occurrences, all were confident that they could rise to any occasion.

Then too, (as so succinctly expressed in the ancient, much-loved motto on their celestial team bikers jackets) they enjoyed the luxury of a near-infallible fallback option: 'When in doubt, wing it!'

The Heavenly venue, now guaranteed to be ready a week in advance, would assuredly exceed even the greatest of expectations; the hospitality arrangements would be celestial five star, the universal media welcomed, escorted and informed as never before. Lesser but equally vital needs, from translation services to timetables to ticketing, were safely assigned to long-serving angels who, in the words of their divisional commanders, "really know their secular stuff."

Among outwardly untroubled archangels, however, one central question remained unanswered; when Opening Day came, would the intergalactic contenders themselves be ready? Really, truly ready?

It wasn't that these most eminent celestial executives were unduly judgmental or prematurely pessimistic. Far from it. It was just that, given the benefit of a certain exalted existential realism, they knew from long experience that mastery of the mysteries of love usually proves everywhere a whole lot trickier than it looks.

❧

Throughout the entire cosmos, the lights of worlds beyond number remained on late, as beings of every constellation struggled with their own local interpretations of the same universal themes.

No galaxy, even the most ancient and accomplished, believed it could successfully compete in every category in the vast lexicon of love. At the same time, however, since star system after star system wanted to know as much as possible of what they might be up against, the same enduringly-perplexing questions went round and round. What, exactly, is the nature of love? Where does it come from, and where does it go? Is there a limited amount, constantly recycled, or is there an endless source, arising forever anew? What does it seek to become?

Almost more importantly, every galaxy sooner or later found itself up against the same all-important concern; is it possible to know too much about love, because the implications are far too scary and demanding and, maybe, ultimately liberating?

❧

As a charter member of what was justly called the Original and Oldest Old Boys' Club in the Universe, the first man on Earth had no difficulty in following up on Eve's earlier request, rapidly making contact with some of his more eminent fellow founders in galaxies across the cosmos.

Everywhere he found a kindred testosterone-tossed dedication to their descendants' success in the rapidly approaching Games: whether proudly chairing selection committees, heading up fund-raising drives, leading their local galactic marketing teams, or simply providing the very best of often-unsolicited advice where and when required.

❦

Far from Heaven, in the blue-black vastness of space, a little blue-and-white planet's initial, near-hyperventilated enthusiasm was quickly being replaced by a more sobering sense of responsibility. It was one thing to be proud of Eve, quite another to realize just what her unanticipated cosmic success had gotten them into.

Now they had to make her proud of *them*. The problem was simple, but not small.

In a universe of a hundred and one billion galaxies – many happily deciphering the liberating hieroglyphs of the heart long before Earthlings had even learned to write – what did Earth really know about love?

Urgently seeking an answer, multilateral organizations around the globe began a series of exploratory meetings to determine all relevant policy issues. Their first provisional set of recommendations would likely be ready (they felt reasonably confident) no more than five years after the Games had been held.

Representatives of the planet's major religions all announced that, while every spiritual tradition rightly emphasized the centrality of love to the creation and destiny of the universe, it just so happened that – *mirabile dictu* – their own particular interpretation turned out to be, however providentially, the most superior. By far.

Other approaches, needless to say, were also considered.

Various political parties (depending on ideological bent or budgetary deficit) proposed either tax breaks or rebates to all those willing to learn to love perfectly and completely within six weeks time.

International celebrities and self-styled personalities, renowned for their performances both on-camera and off, charitably offered their services at minimum wage (and all residual benefits). "Sincerity in love is everything," as one well-connected agent confided genially. "My clients, needless to say, can fake it like you wouldn't believe!"

In a spirit of commercial selflessness, several hundred corporations put their entire R&D staff to work nonstop to discover the underlying design secrets of ever more efficient and effective love. International biotechnology companies competed and collaborated to develop the world's first truly comprehensive love drug, equally potent and performance-enhancing in both the profane and sacred spheres.

Their goal was to come up with something that would provide: all the insight of a sage, the compassion of a saint, the tenderness of the old, the innocence of a child, the stamina of a teenager, and the passion of the long-separated, blended together with the extraordinary awe and giggly enthusiasm of one's first extra-terrestrial sighting.

And all this in one tiny, supremely powerful pill that might, just, give the inhabitants of Earth not only super-human but super-loving powers – intensities such as would allow them to compete with beings from far older and quite likely more subtle worlds.

While such research efforts proved sadly unsuccessful, a few of the more ambitious experiments had unexpected, highly acrobatic consequences for the technical staff involved.

Elsewhere on Earth, regrettably bleak people with even bleaker views hoped that the entire Games themselves would fail. A few wrote highly unpopular letters to the papers, pointing out that the whole thing was obviously just a fantasy, and that love forever brought absolutely nothing but trouble, respectfully yours, etc.

Finally, in an almost forgotten space station orbiting high above it all, a frustrated observer of the endlessly unnecessary wars between the science of poetry and the poetry of science consulted a few treasured antique compendia. And then, quietly curious as to what might happen when timeless insight caught the ever-shifting present by surprise, e-mailed nine short words to Earth's coordinating committee: "Who sees with the eyes of love, sees more."

While there is no record of this uninvited submission having actually been received at the address intended, an unofficial excerpt from the Demonic All-Weather, All-Wave-Lengths Monitoring and Transcription Service shows that the same message was successfully intercepted by the Underworld's overnight staff and immediately passed along to the Devil himself.

An indecipherable observation in Big D's own hand appears in the margin.

Not for the first time in a long and distinguished adversarial career, the Devil appeared to have found himself in a slightly awkward ethical position.

On the one hand he was quite happy, even proud, to admire Eve's unforeseen initiative. After all, (ill-assigned disguise notwithstanding) hadn't he played an admirably stellar role in her so highly dramatic career start?

On the other hand, if these Games Of Love actually succeeded, he, of all people, might just find himself on the dole, and not just him alone. Countless others – senior and junior demons, technical associates and temperature-control experts, acolytes and assorted hot-headed hangers-on, all of them understandably lacking unemployment insurance – all depended on him for their salaries, holiday cruises and steady satanic career advancement.

No matter what happened, it was a dilemma pondered ever more deeply as Big D sat sipping mulled wine on Hell's observation deck.

Try as he might, the current Chairman of the Intergalactic Senior Devils' Association could not suppress a smile. Whatever else Eve might do, her latest surprise was indisputably the biggest leap of faith since God had decided the universe might, just might, be worth the risk, maintenance costs notwithstanding.

All the more reason then, Big D decided, to make contact with his own increasingly irascible associates before matters got completely out of hand. One way or another, it was time for fallen angels to rise to the occasion.

Overview

❧ AS THE FIRST HECTIC days passed, each bringing news of ambitious training plans on one highly advanced star system after another, Scheherazade decided to take SS Serendipity for a spin. As the gleaming white spacecraft rose gracefully in space, the unfolding views only confirmed her suspicions. Grand gestures notwithstanding, not only was Earth not ready; it was also unsure how to get ready to get ready. All this with barely seven weeks to go.

In the light of her earlier travels (and experiences best left for her memoirs), Scheherazade could only sigh. While Earth's current maladies might be complex in origin, the overall clinical diagnosis was not; almost a classic textbook case of that evolutionary infirmity known as spiritual stage fright.

Her work still clearly unfinished, it was time for a phone call. One, she was sure, Eve would appreciate, and Big D secretly approve.

❧

Given his earlier divinations, Abracadabra was inclined to be somewhat more relaxed, even philosophic. Thanks to a friend of a friend, he'd been able to get an excellent deal at an ultra-secret used cloud-lot, replacing his battered but beloved little white airmobile's well-worn engine with a bigger, badder, infinitely more fuel efficient one – just the thing for deep cosmos contacts.

As he whirled about in the first few days, exploring thousands of constellations, he found regional sorcerers and sorceresses all busy in much the same super-secretive way. Nearly every wizard, whether licensed or moonlighting, was already hard at work on all manner of supportive love spells, many drawn from ancient sources, others (potentially more powerful but also far less predictable) having been custom crafted only the night before.

Abracadabra sighed. Sometimes magic words worked, and sometimes they didn't – a simple case of technical difficulties, more often than not. Then again, quite often their potential beneficiaries hadn't a clue how to listen properly in the first place.

It was doubly reassuring, therefore, to reconfirm, as both hours and worlds went whistling by, that even the most outwardly flawless planets weren't even anywhere near perfectly ready. Earth clearly wasn't the only would-be wanna-be in need of greater insight, confidence and purpose.

The prospect making him all the more optimistic, Abracadabra hurriedly dialled ahead to the Ocean of Stars. Dinner with senior sorcerers from several of the most advanced galaxies in the universe was beginning to appear even more overdue. And, if he remembered correctly, also exceptionally tasty.

⁊

Having successfully set things in motion, Eve was able, for a day or two at least, simply to sit back and enjoy the Heavenly show.

Celestial plans and budgets were regularly presented for her signature. A host of angels looked after all but the most seemingly intractable issues, leaving the latter for one or more senior staff to resolve. What had gone on successfully for billions of years now continued effortlessly to evolve, moment by calmly passing moment.

Preparations for the forthcoming Games were taken just as easily in angelic stride, or, more accurately, super-sonic flight. Guest choirs, orchestras, and soloists of every tone, instrument and repertoire in the universe arrived and departed on schedule, providing changing musical accompaniments to (almost) every facet of her celestial day. Eve diplomatically drew a line at the kind offer of impromptu melodies for the official substitute Supreme Being's evening bubble bath, partly out of suitably celestial modesty, partly to protect her customary private hour of contemplative, candlelit silence.

To help in the matter of keeping track of potential participants, angelic observers had automatically been assigned to every galaxy. All in all, the preliminary comments were encouraging, Some of the most hitherto sluggish and cranky planets, having already sent their affections in for repair, were now busily asking previously neglected spiritual advisors how to be better fathers, mothers, pet owners, and so forth. Unknown to one another, far-flung innovative planets had announced almost identical contests for local artists and scientists alike, each designed to explore the myriad, mystifying possibilities of love.

Gazing out over Creation, Eve sighed softly, finally able to appreciate not so much Heaven's boundless grandeur as its infinite serenity; that ultimate inner stillness paradoxically everywhere at the heart of ceaseless movement.

Everywhere, that is, but on a certain familiar, wobbly little world whose slightly hesitant revolutions, however far away, still managed to catch the corner of her all-seeing eye.

Eve's smile was fond, wry – and resolute.

It would be unfair, Eve decided, to take even a single angel away from his or her appointed tasks. After all, in the longer term celestial scheme of things, work on the Heavenly Games of Love was for them not just a fascinating logistical challenge but also an unprecedented career opportunity.

In the absence of official help, however, a little extra-celestial assistance from an adventuress already on contract to help find Paradise (Phase Two) might be just the thing. An adventuress, moreover, with access to some very impressive spiritual expertise in The Great Beyond beyond the Beyond.

There was a discreet cough. "A long distance call, Ma'am."

Eve turned to find the Archangel of All Archangels standing at her side, alabaster wings folded as elegantly as ever, a tiny golden celestial cell phone in hand.

"If my normally unerring instincts are correct, an almost equally determined lady would welcome a private word with you," he announced, eyes beginning to twinkle.

With a small wink in the direction of a far-off little blue-and-white world full of yearning and undiscovered potential, Eve pushed the small silver call button.

The real games of love were only just beginning.

Hot Shots

❦ ONE OF THE BENEFITS of being a senior devil is the comfort that, no matter where one travels, a guaranteed warm reception awaits. Not only does the association provide its members with the most luxurious in no-cost hospitality and accommodations (complete with matchless technical and temptation services), but its exceptionally wily staff can lay on covert planning sessions faster than a soul can fall from grace.

As Big D strode into the vast underworld lounge of a galaxy long known for its discretion, he was pleased to see, among the noisy crowd of his peers, the local head of demonic operations standing by as arranged.

"Your old lady-friend caught us all by surprise," his old acquaintance announced pointedly by way of greeting.

"I seem to recall warning you that God still had an undiminished appetite for the unexpected," Big D replied, his expression both pleased yet circumspect.

"Indeed you did. Indeed you did." There was a thoughtful pause, then his colleague gestured to their associates. "The key question, however, still remains; what is our role in all this? Are these Heavenly Games of Love an opportunity to do our best or our worst? Or both?"

Big D looked around the room, impressed as always by the sheer demonic intensity of these *capi di tutti capi* of so many underworlds. "I don't know about you," the Chairman of the Intergalactic Senior Devils' Association replied in that intensely soft voice which suggested his opponents best get out of his way, "but I'm getting a little tired of being, how shall I say, overly indulgent."

Nodding his thanks to the ancient barman, Big D took the offered drink. "After so many aeons in the battle of good versus evil, with no lasting winner yet declared, it's probably time to do things a little differently!"

"Such as?"

Big D leaned closer, a bright crimson glow in the depths of his eyes, whispering for a time in his colleague's stylishly-pointed ear.

His old friend began to laugh. "Glory be! What you might call a whole new chapter in the book of revelations!"

"Why should God be the only one permitted to behave unpredictably?" Big D asked, eyes twinkling ferociously. He gestured around the crowded lounge. "Seems a damn shame (pardon my language) to see so much truly terrifying power so often going to waste."

A bell rang, calling all the devils-in-chief to dinner.

"Put your plan to the governing council afterwards, over coffee and flaming cognac. I'll second the motion. If it works, it'll do wonders for our reputation."

"Always more than happy to complicate matters," Big D acknowledged gratefully. "Especially if it ultimately helps simplify things."

❦

The Association having voted unanimously in favour of his proposal, Big D excused himself to make a quick call.

"The sealed plans are hidden, as you probably guessed, at the heart of the ever-burning fire in my office. Start general preparations as outlined." There was a pause. "Might be a good idea to double our last order of pitchforks. Chances are, we're going to be busier than ever before!"

"Consider it done, Boss," declared the red-haired, red-robed giant demon who ran the place almost flawlessly in his absence. "Any hint as to what's going on?"

Big D laughed, already savouring a long-awaited, hitherto impossible long-distance call. And some even longer overdue angelic give and take.

"Let's just say it's something I suspect even God would be tempted to call the most spectacular joint venture in cosmic history."

Listening in on speaker phones throughout countless underworlds, billions of demons old and young gleefully rubbed their hot hands together at the prospect of wonderfully fiery tomorrows to come.

Awaiting the Call

❦ IT WAS ASTONISHING, Scheherazade's co-adventurers agreed, how much could be achieved by lounging by a pool if one put one's mind to it. Or, more accurately, gently sets one's routinely agitated, frequency-hopping mind aside and, in the resulting stillness, lets the communication everywhere secretly occurring become clear. All by itself.

When it came to renewing contact with The Great Beyond beyond the Beyond, all six women found, this earliest yet most advanced form of telecommunication worked just fine in every case.

❦

Marina embraced the tall, dark and delightful Dr. Professor O'Bliss. Then they embraced again. If absence makes the heart grow fonder, distance doubles the delight.

The prospect of becoming part of Eve's informal advisory team, he assured her, was a rare and much anticipated honour. Together with carefully pre-selected staff members of the Interplanetary Centre for Joy, he would depart for Earth a.s.a.p.

❦

The small yellow monkey began jumping up and down the moment Leila made contact.

"I was beginning to think you'd forgotten me."

"Not a chance." Leila cast a now even more appreciative eye along the dusty corridors of the Museum of Historical *Culs de Sac*. "How would you like a short-term assignment – all expenses prepaid?"

"On Earth?"

"You betcha. A small matter of improving its chances in the biggest intergalactic love-fest since God first made little green apples."

"Whoopee!" cried Aurora, already performing a practice pirouette. "I love long shots!"

❦

The two close-cropped silver heads on a single body bobbed in greeting, familiar emerald eyes flashing as before. "Don't suppose you've come all this way just for a tune-up?" Chief Inspector Go-Go asked.

"Actually, I've come on behalf of a friend." Qingling glanced around the crowded grounds. All around, scores of excited new arrivals were being registered for entry-level psychic rebuilding. "I was wondering if you two ever offer intergalactic roadside assistance."

"Do we look like spiritual tow-truck drivers?" Chief Inspector Stop glanced sideways at his associate, their smiles growing larger.

"Since the planet in question rarely seems to learn from the Past," Chief Inspector Go-Go observed, "it will be interesting to watch it trying to sit still long enough to benefit from the Future!"

❦

"Howdy!" the tall, wiry skeleton exclaimed, just back from vacation on an ethereal dude ranch with tireless, skeletal horses and wondrously ghostly sunsets.

"What's a-cookin'?" asked the second, rounder one who, given his appetite for just about everything, frequently was.

"I need the help of some deep, dark, secret spies of love." Yazmina was never one to linger long in getting to the point.

"Who doesn't!" both skeletons cackled happily.

"Seriously!" Yazmina prodded them both. "Earth needs the help – instantly, if not a thousand years earlier – of the very best of underhanded old hands."

"It would be a pleasure." The tall wiry skeleton reached out for a ghostly address book only the two could see. "And we'll bring along as many otherworldly freelancers and eerie-realm retirees as we can."

"Gotta warn you, though," the short, burly skeleton added. "Ever since the Games were announced, every big-budget galaxy in the universe has been out competing for spooky professionals."

"When it comes to love," Yazmina sighed, "everybody wants an edge."

❦

Just as Tatiana was trying her best to conjure up a certain playful wonder-worker with serene violet eyes, Valentina herself appeared in projected holographic form.

"You called, oh almost equally gorgeous one?"

"As you surely expected."

"As I undoubtedly did." The celebrated founding director of the Wondrous Winding Gardens of Desire agreed. "Nearly every galaxy in the universe has been in touch, all seeking exclusive use of our unorthodox advisory services." She clearly appreciated the well-deserved compliment.

"In the spirit of the occasion, however, we've decided to offer our services to everyone. Providing, of course, that we're allowed to throw in a few bonus surprises for favourite customers."

❦

At first, only the luminous tops of the Three Crystals could be seen, submerged as they all were in the Interstellar Oracular Training Centre's supercharged hot tub. Having had the foresight to make her ethereal reappearance in the best-looking bikini in The Beyond, Sybilla was as quick to join them as they were to welcome her.

"Earth's going to need all our skills," the Three Crystals announced.

Nestling beside the tallest seer, Sybilla's astrally-projected form leaned back contentedly against the hot tub's bubbling curve.

"In that case, I should probably just relax and enjoy the ride."

God (and Friends)

❧ AS THE REMAINING weeks before opening day rushed by, the famously omnipresent Source of all appeared nowhere to be found.

For their part, those few sages who had fleeting intimations of an ever-changing whereabouts kept an amused, protective silence. Having finally taken time off, all agreed, shouldn't God be permitted to enjoy it in peace? It was a conclusion Eve fully agreed with. Just because she happened to have a unique white-and-gold business card with its own emergency contact number, didn't mean she planned on using it.

God, meanwhile, was enjoying not only the best sleep in aeons, but also dream after unexpected dream opening on ever more inviting new horizons. Even on vacation, in dreams God returned to the job God did best; miraculously, mysteriously ensuring that even greater wonders never ceased.

❧

The celestial realm, if its non-stop staff were permitted to say so, was looking better by the moment.In countless buildings carefully concealed among Heaven's lush gardens, expert angels were hard at work planning, calculating and preparing models and mock-ups, diagrams and designs.

The Angel of Transstellar Transportation had determined his priorities and how to meet them: travel at or above the speed of light for contestants, team coaches and dignitaries; and travel at slightly lower speeds for support staff, Games officials, and judges (selected from the most distinguished spiritual, amorous and philosophic traditions).

Individuals and groups wanting to attend were directed to an approved list of interstellar travel agents offering special discount rates for the occasion and, in the case of those with special needs, celestially subsidized travel programmes as well.

The Angel of Hospitality and Accommodation, together with the Angel of Cosmic Crowds, surpassed even their own high expectations in making sure that contestants and visitors alike would find their stay during the Games to be truly divine. The finest of architects, interior designers, hotel and resort staff, chefs and restaurant personnel throughout the cosmos were quietly contacted and invited to develop everything from the latest in celestial rooftops overhead to all the best that could possibly be enjoyed, day or night, beneath them..

The already-overworked Angel of Facilities, Grounds and Gardens, on learning of Eve's revolutionary proposal, put in a rush call to an old and notoriously unflappable colleague, the Angel of Truly Infinite Resources.

There was no way, the Facilities Angel explained, that Heaven's very first stadium and all its many surrounding sporting venues, could be conjured up within less than two months (Earth time). Unless, of course, he might be permitted to beg, borrow – or steal (an old angelic in-joke) some timely and unlimited help from an unlimited number of knowledgeable celestial sources?

"Have I ever let you down before?" his old friend replied from his office, already shuffling through a handful of preliminary sketches, estimates, schedules and suppliers' samples.

For his part, the Angel of Truly Infinite Resources was already thinking ahead, beyond the finished stadium and toward all the greater complexities of the official Opening Ceremonies. If his calculations were correct, Eve's sojourn in Heaven would officially end at the exact same moment as the genuine, original Supreme Being returned invisibly to duty; righteously recharged and just raring to go!

No matter which celestial C.E.O. Heaven might report to on Opening Day, one thing was clear; everybody currently holding or hoping for celestial tenure had better get everything perfectly right!

Explorations for now complete, Adam caught an unexpected ride to

Heaven with an angelic reconnaissance team. Upon arrival, Eve led him happily to her private suite, drawing every curtain with a single look. The hours then shared, as described in a much-revisited chapter in their memoirs, were literally heavenly. ('A real page burner', as Big D would later say approvingly.) It was not till early evening that the now dazed but deeply contented pair, dining *al fresco* on a celestial balcony, gave a thought to their own little blue-and-white world and its preparations for the Games.

"Lots of high-minded committees," Adam reported. "Unfortunately, when they realize how many galactic superstars they'll be up against...."

In the distance, two hot comets sizzled by, trailing sparkling hints for one another to follow in the dark.

"Not to worry, at least not yet. I've already asked Scheherazade & Associates to get in touch with probably the most unusual strategic coaches around!"

Adam knew when to speak, and when to wait. And also when Eve was up to something, or soon would be.

"They also need a leader."

"You're not thinking of Scheherazade, by any chance?"

"No – but a very good guess since I was actually thinking that, professional explorer as she is, she will undoubtedly know just where to find one. Or two," Eve added, studying him fondly. "Two would be perfect, yes?"

"Are you going to call her?"

"Better yet, I'll ask the Archangel of All Archangels to invite her here."

The two comets disappeared together over the far horizon, happily luring one another on.

"And while we're waiting?"

"You ... me: more pillow talk!"

Adam gazed into the tender, insistent, wonderfully well-known eyes of the woman so significantly chosen by Fate: someone who (temporary celestially superlative title or not) just happened to be, as far as he was concerned, forever the most endlessly fascinating, challenging and beautiful woman of all.

"Have I told you recently how very glad I am we met?"

"Explain it to me again," said Eve.

Big Leap

✿ WHEN THE POOLSIDE telephone rang shortly before noon, Tatiana happened to be closest, towelling herself dry after a leisurely swim. After all, she figured, if she was fated to play some part in upcoming events, why not make the most of this time of waiting by keeping in shape, especially when enjoying a shape already so enviable. It was a conclusion her colleagues clearly shared, as all six cruised unhurriedly through the welcoming blue waves, or took up sinuously advanced yoga postures under a discreetly admiring sun. Both tomorrow and their exotic acquaintances from The Great Beyond beyond the Beyond would arrive soon enough.

"Chez Scheherazade. Good afternoon."

"Good afternoon," came a confident, baritone reply. "I was hoping to speak with Scheherazade, please." There was the slightest of pauses, a sense perhaps of brief hesitation. Or even more intensified resolve. "Is she in, by any chance?"

"Very sorry, but you just missed her," Tatiana responded, quickly speculating on which of so many acquaintances over Scheherazade's already eventful career might choose this particular moment to get in touch. "She's away on business – back in a day or so."

"Did she leave a contact number, perhaps?"

However genial and relaxed the strangely familiar voice seemed, Tatiana sensed it might be wise to know more.

"May I ask who's calling, please?"

There was another pause, longer and more thoughtful, followed by an amused laugh. "Let's say I'm, how shall I put it, a recent sporting acquaintance," Big D replied. "More professionally known as The Very Devil Himself."

To her credit, Tatiana recovered faster than might be expected.

"You can reach Scheherazade by way of the Heavenly Switchboard Operator." She gestured downwards, then up as her co-adventurers paused in mid-exercise or swim. "She's visiting a friend, a certain lady by the name of Eve." There was a fleeting, perfectly-timed pause. "Whom I believe you've already met…."

The burst of laughter at the other end of the line was surprisingly unguarded. "No wonder my job can be so difficult!"

Tatiana found herself laughing in reply. "Since Scheherazade said she was hoping you might call one of these days, I expect it might just be about to become even more so!"

❦

Arriving in Heaven just in time for lunch, Scheherazade was immediately seated between Adam and Eve, the latter thoughtfully having invited a number of angels her special guest had already met.

"Lots of changes round here," the Angel of Uncanny Encouragement declared. "And Eve's managing everything wonderfully."

"Reports and rumours notwithstanding, I never appreciated just how enormous the Universe really is," Earth's first lady confessed.

"It's always been busy," the Archangel of All Archangels confirmed, graciously offering around a platter of low-fat bocadillos. "These days, however, it's becoming incredibly boisterous as well.

"Not that I mind," he added, refilling everyone's glass. "Almost every galaxy is finally thinking long and loud about all it has yet to do. As the hours till opening day go down, the volume unavoidably keeps going up."

"And then up some more," Adam confirmed, enjoying the comparative celestial calm after his own hurried tour of many over-active worlds.

Looking round the crowded table, Eve wondered what God might be thinking of their progress so far. Come one hourly less distant day, she hoped, she would still be found worthy of the chance to ask.

"Do you ever wonder what you've started?" the soft-spoken yet gently-relentless Angel of Uncanny Encouragement inquired.

"All the time," Eve confessed. "Ever since the beginning. And maybe somehow even in dreams before that."

⋅⋅⋅

The lunch guests having scattered to their afternoon responsibilities, Eve and Scheherazade set out on a private stroll through the most beautiful gardens anywhere.

Adam, ever diplomatic and always technically curious, excused himself to explore Heaven's unparalleled engineering establishment.

As they slipped between flowering branches, Scheherazade could see, beneath a gentle slanting light, the faintest signs of strain on her new best friend's thoughtful face.

"Five weeks, terrestrial standard time, to go until the Opening Ceremonies," Eve acknowledged. "A lot can happen in the meantime."

On either side, spiralling, multi-coloured cascades echoed the distant shapes of their native constellations, long ago gifts now blossoming here.

"The advisors you asked for are even now on their way," Scheherazade affirmed, eyes twinkling at the thought of all the unlikely forms in which help would soon arrive.

"I thank you," Eve chuckled, "even though Earth may not. And as to that other, more difficult matter…."

It was Scheherazade's turn to laugh.

Comes the hour, comes the couple. Once again.

"To its great good fortune, Earth just happens to have two individuals meant not just for each other but also for this very moment; caring yet calm, whimsical yet wise. And, not only that…." Reaching into a pocket, Scheherazade dramatically withdrew a duet of photographs. "They're also both specialists in areas, from tombstones to timewarps, offering up their own undying insights into the countless intricacies of love."

The first image was that of a distinguished, unmistakably powerful gentleman, the second a tall, assured woman, her sky blue dress flashing with a hundred stars.

As Eve held the two pictures in her hand, the eyes of the World's Greatest Gravedigger slowly turned in his photo to meet those of the World's Most Beautiful Astronomer, swivelling in tune to meet his gaze. As their eyes locked, both of them winked.

"I feel better already!" Eve exclaimed.

Earth's first lady reluctantly took her eyes off the happy pair. "One more thing. If and when the time comes for Team Earth to strike up the band, as it were, it probably wouldn't hurt to have a real one on hand."

"Something along the lines of a Whole Earth Choir, Orchestra and Marching Band Combo, perhaps?" Scheherazade responded.

"Unorthodox, all-inclusive, inspired – and ideally as deafening as possible."

"Perfect!"

Even Bigger Leap

🙊 RETURNING TO GOD'S office, the two women found the Archangel-in-Chief holding a golden telephone receiver against his chest, his face unreadable. "Call for you, Ma'am." His eyes flickered impassively. "The gentleman did not give his name."

At the other end, Big D shook his head ruefully. For better or worse, he seemed to have a thing for exceedingly beautiful, multi-talented women who could be trusted, without fail, to have their very own, very definite view of things.

In keeping with his own private spiritual practice, the Devil took a moment to voice a small prayer of gratitude for all the many salutary virtues of temptation, even if he still wasn't completely sure, in his and Scheherazade's unfinished story, who would be revealed to be the wily tempter, and who the far wilier temptee.

"Hello?" said Eve; then, at the sound of an effortlessly seductive voice, she immediately began to laugh.

"My warmest congratulations. It couldn't have happened to a lovelier, wiser or, trust me, more irresistible young woman," Big D proclaimed, clearly still as incorrigibly flirtatious as ever. "As Adam has undoubtedly told you," he added, "I've always been one of your biggest fans."

"Never doubted it for a moment," Eve replied, shooting an amused look to an uncertain Scheherazade.

"Just wanted you to know I'm still thinking of you."

"And I hadn't forgotten about you, either." Two could certainly play this game – and very well. After all, both had done it before. "Somehow I suspected you might get in touch."

"From what I hear, you've got a great deal of work ahead before the Games open – and not a few potential problems," Big D responded cryptically. "Including some rather badly behaved characters in some rather disreputable interstellar tax-havens who would be more than happy to see you fail!"

There was a thoughtful silence while the current heads of Heaven and Hell contemplated their options. And their prospects.

Eve smiled across the distance in between. "This wouldn't be the first time I've been underestimated, as you may recall."

"No comment," Big D exclaimed, with a matching, far-off look.

One of the more surprising benefits of her recent promotion, Eve had discovered, was that when she really, truly wanted to know what had been going on anywhere in the universe, it actually turned out to be astonishingly easy.

In the momentary silence she saw, as if on a luminous screen, a replayed image of Big D surrounded by a number of the most illustrious devils throughout Creation, their heads bowed in fierce concentration, together plotting and planning all the most judicious demonic ways 'to honour' (their words) the upcoming Heavenly Games.

"Ah-hah!" Eve exclaimed, watching as her very own private replay as the Underworld To End All Underworlds Conference ended in unanimous agreement to make the most of Big D's unexpected proposal. From Heaven's vantage point, it was clear that God wasn't the only one who enjoyed a good plot or, in this case, an even better joke.

"Somehow I suspect I may know what you're up to!" she teased.

"Somehow I suspected you might!" Big D replied. His deep laughter faded away and was replaced by a more sombre tone. "But please don't tell anyone. After all this time, we certainly don't want to spoil the fun."

"Wouldn't dream of it. Let's consider it our, how shall I say, far from little secret."

"Much obliged," Big D responded, ever more delighted by his old Boss's choice of his new one. Whatever else the former chatelaine of Eden had become, she was clearly still one tough cookie.

"Good luck to all of you," Eve concluded pointedly. "Hang on. Someone else wants a word." She then added, "You old devil, you!"

The Archangel of All Archangels tried extremely hard not to raise either of his extremely expressive eyebrows as Eve swiftly passed the telephone to Scheherazade.

"It's alright." Earth's first lady observed, putting a reassuring hand on her senior celestial advisor's arm. "Just a little matter of one or two more supporting plots thickening as they should."

"Hello again," Big D began. "You certainly seem to get around."

"From what I hear, so do you." Scheherazade's voice was as cautiously noncommittal as his.

"Just another routine business trip. And you?"

"Likewise."

"Related, by any chance, to the upcoming Games?"

"Isn't everything, these days?"

There was a long pause before Big D laughed, so warmly, deeply, demonically-delicious a laugh that, despite the distance between them, she could clearly see the flash of his dark blue eyes. "I decline to answer," he confided solemnly, "on the grounds that it might tend to incriminate me."

Despite all her many-worldly experiences and wisdom, Scheherazade's heart skipped a beat, then two more. "Were I you, I'd be careful, too," she responded, with a smile not completely concealed from either Earth's first lady or a still bemused chief of angelic operations.

One of the fundamental qualifications of an eminently senior devil is, of course, the seasoned ability instantly to hear the unspoken and see the unforeseen.

Big D's heart skipped three beats, then three more.

"I was wondering," he began, his voice hesitant, almost boyish, "if you were planning on attending the Opening Ceremonies?" There was an even longer pause. "And if so … whether you might enjoy an escort?"

Scheherazade looked sideways at Eve and the Archangel of All Archangels, each unable to keep from watching her with a discreet but obliquely-fascinated eye.

"The Devil makes his first celestial reappearance – in quite a long while (to put it mildly) – in order to share with me a front row seat at the ultra-spectacular opening of the inaugural Heavenly Games of Love … now, that's what I'd call a truly heavy date!"

"I take it that means yes?"

"Call me the day before, to arrange where and when to meet," Scheherazade answered softly; suddenly and, without yet quite knowing fully why, happily confident and confidently happy in fully sixteen different dimensions of reality. "If we don't happen to meet by chance before then," she added thoughtfully.

"*Au revoir*, as we frequently say around here," Big D responded gently, before making a small parting request.

Holding the receiver against her shoulder, Scheherazade turned to the Archangel of All Archangels who was doing his best, without much success, to maintain an impenetrable celestial equanimity.

"Your erstwhile associate, as he put it, would appreciate a quiet word," she announced.

I always thought Big D hadn't yet met the right woman, Eve mused to herself.

Some things, however superficially surprising, are just plain inevitable. The Archangel-in-Chief took a deep breath and put the golden telephone to his ear. Better the Devil you know....

"It's been far too long," Big D began, his deep voice still as engaging as ever despite so much time and so many circumstances.

"I was wondering if I could interest you in a little business proposition."

Game Plans

"TRAIN HARD, FIGHT SNEAKY."

— The Angel of Uncanny Encouragement

Taking Charge

❧ ITS MANY GOOD INTENTIONS notwithstanding, Team Earth's international steering committee was starting to wonder if it might just have wandered up the proverbial creek.

On the plus side, a secret training site had been selected and generous donations had underwritten the overnight construction of everything from dorms to classrooms, from love-labs to reference libraries. Covert offshore contributions funded not only runways for private aircraft, but also an enlarged marina for those self-accredited spiritual leaders who, arriving with their own yachts and entourages, had clearly taken vows, if not of poverty, then of minimal clothing and maximum bling.

As the days passed, countless prospective team members, whether invited or self-selected for their enviable prowess in love, began to arrive. As a result, Team Earth soon found itself a kaleidoscopic *mélange* of representatives of every creed, colour, country of origin and expertise, all full of high promise and even higher hopes.

Provisional coaches in as many aspects of Love as possible were chosen worldwide, their sources, including eminent religious traditions (popular and arcane), singers and songwriters, talk-show hosts, genetic scientists and, not least, recent award winners for best actor, actress or director.

Such auspicious beginnings notwithstanding, however, one thing remained clear. No one present quite knew what to do next. So it was that when SS Serendipity swooped down to an increasingly-perplexed and argumentative training camp, its pilot and passengers were greeted with undisguised delight.

Their reception became all the warmer when Scheherazade produced a celestially-sealed note revealing that while, of course, Eve did not feel it her place unduly to interfere in Earth's affairs, its founding lady and temporary deity would nonetheless take it as a not-unappreciated favour (hint!) if all members of Team Earth would immediately and henceforth be guided by the tough-minded, tender-hearted couple now arriving as their suggested co-captains.

Further assistance, Eve's letter continued, would soon arrive in the form of an illustrious advisory board even now reversing course in The Great Beyond beyond the Beyond to return to what, to them, was already Yesterday, if not a thousand million yesterdays before.

"Listen to them," Earth's first lady admonished, "no matter how heretical their approach may seem. Believe me, when it comes to figuring out what to do in a universe as old, bold and busy as this one, it's best to keep both an open mind and a resolutely unlocked heart."

So unexpected and encouraging a note, ending as it did in Eve's fond expression of confidence in her descendants, arrived with perfect timing. As one, the members of Team Earth began to cheer, and then to cheer some more.

It was amazing, the equally-distinguished chief operating officers of Heaven and Hell agreed, what could happen when they finally decided to go into business together. Especially when a vacationing God appeared to have left them to their own devices, both metaphorical and real.

At Big D's suggestion, long-reformed angels, with the sixth sense only a once-shady past can provide, were soon interlinked to Hell's newly installed Transgalactic Bad Guy Tracking and Reporting System. As a result, a host of hitherto unsuspected rebels, renegades and reprobates was quickly added to the growing list, the devils on duty feverishly scribbling detailed notes in the margins.

Then, nodding at such timely improvements in vertical integration and Satanic supply chain management, Big D & Associates settled back to wait, their prospects ever more promising. Given that the old saying, 'Hell is full of interesting people', was everywhere true, all looked forward to discovering just how much more interesting the cosmic underworld was likely to become over the next few short weeks.

Personally interesting and, all sincerely hoped, professionally most rewarding.

❧

On the patio of one of Heaven's better bistros, a certain appropriately globe-shaped angel responsible for Celestial Opportunities reached out to clink glasses with his strategically identical twin.

"So far..."

"So good!" the equally-agile and auspicious Angel of Hidden Agendas agreed.

The two white-winged siblings watched contentedly as fleets of adventurous stars sailed by en route to distant destinations and unfinished destinies which, at this stage, their residents inevitably still found so hard to discern.

"What do you think," the first twin asked, toying with his swizzle stick. "Is the universe still unfolding as it should?"

"If not, then I'd really hate to see it unfolding as it shouldn't!" Crossing his eyes dramatically by way of emphasis, the second finished his glass with a decisive gulp.

"Back to work," the two announced in unison.

Welcome to Training Camp

꩜ A NEW SENSE of inner purpose, and the combined encouragement of the World's Greatest Gravedigger and its Most Beautiful Astronomer notwithstanding, Team Earth found itself uneasy as it awaited the imminent arrival of instructors from The Great Beyond beyond the Beyond. It was one thing to be told that help was on its way, quite another to hear rumours of the forms it might take.

"Here comes the cavalry!" Aurora exclaimed, eyes flashing with delight as she set foot on a planet she'd begun to study avidly. The first to arrive, she kissed Leila warmly on both cheeks, then, sticking out a graceful paw, began introducing herself to Scheherazade and friends, and a first few members of a now clearly even more nervous Team Earth.

Given her own long and often lonely millennia in charge of the Museum of Historical Culs-de-Sac, Aurora was quick to recognize in others even the earliest signs of potentially terminal apprehension. Stage fright was always understandable and, with a little determination or distraction, usually passed. Next-stage fright, however, left untreated, was a condition which could easily prove fatal.

Excusing herself, she wandered casually over to join a number of prospective contestants in the demanding fields of Microscopic and Telescopic Love (more formally known as immanent and transcendent) already deep in unresolved debate.

All eyes turned as the small yellow monkey ambled up, a reassuring look masking the dedication in her dazzling purple eyes.

"Don't worry," Aurora declared, after first politely shaking hands with all. "Think of yourselves as I do," she said, spreading her arms and pirouetting on one leg, the other gracefully extended. "A bundle of truly remarkable contradictions ... and an absolutely fascinating work in progress!"

࿐

Marina, Leila, Qingling, Yasmina, Tatiana, Sybilla and Scheherazade compared notes, finished their drinks in Team Earth's executive lounge, and then went outside to wait. But not for long. One moment the little group was alone – the next, it wasn't.

One of the benefits of the passage of millions of years is that the inhabitants of the Future are easily able to read one another's minds. And degree of thirst. As a result, they each timed their simultaneous arrivals so perfectly as to encounter the Three Crystals returning, now tray-laden, straight from the bar, having ordered exactly the right drinks for them all. Moments later, restorative-of-choice in hand, they surveyed the crowds of candidates gathering nervously in front of them.

"Bright-eyed looking bunch," observed Dr. Professor O'Bliss. "Bit overly earnest, maybe...."

The tallest of two skeletons turned to his fellow instructors. "What do you ladies and gents think? Can we teach them anything solidly ethereal in only five weeks?"

The new arrivals from The Great Beyond beyond the Beyond all nodded encouragingly, at the same time trying hard not to cross their fingers behind their backs.

Nobody ever said spiritual heavy lifting was easy.

࿐

"Strange as it seems, don't worry." Dr. Professor O'Bliss's lazy, reassuring smile reflecting millennia of time-tested training sessions. "Sooner or later, there's always method in the madness of our methods!"

Just as many in Team Earth were about to exchange relieved looks, two distinguished skeletons suddenly stepped forward, enjoying as always the effect their elegantly-pared-down forms seemed forever to have on the unprepared.

"As you can now clearly see...," the first ever-so-smoothly articulated gentleman began, serenely tilting his skull and rattling his bones.

"Appearances are more than deceptive," said the second, clattering in companionable unison.

"We like to travel … lightly!" the two spectres chorused in unison, dancing a little jig and whistling to themselves. "Bodies may come, and bodies may go; but skeletons go on forever. Or very nearly."

"Now, before we all divide up into smaller groups and get to work on our special areas of competitive expertise," the first skeleton continued, "we thought we might just put you in the mood."

"A little film … to show you a much bigger picture."

The two skulls atop their ever-restless bones exchanged quick glances. "Look at it this way; however large your current horizons, we promise to broaden them enormously!"

By prior arrangement, the bright afternoon sun hid itself behind layers of cloud, the area around Team Earth's training grounds turning conveniently black. Seconds later, a gigantic movie screen descended from the sky, its colours deepening to reveal galaxy after shimmering galaxy from a vantage point previously unknown. As haunting music filled the air, countless star systems began singing softly to one another, each playing its part in a vast choir, their shared hymn resounding to a greater, more abiding rhythm still.

A rapt Scheherazade shot upright in surprise, instantly aware she'd seen this unique panorama just once before; a fleeting, privileged glimpse of the universe alive to its own becoming … as seen through God's miraculous, unmoving eye.

She turned to the two figures watching intently in the darkness, the bony sockets of their skulls aglow with a kindred, ancient amusement.

Each skeleton put a serene ivory finger to long-gone lips. "Sssshhh!"

"Let's just say that we too appear to have friends.…"

"In exceptionally high places."

۞

As the film ended in a great lingering chorus of light, the combined voices fading away, the audience sat in an absolute stillness.

The taller of the two skeletons rose. Then rose some more, ivory feet now happily walking on air.

"The point is simple; in a universe this complex, everything hangs together. Every last little thing flows into everything else, depends on everything else, descends from and – eventually – ascends to every last other little thing else."

He raised an eloquently bony finger for emphasis. "Again – and again – and again."

"Which, of course, is how it must be," the second, shorter skeleton declared gruffly. "Otherwise, you'd have bits and pieces of the universe wandering off by themselves, trying to go it alone, and getting lost. And ending up being next to useless, to themselves and everybody else."

"And that," said his lanky associate, "is definitely a cosmic no-no."

"Not least because it really tends to screw up the celestial music!"

"And so, our first lesson is simple," the thin skeleton continued. "If you yearn to be successful in love and at love, then our plain and simple secret is, plainly and simply, look for the hidden connections."

"It's real easy, really." he other skeleton said, rising even higher on exaggerated tiptoe, pointing somewhere in the direction of the stars now hiding happily overhead under the cover of daylight. "Just get up, get out … and follow the celestial dots."

So Much to Learn

&. "LET THE TRAINING BEGIN!" the World's Most Beautiful Astronomer declared as Team Earth hurried into smaller sub-groups, each anxiously awaiting the hopefully-tender mercies of their new-found coaches from The Great Beyond beyond the Beyond.

High above, the sun paused in its endless ascent, peering down to examine the crowded scene below. While Earth might not be the largest planet in its care, it was now certainly the most entertaining.

For a long, unnerving moment, the sun was overcome by feelings of great pride, and then even greater apprehension. Who would have thought that that first, long-ago impulsive leap into fiery luminescence could have led so far, or have such potentially galactic repercussions! Whispering under its breath a small prayer, it doubled momentarily in intensity, shooting off a few billion solar flares by way of encouragement before continuing on its ever-dependable path toward noon.

"Let's hope they manage to surprise us," said the World's Greatest Gravedigger, one roughened hand on his gleaming spade, the other around his lady-love's slender waist.

"Let's hope they manage to astonish themselves," came her swift reply.

&.

To Marina's amusement, the tall, dark and captivating director of the Interplanetary Centre for Joy led in a group of elongated tangerine beings, their heads lime-green and shaped like up-turned horseshoes. The odd arrivals began immediately plying their unconventional skills.

As each of Earth's would-be competitors advanced in turn, offering either left or right hand for electronic inspection, an impassive tangerine-and-green technician entered the results on a proprietary satellite video-link. Instantly received in The Great Beyond beyond the Beyond, this information was analyzed, cross-checked, and then speedily converted into a personalized, totally comprehensive training programme in the most advanced forms of delight-hearted loving ever!

Such specialized prescriptions were in turn speedily beamed back to Earth where an increasingly-impatient cluster of horseshoe-headed attendants were already making discreet side bets as to the individual outcomes.

When the last candidate has been examined and all the results now in, the five tangerine-and-green trainers stepped aside to compare notes. After a brief consultation, all shook their upward-curving noggins: first ominously from side to side; then, more encouragingly, up and down. The most senior approached Doctor Professor O'Bliss and, after nodding approvingly at Marina, whispered softly in his boss's ear.

"The bad news," the founding director of the Interplanetary Centre for Joy announced dolefully, "is that, cosmically speaking, not only does Team Earth face a lot of competition … but you also need a lot of work."

His sudden smile stifled every burgeoning frown and muffled groan. "The good news, however, is that you also appear unbelievably luckier than most!"

Everyone present hoped so, especially since Eve was almost certainly watching.

❧

Thanking Leila for her kind introduction, Aurora stood on the small chair facing an understandably rapt audience, her beguiling purple eyes magnetic in the bright morning light.

"Now," she began firmly, "I'm told that you particular ladies and gentle-men hope to represent Earth in one or more of the admirably esoteric fields of Transitional, Transformational and Transubstantial Love."

The members of her audience nodded carefully, trying to keep a proper balance between excitement and decorum.

"OK." The little yellow monkey stood as tall as she could. "Then first let me tell you what not to do."

For the next quarter hour, Aurora captivated her audience with a series of increasingly spectacular metaphysical misadventures drawn from the Museum of Interstellar Culs-de-Sac's voluminous and dusty archives.

"And so on, and so on," their guest speaker concluded.

After some silence, a gentleman at the back put up his hand. "Then what's the real secret?"

"Are you sure you're ready to find out?" Aurora's eyes twinkled with an ancient, contemplative pride. A moment later, the small yellow monkey disappeared into a sudden cloud of purple smoke.

As the haze cleared, she emerged in the form of a giant sixty-foot high goddess, multi-armed and radiantly beautiful. Her first hand held a banana, the second a clock, the third a miniature computer, the fourth a spaceship, the fifth a map of the entire universe, the sixth a vial of the essence of cosmic tenderness, the seventh a bottle of all the wisdom of all the genies of all Creation, and the eighth and final hand open to support a small, self-possessed male monkey who regarded her with adoring purple eyes.

"You never know what you can become," she whispered. "Unless you try." There was a pause, then a strangely poignant frown. "Take it from me, you're all so much bigger than you seem."

Advice rendered, Aurora returned just as suddenly to her everyday guise, peering up shyly at Leila once more. Spreading upturned paws, she shrugged with a becoming, if slightly impish diffidence.

"Don't be too surprised," she observed wistfully. "After all, don't we all have our own little secrets?"

⁂

Qingling, ever self-assured, had volunteered to take charge of Team Earth's would-be contestants in the highly demanding field of Spiritual Prowess & Intergalactic Progress. The quality most prized was the ability to perform as many rock-solid, gossamer-soft works of faith and labours of love as possible, under all conditions and circumstances.

Most people, if pressed, found themselves capable of carrying out at least one work of faith per month, and (allowing for time off for vacations and bad moods) between six and ten moderately-sized labours of love over a whole calendar year.

To live a life, however, where faith and love were seamlessly interwoven, where every act was a gesture of love and every breath a renewal and expansion of faith, was not always a state so readily attained.

It was little wonder, therefore, that even as some would-be champions of faith, hope and charity awaited the arrival of their designated instructors eagerly, more than a few other members of Team Earth should have begun shuffling back and forth, their fledgling haloes already beginning to flicker as they found themselves increasingly unsure of their own current degree of spiritual completeness.

This was so especially given the rumours that certain competitors (admittedly from especially-advanced civilizations) already enjoyed the benefits of specialized short-term, high-speed theological colleges that trained them in sixteen mutually compatible forms of sanctity simultaneously; and then released them into worlds where love was the second hand of infinity, and faith the invisible impetus of eternity.

It hardly seemed fair.

And so it was, with decidedly mixed emotions, that this little band of wanna-be spiritual stalwarts had watched as a single upside-down figure in a white coat ambled toward them on its hands, peering at them closely all the while from its two distinctive silver-topped heads. A pair of identical but smaller versions followed, also comfortably reversed, and balancing what appeared to be oversized tool boxes on their upturned feet.

Qingling approached, ready to provide official introductions for the two understandably-renowned directors of the Intergalactic Recreation and Repair Centre.

The first head smiled up at her with familiar emerald eyes. "Well, here we are, just as promised," Chief Inspector Stop declared.

The second head turned from its examination of their prospective students, its identical emerald eyes shining with technical anticipation and seasoned professional mischief.

"At first glance," Chief Inspector Go-Go declared, "they're all going to need a lot of work!"

❧

"Generally," Chief Inspector Stop began, "here we believe that major reconstructive surgery is a basic requirement for all those seeking what

I like to call non-stop, all-weather holiness. Especially if there's also the complicating factor of a long undiagnosed spiritual glitch or two."

"Such as?" Qingling inquired, always happy to see a good glitch (or even better, a bad one) come unglued.

"Take your pick," Chief Inspector Go-Go replied, bringing out a very large chart and pointing here and there rapidly. "Doctrinal inconsistency, prematurely elevated sanctimony, shaky heart murmurs, overly-selective sacramental sensitivities, untimely fanaticisms, and so forth and so on."

"Inevitable, perhaps," Chief Inspector Stop interposed, "but always most unfortunate,"

"And so?" Qingling asked.

"We're goin' to fix 'em up, of course," Chief Inspector Stop exclaimed.

"Or try to."

"Take out some qualities, add others, rearrange and completely reverse some more."

"Reconnect where necessary, disconnect where imperative. And so on."

"So, if you'll just get the candidates to line up," Chief Inspector Go-Go declared – motioning to the waiting group, who appeared to recognize that this was one of those moments where their faith, if that's what it was, was about to be seriously tested – "we'll start to work."

"I don't believe I've ever seen a human being changed into a full-fledged, five star saint in much under a year," said Qingling. Her eyes brightened with a curiosity as much personal as professional. "Mind if I watch?"

Chief Inspector Stop looked at Chief Inspector Go-Go, who returned his esteemed colleague's companionable smile.

"Truly sorry," they both exclaimed in unison, 'but we always seem to do our best work in private."

As Qingling obligingly walked away, every prospective candidate was trying, as politely as possible, to let someone else be the first to sign what appeared to be a combination of confidentiality agreement and intergalactic waiver form.

§

While it is generally accepted that all people have what is conventionally known as skeletons in their closets, it is less widely appreciated that, metaphorically speaking, skeletons in turn have their own closets with people in them.

Having been around as long as human beings, watching their fallible, fortune-tossed generations come and go, it is not surprising that the esteemed veterans of the timeless society of skulls and bones should be among the most informed, if close-lipped observers of humanity. They are, as they themselves freely acknowledge, more than slightly unsettling presences.

As a result, when Yazmina proudly reintroduced her two eloquently-bony friends to Earth's provisional competitors in the extra-subtle sub-category of 'Super-Secret and Even More Cunningly Hidden Mysteries of Love', the latter were understandably apprehensive.

A skeleton's empty eye-sockets can be surprisingly compelling, even intimidating; especially if you happen not to know the answers to those life and death questions they appear eternally about to ask. Well aware of this, the two ivory gentlemen did their mannerly best to put their new pupils at ease.

"To start with, we won't try to deal with everything at once," the first began, "even if it usually happens that way."

"And second, you'll undoubtedly find that the inside story," his companion continued, pointing to his own knobbly, see-through chest by way of illustration and emphasis, "can actually be quite a lot of fun."

Together, they bowed to their keenly-attentive audience. "From here on," they announced, "think of yourselves as skeletons-in-training."

A moment later, the two gentlemen put a pair of bony fingers to their absent lips, then together blew a single, piercing whistle – which served not only to bring their audience abruptly out of its trance, but also a host of multi-coloured, professorial skeletons clattering and capering out from hiding.

"Congratulations!" the two eminently senior, ivory-toned instructors exclaimed, fixing their startled students with captivating bony stares. "Each one of you, as of this moment, has been assigned your very own highly personalized, impeccably-skeletal tutor-at-large. Able to reduce things to the absolutely bare bones, as it were."

They looked at each other jovially, and then went on.

"Think of him or her as the one skeleton you've always wanted in your closet: the infinitely non-judgmental cosmic confidant who knows your deepest darkest secrets – and doesn't mind a bit. The one, moreover, who knows all the winsome, wondrous ways of love: hidden or revealed, sacred or profane, paradisiacal or persnickety. And is more than willing to share them free of charge!" The crowd of beaming, gleaming, many-shaped skulls and bones, chattering among themselves, gradually fanned out to approach their individual pre-assigned apprentices.

"Ooops!" exclaimed most of Team Earth's 'Hidden Mysteries' division under their suddenly shallow breath; not quite sure whether to jump with joy or try to run and hide. Who knew that learning about Love, on the thin ivory edge of eternity, could be so profoundly scary!

And Still More to Learn

❧ ITS EROTICALLY-INSPIRED history notwithstanding, Earth's citizens have seldom been fully comfortable with the magical, mysterious energies of Desire. The sternest laws, the most finicky of good and sober intentions, the very latest in pinch-lipped moral prescripts, all prove woefully inadequate before its relentlessly anarchic caprice.

Desire brings complications; and complications (almost always) mean trouble. And trouble has a scantily clad way of redoubling desire.

"On the other hand," Valentina announced cheerfully, pointing sky-wards, "there are those for whom pleasure has long been a wise and trusted guide."

At her words, every passing cloud lit up with portraits of select constellations big and small, all happily free-wheeling their way through Time and Space, their lives and loves dedicated to a profound, all-embracingly sensuous appreciation of everything!

The members of Team Earth stared up wistfully, the same thought crossing every mind. While they weren't entirely opposed to such enviably open-minded abandon, they undoubtedly lacked the stamina.

"Not to worry." The beautiful, violet-eyed director of the now far-off Wondrous Winding Gardens of Desire broke into a reassuring smile. "Ever heard of Comprehensive Cosmic Sensuality 101?"

"Otherwise known as Early-Stage Ecstasy for Earthlings," a second voice confirmed.

Swivelling on her custom-made heels, Tatiana found herself only inches away from the twinkling eyes of the poised, peacock-blue Un-official Ambassador (Plenipotentiary) of Cosmic Hedonism.

"Do you think they're ready?" the cube-headed sage murmured, eyes flickering back and forth across the throng of anxious students.

"What's the alternative?" his second cousin replied, his own gleaming sphere sending sunlight bouncing all over the place.

Rubbing his hands together in anticipation, the third and final, triangle-headed sage then beckoned the crowd in closer.

"No more of this well-intentioned effort of thinking globally, as it's called. You have to begin to understand everything inside out … as if, in fact, you yourself are the entire world!"

The Three Crystals exchanged glances, then harmonies.

"A-one, a-two, a-three."

The shortest sage snapped his fingers, at the same time muttering something which, while indecipherable, would undoubtedly be best not to try to repeat unless you were prepared for the consequences.

In an instant, the third sage's shiny head completely disappeared, replaced by a perfect, if miniaturised version of Planet Earth.

Oceans, lakes, rivers, cities, roads, mountains, deserts, all appeared in precise if minute detail. Swarms of thousands of near-invisible aircraft circled and whirred like extra-tiny mosquitoes, as trillions of electronic signals pulsed from his global brain every second.

Although a collective gasp was definitely called for, his astonished audience didn't have time. The smaller-sized seer snapped his fingers once again.

A split nano-second later, all Earth's would-be competitors found their own heads suddenly gone: replaced atop their individual shoulders by identical versions of a whirling blue-and-white globe, each one reverberating with all the lives, loves and interwoven destinies of its billions of inhabitants.

No longer could anyone feel isolated from the world – for they had become the world. Thinking Earth's thoughts in its own time and its own way, each knowing their home planet for the first time from within.

"Don't worry," all three crystalline sages were quick to reassure their visibly-startled charges, now stumbling about, hands clasped to what only moments ago were their foreheads. "It's only totally overwhelming for the first twenty-four hours. After that, you start to feel a little more comfortable and, in time, even constructive."

"I never realized how truly big Earth was!" a bemused voice whispered in the back row.

"Or how infinitesimally small!" added someone else immediately in front.

"Or how really, really, really hard it is to be a planet," a third voice joined in, tilting its own version of the blue-and-white wandering globe warily from side to side. "Let alone a good one."

"Now they're really starting to learn," Sybilla whispered.

"And unlearn," the Three Crystals announced with one voice.

"What happens next?"

The sphere-headed sage tucked his own scaled-down version of Earth under one arm, taking Sybilla's with the other.

"If we had more time before the Games, the most promising competitors would graduate to learning how to live as if their heads were identical to an entire constellation. Then, after much frustration, cursing and subsequent expansion of awareness, they would move to sporting a complete galaxy (albeit a very small one to start with) atop their shoulders; and then, eventually they would discover the fundamental secret of successfully supporting even an entire universe!"

"Which is?"

"The same secret at the heart of everything, of course."

"Which is?"

"Whatsoever you do, do it with love."

Obstacle Course

"WAKEY, WAKEY!!"

— The World's Greatest Gravedigger

God Says Hello (Again)

✿ HEAVEN, EVE CONCEDED with exhausted delight, was definitely not a retirement home. As the hours before the Opening Ceremonies grew fewer, one all-important meeting followed another at ever-shorter intervals.

Delegations from billions of galaxies arrived to present both their credentials and provisional plans for participation. A host of institutional sponsors submitted (most humbly, to be sure) their respective advertising and marketing suggestions, together with discreet requests for perhaps a mention in the official programme and (if it weren't too much trouble, your Supremeness) a few of the more choice seats for as many events as possible.

Exotic architectural drawings came swiftly to life as buildings of every size and purpose sprang up throughout the length and breadth of Heaven. Tentative schedules were checked and rechecked, tests conducted and time trials undertaken.

The management, commentators, reporters, angelic stringers and technical staff of the Heavenly Broadcast Studio endlessly expanded their comprehensive intergalactic transmission plan. Links were established with even the tiniest star, so that everyone in the universe would be able to watch what was billed as The Most Amazing Spiritual Sporting Event in the History of the Whole Dang Universe!

Under such circumstances, it was not surprising that the senior angels uncomplainingly worked both double duty and triple time, their junior associates (particularly those aspiring to early promotion) making sure that they too were seen to be keeping up the pace.

It was in the midst of all these many labours of love that Eve looked up to find the Archangel of All Archangels standing in the doorway of her private suite, an unexpected postcard in hand.

The image on the front was of a deserted tropical beach, sunlight bouncing happily off a leisurely bright blue sea. A single white-and-gold beach chair was strategically placed beneath palm trees by the water's edge: seemingly empty, but for the glass of something evidently divinely appealing that was suspended in mid air, held aloft by an invisible hand.

Eve turned the card over.

"Having a marvellous time. Hope Heaven's still there. Warmest regards to all. P.S. Glad (for once) I'm not around."

"Don't bet on it," the Archangel-in-Chief said affectionately.

It would be interesting to know what God might think of the Archangel's own suddenly-compelling tropical vacation plans. Assuming, of course, that the Boss hadn't already arranged for them long before.

When it comes to biding time, God bides it better than most.

Weighing The Odds

AS DARKNESS CONSIDERATELY fell once more on Team Earth's preparations, a silent couple slipped through the shadows, their troubled expressions fortunately unseen.

"What are our chances?" The World's Greatest Gravedigger paused, carefully rephrasing his question. "Or should I say – given lack of time, loads of circumstance, and our virtually limitless competition – does Earth really have any chance at all?"

"Friends in high places notwithstanding, there's still so much to do." The World's Most Beautiful Astronomer's slender hand brushed pensively across her star charts. "For Earth to be even chosen as the galaxy's designated representative, we still have to win the Milky Way selection committee's approval."

"And what are the odds of that?"

The world's most beautiful co-captain raised her telescope to the night skies, tracking star after shimmering star, calculating which might be inclined to take Earth's side, and which already had favourites of their own. Survey complete, her eyes returned to Team Earth, its members now heading back to their dormitories, flushed from the day's efforts, yet elated by the unorthodox new skills they were just beginning to learn.

Earth's most alluring sky-watcher shook her head. "One thing's for sure. If this increasingly gung-ho gang of cosmic go-getters doesn't somehow find their way to the Opening Ceremonies, they'll be a whole lot more than just mighty disappointed. It would be like finally managing to get a glimpse of Paradise's long-secret second whereabouts, and then being turned away at the door!"

"Not on my watch," the World's Greatest Gravedigger growled with the fierce, poignant determination of one who had already buried too many dreamers and dreams: some realized, but so many others – so much more often – not. Earth's appearance at the Universe's very first-ever Heavenly Games of Love was one cause he would fight for till the end, and beyond, if need be. For all its faults and flaws, that little blue-and-white ball was infinitely more than a one-way mortuary in space.

At her consort's side, Earth's Most Beautiful Astronomer reached out, quietly taking her new, first and last lover's hand. There were times when the universe felt very, very big, and even its bravest all too small.

A moment later, from Team Earth's hastily finished quarters, the first, increasingly confident notes of an anthem rose in the air, followed by laughter and cheers.

The World's Most Beautiful Astronomer closed her telescope with a smile. "Somehow, I get the feeling our very own Heaven-storming hopefuls are a whole lot tougher than they look!"

The World's Greatest Gravedigger embraced her with one arm and with the other, raised his redoubtable silver spade, shaking it in resolute warning to the silent watching stars.

"And if not, they soon better be!"

Overhead, constellation after constellation whirled onwards, each teasingly aglow with its hidden tales and unrequited questions. The World's Most Beautiful Astronomer followed their path, pointing to one among millions of tiny lights twinkling in the darkness, their brilliance concealing a trillion others still unseen.

"Everything's changed – and yet remains the same." She smiled an irresistibly-astral smile. "The choice is always ours: choose a star and make a wish come true!"

The two turned toward on another. "Onwards," Earth's team captains declared in the moment before they kissed.

"Forever onwards!"

Ocean of Stars

❧ AS A VENERABLE wizard with an unflagging sense of curiosity, Abracadabra had made the most of recent weeks, keeping track of cosmic developments in general and the training progress of Earth's competitors in particular. It had been, all in all, a wonderfully-informative research trip, leaving him both exhilarated and thirsty.

So it was at last, with both relief and anticipation, that he steered his way into the final approaches to the Constellation of Second Sight. Ahead, a cluster of fellow white clouds, moored comfortably in the parking lot of the Ocean Of Stars, confirmed that it still remained a favourite watering hole among senior sorcerers.

Once inside, it was only a matter of moments before he joined in comparing notes. The Games, all wizards agreed, had definitely been good for business. Almost every galaxy in Creation, eager to improve its chances, was more than ready to pay top dollar (or interstellar equivalent) for the most up-to-date sources of cosmic inspiration and foresight.

"Quite, quite amazing," a distinguished past-president of the Intergalactic Geomancers' Association declared. "Two or three quite venerable star systems, ones which I would have sworn were well past it, have since found truly astonishing new energy and purpose."

Abracadabra pushed back his now-empty plate, burped contentedly, then reached for a third goblet of his preferred vintage elixir.

"Interesting celestial developments of late."

"Big D's up to something, too," one of his oldest, most astute associates observed, loosening the buckle on his bulging cloak with a satisfied sigh. "Something fairly drastic, I gather."

"I've heard the same rumours," added a short, bespectacled sorcerer whose family had run strategic psychic listening-stations in a number of constellations for generations.

Abracadabra glanced around the table at his illustrious companions, whose reputations had already made them the preferred choice as strategic coaches for ambitious galaxies in the upcoming Games.

"Not so surprising, in many ways. Once Eve was chosen, it put Big D in an exceptionally awkward position. Cosmic demonic street-cred and all that."

"Maybe," mused an impressively triple-headed gentleman whose three pairs of eyes gazed at each other thoughtfully until finally blinking in syncopated agreement. "And maybe not. What if it's actually part of a larger plan?"

"What I want to know is which galaxy will win the over-all Grand Prize?" The biggest gambler of the bunch looked round hopefully. "Still early days yet, but ... any bets?"

"Count me in," the well-tailored senior sorcerer to his left declared.

"Don't count me out," Abracadabra added softly.

He sat silently for quite a while, visualizing Earth's long history of self-imposed defeats, its wishful thinking, unkept promises and interminable list of hopes unfulfilled. Time slowed as he contemplated its endless efforts to become something more than just another little planet struggling to understand, make something of itself and, finally, find its ultimate place in the great universal scheme of dreams.

"Guts," he whispered to himself at last.

The real miracle of the mythical phoenix, he'd always thought, was not that that bright-winged icon of inspiration and imagination forever arose from the smouldering ashes of its past. It was that it always returned just as unhesitatingly to the flame.

Staring into their drinks, as if seeking to decipher Time's enigmas in swirling bubbles, the assembled diviners all suddenly looked at one another, each sharing the same thought. Across the enormity of Creation, it seemed, virtually every galaxy was now set on a course of getting to know better not just their neighbours but also themselves.

Sometimes, even for the most gifted of seers, it was far more interesting not to know the outcome. Until, of course, the time came to help make it happen.

Joys of Office

❧ EVEN IN EDEN EVE always had hoped that, some day, an emissary from elsewhere in her native galaxy would arrive.

What she hadn't anticipated, however, was that this long-awaited encounter would come to pass in Heaven; or that it would take the form of a delegation from (as they liked to call themselves) the Impressively Grand Council of the Almost-Fully-Homogenized Milky Way.

Ready or not, however, this appeared to be one of those moments whose time had finally come. For better or, in this case, very much worse.

"Hello, neighbours," she began, by way of informal welcome.

Despite having three revolving eyes in the centre of their wide, flat foreheads, and three mouths which spoke individually yet in perfect, harmony, her trio of unexpected guests were still strangely recognizable as distant relatives

A formal afternoon tea was poured.

"May we offer our most sincere congratulations," the leader of the delegation announced, speaking first from only one of its three mouths.

"We were truly proud to learn of your achievement," it continued, now from a second.

"A very great honour that one of us should be selected to be God for a Day," it concluded from the third.

There was a pause while the visitors looked nervously at one another, then at Eve. All three of their sets of three revolving eyes began to rotate faster and faster.

"Now, however, it seems we have to make a decision," the second ambassador began, each mouth speaking in turn.

"As to which planet, chosen from all those who call our whirly-twirly galaxy home...."

"Might best and most successfully represent us in the upcoming Games!"

"Of course," Eve replied diplomatically, reaching for her forehead. In the hurry to leave, God had neglected to mention that a celestial headache, while rare, was correspondingly huge.

"As you know, the Milky Way's a fairly biggish place," the third member of the delegation stammered.

"With lots of quite sizeable and fairly knowledgeable constellations...."

"Many of whom have some surprisingly well-seasoned, yet spiritually-still-quite-athletic planets in their repertoire."

"And so we found ourselves wondering...," The first delegate from the Impressively Grand Council, having drawn out the last word out as long as possible, closed his eyes and leapt into the unknown. "How might you feel if the Milky Way just happened to choose a planet other than Earth as our galaxy's duly appointed champion in the Heavenly Games of Love?"

Now Eve's head was truly beginning to throb.

"After all, your little blue-and-white home has already been astonishingly fortunate, especially given, that is, its comparative youth and size. So ... it seems only fair to let another, bigger, more experienced and (how shall we put it) galactically-better-connected planet have a chance. Wouldn't you agree?"

The three ambassadors abruptly closed their three mouths, swallowed in unison, their three sets of three eyes all blinking rapidly at the same time.

What was there to say? "I appreciate your courtesy in coming all this way to ask my blessing," Eve replied at last.

Try as she might, there appeared to be no way out. In virtually every other matter, Eve would have felt no hesitation in asking the Archangel-in-Chief for a celestial second opinion. In this case, however, the dilemma was clearly hers alone to resolve.

She faced all three visitors squarely.

"As stated in the previously-publicized rules of the Games, every galaxy gets to select 'whomsoever, in its sole opinion, it sincerely believes to be its best and most promising representative.' No questions asked."

Eve paused, her face impassive. "And so, whatever your final decision may be, I must and will fully support your choice."

Ever the generous, (outwardly) unhurried hostess, she poured her guests another cup of celestial tea, silently wishing all the while for both the Rx Angel and the astringent consolations of something very much stronger.

A moment passed.

"Grateful though I am to you for considering how I might feel," Earth's founding mother added evenly, "I'm sure you'll understand if I also say that, right now, I'm slightly more concerned about how my distant offspring are going to react to this news, as and when they find out!"

Official substitute though she might be, Eve did not need the supernatural powers of her office to know that, on learning of its rejection from the Games (especially after so much effort and so close to opening day) in favour of a supposedly more talented planetary cousin, Team Earth was unlikely to respond with blithe unconcern. So colossal a disappointment was, in fact, exactly the sort of unexpected, all-too-public blow to Earth's emerging self-esteem as to send her home planet into a depression lasting hundreds, if not thousands of light years.

The three delegates from the Almost-Fully-Homogenized Milky Way Galaxy all looked thoughtfully at one another, political calculation, personal concern and undeniable tribal loyalty revolving simultaneously in their three sets of three eyes.

"Perhaps we could find a way for your home planet to be an unofficial entrant in, say, some sort of extra-special category," the delegation's leader offered tentatively.

"Perhaps." Eve frowned thoughtfully.

From her vantage point, Earth had always been in an extra-special category. And besides, fatalism wasn't really her *forté*.

Party Invitations

&. APPEARANCES NOTWITHSTANDING, it is seldom easy being a devil, especially a really good one. The hours tend to be long, the associates congenitally rebellious, the clients inevitably unruly and the offices regrettably downmarket.

For those chosen few renegade champions, however, ranging over millions of years across all the galaxies of Creation, for whom the judiciously diabolic and sagely demonic prove a rare and noble calling, it is a destiny like none other.

Shutting down the hotline after a satisfying conversation with his angelic counterpart, Big D couldn't stop smiling. Dues long paid, it was more rewarding than he ever imagined to find himself at the height of his powers, even if, for now, those powers remained well hidden and he, for a at least a little while longer, the proverbial Devil in disguise.

A moment later, he placed the first of a series of calls putting him in conspiratorial touch with nearly every senior demonic colleague in the cosmos.

"Thank you all for your most impressive initial efforts," he began. "Now, if each of you would kindly open your newly-revised copy of The Eminent Master Devil's Compleat Procedures Manual and Retribution Guide, and turn to the chapter entitled Operation Secret Conscience, we can begin to plan our next moves."

&.

Crimson colleagues duly dealt with, Big D's next call was to one of the finest, most resilient gentlemen (above or below) it had ever been his pleasure to cajole.

When his complimentary celestial cell phone rang, the best Adam of the bunch (if he could say so himself) was taking a breather from his own extended journey of intergalactic inspections and consultations.

Pushing bacon and eggs to one side, he answered the call. "Yup?"

"Long time, no see," said a voice from the past, the jaunty face on the small screen still as youthful as ever.

"If by any chance you happen to be free on Games Day evening, I was wondering if you might be interested in a night out with me and the boys."

❦

One phone call remained.

How appropriate, Big D reflected, if his true match turned out to be the one woman in the universe who might just be able to out-match him. On a good day, of course. Divine punishment … or poetic justice?

"Couldn't help wondering how I was?"

"An irresistible urge," Big D admitted gallantly.

"I like it when you give in to temptation," Scheherazade laughed. "It suits you."

Big D did his best not to blush (not that it would have been readily apparent).

"I was also curious how you were faring with Team Earth," he added. "Pardon my curiosity, but will they be ready in time?" Big D listened to Scheherazade's silence at the other end of the line, sensitive as ever both to the many contradictory forces even now at work on that still-unstable little world – and to her.

"They're doing their best – almost."

It was the Devil's turn to be silent.

"The new co-captains are teaching them all they can," Scheherazade said at last. "And the coaches from Tomorrowland are daily pulling new rabbits out of a seemingly endless supply of bottomless hats."

"At the same time, however," Big D interjected gently, "Team Earth is also beginning to discover just how much, Games or no Games, they still have to learn."

"Truer words…," Scheherazade replied, relieved to share her concern with the one person who, whatever else he was up to, could be trusted to keep his eye on this particular blue-and-white ball. "What gave you the final clue?"

The universe's foremost devils have an inherent ability not only to tell the truth, or its opposite, with equal skill and conviction. The greatest of them also know unerringly which to choose, and when.

"If you've been running an underworld as long as I have," Big D ventured quietly, "you get to know a great deal about all the difficulties of learning to love...."

Scheherazade's heart bounced. It didn't always take a cosmic heroine to know when a public observation might just also be a private confession.

§

For two professional chameleons who had each enjoyed more than a few romantic interludes over time, Scheherazade and her charmingly devilish admirer suddenly found themselves quite surprisingly shy.

"See you at the Opening Ceremonies?"

"Wouldn't miss it for the world."

"Any chance we might meet before then?" they both asked.

"We're very busy."

"Indeed we are."

"In that case, chances are we probably will," each concluded.

As Scheherazade and Big D each listened to the other's voice fading away at opposite ends of the universe, both couldn't help feeling that, as an aperitif, understated anticipation had much to recommend it.

Pillow Talk

&. JUST AS THE RELIEVED delegates from the Impressively Grand Council set off on their return voyage from Heaven, a familiar knock on Eve's door heralded Adam's perfectly-timed return. They stood silent in one another's arms, feeling the inseparable comfort and pleasure of thousands on thousands of years.

No one, least of all God, could say that being a cosmic founding couple was easy. There were certainly moments, Eve thought, when courage seemed an overly-demanding virtue. Until, that is, one considered the alternatives.

At last, she broke the spell. "I'm more than tired. Exhausted, in fact. It's been a disconcertingly long day, and the Games begin in only a few more."

"Why don't we have an early evening," said Adam, kissing her neck. "I'll make dinner, and you can tell me all about what's been happening. After a long, hot bath."

There were times, thought Eve, when her consort definitely seemed an angel in disguise.

No doubt, of course, he felt the same way about her.

&.

With a little culinary help from several sous-chefs in the blending of unfamiliar seasonal ingredients, together with suggestions as to the most piquant of celestial sauces, Adam was able to outdo himself in the kitchens of Heaven, much to his own and Eve's delight.

Leisurely dinner over, they stood with their arms round one another, feeling the evening breezes flowing in from billions of stars.

"It all seems like a dream," Adam said at last. His arm tightened on her waist. "But...."

"But it's not."

He turned his head, silently admiring once again the proud, fallible woman he had known (and usually liked, sometimes disliked and always, always loved) ever since their own tumultuous beginning in that now long-vanished land where everything itself had first begun. Everything, at least, on their own little planet.

"What about Earth?" he asked at last.

Eve did not answer immediately, continuing instead to stare deep among the stars, as if seeking across time and space a glimpse of their infinitely far-off home. Seeking an answer to an ancient question that was, for the moment, hers alone to solve.

"Let's just say," Eve replied at last, her measured voice now accompanied by a wicked grin, "that right now I am considering all 'My' options."

That particular expression, if Adam remembered correctly, was almost exactly the look on his beloved's face moments before she blew the doors off Paradise! 'Danger!' the invisible but unmistakable sign might as well have read, 'cosmic superwoman coming through!'

❧

As Adam and Eve were falling asleep, resting up before the inevitable battles to come, he suddenly eased her head from his shoulder, looking deep in her eyes.

"I almost forgot." Adam chose his words carefully. "While you're arranging the Games, don't be surprised if I'm, how shall I say, tempted to help with a little unfinished interstellar business myself."

"I know you are," Eve whispered, affirmation and amusement in her reply. "And, chances are, I also know where you're off to. And with whom. And, more importantly, what you're all planning to do!"

Big D and Associates. No question, it was a corporate title with an unusually promising ring.

"Somehow I thought you'd figure it out," Adam confirmed, "celestial intercepts or not."

The only response, Eve decided, was a beatific smile. Not surprisingly, it came naturally. What was it about the male, she thought; so capable of being simultaneously tough, tender, terrifying and totally terrific?

She held up her right hand, wiggled her fingers gently, contemplating her latest nail polish (the Heavenly Spa was exactly that) under purposely lowered eyelids. "Boys will be boys," she sighed.

In equally fond reply, Adam puffed out his still impressive chest. "Given the importance of the next few days, perhaps a more accurate comment would be: men will be men!"

Eve's hand cupped the back of his neck, bringing him down to her: this cherished, vulnerable, invincible being so devoted to her and she to him; united from the very beginning in their resolve to protect, honour and make the most of this fragile little world entrusted to their care; the birthplace of their past, present and uncertain future, of all the fears and dreams with which their children's children's children continued ceaselessly to arise and to strive.

"Wouldn't have it any other way," Eve whispered; and she meant it.

Avante

GIVEN THAT HEAVEN has been successfully conducting interstellar conference calls ever since Time first learned to speak, it was not difficult for God's temporary replacement to arrange a lengthy conversation with quite a few of her extended family of sister Eves.

Nearly every alpha matriarch was pleased to report that her particular star system couldn't wait to begin! It was also clear that, while obviously friendly, the competition between them all would be fierce. Impressive teams had been selected from galaxies across the universe; advanced training in many categories of love and loving was everywhere nearly complete; and excited fans were making plans either to attend in person (if, that is, both degree of virtue and credit card limits allowed) or to take the day off and watch the opening ceremonies courtesy of the Heavenly Broadcast Studio. It promised to be a day like none other.

But also a day, Eve thought quietly, that might just mark Earth's biggest collective disappointment since that moment, some sixty million years or so before, when an uninvited, hugely unwelcome meteor so decisively convinced the dinosaurs that, despite all their good looks, energy and charm, the universe could well have other plans.

❧

It is a self-evident celestial axiom that angels are invisible most of the time, if only because they have much better things to do than merely hang around and look decorative. It is also true that they will miraculously tend to show up precisely when and where required.

For those few angels either still learning their trade or needing to refresh their skills at multi-level synchronicity there are, of course, special celestial schools to help them recalibrate their internal chronometers.

The beautiful topaz-eyed Angel of Extra-Subtle Service had no such problem. Equally adept at transcending the two-fold illusions of time and circumstance, she routinely appeared wherever the need was greatest. Whenever the cosmic cards needed to be reshuffled, the intergalactic roulette wheel given a faster spin, or the transstellar dice shaken a little more recklessly, she was often the one to lend a stealthy, subtle hand.

Or, in this case, to tap gently on Eve's door with an early evening bottle of champagne and two clearly impatient glasses.

"There are moments when I could get to like this job." Eve took another slow, appreciative sip, starlight flickering in the amber bubbles.

"Lots of extraordinary advantages," the Angel of Extra Subtle Services agreed. There was a diplomatic pause. "Then again, the problems tend to be on much the same scale as well."

Eve let out a sigh. All would ultimately be well, of course. Of that she had no doubt. It was a fundamental part of the overall cosmic warranty. The question right now was: would all be well on time?

The white-winged figure nodded in silent agreement, then asked with mischievous complicity, "So, tell me: how exactly is Earth going to sneak into the Games?'

"I really don't know. Yet!"

Eve scrutinized her upturned palm as if hoping to find some ancient reassurance etched in its weathered, criss-crossed lines. When so much was said, and so little done, the long and winding road to Heaven was a whole lot longer and more winding than one might wish for.

"Around here we much prefer happy endings," the Angel of Extra Subtle Services observed, as she swallowed the last of her champagne. "What if I said that, somehow or other, Love will find a way?"

In celestial vino, celestial veritas?

"Well then, you tell it to get a move on!" Eve laughed, spirits restored. "From where I sit, we Earthlings look like we're running out of time!"

Celestial Interventions

❦ "WOULD YOU MIND calling this number for me, please?"

As expected, the congenitally imperturbable angel in charge of the Heavenly Communications Centre was having the time of an everlasting life, the cosmos everywhere lighting up with last-minute calls and requests.

Teams and tour groups were even now en route from the furthest galaxies. Celestial hotels, even those offering fewer amenities on the outskirts of Heaven, were already filling with dignitaries, as well as delegations of spiritual leaders from all over Creation. Prospective referees and umpires were in almost constant contact across every star-system, putting their finishing touches on the first-ever Official Rules and Regulations of the Heavenly Games of Love.

Not surprisingly, new transgalactic telecommunications records were hourly being set, and just as soon exceeded, as gazillions of simultaneous conversations continued to reverberate across the cosmos. Even so, it was less than a millionth of a billionth of a moment before Eve was connected to a certain hard-to-find place on a little blue-and-white planet; and to the three individuals she very much needed to talk to.

Three individuals who, in turn, also very much needed to talk to her.

❦

"So, that's the Milky Way Galaxy Committee's decision," Eve explained. "You won't be getting any help from the Galaxy itself; at least, not officially. They've chosen someone else."

There was a silence on the other end of the line, followed by two undeterred voices speaking almost on top of each other. "Then we'll just have to show up without their blessing," the World's Most Beautiful Astronomer declared, already reaching for her little book of Friends, Contacts and Fixers in Far-Off Star-systems.

"Down, we may be, but dead, we definitely ain't!" the World's Greatest Gravedigger said loudly. "Trust me, I can tell the difference."

"Lousy timing, all the same." Scheherazade shook her head. "Just when our friends from The Great Beyond beyond the Beyond are becoming really proud of Team Earth's progress."

"It's true," the World's Most Beautiful Astronomer said. "Though our gang may be nowhere near perfect in a whole lot of categories of love…."

"They're finally getting the right attitude," her broad-shouldered co-captain affirmed.

There was a silence between Heaven and Earth while Eve's three far-off associates looked at one another thoughtfully.

"Any suggestions from your end?" Eve asked finally.

The World's Greatest Gravedigger gave the answer he'd known all along. "Only one: a no-holds-barred, let 'er rip, this ain't our last-gasp meeting of Team Earth."

The World's Most Beautiful Astronomer nodded. "Whatever happens, it's ultimately up to them anyway."

The decision didn't seem to trouble Earth's new co-captains in the least: not when their confidence in a little blue-and-white world had just about been out-stripped by its own growing faith in itself.

Eve suppressed a smile. Who'd-a-thunk-it? One big old happy family at last?

"I don't suppose, by any chance," Scheherazade ventured, coming in on a sudden hunch and unspoken celestial cue, "that you might have anything else to add? Totally off the record, of course."

"On the one hand, I'm supposed to be impartial," Eve said slowly. There was a delicate pause. "On the other, if I were you, for starters, I might be tempted to see what that newly formed Whole Earth Choir Orchestra could do by way coming up with a catchy new global anthem."

"A spell-binding number in the key of white, gold, blue and courage, perhaps?" Scheherazade offered with lyrical, kinaesthetic amusement.

"Something like that. And, needless to say, in every planetary language and dialect simultaneously."

"And then...?"

"Let me get back to you."

❦

The next call was a local one. At the Archangel-in-Chief's suggestion, Eve quickly reached one of his most trusted subordinates, a deceptively-dishevelled angelic presence now hard at work in the central planning office of the Celestial Secretariat for Ceremonial Parades.

"Unusual though it may seem, what I have in mind is...," she began, before continuing to provide all the whimsical, well thought-out details of her request.

Even before she finished, the senior angel's bright golden eyes were gleaming with pleasure at this latest, greatest challenge. What his temporary employer was suggesting gave a whole new meaning to the term extra-special effects.

❦

All in all, it had been a long, long day, with even more last minute details and decisions still ahead.

As Eve's head touched the pillow, her third-to-last thought before falling asleep was the hope that, wherever God might be, the genuine, original deity was having a wonderful time. Her second-to-last thought was an even greater hope that, on God's return, Heaven and Universe might be all in one still recognizable piece. No worse, and maybe just a tiny bit better, for her own small unsteady hand at the celestial controls.

Temporary deity though she might be, she hadn't lost her human touch, or the need for one. Her last thought was, "Good night, sweet Adam, wherever you are," as she blew him a kiss across eternity.

Heart to Heart

"TIMING IS EVERYTHING."
— The Angel of Unprecedented Opportunities

"ESPECIALLY THIS TIME!"
— The Angel of Hidden Agendas

Wake-up Calls

᪥ AS TIME WOULD soon tell, it was not a good day to be bad.

It was, however, an absolutely wonderful day to be one of a large number of highly-trained Intergalactic Devils-in-Good-Standing. For Big D in particular, it promised to be the most rewarding twenty-four hours, so far, in a long and engagingly ruthless career.

At that very moment, while Eve remained fast asleep in the finest of Heaven's guest suites, dark and nasty forces were gathering together in secret sites throughout the universe.

The Unheavenly, Hard-Headed and Harder-Hearted Enemies of Love (to give them their proud, if understandably unregistered corporate title) were convinced, like so many long-vanished villains before them, that now was the time, now was the ungodly, all-destructive hour

In little more than a day, all the weeks of celestial preparation would reach their climax, and the seats of a newly constructed Heavenly Games stadium would be filling with spectators from across the universe.

Much more importantly, however (as far as countless cosmic bad guys were concerned), this very same opening day also marked that moment when the genuine, original Supreme Being *Extraordinaire* was scheduled to return from vacation; thereby putting paid to a literally Heaven-sent opportunity to mess with Creation in its Creator's absence.

It would be a shame, all agreed, to waste such a unique chance to lay waste. Not surprisingly, many of the Games' greatest enemies were professional opponents of the good, the true, the tender and the beautiful.

Some had made an impressively early start in doing to their fellow citizens what they avidly hoped none would ever dare do to them. Others (later developers) had taken up violence, malevolence and deceit to supplement unsatisfactorily shady semi-retirement plans. Some looked forward to relatively local planetary mischief. Still others rejoiced in the prospect of more substantial, constellation-sized criminality, while a smaller but far more dangerous number hoped to subvert entire galaxies.

Worse, a supremely uncaring few even aspired, one way or another, to do their damnedest to destroy the first-ever Heavenly Games themselves.

ॐ

The enormous extent of such inconsiderate behaviour did not, of course, come as a complete celestial surprise.

As the Angelic Bureau of Heavenly Strays had known too well, a universe of a hundred and one billion galaxies is capable of producing an impressive number of beings eager to commit, if not every one of the seven deadly sins, then at least quite a few of the seven hundred and seventy-seven lesser ones that make life, if often a little more interesting, also a whole lot more convoluted and problematic.

Now, as clocks throughout countless star systems counted down the hours, various extremely bad influences of every configuration chose to make their move.

At the exact same moment, on galaxies everywhere, temporarily still unseen devils of every description sprang ferociously into action; each one elated that this long-deserved day had finally come, each one proud to play a part in Big D's colossal master plan to subvert the hitherto most subversive.

Just as every darkly-intentioned individual was about to set out on whatever his or her destructive deed of the day before Opening Day might be, each felt a small but decisive tap on the shoulder. In every case, as he or she slowly turned in the first flush of guilty surprise, it was to find a devil facing them with an unreadable, quietly-terrifying smile.

The first words were always the same. "Good morning! Wonderful news! To your great good fortune, I just happen to be the devil specially assigned to your particular case."

There was always a judicious pause while an undeniably demonic smile got bigger and bigger. "Would this be a good time to have a quiet word with you?"

In almost every instance the devil's detailed arguments, being perfectly prepared, proved almost just as perfectly persuasive.

After all, it is very hard to contradict someone who knows your errors (past, present and potential); including all your excuses and evasions (not to mention also knowing all those distracting tricks of the demonic trade which you haven't even begun to think of and which, for the sake of both peace of mind and immortal soul, you would be well advised never ever to begin to try).

Across all the galaxies of Creation, the result was almost always the same. The offer made was sublimely simple, and brutally direct: "Either, learn to care for your neighbour and your neighbourhood – local and cosmic – as yourself or the devil conveniently on hand will be more than happy to provide you with however painful a demonstration as is needed to convince you of the many errors of your ways."

It was usually at this point in their unsolicited conversion programme that the devils' smiles became even more terrifying. And, for those with a keen interest in self-preservation, wholly irresistible.

For some interviewees, the demon's unexpected arrival-on-scene brought sudden yet secretly long-sought relief. Especially when it was explained that, with a change of heart and more than a little cross-training in faith, hope and charity, they too could aspire to become compassionate devils as well, covertly dedicated to the protection and promotion of the many secret pathways to Paradise! Who knows, it was suggested, given time, some might even hope to become angels (although most demons were firmly convinced that while the latter might have more perks, devils had infinitely more fun and far more flexible hours).

࿘

In the event, the great interstellar Demonic Prevention (and Irreversible Transformation) Drive proved extraordinarily successful.

Some ill-tempered individuals who had awoken that morning to glimpse in the mirror a familiar, reassuring image of malice, now gazed at their fellow citizens in new-found wonder and wide-eyed appreciation. Many more (after first bidding their former sins a fond *adieu*) transcended their previous lives completely.

Only the universe's titanium-reinforced hard cases proved resistant to their particular devil's carefully conceived repertoire of protective custody and alternative career choices. For them, extremely personal appointments had been judiciously pre-arranged with some of the most senior partners in Satan & Associates, a unique set of gentlemen for whom all the cosmic skirmishes so far had merely been welcome, if comparatively minor, warm-up exercises.

❦

In his seat at the heart of the Intergalactic Demonic Control Centre, Big D delighted in the success stories arriving moment by moment from every hitherto shadowy corner of every star system, proudly exchanging grateful congratulations with his beaming accomplices.

Most satisfyingly, all fully-accredited devils in the cosmos had out-performed even their own optimistic expectations. In less than twelve hectic hours the universe was already beginning to look a lot less spiritually unkempt.

It was a great day, everyone agreed, to be a secretly-subversive force for good. Campaign medals all round were surely in order, along with a personally-signed letter of celestial appreciation from the honorary Supreme Being herself.

It was truly amazing, Big D reflected thoughtfully, what could happen when you convinced people finally to make friends with the future, with each other … and with themselves.

Rubbing his hands, the Chairman of the Intergalactic Senior Devils' Association narrowed his gaze in anticipation of even greater pleasures to come. "And now, for my next trick," he announced, turning swiftly to his giant red-haired, red-cloaked assistant, the latter leaning contentedly on a huge pitchfork freshly forged and sharpened for the occasion.

"I need to speak to my once and future colleague, the Archangel-in-Chief. And also a certain admirably independent-minded fellow by the name of Adam. You'll find you can now get them quite easily on the hot-line. Both no doubt are already eagerly anticipating my call!"

Given that good, honest deviltry could be such fun, it wasn't surprising that even the best, sooner or later, couldn't wait to give it a try.

Go For It

&. WHEN TEAM EARTH'S co-captains broke the news that an obviously myopic Milky Way had chosen someone else as its representative, cries of disbelief and indignation followed predictably swiftly. So much training, dedication and, most of all, enthusiasm now all seemed for nothing.

Until, that is, the galactically-rejected, universally-dejected team members suddenly found themselves turning as one, staring upward to where the familiar constellation of the Big Dipper, now standing on its handle, had begun shimmering in the darkness like an unanswered question mark of stars.

Sometimes, seeking solutions, we wish upon the stars. And sometimes, though we may not yet fully understand why, they too have their own wishes for us.

And so it was (the Heavenly Games official history records) that, just moments later, Team Earth began, of its own accord, its own long overdue meeting: inspired, inspiring and (as Eve had so often hoped) irrevocably decisive.

"Ten to one, they get it right," the taller of the two skeletons observed, casually examining his newly trimmed nails.

"Billion to one," his shorter associate replied, buffing his own against his chest.

&.

"You gotta admit, the odds seem greatly against us," exclaimed one of Team Earth's superstars, a high-pitched, low-cut, award-winning songstress of hauntingly defiant love lyrics. "Most everybody else has a few hundred million years head start."

"Maybe; maybe not." The World's Most Beautiful Astronomer spoke quietly, scanning a crowd of uncertain faces, their eyes drifting again and again to the Big Dipper high above. "But for now, let's not worry about what others can bring."

"It doesn't matter how young we are," the World's Greatest Gravedigger declared, "or even how much we know we still don't know." Starlight flickered off his sterling silver blade. "What only matters is … what can our little whirling blue-and-white ball of wishful thinking – its many limitations and liabilities set firmly aside – bring to the Heavenly Games of Love? What do we have when we have no other choice?"

"And just how do we figure that out?" his consort concluded.

"If I were them," whispered a certain little yellow monkey with no small exposure to prayer, ancient or modern, unanswered or not, "this is where I'd probably start looking for a little divine guidance!"

Listening in from a seemingly-deserted beach in the most secluded corner of the universe, God quietly drew from an equally invisible pocket the universe's first golden coin (now slightly worn). A moment later, divine laughter accompanied its fall as it landed perfectly balanced on its own thin edge.

Reaching out among so many constellations, the greatest magician in the universe began turning up the lights of a still unanswered question mark of stars.

૱

Somehow, while Team Earth might not have heard Aurora's whispered suggestion, they all found themselves on their knees a moment later.

Many argue that, one way or another, the limitless mystery which we call God ultimately answers all prayers: an achievement which would seemingly leave the original owner and operator of Universe Inc. with little time for much else, given the unimaginable volume of requests.

Others, equally inspired, feel that the act of prayer itself, a humble attentive listening, provides out of itself its own sure guidance. Perhaps, all finally may agree, these are but one and the same: the divine seen from without and within.

In any event, as many have happily testified over the aeons, the response to a heartfelt request for divine direction can come in many forms, literal and metaphorical: everything from a hint to a wink to a word to a totally irresistible celestial shove.

On this so uniquely special occasion, however, it came to every member of Team Earth – still gazing up toward the starry question mark, now flashing insistently on and off high above – as a sudden, shared surge from deep within their mortal, valiant hearts.

Everybody knew all too well what Earth could do at its worst. What could it be … at its best? What did Earth always have to offer – especially when it might have nothing else to give?

For every one of a little blue-and-white world's team members, the answer was suddenly clear: an answer already taking shape millennia before the Games were only a dream.

Other planets might be wiser, richer, better connected or better dressed – or even (being in quite a few cases, so many millions of light years older) able to provide impressive combinations of all of the above. All of these were achievements to which Earth could now only aspire.

But for now they had only that mysterious, Eden-born courage which had got their planet this far; the same determined bravery that led their ancestors onward, day after daring, fearful day, century after terrifying, liberating century.

The choice was theirs – always theirs and always the same: the courage to build – and the still greater courage to rebuild. Going forward valiantly in each new day, never giving up and never giving in, until at last, on some distant morning, even Paradise itself might somewhere, somehow be found anew.

Planet Earth: battered, bruised, bloodied, maybe – but always, always unbowed, and ready for more.

As Team Earth rose to its feet, faces resolved, decision sure, the Big Dipper swiftly rearranged itself into a gigantic, jubilant exclamation mark, flashing repeatedly in approval while nearby constellations, braking in their orbits at the sight, began loudly to cheer.

In return, a single inspired cry went up from every voice, echoing across the evening air, and beyond.

Brushing a tiny tell-tale tear from her eye, the World's Most Beautiful

Astronomer took her beloved by his roughened, gentle hand, turning to face the polyglot gang they now felt even more honoured to lead.

Opportunity (however providentially) had most definitely knocked. And still continued to do so, starlight spilling down over Team Earth's upturned faces.

Carpe diem … carpe Deum …

"In that case, what if we…?"

The deceptively ethereal beauty in a sky blue dress of stars took only moments to summarize her plan, or, at least, its first near- sacrilegious steps. God helps those who help themselves. Especially to Heaven.

"Yes! Yes! Yes!"

As the coaches from The Future watched in an eloquent silence, all the members of Team Earth found themselves looking beyond the many unresolved conflicts of their own little whirling world. Even looking, in fact, far beyond tomorrow's great Games Day itself.

"Are we all agreed on what we have to do?"

The World's Most Beautiful Astronomer raised her telescope high in the air, pointing toward countless horizons forever beckoning but, until now, just as long unseen.

"Wherever that decision may take us?"

The World's Greatest Gravedigger raised his shining silver spade, brandishing it as if to bar any possibility of retreat.

"Once committed, there's no going back!"

Suddenly, coming from nowhere and yet everywhere, Eve's unseen voice filled the air around her descendants.

"Trust me; there never really was a choice of going back."

⸙

"Onwards!" The cry rose in the night sky, loud enough to rock the nearest stars.

"Forever onwards!" all the members of Team Earth repeated together triumphantly, jumping up and down with as much lack of dignity as they could possibly manage.

As their cheering died away, an inimitable voice could be heard. "Great overall strategy – as far as it goes," Eve commented quietly. "But when it comes to tactical details, I'd suggest you give me a call!"

Friendly Persuasions

❧ WHEN BIG D'S much-awaited phone call came through, Adam and the Archangel of All Archangels were separately busy at what, at this stage in the proceedings, each could do best.

Adam's hurried visits to quite a number of his cosmic peers – planetary founding fathers, like him, – had all gone well, his offer of unusual volunteer employment turning out to be absolutely the right proposal to absolutely the right gentlemen at absolutely the right time.

Presented with so unexpected an opportunity, most of his brother Adams were happy to leave their home galaxy's final preparations in their descendants' increasingly capable care. After so long, the sudden prospect of some uniquely high-level, character-building spiritual thuggery proved itself absolutely irresistible.

For those primal parents, in particular, who had felt for some time that their children's children hadn't turned out quite as well as they'd hoped, there were some long-overdue family discussions to look forward to, and even more belated great-grandfatherly advice to provide. All in their descendants' own best interest, of course.

The Archangel of All Archangels, for his part, was delighted to be a co-director of the biggest inter-service combined ops adventure in celestial history.

Ever since Big D's first phone call, the chief Archangel's most trusted, versatile staff had been painstakingly compiling a vast Guide to Major

Spiritual Offenders and Ultimate Enemies of Love, its encrypted pages containing the names and unflattering mug-shots of every truly big-time crook in Creation. Beside each metaphysical con artist appeared a full report of his or her prior crimes, including most significant sins of both omission and commission. To the devils' delight, equally detailed notes outlined each individual's most totally enticing temptation.

The Archangel of All Archangels surveyed his crowded temporary headquarters, quietly enjoying the prospect that millions of years of good, if unrewarded intentions were now about to be replaced by considerably less benign but far more persuasive activity.

"I think it's time to make each of them the one and only offer they can't possibly refuse!"

❧

Abracadabra, wise and ancient wizard though he might be, wasn't feeling quite himself. From long experience, he guessed it was likely a mild recurrence of that malady common to all great seers; namely, that while still feeling reasonably saintly, he was also more than a little bored. Then again, perhaps it was simply fatigue. After all (as his recent bar bills would readily confirm), he'd certainly been doing his particular bit behind the scenes.

The old sorcerer yawned. In a few hours, more or less, he would himself set off to join a number of his associates, together savouring all the excitement of opening day ceremonies from the well-deserved luxury of their reserved box, exotic juice bar and all. There was, at least, no small consolation in that.

All the same, he sighed, it was rather sad about Earth. He could well understand that the Milky Way Galaxy might feel safer with a more conventional, less impulsive planet representing it. And yet....

Abracadabra shook his head. Rational explanations notwithstanding, something still didn't feel quite right. He could have sworn that, one way or another, a little blue-and-white planet, its perennial recalcitrance and self-doubt notwithstanding, was somehow going to find its way to the Games.

In fact, the old wizard mused, he would have bet his second best magic wand on it. Maybe even his first, if the occult airwaves hadn't already been so infuriatingly crowded with top-secret transmissions.

A deep 'harrumph' seemed the only proper response. In the old days, Abracadabra muttered in exasperation, the universe, while admittedly far less interesting, had never been quite so damn noisy.

✌

"Good evening, gentlemen. Or, better yet, a great one!"

Big D's most trusted and ferocious devils stood relaxed and waiting, chatting casually with their underworldly counterparts from other star systems. "Everything ready?"

"You betcha!" Adam replied, delighted by the reinforcements from the Honourable and Ancient Intergalactic Founding Fathers' Association whom he'd managed to round up on exceedingly short notice.

"Need you ask?" the Archangel of All Archangels added more than a little curtly, as might be expected from one alpha celestial male to another. His staff, it went without saying, were invincible. Not to mention impeccably well-behaved. At least, that is, until now.

Big D laughed. "Save your strength – you're going to need it. It promises to be an extremely long night."

All three redoubtable gentlemen synchronized their watches, each displaying not only historical, current, prospective and eternal time simultaneously, together with all their points of ceaseless interaction, but also a compass featuring all the magnetic interconnections of intergalactic good and evil.

"The invitations to what we have so enticingly, if euphemistically called The Party To End All Parties have all gone out as planned. All our esteemed guests should be arriving at the newly finished Cosmic Rehab and Recreation Centre around 9:00 p.m. A near infinity of tempting ways in – and absolutely no way out!"

The other two could hear the fiery determination in their colleague's voice. After millions of years of putting up with the universe's worst, this was a moment when revenge was a dish best served with a triple helping of salsa.

"Dress lightly," he went on. "The evening promises to be hot!"

"Can't wait." Mild-mannered and kindly-disposed though Adam might often appear, he and his long-suffering cousins had quite a few ancient, even primordial scores to settle.

"See you there," the chief Archangel said, before adding slyly, "I trust you remembered to order enough pitchforks for my mob of high flyers. Along with the appropriate instruction manuals, of course."

"Glad to see you haven't lost your celebrated sense of humour," Big D laughed, delighted at the renewed pleasure of a little long-lost, celestial give-and-take between equals.

"A joy to work with you again, too," the Archangel of All Archangels replied, meaning it sincerely.

"Aeons overdue," his old associate agreed.

Big D's tone changed. "If I'm five minutes late, start without me." His voice lightened as he made no attempt to hide an almost boyish, anticipatory look. "Chances are, I may have to make a brief stop along the way."

Better able than most at reading between unseen lines (especially familial), the Archangel-in-Chief immediately had an image of a certain enchanting and (luckily for her, in this case) enchantingly independent woman; a gracious and gutsy lady exceedingly well-thought of by his currently absentee Boss.

He chuckled despite himself. "Some things never change!"

"Don't be too sure," his demonic counterpart confided softly. "This one's a keeper."

The Archangel-in-Chief chose to misinterpret. "Always felt you needed one."

Big D grinned. Much as he cared for his sometimes cantankerous celestial colleague, Heaven obviously still wasn't big enough for both of them. At least, not at the same time.

What a wise move it had been to leave home early!

Adam, listening to the exchange, couldn't help smiling. When it came to getting the really difficult job done, whom you worked with made all the difference.

"Hi ho, hi ho," he began to sing under his breath, "it's off to Hell we go!"

❧

Abracadabra was about to make himself a fresh pot of elixir and while away the remaining hours with divinatory solitaire, when his latest and, as far as he knew, completely unlisted cell phone rang decisively.

"Care to help a damsel in distress?" Eve asked rhetorically. "Care to save a universe from itself?"

Reaching instinctively for his magic wand, Abracadabra glimpsed a now youthfully ancient face in the mirror. "Surely it's a fine and lovely day to do great and daring deeds," Eve exclaimed.

"Must be my destiny," the distinguished old wizard agreed. While it can be a pleasure to foresee the future, it's far more fun to be part of it.

"How many people can you fit on your little white cloud?"

Abracadabra's answer was instantaneous. "Ninety to a hundred, more or less – depending on weight and size – plus one carry-on bag each."

There was a silence at the other end of the Heavenly line while Eve performed some quick calculations. "How soon can you round up a hundred more?" she asked after a moment. "Plus another ten medium-size cargo clouds to carry uniforms, equipment and the band instruments."

"Would an hour and a half be too soon?" Abracadabra inquired.

Whatever the need for this rather specialized form of transportation, he could think of more than enough magical old friends and white-cloud jockeys who would be elated at the prospect of unexpected adventure.

"Ninety minutes would be perfect."

Discretion and curiosity struggled for supremacy. "I don't suppose, by any chance, you might just happen to have a flight plan already in mind?"

"What would you say if I told you your first stop was a certain secret site on a little planet called Earth?"

Abracadabra began to laugh as well, a prophetic blend of relief and even greater anticipation.

"I'd say that I was right all along!"

Details, Details

❧ DESPITE HEAVEN'S increasing demands, Eve's promised return call to the World's Most Beautiful Astronomer and its Greatest Gravedigger was only slightly delayed. In the meantime, Team Earth was doing its best to await further divine guidance with newfound calm and grace.

"My apologies for keeping you in suspense," Eve began, "but Heaven is unbelievably preoccupied right now: every angel all in a whirl, every one of them with equally-urgent things to do before morning."

"It all must be impossibly exciting," the World's Most Beautiful Astronomer said longingly.

In the background, Eve could hear Team Earth crowding round, trying hard not to appear to be listening in. "It is," she confirmed, suddenly feeling very small, and suddenly very human. "It truly, truly is."

There was a long silence as Eve pictured her distant descendants now imagining Heaven's non-stop whirl. "And what's even better, in a very few hours, you'll all be able to enjoy it for yourselves!"

Eve rose, turning toward the nearby window opening on the vast, now-empty stadium, seeing in her mind's eye an entire universe already on the move, readying itself for a day like none other.

"I have just made some rather extraordinary travel arrangements," she continued. "To be sure, an unconventional means of transportation. Scary at first, but exceptionally swift, energy-efficient and environmentally friendly."

Reaching for the little gold encryption device which God had so considerately left behind, Eve switched it on so that only she and Earth's two co-captains could hear. "The chief pilots for what might best be called Wizard Airways will be there shortly, so you'd all better be packed and ready." Eve took a deep breath; then, contemplating the audacity of her plan, took a deeper one still.

"Now," she began, her ancient voice surprisingly clear and unwavering, "if you're willing to follow the suggestions of someone who only looks like a harmless little old lady much of the time, here's what I have in mind…."

ﻬ

One of the more convenient benefits of being omnipotent, God was happy to say, was that, if by seeming chance a certain magic celestial coder/decoder device just happened to have been left behind at the office, there were fortunately still many other divinely undisclosed ways to overhear anything and everything in the universe, anywhere and everywhere.

Now, listening in as Eve completed her instructions to Team Earth, the genuine original Supreme Being couldn't keep from laughing. Conscientious and determined as God's well-chosen substitute might be, it was heartening to reconfirm that she also retained a uniquely dramatic flair for the unexpected.

ﻬ

Just as Scheherazade was preparing to depart for Heaven on an already-eager SS Serendipity, the fabled director of the Wondrous Winding Gardens of Desire detached herself from the rest of the team's coaches, a satisfied smile in her deep violet eyes.

"It seems your none-too-secret subterranean admirer is resurfacing on my private line," Valentina announced, offering up the very latest in small, heart-shaped electronic devices (ruby ring tones optional). She waited a moment. "Sort of lends a whole new meaning to the phrase 'designer cell phone', yes?"

"Busy times!" Big D began.

"Very," Scheherazade answered, blushing slightly despite herself at the sound of his voice, and yet still able in her reply to convey multitudes of meanings simultaneously in one brief two-syllable word.

"When do you expect to arrive in Heaven?" Big D asked. Given the circumstances, and the lady in question, there was really no time to waste. "As fate would have it, I have to work late tonight," he went on. "But I was wondering whether an early supper...."

"A little something to see you through the midnight shift, as it were?"

His answer, coming as it did from the most discerning and prophetic devil in the entire universe, was not unexpected. "Actually, I've been preparing for this particular evening for a long, long time."

"I know," Scheherazade said softly, because she did; somehow easily hearing both his revealed yet hidden meanings at one and the same time. Suddenly, she, too, couldn't wait.

"Would seven p.m. be too early?"

It definitely wouldn't be too soon for Big D either.

"There used to be a quiet, unpretentious little three star diner just on the western outskirts of Heaven."

"*Le Promis de Paradis.*" No need now to ask whom he'd taken there before, grateful though Scheherazade was to all those who'd helped make him finally ready for her. "It's still there. Passed it once or twice on the way."

Big D, in turn, wasn't about to wonder aloud about all the penultimate tables-for-two in her own unmistakably-eventful past.

"*À ce soir,*" he said gallantly.

In Excelsis, Hectic

ᴥ THE FLEETING HOURS of the final afternoon before opening day proved everywhere as busy as expected.

In Heaven, Eve held last minute meetings with everyone from the senior members of the Celestial Officiating Committee to the beatifically unruffled angelic directors in charge of hospitality, logistics and media relations; not to mention quick, reassuring discussions with those staunch advisors, the Angel of Divine Back-Up, the Angel of Truly Infinite Resources, and the Angel of Uncanny Encouragement; and, last but not least, the immensely calm Emergency Services Angel, who reported that everything unplanned that might possibly occur had already been successfully anticipated and prepared for.

She also had an exceptionally quiet word with the deputy head of the Celestial Secretariat for Ceremonial Parades. Everything she had suggested, he whispered, his tones blending deference with delighted conspiracy, was now nearing completion.

Expressing her thanks, Eve added, "Don't be too surprised, however, if I may have a few last minute requests."

The deputy head of Processions, Capers and Carnivals simply nodded. When one worked for God, contingency planning was second nature.

ᴥ

In guest rooms throughout the Games complex, representatives from all the galaxies were busily putting the finishing touches on their uniforms, expressions and professional skills. Team after team after team practised their respective native walk, waddle or waltz in preparation for tomorrow's great winding entry into the glorious Heavenly Stadium.

Every team, understandably, tried to get in at least a little advance practice in their own particular area of expertise in the many fields of love. Almost all, equally understandably, found themselves both too thoroughly giddy and too nervous to remember exactly what it was that they were undoubtedly very good at.

A whole lot of first-time visitors from a whole lot of star systems found themselves taking a whole lot of very deep breaths. Dignitaries from hundreds of galaxies mixed and mingled, glad to meet one another for the first time. Business cards of every colour and kind were enthusiastically exchanged, mutual advantages begun to be calculated, and mutual opportunities anticipated.

Seers, saints and sages from all religious and spiritual traditions throughout the entire universe gazed thoughtfully and, for the most part, benevolently on one another. Everyone had come, they all concurred, to look, listen and, who knows, maybe even learn. After all, they agreed, wasn't it axiomatic that everything and everyone was everywhere ultimately united in cosmic love?

Whatever the similarity of their differences, all these worthy folk were especially looking forward to what promised to be the professional highlight of the Games: an exclusive spiritual meet 'n' greet party hosted by the genuine, original Supreme Being shortly after that exalted mystery's return from vacation.

Behind the scenes, practising his swing in an understandably well-soundproofed room, the Angel of the Golden Hammer and Gong readied himself, again and again and again, in his own inimitable way.

Meanwhile, throughout the cosmos, every individual, old or young, prepared to celebrate this very first shared trans-celestial holiday by getting up early. If, that is, they somehow managed to get to sleep at all.

❧

Under the watchful eye of the Archangel of All Archangels, the joint task force of angels and devils was together putting their finishing touches on all the torments and ultimate transfigurations that awaited the arrival of the unsuspecting baddest of the universe's really, really bad.

Adam shook his head in admiration. The prodigious construction efforts of the past few days had clearly paid off, this fully-equipped, totally modernized version of Hell being even more terrifying than the original. Now it was simply a matter of waiting for their guests, the better to reaffirm the truth of that old demonic saying, Hope springs infernal!

A moment later, Big D's giant red-haired assistant handed Earth's founding father his own newly-upgraded phone linking Heaven and Hell. ("Apps like you wouldn't believe!" the joint engineering task force brochure rightly proclaimed.)

"Just wanted to wish you good luck." Eve's concern was not entirely hidden in her voice. "I'll be thinking of you."

"And I even more of you," Adam answered swiftly, unsurprised by the thoughtfulness of her call in the midst of her own so-much-greater preparations.

There was a long, universe-size silence.

"Everything proceeding on schedule?" Adam asked, lowering his voice.

"More or less…."

"Wish I were there to help," he said tenderly, knowing all the while that his true work, right now, was right here.

"My hero."

"As always," Adam agreed.

"As ordained," Eve responded, before bursting out laughing.

"See you in the morning."

"Can't wait!"

À La Carte

❧ SHE WORE A DECEPTIVELY simple little black number with pearls and three strategic drops of a new perfume. He was elegantly dressed, as ever, for anything and everything. *Le Promis de Paradis* was empty but for the two of them. Together, Scheherazade and Big D savoured their first sip of a shared half-bottle of *Fleurs de Demain*, watching quietly as fleets of last minute arrivals streamed by in the distance, en route to Heaven and a brief rest before tomorrow's momentous beginning.

For each, just the right amount of unfinished business still remained.

"To you," Big D said suddenly, raising his glass, dark eyes a deeper blue than ever before, his voice rough with unconcealed tenderness. "You've certainly helped to stir things up around here." He gestured thoughtfully towards Heaven's far-off towers, their blazing lights a reassuringly visible sign of unseen angels working later and harder than ever.

Scheherazade dipped her head in appreciation, grateful for the unexpected accolade, though not really surprised at either its source or its warmth.

As she contemplated her companion's unwavering gaze, it now seemed such a long, long time ago that a certain little white-and-gold bird had flown through her window one bright spring morning, bringing with it the gift of a challenge she was temperamentally unable to refuse.

Ah, well … the universe did not lie. Explorations and adventures she had been promised, and explorations and adventures she had had. Perhaps not quite on Eve's exalted scale, of course; but, all the same, not bad for an equally-dedicated, if somewhat less notorious cosmic heroine.

"From what I hear, you haven't been all that shy and retiring yourself," she said. "Nor any of your dependably unruly personal staff, or their equally-rebellious interstellar associates too, for that matter...."

"It's a grand and glorious day indeed to be a fully-licensed devil-at-large," Big D agreed. He glanced at his discreetly-designed multifunction watch. "Or night, I should say."

"Of all the charming, many-talented gentlemen over time it has been my pleasure and continuing edification to meet," Scheherazade began, "you are, by far, the one best able to look after himself. All the same...." She reached out, softly placing her hand over his. "Please look after yourself. This evening in particular."

Big D's hand came down just as gently on hers, his eyes flickering moment by moment between ever-fonder appreciation and ever-greater demonic anticipation.

"If my adversaries only knew what – or rather, who – awaits me after my soon-to-be-conclusive encounter with them," he declared, "I suspect they'd all surrender immediately, if not sooner!"

"For a devil, you say the sweetest things," Scheherazade replied. She smiled from beneath artfully lowered lids.

"Especially when true," Big D agreed.

She looked up, eye to increasingly-appreciative eye. "Rather flattering (at my age) to find myself part of, how shall I say, so mutually satisfying a cosmic renewal programme."

"No question, maturity brings its own rewards," Big D acknowledged. He leaned over to kiss her cheek.

"Seems to," Scheherazade agreed, turning her head so that their lips met. "Definitely seems to."

For two temperamentally-independent individuals from opposite ends of Creation, they found themselves surprisingly comfortable. If she knew the universe's ins and outs, he was just as wise to its ups and downs.

Their brief hour together had passed all too quickly, shy personal confidences interwoven with inevitable, more professional speculation on the chances of a number of impressive galaxies. Whatever the outcome of the Games, both agreed, there had never been so much interstellar aspiration, dedication and outright idealism assembled in one place in so short a time.

"Tomorrow's really only a beginning, of course." Big D glanced speculatively towards Heaven, distant and beguiling as ever. "Even so, I can't help wondering what the universe is going to look like in the days and weeks after the Games are over."

"Let alone a thousand years from now," Scheherazade mused.

"Or even a million...." Gazing out over vast stretches of increasingly-excited, sleepless stars, Big D began to laugh.

"What's so amusing?"

"Eve, of course! Adam's always been a great go-getter and a perfect gentleman." Big D paused, clearly savouring deeply private memories. "But from the moment I first laid eyes on her, so radiant and poised, glistening in the very first light of that very first dawn ... somehow I always knew she had true potential."

"Obviously, in retrospect, so did she!" Scheherazade looked slightly enigmatic, even conspiratorial.

ৡ

A quick coffee completed their meal.

"On the house!" the *maître d'* bowed, declining Big D's request for the bill. "Very nice to see you again, Sir, after so long." He shook Scheherazade's hand eloquently and approvingly.

ৡ

"So, I'll see you in the morning", they both said at the same time, each just as reluctantly. Scheherazade reached up, instinctively putting her arms around him.

"Be careful," she whispered.

"Be carefree," Big D whispered in return, inhaling her scent. Lips against her neck, he added softly, "Your perfume is ravishing – and somehow strangely familiar."

"I thought you might like it. A recent choice," she laughed. "A new private custom blend called ... Gotcha!"

"Why am I not surprised!"

As she drew from her purse the small glittering heart-shaped fuchsia-red bottle, he reached out, turned it over to reveal a bright but tiny label on the reverse.

Under their gaze, the fine print suddenly got a whole lot finer.

"An exceptionally-limited edition of an intriguingly-rare and exotic fragrance, exclusively and compellingly prepared from imported floral essences in our own secret in-house laboratories. All galactic rights reserved. Silver-Tongued Devils Ltd., a division of Big D Enterprises, Inc."

Scheherazade beamed. "You never miss a trick, do you!"

"Neither do you," said Big D, as he took another deep, satisfyingly-dizzying breath. "Neither, thankfully, do you."

Hot Times

"À VOTRE SAUTÉ!"

— one of Big D's favourite toasts

Bienvenue!

꙳ GIVEN THEIR LONG contrarian careers, it was not surprising the distinguished members of the Intergalactic Senior Devils' Association should be proud masters of those underappreciated virtues of illusion, delusion and discombobulating confusion. Nor was it surprising, given recent events, that such talents should have found their finest expression to date in the unanimous decision to design, build and diabolically furnish what was to be the first ever Interstellar Temple of Totally Irresistible Temptations. Entry by personal invite only.

After all, they agreed, surely it was only a matter of simple satanic courtesy (suitably in keeping with the egalitarian spirit of the up-coming Games) to provide a little timely entertainment for those many cosmic ne'er-do-goods more inclined to somewhat less-exalted enthusiasms.

When it really counts, devils have a special soft spot for the truly hard core.

꙳

As so often in its history, the Association's celebrated Demonic Apparitions division not only met but more than exceeded expectations. Its round-the-clock construction work on the gigantic special-purpose complex was completed not only under budget but also well ahead of schedule. As a result, excited devils from all manner of colourful galaxies chose to check in early, the better to begin their own advance preparations. More importantly, it gave them all a chance to re-read the case histories of the many illustrious cosmic villains soon to arrive to claim what promised (according to their invitations) to be their very own well-deserved and long-overdue rewards.

Even as the devils compared notes, the worst of the universal worst, the *crème de la crème* of cosmic sour cream, were already en route, more than ready to enjoy what was the one opportunity they couldn't possibly refuse.

Ready, in short, for what was advertised, correctly if not completely, as the universe's first-ever, highly-exclusive, all-inclusive Cosmic Bad Guys' Come-As-You-Are, Opening Night Surprise, Surprise, Surprise (!) Party. All expenses paid. ("We just never told you by whom....")

ƺ

A few of the younger devils were beginning to consult their watches when, precisely on time, Big D arrived in an elegantly-tailored dinner jacket, red rose in his lapel and an understated flourish of sparks and crimson smoke.

At his appearance, Adam and the Archangel-in-Chief detached themselves from an informative conversation with a cluster of nine-headed demons (the latter being specially assigned to galaxies whose worst citizens possessed a similarly disconcerting number of inventively ill-intentioned noggins).

"Having a good evening so far?" the Archangel of All Archangels inquired smoothly.

Like many separated twins, the two oldest angels in the universe enjoyed reading each other's minds. Given their respective professional responsibilities, however, both were inclined to be exceedingly careful about revealing just how much each really knew about the other.

"Almost beyond expectations, but fortunately, not quite!" Big D replied, the words underscored by the slightest hint of lipstick on his collar. "Very thoughtful of you to ask," he acknowledged graciously.

Glancing around, his eyes glowed with a dark radiance that promised well for his many friends, less so for anyone who might seek to spoil his evidently-superlative mood. After all, how long ago had he secretly begun dreaming of the possibility (even perhaps, the ultimate inevitability) of this evening's so improbable entertainment?

Ever the good host, he turned back to Adam, the latter raptly gazing around the vast hall, entranced at the seemingly-endless variety of multi-coloured, multi-form devils the cosmos appeared so effortlessly able to conjure up.

"Finding whatever you need; everyone being helpful?" asked Big D.

After so many bad centuries and worse people, everything finally appeared to be working out just as he and Eve had often hoped, albeit not in this spectacularly-unexpected way.

In the past twenty-four hours he had met more charming, thoughtful, multi-talented demons than he would earlier have believed existed. He had also had time to catch up with at least some of the representative brother Adams from star systems near and far; all of them arriving for the same great purpose: namely, the universe's first-ever unrestrained, unrestricted and undeniably long-overdue Cosmic Criminals Comprehensive Clean-Up Campaign.

Otherwise known as Project Total Redemption.

The evening's three heroes – the senior devil *extraordinaire*, the knight grand commander of the ancient, exalted order of archangels and, last but in no way least, the debonair man-about-Earth and beyond – stood together a little longer in amiable, anticipatory silence, surveying the vast intermingling crowds of demons and planetary founders now turning toward the stage as they sensed their moment had finally come.

Big D reached out, shook hands with his two co-conspirators in this evening's work of super-heated, super-charged salvation. "Good luck!"

"And good hunting!" the Archangel-in-Chief added in a voice of tungsten-hardened steel. Even though Heaven might be home, the past ten billion years (give or take) hadn't been all rhapsody and rosebuds. Tonight, of all nights, promised to make up for some very disappointing millennia and equally dispiriting people.

Big D strode to the giant red podium, ringed by some of the oldest, earliest of Adams and by the most eminent senior devils in the universe, the latter resplendent in their distinctive crimson tunics, complete with glowing gold badges of high office. As one, the assembled company together twirled their gleaming, freshly-sharpened silver pitchforks with fearsomely-nonchalant expertise.

"I'm a man of few words, when I want to be." Big D spread his arms in greeting. "So, I would like simply to thank you all, most profoundly, for your countless unselfish contributions to the cosmos over so many aeons. And, just as importantly, to welcome every one of you to what promises to be a memorably-warm evening. Enjoy yourselves!"

He turned, bowing magisterially to the encircling crowd. "And now," Big D snapped his fingers with a magnesium flash, "let the Flames begin!"

Turning Up the Heat

੬ AS PLANNED, the great assembly of impatient Adams and devils made a tactical, if only temporary, disappearance.

Below, deep in the ultra-modern engineering control room of the Interstellar Temple of Totally Irresistible Temptations, some of the burliest members of the Demonic Firemen's Union reached out to push their ceremonial startup buttons, firing up the latest in high speed, high-intensity blast furnaces and sending the temperatures in the carefully designed 'guest' rooms steadily rising.

While the old-style towering bonfires and giant hellacious bellows still worked just fine, this latest technology was a more fuel efficient, environmentally-friendly refinement of the time tested fire-breathing tradition. Indeed, as aeons of happily-successful underground experience would confirm, whenever one needed to bring a recalcitrant evil-doer to just the right degree of fast-purifying torment, the ancient yet simple means of heat and humidity were always and forever the best.

Give the devils their due: whatever their reputation (usually sadly misunderstood and woefully undeserved) they definitely knew their job. Especially when it was, at long last, the absolutely perfect time to set about recycling a host of the most discordantly-unrepentant sinners.

੬

One by one, the most self-serving monsters of the universe arrived at the temple's neon-lit entrance. One by one, each had the same fleeting illusory pleasure of being met by what seemed, miraculously, the perfect embodiment of their perennial favourite among all the sins it was possible to commit.

Judging by their high spirits, every one of them was sure tonight promised to be utterly unforgettable – a conclusion with which the increasingly impatient members of what Big D liked to call his official demonic deception-reception committee could only agree.

Thanks to brilliant advance planning, it didn't take long before millions of cosmic miscreants were successfully introduced to the first in a series of perfectly-orchestrated stages of their irrevocable transformation.

For each of the so-called guests, the doorway to unparalleled delights opened for just long enough to allow entrance to a suddenly darkening, disorienting passageway known, all too correctly, as the Well-Calculated, Increasingly-Uncozy Corridor of No Return.

Its fast-moving floor carried them directly into the Great Hall of Unavoidable Confrontations – a vast chamber decorated with suitably sombre portraits of celebrated villains of cosmic history, together with the exact date and location of their enforced removal from office, and a flattering photograph of the specific demon responsible for their deserved and timely fate.

As the visitors' eyes travelled along the huge gallery of earlier satanic victories, they eventually came to rest on Big D. He was leaning nonchalantly against a modest dais at the far end, elegantly unperturbed in the face of so much evil.

Since many of the involuntary arrivals liked to think of themselves as fairly fearsome beings (despite a complete lack of basic demonic professionalism) there was a good deal of swearing and swaggering, stamping of feet and pawing of suddenly shaky ground, along with competitive demonstrations of outraged bluster.

"This ain't what we wuz all promised!" "Where's all them delightfully nasty rewards of crime outlined in the brochure?!" "We bin robbed!"

"And while we're at it, who the hell are you?" one of the largest, loudest intergalactic bad guys yelled out to their eminently laid-back host, all the while trying to decide whether to advance on him as menacingly as possible. Given providentially good eyesight and an even better sense of self-preservation, he decided not to.

"Excellent question," Big D replied, gently smoothing the lapels of his dinner jacket and adjusting his *boutonnière*. "Thank you for asking."

His expression changed, becoming one of unrelenting, bleak ferocity (a seldom used response; one which, in private moments, he liked to call "my very own, sure-fire stare-way to Heaven!").

"My name varies widely, depending, of course, on language, degree of guilt and galactic location. Loosely translated, however, its real meaning remains everywhere the same: in short, the secret face in the secret mirror; otherwise and more accurately known as The Devil You Want Never To Meet, But Know That One Day You Must!"

He gestured around the Great Hall, now empty of the many chimerical temptations that were earlier on such tantalizing display. "My apologies for so convincing an illusion, of course. But we had to get you here, one way or another."

There was a well timed, instructive pause.

"For your own sakes, let alone for the continued well-being of the universe."

As a renewed wave of malevolent grumbling swept the room, Big D spread his hands in the scariest of benedictions.

"Welcome back, one and all, to the nursery school you so obviously missed. Come morning, however, I can guarantee that every one of you will have become a successful (if initially reluctant) beneficiary of the universe's first ever all-night, all-galactic, co-op retraining programme!"

Big D's eyes grew more fierce and determined than even his oldest demonic companions could remember.

"And I can also promise one more thing," he added cryptically. "When we're finished with you – or, more accurately, by the time you've finished with yourselves – nothing will ever look the same again!"

An instant later, briefly hidden by an enormous cloud of suitably-sulphurous crimson smoke, Big D exploded upward, a thousand times greater in size. Flames danced merrily in his huge but narrowed eyes, lightning bolts hundreds of metres long shot from his hands to crackle and sizzle in the air above his terrified audience. There was no question but that a certain persuasive flamboyance could still be most helpful in his line of work.

Simultaneously, as hundreds of thousands of unseen doors suddenly opened with a crash on every side, well-prepared devils from galaxies throughout the universe, materializing as if by magic, began to advance confidently towards their individually pre-assigned prey.

"For personal redemption and public restitution," Big D inquired ominously, "who wants to lead the way? Who among you just can't wait to enjoy the many restorative features of the very latest in fashionable demonic detox; courtesy of our very own custom-designed hot-as-you-can-stand-and-then-some Satanic Spa and Spiritual Sauna Complex?"

Turning to his assembled forces of satanic reconstruction and renovation, the Intergalactic Senior Devils' Association head honcho offered a near-imperceptible nod in Heaven's direction.

"It's ... show-time!"

Under the circumstances (as his once and future Boss had already discovered) the phrase was one eminently hard to resist. Then again, Big D acknowledged, a certain fondness for melodrama seemed a pardonable family trait.

&

At the signal, countless demons of every size, shape and local expertise began to rush their selected charges toward pre-arranged changing rooms, all easily identifiable by glow-in-the-dark signage showing the specific galaxy, constellation and home planet.

Like central hubs with radiating spokes, these in turn each opened onto a custom-built, custom-purpose steamroom, outfitted with deceptively fragrant cedar benches, each with corner units of hi-tech heated stones, and each with temperatures inexorably rising.

"I think you'll find them an improvement on our earlier, more rudimentary models of Hell; less crowded, more stylish and hygienic, not nearly as noisy or noxious, and certainly way more personal," Big D explained helpfully. "Then again, the standard operating procedure remains much the same...."

As the universe's meanest and nastiest were moved towards their hot and humid fates, a cheery demonic chorus echoed inauspiciously in their ears.

"More heat than you can possibly withstand, and just the right amount you need!"

Make 'Em Sweat!

🔥 IT'S RARELY VERY appealing, if you've been really, really bad, to have your darkest secrets exposed.

It was not surprising, therefore, that so many involuntary overnight guests of the Satanic Spa and Spiritual Sauna Complex should find themselves less than happy at the prospect of being (but for the skimpiest of towels) completely and utterly naked. At first literally, and then, as time passed and temperatures rose, more and more figuratively as well.

As the cosmic criminals each sat in their individual steamrooms, the first drops of perspiration appearing on reddening skin, their strangely familiar and irritatingly imperturbable devil sat opposite them: cool as an arctic snowball and reaching out occasionally to add just the right amount of water to the nearby sizzling stones, contentedly increasing the heat that seemed to bother him not a bit.

The steady silence, whether tactful or tactical, was itself also distinctly unsettling.

"What happens next?" asked more than one anxious offender, usually sooner than later.

In every case, the answer was always the same. "Are you completely sure you want to know?"

It wasn't the first time in the history of the universe when an uneasy soul with a history to hide began to wonder whether devils might be most dangerous when seemingly most diplomatic.

🔥

Adam, on the other hand, like so many other founding fathers gathered together for this special occasion, was having one of the most rewarding nights of his long life, happily stalking the humid corridors, personal planetary checklist in hand.

All the past weeks of highly complex planning were now about to pay off. All those karmic career criminals whose names appeared on demonic lists marked Baddest of the Local Bad – lovingly prepared in concert with an equally long-frustrated Celestial Intelligence Agency – were now fated to receive a profoundly disconcerting uber-parental visit.

Allowing for some understandable regional variations, the individual approach was usually much the same.

The sauna door would open with a bang to reveal the evil-doer's specific planetary Adam, standing before him stern-faced and silent. After a long, dramatically-extended pause during which the surrounding heat seemed to increase by hundreds of ever-more-painful degrees, the sweating culprit would inevitably flinch back as his own earliest and greatest of grandfathers pointed a solemn accusatory finger.

"You," his most ancient of ancestors would invariably begin, in keeping with the pre-agreed script, "are such a complete and utter disappointment to your great-great-granny and me!"

At this point, the local Adam (depending on which mode of remonstrance would seem regionally most effective) would choose to reason, rant or roar.

In every case, the diatribe was the same. "Do you think Eve and I left a perfectly good garden (at no little cost or inconvenience) the better to found an entire world … just so that you could set about abusing it for your own disgracefully selfish ends. Trust me; you have a whole lot of explaining to do!"

No matter planet of origin, every Adam delivered this long-overdue line with aeons of pent-up frustration, and a barely-suppressed hint of primal rage.

It's one thing to lose a paradise. It's another to trip over someone still blocking your way when you're getting closer to finding it again.

"Do you have any idea," the script continued, "just how much pain and suffering you've caused across the years? Just how many hard-won planetary resources you've stolen, wasted or otherwise diverted from the common good?"

Then, most Adams generally found it opportune to step forward, seize their wilting and horrified descendants by the throat, and shake them mercilessly to and fro.

This personally satisfying, if politically incorrect, technique almost always seemed to impress. And, in more than a few cases, led almost instantly to that ultimate inner surrender which was all along the secret purpose of the devils' highly organized, if unorthodox, spiritual re-awakening programme .

In the event, however, that these kind words of primal guidance failed to bring about an immediate change in closed and darkened hearts, the Adams of the universe just as decisively moved on to the next deeply-disappointing descendant, abandoning the unrepentant culprit to the tender, implacable mercies of his or her very own personal devil.

In doing so, they were confident the bad would be in good hands. If, as widely reported, 'it takes one to know one', then its inevitable corollary was even more appropriate now. After all, who better than a true demonic professional to show the merely amateur desperado the many inescapable errors of his ways?

As one of their more celebrated cosmic bumper stickers puts it so matter-of-factly: 'Devils are totally hot!'

Far underground, senior engineers of the Demonic Firemen's Union continued to monitor their complex controls, delicately adjusting all the different degrees of heat in the individual steamrooms high above. It was a matter of professional pride to get the 'slow roast' temperature just right. After all, the aim was to soften resistance, not to broil.

Where warranted, special hallucinatory oils long helpful in ethical awakening were imperceptibly added to the mix together with, if only for old time's sake, the faintest hint of sulphur.

Overhead, in the Satanic Spa and Spiritual Sauna Complex's many hot and hazy interrogation rooms, the same sure-fire scene was repeated again and again.

Each carefully-chosen devil sat directly opposite his designated guest in silence, dauntingly patient and serene, rising only as the spirit moved to add a little more water to the blazing stones, sending up fresh bursts of steam. As the heat grew, the air began to shimmer and the room itself to pulse with an unsettling staccato rhythm of its own. At the right temperature and moment, everything most improbably but irreversibly changed.

As the (until now) only strangely familiar demonic figure opposite gently smiled, his features began simultaneously to blur, to dissolve and then, at last, to reform: revealing a ferociously guarded face which returned his unnerved guest's stare with an expression at once threatening and wary; an expression, moreover, both deeply unfamiliar and yet, at the same time, all too impossibly and alarmingly wellknown.

It was as if the cosmic criminals suddenly found themselves confronting, for the very first time, the face with which they for so long and so darkly challenged the world; an inescapable personification of all the hurt and suffering inflicted on others, and all the unacknowledged damage done also, inescapably, to themselves. It was, in every case, not a pretty sight.

Taking his cue from that first, undeniable shock of self-recognition, the presiding devil (cool as a sadly-absent breeze) immediately began turning up the heat. Instantly, the chosen culprit in his care began to sweat, then sweat some more: not only physically but also emotionally, mentally, financially and, sooner or later, spiritually as well.

In every case, the unrelentingly but unseen flames (together with fast-acting vapours) helped to release long-unacknowledged responsibilities for all manner of past sins. Whatever the scale and scope of the crimes, all was included and all was revealed.

Where a little prompting was required, the demon opposite casually recited from irritatingly perfect memory each and every sin of which his particular assignee was guilty; his face, all the while, reflecting back every ineffective effort to conceal, deny or run like hell.

No matter how much the hapless guest tried to dodge, it was to find his very own demon blocking him at every turn. For, as every well-trained, self-respecting devil knows, it is hard to escape from your own conscience, once awakened, for very long. This was so especially when it just happens to be sitting only a few steps away, in living colour and in at least three, if not more, fully informed, genially accusatory dimensions, and quite literally staring you in the face, contentedly waiting you out.

As one of the older, taciturn demons summarized the predicament, "Consider yourself lucky. Under other circumstances, I could have been a hard-hearted stranger. Tonight, however, the everyday axiom has been reversed: better the devil who knows you, than the demon who doesn't!"

Throughout the Satanic Spa and Spiritual Sauna Complex, the most malign megalomaniacs from every corner of the cosmos – now inescapably mirrored in the watchful faces opposite them – were gradually beginning to see themselves clearly for the very first time. As each changed, so too the expressions of the individual devil transformed, reflecting back a new, continuously-shifting experience of themselves.

Denial gave way to guilt, guilt to regret, regret to remorse, remorse to repentance, and repentance to a far greater clarity still – a clarity that, for the very first time, revealed all they had been, and, even worse, all whom they'd harmed, including, foremost, themselves.

Gradually the atmosphere changed. Sooner or later, as each guest looked up,, it was suddenly to find, in the face opposite him, a new, unaccustomed emotion: an expression of almost serene acceptance, a steady generous calm that rendered all past false posturings and ignoble deeds now pointless and forgotten.

It was as if those who had once viewed themselves as gods, now, drained and humbled, began to know themselves at last, in all their littleness and limitations, through the all-seeing, all-forgiving eyes of God.

The common response, as and when words finally came, was a soft, heart-felt, "Thank you; thank you so very much!"

"Don't mention it," the personal devil in attendance usually replied, eyes still twinkling with sweet, subversive compassion. "Nobody ever said sanctity was easy."

It was at this point that this long-suffering figure stood up and, with a long slow wink, carefully recomposed both his features and his form, revealing himself as what he'd so secretly been all along; an individual, if more than slightly unorthodox guardian angel in disguise.

The individual host then pulled out a suitably laminated, water-and-heat-proof business card which, in addition to providing his personal contact number, also revealed, beneath the embossed crest, his title and organization of origin: Registered Angelic Associate, Intergalactic Grace Relations Board.

His next words, spoken sooner or later in almost every steamroom/cedar-lined confessional of the Satanic Spa and Spiritual Sauna Complex, were everywhere the same.

"From here on, you might find it helpful to think of me as your personal celestial parole officer. Do right in future … and all will be well."

There was a judicious pause. "However…."

The figure opposite suddenly reverted in a blazing red flash to his most archaic and aggressive demonic form, instructive pitchfork tines pointed straight at his ward's bare and vulnerable throat. "Mess up again, and you'll be back to anti-matter!"

In an unfinished universe, even guardian angels have their limits.

It was not surprising, therefore, that when (according to plan) a knock on the door shortly followed, and a given individual's planetary Adam next entered with a long and precisely predetermined to-do list in hand, he should now be welcomed by the newly redeemed with open arms and an even more open mind.

"You've clearly got a lot of cosmic catching up to attend to," was the usual admonition that accompanied the outline of suggested penance, both private and public, and subsequent altruistic endeavours.

Having been bad for too long, the prospect of having to be truly good for the next few millennia by way of compensation did not seem unduly troubling. For most, in fact, it brought a kind of relief. Sooner or later, even for the least conscience-stricken career criminal, the universe had a way of becoming an all-too-problematical place.

As this evening's exquisitely tricky developments had amply confirmed, there was always a watchful, wholly unpredictable devil lurking about, complete with secret stopwatch and an all-too-personal personnel file.

Three Cheers for Adam

🝮 AS BOTTLES OF THE finest *Chateau des Enfers Eternels*, especially reserved for the occasion, sprayed through the heated air, the collective mood was understandably triumphant. The universe, all senior devils agreed, was (for now at least) a much nicer place than twelve hours before, most of the hitherto unrepentant having so satisfyingly succumbed to the relentlessly-tender mercies of their individual interrogators and exorcists.

A heedless, hardened few, however, had yet to meet their fiery fates …if not for very much longer.

🝮

From their vantage point in the underworld's highest-tech control centre, Big D and the Archangel-in-Chief had tracked the progress of enforced super-heated deliverance, casually making bets on which of the ultra-obstinate might hold out the longest; and which would definitely require (as Big D put it with no little professional enthusiasm) "a little further cognitive behaviour therapy."

As they watched, hundreds of satisfied demonic engineers gradually began shutting down many of the individual rooms now empty and cooling. The hands on every clock, all set to Celestial Central Time in anticipation of tomorrow's great event, were all nearing midnight.

"Twelve hours, more or less, till the Heavenly Games are set to open," Big D mused aloud. "And I'd like to get to the stadium a little early…."

Not only was he not about to disappoint Scheherazade, he was also keen to see first hand the latest celestial developments. It had been, after all, quite a few aeons since he'd had the pleasure of enjoying the view from above.

"I should be upstairs by morning myself." The Archangel-in-Chief raised his eyebrows. "God's due back later in the day, and, as you might guess, Eve has a fair amount of paperwork to get through before then."

"Whatever I may have said in the past," Big D said, trying hard (but not too hard) not to laugh, "I really don't envy you your job."

Heaven's C.O.O. shrugged and spread his hands. "What can I say. It's a living!"

Smiling in quiet mutual appreciation of their respective lots, the two returned their gaze to the controlroom monitors and the images of their remaining unrepentant, evil-tempered adversaries.

Big D and the Archangel of All Archangels read one another's minds, both reaching the same conclusion.

"Back to basics?"

"Always worked in the past," Big D said, leaning over to whisper instructions in his senior technical expert's ear.

"Fast and furious?"

"Always more fun – for us, that is!"

"I must say, I've always liked your style," said the Archangel-in-Chief. "Cunning, elemental, entertaining and bold."

"Old family motto," Big D replied. "K.I.S.S. ... Keep it Simple, Satan!"

❦

While Adam would have further work to do later that memorable night, for the moment he was free to relax. Thanks to his own earlier impressive oratory, a gratifying number of misguided descendants had not only come to see the error of their ways, but were already considering new, more selfless steps toward both their own recovery and planetary restitution.

After so many thousands of years, Adam decided, a not-so-little taste of a little something in celebration seemed very much in order.

Given their motto (Nothing Unrevealed, Nothing Unrewarded!) it was not surprising that the Intergalactic Senior Devils' Association should have reserved a particularly luxurious lounge for all those Adams who together played such a seminal role in this extraordinary evening.

Long and winding road that it had been since he and Eve had first left Eden, it was all the more enjoyable now to put his feet up for a few moments, order a drink from one of the hovering white-jacketed devils-in-training, and compare notes with other members of his select fraternity.

Earth, much to his relief, turned out to have produced no more nor less a grand total of villains than any other comparable planet.

There were, of course, a few exceptions: constellations crippled by vastly excessive chaos and criminality from the outset, and those (even more rare) who seemed annoyingly proper and pure ever since the moment they first began to coalesce (as their inhabitants never ceased to explain) from a loftier, more righteous brand of stardust.

Live and learn. Learn and – however so late – begin to live!

Everywhere in the universe, it seemed, nearly everybody had an inherent penchant for getting things wrong, the better eventually to get them right. Wouldn't it be wonderful, Adam mused, sipping his single malt, if there was some way to speed up the process? If, somehow or other, people could simply manage to see the truth for themselves?

Comes the hour, comes the epiphany.

Slamming down his glass with a bang, Earth's greatest grandfather began counting the hours till morning. Then counted them again. Then shot to his feet with the certainty that this one last night, before Games Day and God's return, might just offer a little blue-and-white planet its most literally Heavenly opportunity of all.

If, that is, he could get hold of Eve, with all her earthly moxie, and time-limited celestial pull.

T'was the Night Before Games Day

❧ IF ONE HAS BEEN married to the same man for a few hundred thousand years, sooner or later one develops a reasonably clear-eyed understanding of both his strengths and weaknesses, as well as an appreciation for just how unexpectedly, endearingly brilliant he can be.

When Adam called, Eve was preparing not for bed, but rather to spend her last hours in Heaven fully awake, dedicated to keeping a solitary vigil in the splendour of God's private chapel and to a parting contemplation of all the sacred, unfinished mysteries of the universe asleep.

Morning would come soon enough, and with it all the thunder and wonder of the opening ceremonies of the great cosmic festival of love. Now, though, if ever there were a time for her to lose and find herself in prayer, it was in the approaching wee small hours of this one final night.

Under these circumstances, Adam's suggestion, coming as it also did with uncanny celestial timing, proved perfectly irresistible.

If, as he said (quite reasonably, she thought) their descendants had so far not managed to achieve their lofty, oft-touted ambitions to build Heaven on Earth, maybe, just maybe, it would be simpler (given her still infinite powers) to reverse the process and actually bring her native planet a whole lot closer to the celestial realm itself.

After all, if the citizens of Earth could somehow obtain a much closer view of that wondrous, ineffable destination to which, generation after generation, all continued to aspire, might not it dramatically improve both their everyday behaviour and their chances of getting there sooner?

"I'll see what the Sun has to say. One thing's certain: it's sure going to come as a surprise!"

"Remember, you're in charge," Adam responded encouragingly. "You can do anything you want."

Eve's laughter danced through the vast interstellar space between them.

"I always so like it when you talk that way."

ॐ

As Scheherazade drew nearer to Heaven, SS Serendipity contentedly on autopilot, a warm, remembered voice suddenly came through her headphones.

"Welcome back," the Angel of Uncanny Encouragement exclaimed. "You'll find the place a whole lot busier than your last visit. Booked to overflowing, in fact!"

After a brief conversation, the two old friends arranged to meet for a nightcap as soon as Scheherazade had checked in (despite her minimal protestations) to a specially-reserved and redecorated celestial suite, complete with the finest of views and clairvoyant seraphim on call twenty-four seven.

"Make yourself at home. You deserve it, after all you've done one way or another. And besides," the sapphire-eyed angel added, "you'll find there's more room should you happen to encounter a certain incorrigibly charming rogue who still knows his way around these parts."

And not a few others, Scheherazade thought quickly. "Your gang thinks of everything," she answered, unsure whether to feel flattered, amused or exposed.

"We try; we definitely try," the Angel of Uncanny Encouragement replied affectionately, "particularly when it comes to destiny."

ॐ

Throughout the universe's many star systems, little children and adults wise enough never to outgrow a childlike capacity for wonder found themselves kneeling before sleep, fervently sending Heavenwards a small, but hopefully mighty prayer for the success of their own home team in tomorrow's great Games of Love.

Dawn was only a few hours away and the Heavenly Broadcast Stadium, while still technically off the air, was already preparing the way with a commercial-free selection of the most inspiring composers over the past two billion years. Listening in, even the most cynical of constellations (having nonetheless double-set their alarm clocks like everyone else) found themselves secretly wishing that they too might have made more of an effort, no matter how seemingly naïve, in their more youthful, more idealistic days.

Love might be hard to explain … but it was even harder to deny.

While the entire universe would, of course, be able to watch the entire show, it was ultimately only a truly lucky few who would actually get to march together in tomorrow's grand parade. And so, as the inhabitants of a hundred and one billion galaxies turned in for the night, old and young alike were united in the same shared wistful yearning: "Sure wish I were going."

❧

"We're nearly there."

Abracadabra's voice crackled through the wizardly WiFi network linking a stealthy fleet of little white clouds skittering through the darkness, racing on toward their destination's distant, unmistakeable glow.

The World's Most Beautiful Astronomer raised her dozing head from the shoulder of The World's Greatest Gravedigger, quickly following his gaze. Around them, as many members of Team Earth as Abracadabra's personal cloud could hold were gradually stirring. Behind, on the other wispy yet surprisingly sturdy ultra-speed aircraft, the rest of their band of competitors, together with their small group of coaches from The Great Beyond beyond the Beyond, also began to awaken.

Marina, Leila, Qingling, Yazmina, Tatiana and Sybilla, strategically placed next to the various sorcerers guiding their individual clouds, reached into their carry-on cases for lipstick and mirrors. On a first visit to Heaven, a lady should definitely look her best.

❧

Throughout the limitless celestial corridors, angels who had until now carried out their many demanding duties with characteristic insouciance, found themselves suffering from a sudden attack of nerves.

To employ their specialist skills incognito, as was their wont, was one thing. To do their celestial thing before keenly-attentive onlookers from more than a hundred and one billion galaxies, however, was something else again.

The all-powerful Angel of the Golden Hammer and Gong, practising his swift yet mighty swing in preparation for Opening Day, very nearly lost his grip on the handle several times. The vision of his favourite, perfectly-pitched musical instrument forever soaring on soundlessly in space alone, filled him with horror. With it would go, he was sure, both his celestial musician's licence and a reputation upheld over millions of years.

For their part, the angels in charge of the Celestial Office for Spiritual Sound and Light Shows (Custom Fireworks Branch) now doubled their budget, their staff, and their overtime hours, the better to perfect an unprecedented display featuring the skylit logos of every star system, all set to the fluidly interwoven sounds of corresponding anthems. The required software, they were beginning to find, was almost more intricate than its intended effects.

The organizers of the next day's Grand Processional, on the other hand, had to make sure that their carefully considered instructions and second-by-split-nano-second schedule had been accurately translated into a trillion languages. And then to ensure that those same translations had each been delivered to exactly the right teams.

Under the circumstances, it wasn't surprising that more than one celestial veteran was overheard to mutter that, however glorious Games Day promised to be, he (for one) would be more than glad when the genuine, original, no-nonsense God got back from vacation and the universe returned to what had hitherto passed for normal.

It was a sentiment Eve would surely have sympathized with, were she not already busy trying to get the show (or, at least, a critically important part of it) on the road. Quite literally.

❧

That normally soft-spoken, non-stop ball of fire known locally as the Sun (despite being only one of millions upon millions of similar stars in a relatively mid-sized galaxy) was, in fact, extremely proud of its distinguished, if astronomically modest career. Not only had it managed to sustain a dauntingly wide range of often bizarre life forms over billions of years, but had itself been the happily storied subject of all manner of myths and legends on its dramatically different encircling worlds.

Fond of all its stepchildren, it had a particular, if undisclosed affection for that little whirling blue-and-white ball which, although two-thirds water, for some reason chose to call itself Earth. Strange indeed, the Sun had occasionally mused, how often it was the near runts of the litter that showed the most potential.

It was not surprising, therefore, that the so unexpected accession of Eve to the Heavenly throne should have been a cause for unusual solar celebration. Ever since her first day in office, in fact, the Sun had been putting out some of its most inventive fiery coronas in honour of what it increasingly enjoyed calling a family achievement.

On the other hand, it still wasn't quite sure what best to do, if anything, to mark the actual opening of Games Day itself. Various moons, depending on location, timing and cyclical mood swings, wondered aloud about a series of spectacular eclipses. On reflection, however, they rejected that idea as too routine. Wouldn't it be lovely, they all agreed, if they could come up with something bigger; even, perhaps, some sort of transgalactic showstopper?

It was a conclusion which, thanks to Adam, Eve had already reached.

$$\cdot \clubsuit \cdot$$

"I would expect that by now you must be getting a little bored with your daily routine," Earth's first lady began by way of introduction on her fully encrypted cell phone, "keeping a slightly glazed eye on all those mathematically predictable, ever-soepetitive orbits."

"*Noblesse oblige*," the Sun replied, stifling an involuntary yawn.

"Let's just suppose," Eve began delicately, "that I could arrange for something out of the ordinary? A little cosmic sight-seeing tour, perhaps?"

The Sun perked up, huge explosions of helium betraying its sudden excitement.

"You mean … break out of my perennial rut; broaden my horizons, maybe even finally find out what all the other fiery furnaces get up to on Saturday night?"

"Something like that," Eve acknowledged.

The super-hot pivotal point of the entire solar system glanced hurriedly around to where Mars was curiously contemplating its latest over-dressed visitor from Earth, Saturn was retrofitting its rings for a gigantic carnival merry-go-round, and Pluto, as usual, was humming to itself while staring off hopefully into the far distance.

"But what about my nearest and dearest, all my orbiting relatives and dependents? Can't very well leave them here without me: all by themselves, alone in the dark, whistling Dixie…."

"Wouldn't dream of it," Eve chuckled. "Of course, you'll be taking them with you – planets, moons, asteroids, *le tout* solar shebang!" She looked at the clock on the Heavenly bedroom wall, its hands nearing midnight. "But you don't have much time, given that all of you – including, most especially, Earth – have to get where you're going before noon!"

She turned, beckoned to the smiling Celestial Aerospace Engineering Angel standing confidently in the doorway, supra-light-speed flight plan in hand. "Fortunately, you're going to have some superlative assistance."

Eve lowered her voice, began to speak softly but firmly. "Now, here's my ultra-secret plan."

When Eve had finished, hanging up after wishing one and all a good and speedy trip, the Sun could only shake itself and take a deep breath. And then get on the solar hot-line (reserved for regional emergencies or extraordinary cosmic developments) connecting it to all its rhythmically circling associates.

"You ain't gonna believe where we're going!"

Eve's next call reached Adam in the midst of an increasingly loud, if slightly preliminary celebration with his fellow founding fathers from across the universe.

"Hello, my hero," said Eve. "Just a quick word to let you know: our exciting aeronautic experiment, which the technical staff here are already calling Operation Up Close and Personal!, is now happily underway."

"So lovely to see you at the height of your powers," he replied, meaning it more than anyone else, anywhere, could truly appreciate.

"Almost," Eve replied teasingly. "Almost … but not quite." She paused. "Just wait till you hear what I've got in mind for tomorrow."

Shock Therapy

ONE BY ONE, long, slow bells tolled the fearful hour of midnight.

In the labyrinthine maze best known to its dedicated, hot-tempered staff simply as Demon World, all was prepared. As the compulsory registry at the entrance to the all-red lobby noted: "To all our far-from-distinguished guests, welcome! We sincerely hope you'll find it truly Hell to be here."

❦

"And now," Big D announced, reviewing the scene with infectiously cheerful malevolence, "a reward too long overdue!"

The most eminent senior demons in Creation – whether shaking their heads mock-sorrowfully or sharpening their pitchforks one last time for good luck while exhaling trial bursts of fire – all turned as one.

In the centre of a circle of well-orchestrated and highly-unnerving flames, the last remaining oligarchs of evil throughout the universe sat side by side. As every satanic peer was delighted to see, this was a truly historic assembly of the unrepentant and unredeemed: all those who, having the most to answer for, were also the least likely to answer to anyone anywhere, about anything.

At Big D's side, the Archangel of All Archangels began to mutter. "Charming and cavalier though you appear much of the time, I think our guests are starting to suspect you might also have what could be called a truly wicked sense of humour!"

"Good guess," his old sparring partner agreed.

Hell's demonic engineers, twirling and tweaking their ultra-modern controls, were having the most fun they'd had for millions of years.

Many had secretly felt that (when priestly push came to satanic shove) their traditional, if admittedly somewhat primitive tools and techniques had always been impressively effective. One thing was sure: those ancient fiery fates definitely had a way of getting people's attention. Given current cosmic air-quality restrictions, therefore, they had been all the more surprised and delighted at the chance to fire up their latest computers and run Big D's gift: an entirely new, five-dimensional demonic holographic video projection game, nostalgically called The Fyres of Olde Hell.

Their new toy (instantly nick-named, of course, Hieronymous) came complete with astonishingly vivid illusions of antique demonic blast-furnaces, fed with a steady stream of howling, tormented souls by gangs of grinning devils exalting in their ancient craft of cosmic retribution.

Once suitable sound effects and special-blend acrid aromas had been judiciously added, it was gratifying to see just how quickly many of these assembled nasty guests turned a truly convincing shade of pale and got on their cell phones to speed-dial their lawyers and accountants.

All of whom, as and when they were unwise enough to arrive, were quickly escorted into separate chambers where particularly persuasive crews swiftly disencumbered them of all the secrets (including the exact whereabouts of ill-gotten gains in almost every galactic currency) which they had, until now, so successfully concealed on their clients' behalf.

The proceeds from this initiative, Big D's auditors were pleased to report in the weeks following, were enough to support all philanthropic projects throughout the entire universe for the next five million years. Happily too, even after such involuntary largesse, enough was still left over to fund scholarships in perpetuity for enterprising candidates for Heaven's two distinguished professional training colleges, the Academies Angelic and Diabolic respectively.

As Big D later summarized events, simply yet eloquently, at the banquet in honour of his hard-working investigative colleagues: "Crime pays … especially when the cheque's payable to the order of Demon Inc.!"

There was a pause. "Or, as I sometimes like to think of us, God's discreet little off-shore collection agency."

The simulated but all-too substantial experience of The Fyres of Olde Hell, together with the sudden unavailability of their usually reliable sources of money, muscle and alibis, began to have an immediately discombobulating effect. The heat made the hitherto untouchable figures increasingly uncomfortable within their own skins. They suddenly found themselves supremely vulnerable.

It was not, each began to discover, an especially encouraging feeling. This was so particularly when all around them (or so it seemed) damnably unbribable crimson devils of every size and shape continued merrily to throw more and more wretched souls (whose faces bore an increasingly close resemblance to the cosmic criminals' own) howling and screaming into the everlasting flames.

"From past experience," Big D observed cheerfully, "I would guess we're nearing the point where our amoral guests begin to complain that there ain't no justice!"

"Not, at least, the kind they'd prefer," the Archangel of All Archangels acknowledged.

"Such an ironic fate," Big D observed humbly, "to have fallen into the hands of the ultimate outlaw." He put an affectionate hand on his colleague's broad shoulder. "Even, one might say, divinely inspired."

The Archangel-in-Chief glanced around, his eyes dancing with reflected flames. "Despite my obligatory charitable instincts, I must confess this evening is infinitely more entertaining than I'd anticipated. Watching our guests running out of options – at long last – somehow secretly appeals to my underdeveloped satanic side."

Big D looked sideways at his old associate, at the same time graciously concealing a deeply-enigmatic smile. "Not to worry. Enjoy yourself. After all, it's in a good cause."

The high priest of the cosmic low church pointed to the astonishingly realistic image of a dictator revolving slowly on a spit, anguished tears flowing from his eyes, much to the horror of his real-life counterparts who recoiled away from both the gruesome scene and one another.

"In our business, it's called tenderizing."

ϟ

Ever a brilliant judge of time and circumstance, Big D discreetly checked his designer watch. "I think they should all be just about done by now. All nice and pliable."

Around him, the inner circle of senior devils began flexing their pitchforks in eager anticipation. For their part, the larger audience of celebrated cosmic no-goods, already exhausted by the prospect of good old-fashioned hellfire and damnation, seemed even more alarmed.

"First the fire," said Big D, cheerfully underscoring the well-proven process, "then the fury!"

"Followed, no doubt," the Archangel of All Archangels continued smoothly, "by the Ultimate Celestial Squeeze?"

Nodding enthusiastically, Big D immediately began pointing out various of the universe's very worst of the worst to pairs of senior devils who, in turn, took keen pride and pleasure in happily hauling them away.

"Given our guests' evident lack of enthusiasm for our spiritually invaluable services," he observed, "I'd say we still have truly a Hell of a lot of work to get through by morning!"

Deliverance is usually an elective; postponed long enough, however, it is guaranteed to become a compulsory course, though seldom begun at the time, place or manner of one's own choosing.

Squeeze Play

ℬ WHILE THERE ARE (fortunately) nearly as many ways to separate sinners from their sins as there are sinners in the first place, all the universe's great spiritual traditions place near-equal emphasis on the same abiding antidotes – contrition, confession, repentance and reconciliation.

In the event, however, these deeply personal, highly-demanding transformations have an unfortunate habit of proceeding in their own sweet way and their own sour time. While the rewards may be eternal, resistance to the steps necessary to achieve them can often seem almost as long.

It was not surprising, therefore (given their goal of ridding the cosmos of the last of its major monsters in the few short celestial hours that remained), that Big D and the Archangel of All Archangels should have opted for the most ferociously effective of spiritual makeover techniques.

"While I may be philosophically predisposed to the long view," Big D opined, quietly slipping on his crimson work gloves, "in practice I'm a really big fan of short-cuts!"

ℬ

As the simulated flames of an amazingly realistic-looking Hell crackled and roared, the champions of Heaven and Hell together took hold of one of the greatest villains on the contemporary intergalactic crime scene. Self-styled warlord of a small but merciless planet which held the rest of its constellation to terrorized ransom, he had been for too long an entirely unscrupulous master of all the more lucrative forms of spiritual skulduggery, everyday intimidation and local grand larceny.

"You're definitely on our wish list!" Big D growled, taking their victim by his legs.

"Top of the persuasive pops!" the Archangel of All Archangels yelled, grabbing his horrified head.

They looked at each other across the writhing body of their first candidate for unholy come-uppance: screaming and writhing above what seemed an inescapably bottomless pit of fire, its red and yellow flames reaching up as if to rip him from their hands.

"By the feel of him, he seems loosened up enough," Big D observed in a voice all the more terrifying for appearing so unconcerned. At his signal the two of them began, hand over hand, to spin their increasingly disoriented and disbelieving victim in opposite directions, twisting and turning him ever more tightly on himself.

At last, as the culprit's howls grew louder and his body thrashed in their unrelenting grip, his many and manifold toxic sins, complete with any intention to repeat them ever, ever again, began to ooze from every pore of his body, rising in clouds of foul-smelling steam from the sizzling flames beneath.

"Nasty work, this," the Archangel of All Archangels, declared, enjoying the opportunity of being of service to an ultimately greater end, exceedingly malodorous side effects notwithstanding.

"And you angels thought we devils had it easy," Big D retorted, giving his nearly unconscious but now also almost completely purified guest another sharp tug and twist to hasten the inevitable positive outcome.

When, at last, the two put down their first candidate for what was more formally called Complete Compressive Cosmic Cleansing, laying him gently in the care of two exceptionally compassionate devils in the first of many spiritual recovery rooms, his face, for the first time in millennia, was clear and serene.

"So far," the Archangel-in-Chief observed contentedly, "so very much the better."

An instant later, he and Big D turned impatiently toward the waiting line-up of petrified evil-doers, and the flaring flames that were their impending fate. "Next!"

All the truly sophisticated planning and forethought that had gone into the creation of the The Fyres Of Olde Hell appeared to be paying off most satisfactorily.

Over their own smaller but no-less-convincing versions of the illusory blazing pit, the other members of the Intergalactic Senior Devils' Association, together with bulked-up, strong-armed angels specially seconded for the evening's operations, twisted and twirled their own individual villains, wringing out all manner of noisy confessions and noxious vices and leaving them completely limp, but all the better for the totally exhausting experience.

As the numbers of the unredeemed dwindled, the engineering staff effortlessly switched their attention from stoking their fires to printing out long lists of personalized rehab plans for each successfully remodelled miscreant. Given the scale of their previous offences, all of those who had so recently enjoyed the joint angelic-demonic wringer would now be making spiritual reparations over anywhere from the next five to fifty thousand years.

Who knows, given time, some might even seek to become apprentice angels, or at least be allowed to fill in the application papers for an internship unlike any other.

All in all, to its distinguished organizers' delight, the great cosmic criminals clean-up campaign was proceeding even more successfully than anticipated.

Quietly excusing himself from the wholly justified, if slightly premature celebrations with his fellow founding-fathers, Adam wandered off through the maze of Demon World, his innate, unfailing curiosity leading him to see what else might be going down (as it were). And whether there was anything he could do for further edification and amusement.

As so often before, his timing was close to perfect.

As if predestined, loud and familiar shrieks, howls and groans guided him unerringly to the evening's *Theatre Deluxe de l'Enfer*. Occupying centre stage, struggling mightily over the flames and continuing to resist the ministrations of Big D at his head and the Archangel of All Archangels at his feet, was the unmistakable figure of one of his own blue-and-white planet's most notorious inhabitants; someone unfailingly untroubled by the world's criticism and reproach … since, as far as he knew, he himself *was* the world.

"Recognize him?" Big D asked, looking up.

Adam didn't need a second glance. He began to glower, his face darkening with long-suppressed fury at so many injustices done over the ages by a few of his descendants to all his descendants.

Both Big D and the Archangel of All Archangels found themselves taking a quick step back.

"May I?" Adam asked, his voice implacable.

He gestured to the figure suspended between them over the flames; one who, for the first time in an endless career of uncaring conquest, was now beginning to show signs of panic. Past glories and grandiose prospects all suddenly disappeared, as Earth's worst tyrant ever awoke from his illusions to find the planet's first man standing over him, resolute and enraged.

Taking his descendant's head firmly in his hands, Adam shook his own in sorrow both mock and real. "Excessive testosterone is no excuse: you have to be worthy of it – and use it wisely!"

Big D, an image arising of Adam's own admirably unbreakable world record for begats over the millennia, had some roguish thoughts of his own. Catching the Archangel-in-Chief's eloquently raised eyebrow, he was delighted to see he was not alone.

To everything, a season.

"On three…," Adam declared.

He and the Archangel of All Archangels began simultaneously to spin its truly worst exemplar in opposite directions with a vigour and effectiveness leaving even Big D slightly dizzy, if full of professional approval.

When it came to his first attempt at the ultimate celestial squeeze, it was clear Earth's founding father had an uncommon, hitherto-unrevealed skill. One that might even have made him a very good devil. Under very different circumstances, of course.

ॐ

"That was most satisfying." Scanning the remaining list, Adam quickly picked out the names of a number of lesser lack-of-lights from Earth yet to be dealt with. "I've still got a few hours free. Mind if I hang around and give you guys a hand?"

Big D pretended to check his watch, then smiled warmly. "Always grateful for a little unpaid assistance."

An instant later, he turned away, murmuring to the Archangel-in-Chief. "You know, somehow I've always really liked that guy." His face clouded with lingering regret. "However inevitable, I still can't help feeling sorry about my earlier intrusion on that untroubled little ante-room called Eden...."

The Archangel of All Archangels put a reassuring hand on his expat brother's equally-broad shoulder. "Then again," Heaven's own C.O.O. chuckled quietly, "if it weren't for the three of you pushing each other's God-given buttons so successfully, Adam and Eve wouldn't have had their recent invitation to come up in the world, as it were, and none of us would be enjoying this evening's entertainment."

"Why are you whispering?" said Big D.

The Archangel of All Archangels glanced cheerfully upwards. "Someone might be listening?"

Galaxies of Dreams

❧ EVE LINGERED ON Heaven's highest balcony, contemplating the darkened vistas of an entire universe asleep. Or, at least, trying to sleep.

Half an hour ago, the stars in every galaxy had spontaneously decided to dim their lights on this one special night, the better to help their widespread residents get at least a little rest before morning. All, of course, to no avail, as thoughts of the momentous day ahead kept everyone in Creation wide awake. Even the few off-duty angels, their preparations for the Games complete, either tossed and turned, or wandered Heaven's freshly polished corridors, well-thumbed programmes for the opening ceremony in hand.

Leaning against a glistening railing, Eden's first woman stared into time and space; willing herself once more to see the ceaseless, sleepless cosmos with God's all-knowing, all-understanding eyes.

❧

At the very same moment, savouring the very last night of anonymity in an intriguing, if undisclosed, location, the genuine, original deity was quietly watching over the very same universe with renewed optimism and resolve. All in all, it would be good to be back on the job.

God's horoscope for the coming twenty-four hours (a hugely complex and delicate calculation involving, needless to say, the intersections and influences of every sun, moon, planet and asteroid) was, reassuringly, the most auspicious since that memorable nudge, long, long ago: "This would be a perfect day to turn up the lights!"

Gazing on Eden's first woman, so beautiful and brave in her solitary contemplative stillness, God's heart swelled with a fierce, protective pride. All things divinely considered, it seemed timely – in a discreet gesture of appreciation and encouragement – to lend an unseen, helping hand. At the thought, a white-and-gold cell phone rose in the air, already beginning to dial one of the most gifted among God's countless unlisted contacts.

&a.

Congenital non-conformists, though unpredictable, can be the most valuable employees. Especially if they have an ear for secret harmonies.

True to form, the Angel of Tender Yet Truly Terrifying Rhapsodies was a presence rarely seen during Heaven's day-to-day business. Interstellar symphonic conductor, favourite composer of the most progressive angels and revered custodian of galactic reveries past and yet to come, he came and went as situation, mood and weather forecasts required.

By prior agreement with 'the Boss', his uniquely hypnotic talents were kept in reserve (as his business card warned) for extra-special operations, on truly extra-special occasions.

Such as now.

"Good evening," the troubadour announced, introducing himself to Eve by his full title. "My apologies for appearing so suddenly, but a little bird told me my talents might be welcome at this late and restless hour."

The tall elegant figure in top hat and tails gazed over her shoulder, to where even the far-off galaxies' purposely dimmed lights could not conceal the pacings of trillions of over-excited insomniacs.

"Fortunately for us both," he confided, "I seem to have been in God's bring-forward file."

Eve began to laugh, no longer alone. She regarded her visitor carefully. "I've met quite a number of angels over the past few weeks. Wonderful beings, all; and yet you seem even more sensitive." She paused, then had to ask, "So, why the sobriquet 'truly terrifying'?"

The latest in a long line of angelic surprises smiled. "Something to do with a disturbing old saying round these parts, perhaps? 'Those who see with the eyes of Love'…."

"'See more'!" said Eve, completing the aphorism and, in the same moment, seeing his quiet forcefulness with new understanding.

"Scary thought indeed," her guest agreed. He gazed gently at Eve, sensing so much that was on her mind. Like the universe itself, she too could definitely use a few hours sleep.

Reaching down, this most unusual of angels began opening his well-worn yellow violin case with its countless intergalactic travel stickers at his side. "This should do the trick!"

❦

Swinging gently back and forth on the luxuriously-cushioned chaise longue, Eve watched a succession of fascinated stars appearing and disappearing rhythmically from view.

The mysterious figure sharing Heaven's balcony bowed formally three times: to Eve, to the surrounding universe and, finally, to whatever or whomever only he could see. Murmuring a small prayer, he raised his bow and began to play. If his wardrobe was black and white, his music was anything but, every lyrical colour in Creation flowing softly from the strings, rising and falling in a long-unheard celestial lullaby.

Eve felt her eyelids grow heavy, her breathing slow. She stretched out on the swaying settee, sighing as the haunting sound of a solitary violin reached out through space to billions of suddenly-enchanted worlds.

"I like to call it, Ode to an Elusive Paradise," God's premier *artiste* whispered to the half-dozing woman beside him, her eyes closed in a bemused, now almost childlike reverie. As he played on, his bow weaving a magic spell over all, a hundred-plus billion surrounding galaxies followed Eve into sleep, their residents also awakening inwardly to the same shared dream of their own fateful beginning.

Before their slumbering eyes, the undivided seed of the universe split into darkness and light, emptiness and form; the cosmos dividing and subdividing in ceaseless, unending profusion, nourished by its unfinished past, drawn by its insistent, unrealized future.

One by one, a special group of scattered kindred spirits answered the celestial soloist's call, not to dreams, but to action. In one of the most learned galaxies anywhere, a little old man dusted off his great-great-grandfather's trumpet, and sent up an exuberant crescendo of sound. A long-retired trio of piano and woodwinds, their distant world now composed almost entirely of empty concert halls, looked at one another in surprise and joy and began softly replaying their once-famous sonata.

On a thousand different galaxies, bass players began to thrum the underlying, unmistakable rhythm of Creation. Drummers in myriad star systems bounced drumsticks and brushes as one. Long-separated saxophones improvised lyrical duets over billions of miles. Moment by moment, solitary flutes added their notes from every compass point of Creation.

Bow in hand, God's most discerning concertmaster paused, waiting attentively as more and more musicians, unable to resist, joined in from all over the universe. Smiling, he glanced down at Eve, still asleep and, as the unrehearsed concerto reached its close, lost in delight.

Moved by the sight far more than he could say, the tall, elegant figure doffed his top hat, halo and all, inclining his head in silence. No artist, even a celestial one, ever minded being appreciated, especially by one herself so uniquely deserving of honour. Turning to face the universe once again, God's latest emissary raised his bow, his commanding gesture catching every eye.

"A-one, a-two, a-three ... wing it!"

A split-second later, the far-flung members of what was soon everywhere to be known as the Big Bang & Be-Bop Symphony Orchestra found themselves (to their own great astonishment and glee) launching into the first exhilarating, impromptu notes of "Onwardsl Onwards! (Like It Or Not Sometimes) Forever Onwards!", their own smaller energy echoing the ceaseless momentum of Creation itself.

⁊

Throughout the crowded celestial operations offices, even the most single-minded angels found themselves pausing in their assigned tasks, sustained and uplifted by this improvisation on the music of the spheres.

Deep in the illusory depths of The Fyres of Olde Hell, Big D stopped in the midst of extracting the very last drop of remorse from one of the few cosmic culprits still left. Turning to the Archangel of All Archangels, he found him, too, pausing in his own relentless service to the secret light at the heart of darkness, listening intently as the spellbinding rhythms of the Big Bang & Be-Bop Symphony reached them clearly even there.

Even the luckily unlucky fellow corkscrewed between them perked up, responding to the far-off tune with the beginnings of a hesitant, hopeful smile.

"I always enjoyed that Rhapsodies fellow," Big D confessed. "If I remember correctly, he wrote a wonderful little duet that was played in Eden."

"If I remember correctly," the chief Archangel replied, eyes twinkling, "it was even played just at that moment when someone – looking very much like you – helped Adam and Eve find the door marked Top Secret Exit."

"One lends a hand where one can," Big D conceded modestly.

Elsewhere, as the informal intergalactic band played on, a small formation of little white clouds neared their penultimate destination, a secluded motel parking lot in Heaven's furthest, least-developed subdivision. So many visitors and competitors having already booked the best suites weeks before, it was the only suitably discreet and affordable accommodation Abracadabra could find.

Dozing in their seats, lulled by the forward rush of billowing clouds, Team Earth and its escort of exotic special advisors all found themselves humming the same new, increasingly-insistent melody, the encouraging strains of "Onwardsl Onwards! (Like It Or Not Sometimes) Forever Onwards!" accompanying them on their secret and (from some points of view) recklessly unorthodox mission.

Trillions of miles away, the red-eye special to end all red-eye specials, better known as Sun and Associates, hurtled onward, racing at breakneck speed toward the sporting event of all sporting events in the vacation destination of all vacation destinations. For a certain little blue-and-white planet and all its many wide-eyed passengers, it was the chance to root for their home team in the most improbable of away games.

As the Big Bang & Be-Bop Symphony played softly, that Ageless Divinity simultaneously everywhere yet nowhere to be seen quietly surveyed a sleeping Creation.

"Busy day, soon. We could all use a little rest."

Setting the supremely-melodious alarm on an invisible wrist-watch to 7:00 am, and turning the little dial that determined the choice of weather for the entire universe to 'gentle showers', God propped an unseen head on an equally unseen hand.

Taking his cue, the Angel of Tender Yet Terrifying Rhapsodies bowed gratefully to his ensemble of unexpected guest artists across time and space. As the celestial symphony faded softly away, the stars in turn slowly dimmed their lights once more in their own companion harmony.

A soft, warm rain began to fall steadily throughout all the galaxies in Creation, lulling its sleeping inhabitants murmuring in their dreams, washing countless worlds clean and leaving them refreshed and ready for morning, bright and sparkling at the beginning of The Day of All Days.

Finishing Touches

"COINCIDENCE IS GOD'S WAY OF REMAINING
ANONYMOUS."

— Albert Einstein

"ALBERT EINSTEIN IS ALSO ONE OF GOD'S WAYS OF
REMAINING ANONYMOUS."

— God

Last-Minute Rush

🙤 IF ONE REPORTS directly to God, it is generally a good idea – especially if that august presence has been off-duty for some time, and is returning only hours before the most significant event in recent celestial history – to make absolutely sure everything has been thought of twice and then taken care of at least three times.

Under the circumstances, then, it was not surprising that countless celestial coffee pots should have been emptied and refilled before angelic chimes rang in the magic hour of 7:00 a.m. A mild caffeine buzz has never been known to interfere with an angel's ability to achieve lift-off. Quite the contrary, in fact: an extra double-double on this particular morning might even be welcomed as a kind of flight insurance.

For the final time in five increasingly-hectic days, the Celestial Co-ordinating Committee met to review the countdown to that moment when God – reclaiming a rightful place on the Heavenly throne – would declare the official opening of this, the grandest intergalactic gathering ever.

One by one, each senior operations manager gave a confident nod.

As the Angel of Intergalactic Special Events watched with cool professional calm, his associates in charge of Transstellar Transportation, of Celestial Hospitality and Accommodation and, most importantly, of Cosmic Crowd Control, each reported that everything was proceeding according to plan. Likewise, the Angels of Facilities, Grounds and Gardens, of Protocol and Visiting Dignitaries, and, last but certainly not least, of Truly Exceptional Scheduling and Officiating, quietly confirmed that all was in good order and their staff ready for every eventuality.

"If not, then there's always us," the Angel of Divine Back-Up declared, gesturing to his equally untroubled colleague, the Angel of Truly Infinite Resources.

"Fifteen minutes till the pre-Games show goes live," declared the Angel of Multigalaxy Media Relations, popping his head around the corner of the door.

As one, the members of the most eminent celestial workforce scooped up briefing books and schedules, hastily winging away to their respective operations offices.

§

Throughout the vast landscapes of Heaven, individual competitors from a billion star systems reviewed their personal programmes of wisdom and worship, *eros* and *caritas*, passion and compassion over and over in their mind's eye. Team leaders reviewed the overall lineups of their squads, assigning places for the Grand Processional. Section leaders double-checked the parade sequences which, each hoped, might best express their own particular grasp of the infinitely complex energies of Love.

In changing rooms throughout Heaven, support staff began laying out team uniforms, ecstatically coloured in every possible combination of cosmic hue and tone. Billions of banners, all boldly emblazoned with their team's top-secret heraldic rallying cry, were covertly shaken out, tested in the wind, then carefully re-furled in preparation for their dramatic public unveiling when the long-awaited moment finally came.

§

"Excited?" the World's Most Beautiful Astronomer asked, reaching out to take her co-captain's hand, its palm hardened and calloused by time and Time's work.

The World's Greatest Gravedigger turned, gazing toward Heaven's distant shimmering towers. "And much else besides...."

His beautiful grey-eyed, long-sought soul mate waited in silence.

"When I think on all those I have ushered to their rest during our long careers," her consort ventured after a time, his voice uneven with emotion. "So many who, in their own brief days so much like ours, offered up their solemn rituals and their rites, whispered their serene or urgent prayers; all those who yearned, just like us, for the smallest glimpse of this wondrous glory outstretched before us now."

The two sat in silence, feeling the presence of generations of ancestors, each one a single life uniquely lived, however briefly, badly or well. A life personal and precious – and yet one to which, with reluctance or resolve, each had had at last to bid farewell; mourned on their way by others who would themselves, all too soon, be gone and grieved in turn.

"Mixed emotions," the World's Most Beautiful Astronomer whispered, resting her head on his shoulder.

"Very."

There was a long stillness while the two contemplated all things born, and forever reborn, of the dust of vanished stars.

"And if I said that, appearances notwithstanding, somehow they too are here! All of them; even now; present after all?"

The reply of the World's Greatest Gravedigger was edged with the bittersweet tenderness of time for all Time's children. "Appearances notwithstanding, I would agree."

A single valedictory star shot across the sky, pausing in silent tribute – and triumph – before seeming to disappear en route to its own simultaneous resurrection somewhere else in eternity.

"And so, it seems, do they!"

❧

Bright-eyed as never before, Abracadabra made the rounds of his fellow wizards now gathering outside Team Earth's small motel, genially inquiring if all had had a good night's rest. More importantly, he quietly verified that every little white cloud had been fully refuelled for whatever this day might bring. After all, it would be more than slightly embarrassing to run out of steam (technically known as swirling vapours) just when you had finally reached Heaven and were all set to make the most of it.

"So now, what's the plan?" asked a merrily roguish sorcerer from a venturesome planet thirty-three thousand galaxies down the road from Earth. (His little white cloud was, needless to say, one of the fastest, albeit least muffled) "Something bold, brash and beautiful, I trust!"

Abracadabra put his long wizardly finger melodramatically to his double-sealed lips. "I can only say that I'm anticipating a distinctly important call from an even more important, distinctly far-sighted lady."

"If the woman in question is who I think," his customarily over-impatient colleague replied instantly, "I'm all the happier to be patient."

One of the many admirable things about advanced seers is that, on truly significant occasions, they're more than willing to be guided by the barest of hints and signs, and an unerring openness to surprise.

§.

Thanks to the dedicated efforts of so many angels with advanced engineering degrees, the Heavenly Broadcast Studio had been totally deconstructed, and then swiftly rebuilt in a new location overlooking the site of Heaven's first invitational extravaganza.

Once more, the freshest of flowers graced its transparent walls. For this occasion, however, each of these blooms had been especially cultivated (at great haste and in total secrecy at the Celestial Horticultural Solaria) so as to display the complete range of team colours.

As viewers far and wide awakened, countless screens across the cosmos gradually filled with images – some familiar, most unfamiliar, but always hypnotic – drawn from individual and collective histories of the entire universe.

Moments later, a pair of eminently distinguished angels, speaking with one voice, yet heard simultaneously in every language, began reviewing the miraculous sequence of events leading up to this morning's transmission. Behind them, a medley of massed bands and choirs provided accompaniment to these first few hours of pre-Games commentary.

§.

One of the more enjoyable features of Heaven is that, given its invisible pre-screening operations, complete security comes with the territory. Unlike other places in the universe where lingering suspicions might still be sadly justified, here there were no irritable pre-entry line-ups, no need for iris scans and private pat-downs, however sensitive and discreet.

As a result, by mid morning the vast stands of the great Games stadium were already filling with fortunate visitors, distinguished guests and team support staff from all over Creation. The greatest of the great and the humblest of the humble (so often the same) would soon follow.

In their forming-up areas, the first teams began to take their places, rehearse their paces, adjust their faces, review their graces and, quite frequently, make a quick precautionary trip to the nearest celestial washroom.

Scheherazade, having spent a wondrously dream-filled night in her celestial guest suite, rose to meet the Angel of Uncanny Encouragement over breakfast.

"Enjoy the unexpected concert?" the latter asked immediately, having herself spent the whole night watching thoughtfully as the universe, outwardly asleep yet inwardly awake, found itself rested and enthralled by the Angel of Tender Yet Truly Terrifying Rhapsodies and his newly formed Big Bang & Be-Bop Symphony Orchestra.

"It was superb! An incantation of stars." Scheherazade stretched, feeling refreshed and renewed as never before. "Mood music on a scale and scope I'd never thought possible."

The Angel of Uncanny Encouragement opened her arms towards the endless vistas of circling galaxies, the lights of their constellations now restored to their full glory. "Intermittent bad press notwithstanding, you'd be amazed at what we can do around here when the need arises."

"No, I certainly would not," came Scheherazade's split-second reply. "Not today!"

There was the sudden chime of the celestial intercom.

"A very good morning of an even better day to you both!" Eve's tone, while warm and gracious, was slightly harried; the voice of one who, while still enjoying all the rights, powers and privileges as the first and so far only official substitute Supreme Being, had only a few more especially hectic hours to make the most of them.

"As I seem to be somewhat behind schedule here, I was wondering if you would perhaps care to lend a hand in the little matter of a long-overdue appointment with destiny?"

Scheherazade and the Angel of Uncanny Encouragement looked at one another. What are cosmic friends for?

"Would you please convey," Eve began, "a vitally important message to Team Earth."

Given that there's nothing long-serving angels like more than completely unexpected professional challenges, Eve's next meeting went well. "I know you're all tremendously busy with today's programme. But I was wondering," Eve declared, "if you might possibly take a moment to bring your shared expertise to bear on a little something I have in mind?"

The Celestial Aerospace Engineering Angel, the Angel of Celestial Spectacles and Cosmic Fireworks, together with their accomplice, the Angel of Truly Infinite Resources, all bowed eagerly.

"If, say, you were to take a small gathering of little white clouds," Eve continued, unfolding a small sketch hastily scribbled on a spare celestial restaurant napkin. "And then add the following dramatic effects…."

The trio of celebrated experts moved closer, the better to see.

"And, before I forget, we'll also need billions of these." She produced a smaller sketch. "All completed and delivered in less than three hours from now."

"No problemo," the first two Heavenly technocrats replied in unison.

"Ditto," the Angel of Truly Infinite Resources confirmed. "We use Celestial Express!"

Feu d'Esprit

𝕾 THE MOST SECRET of Abracadabra's unlisted cell phone numbers announced the awaited call with a suitably wizardly warble.

"At Your service!" he exclaimed, his voice blending obvious pride and even more evident relief. "As always."

"Everything's arranged," Eve began, then giving the details of what was to become, long afterwards, the most enthralling chapter by far in the ancient sorcerer's memoirs. "Adam and I will meet up with you all just before lift-off."

Reaching up, Abracadabra swept aside his ancestral pointed hat in tribute. Even the best magicians know when to bow before the truly great.

𝕾

While Scheherazade took the opportunity to brief her six friends on one more journey to come, the Angel of Uncanny Encouragement had a quiet conversation of her own.

"So, if everything goes according plan...."

"Gives a whole new meaning to the term personal best!" the World's Greatest Gravedigger declared, pointing to where Team Earth was seeking a little last-minute wisdom and counsel from a group of auspiciously-nonchalant tutors from The Great Beyond beyond the Beyond.

"Thank God," the World's Most Beautiful Astronomer replied. "Both of them!"

At the Angel of Uncanny Encouragement's signal, all the members of Team Earth gathered around.

"I have good news – and then even better news," the tall, gracious figure began. "First, since you've come all this way, Team Earth is getting into the Heavenly Games of Love after all!"

There was a brief silence, followed by a gigantic burst of applause accompanied by cries of delight.

"And second," one of Heaven's favourite angels continued, "thanks to a certain well-placed woman of influence, you're going both in secret and in style!"

❧

Impatient though she might be for Heaven's Games to begin (not least so that their own more personal, no less satisfying ones might continue) Scheherazade knew better than to call Big D.

First, he was at work, doing now what she was happily confident would very soon prove to be only one of the things he did best. Second, the best heroines, when suitably inspired, can instantly transmit their unspoken intentions as they wish.

He and she would meet up near noon, as planned, somewhere in the vast glittering stadium of Heaven. After all, when two spirits finally find each other after a few million years, they can usually be trusted to be able to do so again after only a few further hours apart.

❧

Much to the eminent members of the Intergalactic Senior Devils' Association's satisfaction, Demon World was by now almost deserted. Only a skeleton crew manned the engineering consoles of The Fyres of Olde Hell, their job to ensure that the remaining few sinners now ripe for remorse each got their very own well-deserved dose of simulated fire and brimstone. Big D and the Archangel of All Archangels could be trusted to do the rest.

In the meantime, all the devils who had worked long and hard to help save so many perennial renegades and reprobates from themselves, could now enjoy a much-needed shower before changing into the very latest in demonic formal regalia. After so many millions of years of stealthy celestial service – dedicated, devoted, yet all too often misunderstood – it was heart-warming to know that the universe's long-suffering satanic staff were soon to get their much-deserved reward. It would be a suitably public form of karmic compensation which, impish and impious as ever, they were already beginning to call their very own Heavenly homecoming celebrations.

⁊

"Still here?"

The Archangel of All Archangels looked up from the dark and sobbing soul who, twisted into an unresisting pretzel above the flames, was just about at the point of surrendering the weight of past sins in exchange for a new, if exhausted beginning.

"Still here," Adam confirmed. "Eve's as busy as you would expect under the circumstances." He paused, glancing at Big D knowingly. "So it seemed a good idea to keep out of her way."

"Your timing couldn't be more perfect," the universe's most dis-tinguished demon announced, rubbing a slightly sore lower back with one hand while steadying his soon-to-be-grateful victim with the other. "It's been a long night. Care to take over for a while?"

⁊

As Team Earth began to gather itself for all that lay ahead, a certain small yellow monkey, listening to the faint murmur of crowds filling a distant celestial stadium, found herself feeling increasingly pensive; even, perhaps, distressed.

The two skeletal deep-space spies (being Aurora's favourites among her kindred unorthodox coaching staff) quietly eyed one another, then ambled over to see what they could do.

"Very stirring day," Aurora said noncommittally.

Messrs. 'Skull and Bones' both agreed it was.

"But I can't help wondering…," she sighed, before going on to reveal at least a little of all she couldn't help wondering about. It was hard to tell whether the single small tear in one eye was of sadness or hope.

The two skeletons looked at one another, then toward the Heavenly Games stadium, then back to all their other colleagues from The Great Beyond beyond the Beyond, each deep in conversation with an excited group of Earth's team members.

"I don't think any of us really knows, the taller of the two skeletons said at last. "At least, not all the intricacies."

He stared at his shorter twin, both of them reaching the same conclusion at the same time.

"Given our present location," the second skeleton exclaimed, "why don't you just ask directly?"

"Why not indeed!" Aurora, suddenly beaming, stuck out a small, determined chin. "After all, I've always secretly wanted to."

❧

The Fyres of Olde Hell had done its duty. The triumphant tally on the Satanic scoreboard proclaimed the night's decisive victory: Supreme Grand Council of Insterstellar Demons: 92,649,777; Forces of Evil: 0.

The Archangel of All Archangels reached out, offering his underworldly twin a proud and grateful hand. "My, how shall I say, warmest thanks for so memorable an evening. Must admit, I've always been curious to see you in action."

"*Au contraire.* It was my privilege and equally-anticipated pleasure to work so closely with you," Big D answered, well knowing he could not have pulled off this first, comprehensive cosmic criminals clean-up campaign without his long-separated brother's ferocious celestial energy.

They looked at each other, silently calculating the synergistic benefits of so many unsavoury sinners saved at once. It probably guaranteed the universe at least a few million trouble-free light years ahead, both decided. All thanks to a single, if exceptionally hot and arduous, evening's work.

"We must do this again sometime," Big D declared, a wry twinkle in his dark blue eyes.

"Chances are, we will probably have to," the Archangel of All Archangels smiled, "because I am certain of the evolutionary inevitabilities of ignorance, awakening and grace. But, thanks to you and your illustriously- scary associates, not for an aeon or two."

"Always wanted to hang up a 'Gone Fishing' sign someday," Big D confessed, already pondering which hook to use, metaphorical or real. (Old habits, etc....)

They both turned abruptly to Adam, who was contentedly watching these two august professionals, glad to be in their company, yet grateful his own responsibilities were decidedly much less grand.

"Don't you have to be somewhere – quite soon?" the chief archangel asked. If his past experience of the two was any guide, whatever Eve might be up to, Adam would be more than up for it as well.

At this affectionate farewell, all three gentlemen, each so admirable in his way, reached out to shake one another's hand. As their still-warm fingers touched, the temporary labyrinthine multiplex maze known as the Interstellar Temple of Irresistibly Terrific Temptations, also known as the Satanic Spa and Spiritual Sauna Complex, also known as The Fyres of Olde Hell, more simply known as Demon World, began to vanish into smoke and thin air, its restorative purposes all fulfilled.

As one, the three so different heroes of God's grand plan – Adam, now truly first intergalactic man among men; the Archangel of All Archangels, forever proud yet humble champion of the celestial realm; and Big D, the pre-eminent poker-faced devil with grace up his sleeve – all turned and, shoulder to shoulder, strode slowly through the embers and dying flames and out into Heaven's fast-dawning light, gently cradling in their arms the very last and worst of all Creation's exhausted, well-steamed sinners, now successfully reconditioned, repentant and redeemed.

Au Revoir

❦ WHEN ONE IS responsible, however temporarily, for the well-being and happiness of an entire universe, it should not be surprising how much paperwork can accumulate in even one, albeit very long, celestial day.

God's tireless support staff, however, seemed to have had no difficulty in keeping up. One by one, Eve was presented with a series of dossiers for appraisal and signature, each dealing with some vital matter still nominally under her control.

"An almost flawless performance, if I may say so," proclaimed the demanding yet ever-unruffled Heavenly Office Manager. "You seem to have a natural talent." He peered over his ancient bifocals. "If ever you find yourself considering a career change, I'm sure there would be a fairly senior opening in our humble establishment."

"Thank you for so thoughtful a compliment," Eve responded swiftly, gratified at the accolade even if she didn't feel she was truly corporate material. "Somehow I suspect I'm needed closer to home, at least for a few more thousand years."

"Already guessed as much," the senior celestial bureaucrat confessed, reaching out in his own small benediction. "All the same, you will be greatly missed."

Touched beyond words, Eve clasped his hand with both of hers. "Be assured, I'll never forget you all."

As the Heavenly Office Manager ushered himself out, the still official substitute deity-for-a-day checked her own to-do list; then, smiling quietly, put in a last-minute call to the Angel of Heavenly Grounds and Gardens.

Her next meeting, a final farewell review with the senior angels of the Games' Celestial Coordinating Committee was, predictably, far more lively.

Over the background hum of awe-struck crowds streaming into the nearby stadium, an array of angelic super-stars proudly reported success in every area of their many responsibilities. Everything, they were glad to say, appeared ready for noon, God's return, and the formal opening of the first Heavenly Games of Love. It was the very best thing they had done since Time itself had been teased out of hiding to join in the fun.

As Eve blushed with delight, some of the celestial realm's ordinarily most composed and stately figures began jostling one another in shared excitement, every eminent angel wanting to make absolutely sure before Eve left that each had a commemorative photograph of themselves taken side by side with the woman proven to be the ultimate of all possible temps.

The Official Celestial Photographer, although already overdue at the site of the Games, was more than happy to oblige, in the end handing over his camera to a willing apprentice so as to ensure that he too had his own special memento.

᠒

In the mirrors of six separate rooms in a small motel in Heaven's secluded suburbs, six dazzling ladies checked themselves approvingly one last time. Thanks to Eve's quiet foresight, Heaven's extensive coterie of angelic fashion designers had been at work over the past few weeks on six completely different versions of just the right little dress (plus, of course, perfectly coordinated accessories selected from sources across the entire universe) for just the right lady to wear.

'With my gratitude for your daring contributions to so supremely special an occasion,' the accompanying card read. 'Much love, Eve.'

Exiting their rooms, Marina, Leila, Qingling, Yazmina, Tatiana and Sybilla found their friends and escorts from The Great Beyond beyond the Beyond gathering outside, their wondrously individual faces all showing the same excitement.

Last-minute suggestions fondly given, Team Earth's eclectic band of time-travelling advisors now prepared to leave their charges – come what may – to their own initiative and whatever this great day's fortunes might bring. They, in turn, hastened to their reserved seats at the centre of the great Heavenly stadium.

"Such a wonderful morning!" Valentina exclaimed, taking one arm of the peacock-blue Unofficial Ambassador (Plenipotentiary) of Cosmic Hedonism just as Tatiana happily took the other. "What a perfect day to know somebody who knows Somebody!"

"Most propitious." The three crystal-headed seers, looking especially distinguished in matching tuxedos, ran their far-seeing eyes approvingly up, down and around Sybilla's felicitously-breezy gown.

"Truly a fine and lovely day for surprises," the turquoise-eyed queen of second sight agreed.

ॐ

Alone for the first time in several hours, Eve sat at God's vast desk, thinking some of the longest thoughts of an already very long life, and quietly turning over and over in her hand a little white-and-gold business card.

In the silence, as the words she needed to say began to come, she reached her decision and then for the celestial telephone. After a brief but fervent prayer, she began carefully to dial God's private cell number.

ॐ

"Supreme Being here! Good morning, and thank you for calling. Unfortunately, I'm in a meeting at the moment, and unable to answer your call. Please leave word, and I'll get back to you just as soon as I can."

Eve frowned momentarily, then began to smile. After all, this wasn't exactly the first occasion when the two of them had had some difficulty communicating, but this time the silence happily provoked far less anxiety. If God could trust Eve to look after herself these days, then presumably she could rely on God to look after God.

She began to speak softly after the tiny celestial harp-beep. "I just wanted You to know that I have to leave work slightly ahead of schedule." She paused, thinking of their conversation before God went off on vacation. "But, somehow, I don't think You're going to mind!"

The rest of the recording was something God not only ensured was immediately transcribed for the Eternal Celestial Archives, but which the genuine, original deity inevitably also enjoyed replaying on those increasingly rare moments over the next few billion years when having an off day.

§

It was fortunate, given so long and demanding a night, that archangels are, by definition and prior arrangement, physically, mentally and spiritually indefatigable. Even so, freshly bathed and wearing his best dress uniform, the Archangel of All Archangels yawned momentarily as he first knocked, then, at her call, entered Eve's presence.

Under his arm, she could see the briefing book inscribed in letters of gold, 'Grand Master of Celestial Ceremonies, Heavenly Games of Love', its pages marked with additional notes helpfully inserted by his hard-working staff.

"Thank you so much for last evening's efforts," she said, in gratitude. "It will make such a difference to the universe."

"No trouble at all – a welcome change of pace, in fact," the Archangel-in-Chief replied gallantly. "And, if I may say so, Adam was truly im-pressive, a tremendous help in every way. Made all the difference."

Eve's reply was the widest of smiles. Some things she had known long, long before reaching Heaven.

The Archangel of All Archangels glanced at the pile of dossiers neatly stacked on God's desk. "Please don't quote me," he whispered, "but I could almost be tempted to say you were leaving this place even better than you found it."

"Our little secret," Eve answered, already beaming. "But thank you for the compliment."

Under the circumstances, a celestial non-compete agreement, however flattering, seemed unnecessary.

§

On the big screen monitor to one side, more and more delegations could be seen steadily arriving to take their seats in the great Heavenly stadium. Hosts of angelic ushers hurriedly checked off each new arrival, at the same time offering both their most beneficent smile and a copy of the great day's programme in whatever language was appropriate.

"As I understand it, God's return is scheduled for the start of the opening ceremonies." Eve regarded Archangel-in-Chief thoughtfully. "I would guess that you, for one, are more than ready."

"We go back a long way," the archangel replied diplomatically.

Eve turned, gazing out for close to the last time over Heaven's endless vistas, the glistening stars hiding countless more. Lost in thoughts older than her own distant beginnings, she bit her lip.

"It looks like I may have to leave here somewhat earlier than planned."

Given his faultless celestial intelligence network, not to mention his own exalted powers, it was a comment Heaven's greatest *consigliere* was already expecting, and an opportunity he couldn't resist.

"I seem to remember you saying much the same thing some several million years ago, on the borders of quite an incomparable, barely-used garden, as I recall," he teased fondly.

Eve grinned triumphantly in return.

"Plus ça change...."

⁊

The muffled sounds of the Angel of the Golden Hammer and Gong beginning his practice swings in Heaven's basement reverberated through the air.

"He's at it again!"

"Definitely a fellow who loves his job." A moment later, the Archangel-in-Chief's expression changed, now both supportive and studiously detached. "I suppose I could make a guess at where you're going. And even what you're planning to do."

As so often now, Eve found herself reading effortlessly between the angelic lines. "But since we both know you enjoy surprises...."

The time-worn face of Heaven's most indomitable angel softened, an ancient, abiding tenderness in his deep-blue eyes. "Good luck!" he whispered softly. "To you both."

Eve couldn't help smiling. "I seem to remember you whispering that to us once before – despite yourself – a long ago and under quite different circumstances."

This time they both laughed.

Eve turned away, gazing around God's office, thinking of all her recent days and nights so unexpectedly passed here, in the company of so many inventive, resourceful and, above all, profoundly thoughtful new friends: a uniquely divine privilege which, when all was said and even more was done, was still but a wondrous prelude to all the work that continued everywhere to stretch so very far ahead.

Blinking back tears, she leaned forward to kiss the Archangel of All Archangels on his cheek.

"Do you suppose I could get a receipt?" she asked. "Returned, in good order, one universe."

❧

In his long and so widely-travelled career, the Celestial Aerospace Engineering Angel had never brought in a project late. Nor was he – appearances notwithstanding – about to now. His quick call to the offices of Heavenly Air Traffic Control was as reassuring as he expected.

"The highly unusual shipment you're enquiring about is still on time, with about five minutes to spare," a relaxed voice advised. "They're obviously not used to flying in formation at these speeds," the air traffic control manager went on, "but, with a little help from some quite enthusiastic tail winds, they should take up their prearranged holding pattern in, say, just under an hour."

"Many thanks – and obviously not just from me."

"Much appreciated. As you can expect, we've had to re-route several regular flights so as to clear the way, not to mention delaying quite a few celestial charters." There was a pause. "Everyone in the tower says, 'Well done!' This is definitely a cargo-carrying first."

"Truly special circumstances," the Aerospace Engineering Angel smiled. "Truly special delivery!"

❧

Reunited at last after such eventful days for both of them, Adam and Eve exalted once more in the simple joyful familiarity of one another.

Though infinitely grateful for all that Divine Providence had done in guiding them here, they were equally glad to be going. With Eve's celestial duties almost complete, their Earthly ones now even more clearly called.

Be it ever so unfinished, there was no place like home, wherever they might next find it.

Side by side, they stood quietly in God's office, looking out over all the splendours of Heaven and toward the immense new stadium, its seats rapidly filling.

"What an unbelievable past few weeks!" Eve exclaimed at last, recalling those first faltering steps at the base of the Heavenly throne.

"So much lost time to make up for; so much to learn; so much to set in motion."

She shook her head in wonder. "Not bad, all things considered, for a little girl from a hitherto-unknown little ball of earth, air, fire, water and – when it really counts – good old-fashioned gumption. Not too bad at all."

Adam put his arm around her. "You were absolutely, totally, utterly perfect!"

"Highly unlikely, but I'm forever glad you think so!" Eve rested her head on his shoulder with contentment, pride and not a little tiredness. And far more than a little anticipation.

Turning her face, she looked deeply, tenderly into the mirror of Adam's all-accepting, all-affirming eyes, seeing in them every moment of the long, shared history of their love, with all its still unfinished consequences and challenges.

"Especially when the best is yet to come!"

"Yours till eternity," Adam whispered. "And beyond."

ꙮ

Hand in hand, Earth's first couple prepared to take their leave of Heaven, a shimmering honour guard of sad but grateful angels to see them on their secret way. As Eve glanced back, everything in the ultimate of all executive offices was as it should be, everything exactly as God had left it before disappearing on vacation.

Everything, that is, except for a welcoming profusion of flowers around the room; and, on God's desk, artfully arranged by her own slender hand, a small golden bowl of Heaven's rarest, most inviting apples.

For old times sake.

Heavenly Games of Love

"ASK NOT WHAT YOUR UNIVERSE CAN DO FOR YOU, BUT
WHAT YOU CAN DO FOR YOUR UNIVERSE!"

— The World's Most Beautiful Astronomer

Back in Time

𓀀 ONE OF THE drawbacks of omniscience is that it is difficult to be surprised, let alone pleasantly so. Even celestial rules, however, have their exceptions.

Eschewing angelic motorcade, sirens and outriders, slipping invisibly back into Heaven through an entrance known only to God, the genuine, original Supreme Being *Extraordinaire* happily surveyed all its many recent changes. Bright, shining, freshly washed and scrubbed for Games Day, the celestial realm had never looked lovelier.

On every side, myriad angels flitted past on last-minute assignments, their faces understandably a touch tired, but all of them more enthusiastic and inspired than the Creator could ever remember. In the distance, as the hour neared noon, the great stadium began to echo with the first notes from the newly-formed Heavenly Games Symphony Orchestra playing the most up-beat, down-home sacred music of the last hundred million years.

Humming along for a moment, God reflected on how delightful it was to be able to delegate with confidence.

𓀀

With the stands now almost filled, the respective leaders of every competing galaxy began to settle self-consciously into their seats, all sporting their individual team colours, all waving their individual flags.

Next to come, sages, seers and saints from a billion star systems quietly filed in to their section close by, their air of nonchalant modesty and ease befitting their advanced states of enlightenment. On looking around, one distinguished member of the Cosmic Alliance of the Friends of the Friends of God couldn't help whispering to her closest colleague, "Say what you like: however long it takes to get here, there's no place else I'd rather call home!"

Moments later, Eve's closest cosmic relatives from the Ancient and Honourable Sisterhood of the Interplanetary Dawns of Creation were ushered to their rightly privileged places, all nearby rising in a spontaneous, swiftly-spreading tribute.

❧

As countless banners streamed against a pure blue sky, a host of senior angels nervously took up their positions on either side of the great golden podium.

Showered, shaved, and now sporting a suitably rakishly cut blazer and open-neck white linen shirt, Big D slipped into his waiting seat beside Scheherazade. The briefest of kisses between them, however discreet, was enough to reconfirm for both all the promise of many shared possibilities.

"How does it feel to be back?" she asked, fondly and archly at once. "After so long."

Big D looked around with a laconic, matching grin. "The joint seems slightly bigger than I remember."

He ran his eyes over Scheherazade's floral silk dress with its patterns of orchids which, as a parting gift, Eve had expressly requested be designed both to conceal and reveal. "And the company now far more beautiful … and challenging."

He paused, making the most of an already satisfyingly-slow examination. "It would seem that a certain rather sharp-eyed lady from a little blue-and-white world has a very good idea of your style."

Scheherazade looked back at him steadily from under perfectly-lowered eyelids. "And yours."

❧

The especially quick-witted, fast-tongued archangels serving as commentators in the Heavenly Broadcast Studio were nearing the end of their scenesetting interview with the Games' Celestial Coordinating Committee.

"And roughly how many current residents of the universe does your staff anticipate will be watching today's opening ceremonies?"

There was a brief pause while a number of ethereal sources were consulted. In view of God's pending return, it was probably a good idea to be as accurate as possible.

"Every single one," the Keeper of Celestial Statistics announced decisively. Putting up his palm to forestall interruption, he added proudly, "including, of course, the invisible, ever-inquisitive presence of anyone and everyone who has ever lived!"

Given how much these galactic precursors and pensioners (whatever their current form and fate) had done to help prepare the way to this day, it was clear they were as eager as their descendants to witness this great festive outcome of their own earlier lives.

"Heaven has put on more than a few memorable performances in its time," the first commentator observed at last, his tone as awed as only a reported-on-everything-under-a-trillion-suns celestial media veteran's could possibly be. "But this, surely, must be the cosmic audience of all possible audiences."

He braked abruptly in mid oratory, as every member of the Celestial Coordinating Committee stared past him at the central, wider than wide-screen television monitor.

In the next instant, as partial images coalesced to became the unexpected picture of a nearly exhausted, proudly sunlit little convoy streaking dauntlessly toward Heaven, every last angel began jumping up and down, laughing in sudden delight.

"Eve…!" exclaimed one celestial committee co-chair, his composure disappearing in an astonished wing beat.

"Strikes again!" said the other, completing a unanimously approving verdict.

※

Earth's dazed and disoriented residents, together with their cousins on the other nine (at last count) planets making up what was possessively known as 'our' solar system, breathed a huge sigh of relief as their very own central star finally ceased its mad dash through the universe and began slowing to a perfectly-positioned halt, high above Heaven.

All the orbiting planets gradually sorted themselves out from the flying V formation which had been so aerodynamically helpful in reaching their destination on time, and began to reassume their usual positions in the great circling scheme of things.

Meanwhile every newly-arrived eye was fixed firmly, if incredulously, on all the wonders below.

For a great many of the voyagers, given that a certain realm long thought to be more fanciful than real now lay spread out before them in all its undeniable glory, major spiritual readjustments seemed unavoidable. For others (not a few gleefully turning to their neighbours to whisper, "See, I told you so!") their first glimpse of this vast celestial haven was simply the sight of an inevitable destination at which they had somehow managed to arrive much earlier than expected.

The Sun, beginning to catch its breath after so unprecedented a trip, was doubly glad to be 'home'. A very long time had passed since the Big Bang, and it had always secretly wondered what might have become of its original birthplace.

The Moon too, lesser light though it might be, was so thrilled by both the journey and the goal that it couldn't stop waxing and waning every few minutes, standing on its head from time to time to enjoy an even more unusual view.

For his part, the Celestial Aerospace Engineering Angel warmly shook hands with his staff, all of them now reviewing further pages of ever more intricate calculations. Given that the residents of Earth were now (thanks to Adam's inspired suggestion) about to get their own privileged view of wonders yet to come, it was clearly essential that everybody on board the planet be in the very best possible position to see the show. After all, it would be a colossal setback to get every Earthling miraculously to Heaven, only then to find that many couldn't quite make out what was going on. Definitely not the sort of supreme cosmic anticlimax any self-respecting celestial technocrat would want on his or her angelic record.

Glancing firstly at the clock, then at the new arrivals, then the clock once more, the Celestial Aerospace Engineering Angel carefully reconsidered what looked like his two main options.

The simplest solution seemed to be to set Earth's rotation to fast-spin mode, so that everyone on the planet could see Heaven for at least five minutes every hour or so.

Clearly however, this approach was not without problems: first, the fitful, repetitive brevity of each individual's intermittent glimpse of the celestial realm; and, second, given the high rotation speeds required, the near certainty that everyone would grow increasingly dizzy with every look.

The preferred choice, he decided, was hastily to rearrange the solar system so that, as other planets swung closer to help stabilize an Earth poised in stillness on its own axis, everyone on the planet could be swiftly moved to specially arranged seating on the sunlit side facing Heaven. From there they could all see everything at once, without interruption, throughout the entire opening ceremony, and, with a few further additions in the way of meals, washrooms and sleeping arrangements, even possibly for the entirety of the Heavenly Games themselves.

Given the Angelic Engineering Society's ancient motto – The difficult, we did yesterday; the impossible takes even less time – all this was successfully accomplished in the twinkling of a celestial eye.

Seated side by side, billions of Earth's residents – now rearranged into a happy jumble of individuals from every country, language and favourite flavour of ice cream – together enjoyed their very own planetary equivalent of front row seats for both God's return and the much-heralded Opening Ceremonies. Before them, Heaven was spread out in all its radiance. Directly below, the spectacular Heavenly Games stadium continued to fill with crowds from across a universe now more imaginable in all its magnificent scope and scale.

All in all, the sleepless but energized visitors from Earth agreed, it promised to be a totally incredible day. Even if, so far, no one from Eve's native planet had caught even the faintest glimpse of that singularly accomplished great-great-grandmother they all hoped to see.

Where, exactly, was Eve?

And, almost as important, where was Team Earth?

Given the occasion, the Angel of the Golden Hammer and Gong had earlier decided, a little extra musical something was definitely in order. Gleaming mallet in hand, he had quietly disappeared through the double-padded doors of the Celestial Music Studio. Finally, after experimenting late in the night until satisfied, he found himself scribbling down the notes of his subsequently-celebrated Composition for Hammer, Gong and Heavenly Games Orchestra; a loud but lyrical interplay to announce God's Heavenly return *fortissimo, brio con molto brio.*

Complete with a final touch more *brio*, just in case.

Checking his carefully re-synchronized watch, he stepped toward the huge, quivering metal circle, the great golden hammer similarly trembling on his shoulder in anticipation.

Now, as viewers throughout the universe leaned closer to their screens, the Archangel of All Archangels and his senior associates appeared from their changing rooms off the celestial lounge and began making their way to their seats at centre stage.

The past few weeks might have been hard on everyone (a labour of love second only to the on-going alchemy of Creation, many agreed) but today, truly, was a great day to be an angel!

❧

As the Archangel-in-Chief neared the podium, carefully adjusting his wings one last time, he caught a fleeting glimpse of the genuine, original Supreme Being off to one side (once again appearing out of nowhere, as so often mischievously inclined to do) and now waiting in that effortless serenity to which even the greatest of God's long-serving admirers still aspired.

The Archangel of All Archangels gave an imperceptible, distinctly approving nod. Wherever the Boss had been on vacation, or whatever the Boss had been up to, it certainly seemed to have worked. However ultimately unreadable, God had never looked better, nor (as Heaven's second-in-command was profoundly relieved to see) quite so relaxed and renewed.

Their eyes met, the near-complete cosmic renaissance acknowledged in a single, all-encompassing glance.

A hundred thousand angels rose to their feet, lifting their trumpets in celebration of Sanctity's safe return. Moments later, the Heavenly Games Symphony launched into its own proud welcome, the indefatigable Angel of the Golden Hammer and Gong bringing those two mutually irresistible forces together once more in a joyful explosion of sound.

God was back!

Hello Again!

&. "LADIES AND GENTLEMEN. Welcome to Heaven!"

The Grand Master of Celestial Ceremonies waved an appreciative hand in reply as the first of many ovations that day reverberated throughout the universe.

On so dazzling an afternoon, there was no need for the earlier scene-setting melodramatics of darkening skies and dancing lightning bolts, effective though these celestial show-stoppers could be. Of one accord, every star in Creation spun the dial of its own intensity, the better to set the universe aglow.

The senior archangel turned, bowing eloquently to the silent radiance on his lef "And, on behalf of everyone in the universe … welcome back!" His next words were carefully chosen just for God, and delivered *sotto voce* with an amused conspiratorial smile.

"Heaven really wasn't the same without You." A judicious pause, a fleeting memory of fire, brimstone and Big D at his uninhibited re-demptive finest. "But it sure was a Hell of a lot of fun!"

Across the cosmos, trillions of far distant cousins got their first glimpse of the ultimate common ancestor of them all; a divinity lately taken for granted, now reassuringly back in charge, invisibility foregone for this special occasion and happily concealed within a shimmering ball of light.

At the universe-wide applause of gazillions of hands, all clapping as one, God broke into an even more resplendent smile.

"Thank you. Thank you, one and all. And may I simply say … it's great to be Home!"

"God looks fantastic!" Scheherazade exclaimed, remembering the hint of divine fatigue overshadowing their first meeting.

"More than fully re-energized," Big D replied evenly, a memory returning of just how deceptively laid back the Boss had seemed only moments before scaring the spiritual pants off all the earliest archangels (then still in training) with the biggest unannounced bang of a cosmic lifetime.

So far.

The two read each other's mind with a smaller, though simultaneous explosion.

"God hasn't finished with the universe yet!" Scheherazade exclaimed. "Not by a long shot!"

Big D took her outstretched hand. "Given all I know of my earliest and abiding mentor, I suspect God hasn't finished with God either!"

Unhurriedly, unrestrictedly, God surveyed all the transgalactic team members listening raptly in the wings, the countless cosmic invitees applauding in the stands, and all the viewers watching in fascination from all their far-flung native worlds.

"Welcome to Heaven!" the unsourced source of all repeated to the universe at large, happily taking up where the Archangel-in-Chief had left off. With this suitably heartening prelude, God turned toward that specially reserved section of the stadium where a select group of legendary ladies sat hand in hand with their planetary consorts from so many star systems.

"And, thanks to so many truly irreplaceable pioneers, welcome, as well, to our very own, first-ever Cosmic Family Reunion'!"

For planets as for persons the ancient secret remained true: our unresolved, seemingly long-forgotten pasts, once rightly honoured and understood, become the liberating source of both salvation and renewal.

As the charter members of the Ancient and Honourable Sisterhood of the Cosmic Dawns of Creation all blushed and stamped their feet in appreciation, their descendants across the universe joined in as loudly (given the considerable distances involved) as they could.

For his part, the less-than-dulcet Angel of the Golden Hammer and Gong quietly positioned a second great brass circle opposite the first, the better to swing resonantly back and forth between the two when the time came. If there was the slightest chance that God might seek to use so extraordinary an occasion to share one or two particularly liberating insights with a cosmos whose attention span remained fairly short, then it was likely a wise precaution to be ready to lend a supportive hand, preferably as deafeningly as possible.

&.

"I would like to begin by thanking all the extraordinarily devoted staff of Heaven Inc. who, working so tirelessly together, have made these inaugural Games possible!" Making the most of a return to centre stage, God surveyed the bright-winged, even brighter-eyed, celestial team of wonderworkers arranged on either side.

"Then again, having long observed my incomparably light-fingered associates in action, I never doubted their powers, or the outcome, for a moment."

For the celestial contributors to what was the greatest spiritual profit-sharing plan in Creation, it was a remark which was heart-warming to hear before an audience of the entire universe. While it is a basic rule of celestial etiquette to accept God's grace as gracefully as possible in return, even the most senior angels were seen to wage a briefly-lost battle in the struggle between looking suitably humble or totally blown away by their own recent record-setting performance.

Across the universe, as well, God sensed the quietly deepening pride of the star systems in all they had just accomplished. There was even the beginnings of a new dedication to an adventure infinitely (and so much more enjoyably) greater than themselves.

"As I look around today, I can't help but feel glad to have finally taken a little executive downtime." There was a judicious pause. "And to have left the universe so constructively in your care."

The great ball of light grinned from ear to invisible ear. "And so it seems, given your justifiably self-satisfied smiles, do you!"

On a now stationary Earth poised perfectly to see all that was happening just below, two doughty, well-preserved ladies originally from opposite sides of the planet turned to one another, mottled hands clutching their freshly buffed, flower-bedecked aluminium walkers.

"Such an inspiring welcome," said the first. "And God looks so much younger than I expected."

"Must go to a really great spa, I imagine," the second replied.

The two stared at each other.

"Isn't it strange that God hasn't mentioned Eve?" They looked at each other again, weathered faces wrinkling into smiles of expectant complicity.

"Probably knows something we don't...."

❧

"As everyone here is aware," God continued, surfacing from thoughts older than time, "there is someone else we need to thank. A beautiful, passionate and providentially independent woman who – appearing as if out of nowhere at exactly the right moment – has not only made the impossible possible, the most unthinkable profoundly real, but also, as I look around Me today, Heaven all the more truly heavenly!"

The great wrap-around screen darkened and as a faint far-off flute sent its first awakening notes toward the sky, the image of a solitary little blue-and-white world appeared, floating bemusedly in space.

A succession of close-ups followed: first, of Adam and Eve, resolute faces turned towards so many tomorrows yet to come, a foregone Eden vanishing in their wake; then of their countless descendants, fated and blessed to explore a world both too little and too large, one forever demanding from them all they could give.

An instant later, Eve's face appeared in a rapid series of snapshots taken unawares: on the grounds of a distant retirement home; ascending the Heavenly throne; in brief discussion with a vacation-ready God; in urgent meetings with senior angels and, finally, alone with her thoughts and the possibilities of one truly extraordinary celestial day.

Fittingly, the last image was of that moment when, kissing Adam tenderly, she had walked out into celestial brightness, extending to the universe at large that unexpected invitation which, ever since, had kept its citizenry at once so extraordinarily busy and unbelievably inspired.

Earth's first lady, in all her unfinished, unvarnished, glory.

❧

"Eve! Eve! Eve!" The first to begin the thunderous chant were all the team members. Were it not for Earth's first woman, none of them would now be here, looking forward to their competitive prospects amid such overwhelming celestial splendour.

The inhabitants of Earth itself – now side by side on the front third of a little blue-and-white planet miraculously poised so close to Heaven – joined in as deafeningly as they could. Even if it was rather difficult to be heard over the combined voices of a hundred and one billion galaxies, all repeating the same increasingly urgent demand.

"Eve! Eve! Eve!"

God held up a glowing hand for silence. "Much to everyone's regret – including, not surprisingly, My own – I'm sorry to tell you that the lovely and enterprising lady we all so much want to see appears, most unfortunately, unable to be with us for the moment."

A disappointed groan escaped every mouth on every galaxy.

"Although we haven't yet spoken directly, Eve left word on My voicemail only hours ago. And while she sounded well and in good spirits, she was apparently called away on, as she put it, a rather urgent family matter. In her message, however, she asked Me to convey, to each one of you in every star system, her deepest gratitude and profound best wishes. In her own words, her recent sojourn in Heaven was 'the honour and privilege of a cosmic lifetime; an opportunity to give back what little I could to so vast and wondrous a home to us all.'"

As the thunderous applause began to fade, the C.E.O. of Universe Inc. turned to the Archangel of All Archangels. "Then again, knowing Eve, I wouldn't be totally astonished if somehow she managed…."

The Archangel-in-Chief chuckled. "I'd only be surprised if she didn't!"

Let the Games Begin!

§. AT THE CENTRE of the overflowing stadium, team members from competing galaxies straightened hurriedly in their seats as God turned on them a disturbingly all-knowing gaze.

"I would like, in particular, to extend My warmest welcome to so many Champions of Love who have come here from every corner of Creation, to delight, challenge and edify us in days ahead."

During the fierce applause that followed, God cast a quick glance at the final briefing notes over which countless angels had held so many exhaustive, wing-thumping confabulations.

God paused, simultaneously looking at every competitor with pointed, individual appreciation. "As One who has had the exhilarating, if also rather humbling experience of coming up with what was then, admittedly, a very much smaller Universe in just under seven days, may I say how deeply impressed I am by your dedication. It is, therefore, with no small professional empathy that I wish all of you now both the greatest good luck and every spiritual success!"

As all rose cheering to their feet, the senior celestial staff keeping watch over the day's events carefully ticked off yet another successfully-accomplished step in their seemingly endless schedule. To one side, the Archangel of All Archangels pushed a small golden button to transmit a series of carefully-orchestrated signals.

Everywhere around the Heavenly Games Stadium, a host of angels sprang into much-rehearsed action.

§.

When heard for the first time, the drawn-out roll of a million drums, even in a space as large as Heaven, can be surprisingly loud, especially when supporting the ascending peals of two million trumpets.

In the silence that followed, the Heavenly Games Symphony began softly to play its own special tribute to the One whom they acknowledged as the concert master of all concert masters. As unforgettable as its source, the melody unfolded as a series of increasingly elaborate variations on that infinitely poignant, fierce, primal song which God heard, everywhere arising like a waking infant's cry, in those first moments when dreaming the universe into being.

No matter their whereabouts, all listening found themselves falling into that same shared timeless reverie.

Moments later, as they looked up and gasped, the air above the stadium filled with a vast, multi-perspective vision: the great cosmic lotus flower that was the universe unfolding from its primordial source; energy and dark energy, matter and dark matter, rhizome and eternal reward – all opening outward and upward together as one.

For a moment, both the commentators in the Heavenly Broadcast Studio and their viewers across the cosmos shared the same awed silence, looking on in wonder at that ever-expanding mystery from which they too arose and of which they were inseparably part.

Clearly moved, God turned to pat Heaven's second-in-command on the back with a firm, if invisible hand. "My unqualified congratulations. That must have taken some work, speaking from experience."

The Archangel-in-Chief blushed with pleasure. "Well, some of Your greatest angelic admirers struggled through more than a few all-nighters on it. We borrowed the original blueprints. Hoped You wouldn't mind!"

"Couldn't have done better Myself," God replied generously.

The senior archangel inclined his head in appreciation. Then he pointed to the far horizon. "All the younger, less arthritic members of Your staff also wanted to show their appreciation."

As every eye looked upward, drawn by a steadily increasing whirr, the first of many of perfectly-choreographed flights of angels began winging happily overhead, keeping stately position with one another in the introductory fly-past of an All Angels Air Show.

Wave after wave of well-scrubbed cherubs and seraphim, their wings freshly whitened and pressed, their faces beaming, flew towards the great stadium in succession, all looking directly at the majestic luminous ball of light at the podium as they passed, and then bowed their heads in homage.

Moments later, their first combined warm-up display complete, the junior angels began to divide into aerobatic groups. Weaving merrily in, out and around one another, their agile wings sparkling under Heaven's unrivalled light, they swooped low, then sailed upward in precise, coordinated patterns, one by one forming the long-revered outlines of the central spiritual images of every religion in the entire universe – a limitless, timeless interwoven splendour of far-flung faiths and forms.

At the sight, the whole stadium leapt to its feet in applause, many pointing happily to their own particular theological icon, others gazing admiringly if not also slightly enviously to ones even more unorthodox or grand.

"Remind Me to give everyone a raise," God proclaimed, looking both astonished and enthralled by this unexpected display of unquestionably-inherited skills. "And an extra week off, when this is all over."

"Just wait a bit," the Archangel of All Archangels interposed, already hovering several feet off the ground, excited as he was at the prospect of the rest of the best that was still to come. "You haven't seen anything yet!"

No sooner had he spoken than the angelic flights divided, racing in equal numbers toward all forty-four corners of Creation. Then, suddenly, reversing, they shot toward the centre of the stadium, simultaneously switching on the coloured smoke canisters hidden beneath their wings. As countless angels criss-crossed at every altitude, every colour in the universe swirled out, over and over and over, across the skies.

The musicians from carefully selected star systems began the first bars of a hitherto unknown, yet hauntingly familiar Heavenly Games Anthem.

Missing each other by the merest of micro-seconds and millimetres at every altitude, millions of angelic sky-writers, each one trailing his or her carefully-chosen coloured plumes of smoke, began to write their collective masterpiece above the cheering, awe-struck stadium.

Letter by letter, line by flying angelic line, the Heavenly skies filled with a vast, illuminated invitation, written celestially large in every language of every galaxy in the entire universe:

Welcome
One and All
to
The First-Ever, Truly Universal
Cosmos-Wide
Heavenly Games of Love

Viewers watching everywhere continued to applaud as the angels, of one accord, turned off their smoke ejectors and began reforming into their original squadrons. As they waved a final time before flying off in rhythmic succession, their vast celestial display itself began slowly to dissolve behind them, a swirl of colours arcing across the sky.

God reached out, invisible hand clasping that of the Archangel of All Archangels. "Now that's what I would call a show-stopper of a celestial show-starter!"

"Thanks, Boss," said the Archangel-in-Chief, finally letting out his long-held breath as the last flight of millions of criss-crossing angels exited without aerial mishap. "We aim to please."

"Always a good idea," God agreed.

§

Staring down on all the rainbows curving happily across Heaven, the residents of Earth had a perfect view of excited teams from countless unknown galaxies, all now lining up for the Grand Processional. To their dismay, Team Earth was still nowhere to be seen: nor, indeed, was there any sign of that intrepid woman responsible for the improbable Heavenly Games in the first place.

From a traditionally divided planet now so tantalizingly close to Heaven, a determined cry rose of its own accord. "Eve! Eve! We want Eve!"

God, inevitably, heard the intensifying chant long before anyone else, gazing upward with a fond, if eminently unreadable smile.

"As Someone who has already had a certain number of, how shall I say, singularly instructive encounters with this particular woman," God whispered, "I trust I may be permitted a small observation. Be careful what you pray for!"

Wisdom of Eden

❧ ONE OF A WIZARD'S noblest aspirations, after so many millennia of arcane training and experiment, is the chance to perform his particular style of magic in front of as large and captivated an audience as possible. One of his greatest fears, on the other hand, is to find himself centre-stage at the precise moment when his personal bag of tricks suffers what is known in the trade as a critical occult equipment failure.

Since the eyes of the entire universe would soon be firmly fixed upon Abracadabra and his fellow magicians, it was not surprising that they all triple-checked the engines, transmissions and, most especially, the steering and brakes on their individual little white clouds.

Given that their first-ever public appearance in Heaven was to be as pilots of a distinctly-innovative form of transportation intending to arrive exactly and precisely on time before a preternaturally meticulous deity, it would definitely do their reputations no good to find themselves suddenly veering off on a tangent or, worse, not being able to stop at the very last moment. It was also understandable that, as an added precaution, comprehensive travel insurance was sought in the form of time-tested spells recited forwards, backwards and sideways.

As Abracadabra put the matter: "If and when one's opportunity to appear before God finally arrives, it could be considered not only extremely bad manners but even exceptionally gross spiritual negligence to blow it in the last thirty seconds!"

❧

On the grounds of their celestial suburban motel, the members of Team Earth looked furtively at their watches and then at each other. The many-hued members of the Whole Earth Choir, Orchestra and Marching Band Combo re-tuned their instruments and voices, then quietly hummed their individual parts in the still-secret global anthem so hastily composed, arranged and (everyone hoped) more or less mastered. In the distance, countless flights of angels soared over the Heavenly Games stadium in their impossibly colourful tribute, the vast crowds continuing to cheer them on.

Shading her eyes against the celestial brightness, the World's Most Beautiful Astronomer turned to her co-captain. "Cosmic multimedia notwithstanding, so many of our descendants will still surely wonder what it was really like to be here on this day."

Leaning elegantly on his ceremonial silver spade, eyes eloquent with resolve, the World's Greatest Gravedigger reached out to take her hand. "Just as so many of our ancestors must be wondering, even now, how it is that we, and they, by proxy, ever managed to get here at all!"

The two perfectly matching halves of the human heart gazed on one another, united in tenderness and triumph. "And both, in their ways – Earth's fast-disappearing past and it's even more urgent future – undoubtedly very glad we did."

"Whatever comes?"

"Whatever comes!"

After a suitably lingering, death-defying, life-after-life-affirming kiss, the two leaders of Team Earth turned, drawing their charges into an expectant semi-circle.

At almost the last moment before leaving Heaven, Eve had placed an ultra-rush order to the secret source (never seen in public without her giant sunglasses) of the ultimate in celestial luxury wear. "Lots of those – and one of this and one of that: to your own design."

Now, only a few hours later and with only minutes to spare, and just as Adam and Eve arrived at the small celestial motel, the near-breathless Angel of Unconventional Elegance rushed towards them, unflustered assistants in tow, their arms laden with an array of blue, white and gold hand-tailored suits and dresses.

"Enough for every member of Team Earth, in all the right sizes of course," the casually immaculate, immaculately casual angel announced proudly.

"And, for you…,"

From behind her back, she produced a delightfully short but not too short-skirted cocktail ensemble in subtly tropical tones of tangerine, aquamarine and cream, accompanied by the perfect complement of gold earrings in the form of miniature fig leaves.

Adam, for whom she provided a more restrained white dinner jacket and aquamarine trousers (debonair bow tie optional), beamed as Eve held the eventfully diaphanous dress against herself for his approval.

"Always knew you were the one worth waiting for," he said gallantly.

"As if you had a choice," Eve replied.

Adam bowed, then, slowly bringing his hand from behind his back, he held out a gleaming golden bracelet to match her earrings, its surface engraved with a pattern of intertwined hearts.

And fig leaves.

"Thankfully, no choice at all."

Standing to one side with his fellow wizards quietly watching Adam and Eve encouraging the members of Team Earth, Abracadabra couldn't help wondering what Eve could possibly say to ready her descendants for this, their very first appearance before a cosmos-wide audience enjoying, in many cases, far greater age, experience and advanced expertise.

Whether person or planet, he acknowledged, it's never easy to make something of oneself and find one's worthwhile place in the great universal scheme of dreams.

Had he overheard an earlier conversation, however, between Eve and two figures making an unexpected, if not perhaps entirely unplanned appearance, the old sage would have found himself reassured.

Choosing their moment with care, the authoritative, globe-shaped twins whom Eve last saw on her way to Heaven's highest office, had suddenly reappeared merrily out of nowhere.

"Thought we'd like to come along on so special a day," the Angel of Unprecedented Opportunities began.

"And wish you both good luck!" said the Angel of Hidden Agendas.

They stared at Eve appraisingly, fleeting images of past and future flickering behind their identically thoughtful gaze. "Team Earth's ready?"

"Almost." Eve looked at Adam. "Except for a few last-minute remarks."

"May we respectfully offer a small suggestion?" the twin globe-shaped figures asked simultaneously. "A little advice from two fairly well-connected celestial insiders."

"Be tough with them," the Angel of Unprecedented Opportunities (and Heavenly big sticks) said with a smile. "Earth's got a long way to go."

"Be gentle with them," the Angel of Hidden Agendas (and cosmic carrots) continued with an even bigger smile. "Earth's got a very long way to go."

In the ensuing silence, Eve reflected on the interwoven fates of worlds beyond number, each with its own histories and hopes, its devotions and even more urgent demands upon an omnipresent divinity inseparable from the unfolding universe itself.

Taking her time, the now former official substitute Supreme Being *Extraordinaire* gazed back and forth between the two angels. "Why not use both approaches?"

"Actually, that's really what we had in mind," the angelic twins answered in unison.

"Me too," said Eve.

&❧

It was fortunate that a freelance technician accompanying the Whole Earth Choir, Orchestra and Marching Band Combo, having turned on his digital recorder so as to interview a number of his favourite musicians, was so mesmerized by Adam and Eve's sudden appearance live and in person that he forgot to turn it off.

As a result, her ensuing brief but heartfelt *cri-de-coeur* to the members of Team Earth was inadvertently captured not only for posterity, but also as the centrepiece of an immediate, record-breaking best-seller (available from the Heavenly Games official souvenir shop and select satellite outlets throughout the universe), its sales quintupling exponentially as the Games went on, fulfilling Eve's every hope and wish.

"Once upon a time…"

There was complete stillness as Eve, Adam at her side, spoke softly of that earliest beguiling yet restrictive paradise and of their mutual decision, in the face of the real false tempter they later came to know as Fear, to forsake its unearned bounty in search of larger lives and a destiny as yet unknown.

As faint wisps of coloured smoke from the All Angels Air Show drifted towards them, Earth's first couple gazed on one another, their eyes bright with the tenderness of a love now crowned by these past few improbable weeks amid the mystery and majesty of Heaven itself.

High above, an unsuspecting little blue-and-white planet counted the moments, in wonder and impatience, until the great show would begin.

"For all our faults and flaws," Eve continued softly, "Earth's come a long way since Eden." She glanced upward to where a familiar sun, now so unexpectedly far from home and wearing dark glasses against the celestial glare, was happily settling in. "In more ways than one."

Adam turned to his descendants. "Ultimately, however, whether planet, constellation or most ancient of galaxies, we all share the same inescapable challenge: to open the way, day by newly-dawning, well-lived day, to all the universe has yet to become."

He turned in tribute to the World's Greatest Gravedigger and its Most Beautiful Astronomer, their hitherto separate powers and passions now reinforcing one another. "Even in death, we are born explorers. Made from the same elements as the remotest constellations, we are fated to seek our fortunes in the stars."

Studying Team Earth in silence, the sounds of cheering rising anew from the distant stadium, Eve appraised every keen and confident face. Eyes misting, she reached out, taking Adam's hand, and with her other hand gesturing towards the great panorama of billions of stars shimmering in their own secret harmony.

"Day by day, throughout generations of joy, sorrow and ceaseless exploration, one force alone – one limitless, numinous power above all else – has sustained, upheld and drawn our countless descendants on.

"Today, as we go forward together, carrying the banner of our fragile, irrepressible little planet to these universal Heavenly Games of Love, Adam and I rejoice to see and celebrate in you, our children's children, that imperishable gift brought safe from Eden and now so much your own … the invincible courage of the human heart."

As Eve finished, there was a trembling in the air, as if generations past and those in crowded, ever more challenging millennia yet to come were already applauding, however silently and unseen.

In the same moment, all the men and women of Team Earth began to cheer – with a new, now unconquerable determination.

Invited or not, a little blue-and-white planet no longer in exile from itself was ready to take on the entire universe, whether or not the universe itself was up for the encounter.

⁊

"Never fails – no matter what part of the cosmos," Abracadabra muttered to himself, blowing strongly on his large white handkerchief. "It's always stirring when time's toddlers finally decide to take matters in their own hands and become heroes and heroines on their own."

Around him, a hundred sorcerers synchronized both their watches and (just to be doubly safe and sure) their magic, moral compasses as well, then moved in unison toward the pilots' seats of their own little white clouds.

Taking their cue, the Whole Earth Choir, Orchestra and Marching Band Combo struck up a sizzling rendition of one of the Fountain of Eternal Youth Retirement Home's perennial favourites (aluminum walkers notwithstanding): "Here we come; get out of the way!"

Elsewhere, on an impatient little planet poised precariously above Heaven, hosts of angels began distributing billions of sealed blue-and-white bundles to every one of its increasingly mystified residents.

The celestial beguine was about to begin.

Grandest of Grand Processionals

❧ FORTUNATELY FOR ALL, God's good time is both infinitely fast and exquisitely slow, effortlessly adapting itself to everyone and everyone to it. Under any other conditions, clearly, it would have been impossible for so many billions of carefully chosen galactic teams to parade past the celestial reviewing stand not just once, but eventually, twice in the course of what even God forever remembered as an incomparably eventful afternoon.

If Big D's preferred *modus operandi* was to speak softly but carry a big pitchfork, the Archangel of All Archangels had his own preferred choice of incentives.

"Ladies and gentleman, boys and girls, and each and every being, seen and unseen, in the entire Universe…."

A wash of colour still filling the skies, the Heavenly Games Symphony once more playing their signature anthem's hypnotic refrain, God's chief operations officer happily returned to his starring role as Grand Master of Celestial Ceremonies.

Surveying the waiting teams, overflowing stadium and, by proxy, the entire universe, the Archangel-in-Chief was pleased. After so many days and nights of non-stop preparation, even the most calm, cool and outwardly collected galaxies were plainly ready (as his crimson counterpart might put it) to let off a little steam.

"In a few moments, contenders from worlds beyond number will begin to strut their much-rehearsed stuff before us all." The Archangel-in-Chief paused, gazing once more on the seemingly endless lineup, its pride and excitement clearly equal to his own.

"Please join me in giving these wondrously-talented, magnificently-prepared and now understandably adrenalin-rushed champions of Love a suitably Heavenly show of appreciation!"

As the audience responded unreservedly, even the dignified members of the Celestial Coordinating Committee, together with every other angel throughout the length and breadth of Heaven, joined in exuberantly as well.

If there were days when it was difficult, even occasionally secretly depressing to be an angel, there were others that proved, quite simply, absolutely terrific! Especially when God led the prolonged ovation, the great pulsing ball of light echoing the universe's clearly unanimous applause.

※

"I have to give him credit," Big D admitted, turning to the beauty at his side. "Uniquely demanding though the celestial realm may be, my archangelic brother really knows how to run the place."

Scheherazade raised an amused eyebrow. "Envious?"

"Hell, no!" Big D smiled, surveying the latest in Heaven's clearly remodelled towers before nodding contentedly. "All in all, I prefer to think of myself as more of an independent contractor."

His very own form of divine retribution (and well-matched reward) regarded him fondly, if not a little mischievously.

"Temptation … and Associate?"

Sometimes silence, accompanied by an irresistably devilish smile, was both the correct and most mutually satisfying answer.

※

The moment everyone had been waiting for (some constellations, of a certain age, much longer than others) finally arrived. As the Heavenly Games Symphony began to play a rousingly evocative blend of love songs and martial fanfares, the first of the contenders led off the great parade.

Justly known for its size and variety, the famous, much-visited Great Galaxy of Aa-Haaah!'s team was correspondingly large, its fans cheering wildly as their very own spiritual athletes made their first appearance.

Love, like galaxies, comes (and goes) in countless forms.

Since each contender sought to show which particular aspect of complex cosmic love it thought itself especially good at, each carried aloft (in addition to their native flags) a great coloured banner emblazoned with the proud assertion of their own singular strength.

In the case of the Great Galaxy of Aa-Haaah!, for example, their representative ensign bore three interwoven quintets of stars above the words 'Love of Anatomy; Anatomy of Love'. Which was not all that surprising, given that everyone in their many constellations enjoyed no fewer than fifteen cheerfully interdependent bodies in the course of lifetimes lasting never less than fifteen thousand years.

No sooner had the applause begun to fade, than elsewhere in the stadium another group of galactic fans rose excitedly to their feet. Waving their small bright-coloured matching pennants, they too cheered in turn as their own home team advanced, the next in sequence now beginning to stream steadily past.

゠●

For those without a previous interest in emerging worlds, or who had yet to venture very far in the cosmos on vacation, the range and variety of galaxies making their first appearance was truly astounding.

The constellation representing the Galaxy of Deeply Discerning Affection, with its proud purple-and-grey banner proclaiming their expertise in 'Extremely Thoughtful Love!' was a distinct crowd-pleaser, not least because every competitor gazed warmly yet provocatively back at the huge audience from each of his or her twenty-seven hundred different heads.

"It's a wonder they ever get any sleep," Chief Inspector Go-Go exclaimed in awe, turning to his twin conveniently sharing the same seat in the stands.

"They probably take turns," Chief Inspector Stop replied automatically, then paused as he began to contemplate all the potential benefits (and hazards) both personal and professional, of so expanded a cerebral outreach programme.

Ten minutes later, after many more contenders went by, the far-off Galaxy of Gloriously Quantum Excess was the next to receive a particularly enthusiastic welcome, merrily coming past the reviewing stand behind its bright-cherry banner affirming 'Never Ever Too Much Love!'.

The white-and-pale-green-striped competitors from the Galaxy of Interstellar Hospitals and Hospitality, whose hotelier-trained residents provided the very latest in all-expenses-paid health care to their many surrounding star systems, got an especially appreciative round of applause. Their banner, 'Better Living Through Love – And Unparalleled Room Service', was among the most gratifying so far. At the sight, a number of normally circumspect senior night-shift angels found themselves nudging one another, wondering quietly on the chances of renegotiating their contracts.

Galaxy by galaxy, big or small, distant or near, they each passed by proudly as the Supreme Being, seemingly equally enchanted by all, raised a radiantly serene hand in greeting and benediction.

ૐ

Given the occasion (and, perhaps, the restraining presence of so many spiritual dignitaries and even more sharp-eyed angels) when the next galactic team advanced in turn toward the reviewing stand, everyone watching did their best to maintain a tactful, if awkward silence.

It was already widely known that the Milky Way (rightly concerned lest it be accused of celestial influence peddling) had eliminated Eve's native planet from consideration as its chosen representative. Not surprisingly, therefore, many more than just the cosmic *cognoscenti* were profoundly curious as to what this previously unheralded, now suddenly so newsworthy galaxy might come up with a worthy alternative.

Under the circumstances, its compromise candidate – a team from one of the most metaphysically correct constellations in Creation, the ever-cautious Planet of Decisively Diplomatic Doubletalk (better known as Duck, Hedge & Weave) – really didn't stand a chance, regardless of how predictably well-rehearsed its advocates might be.

A default selection by a galactic governing committee hell-bent on offending no one no how, their huge beige-on-beige banner bore a suitably spin-doctored expression of vigilant bureaucratic equivocation: 'Love – An Understandably Complex, Highly Contentious Conundrum (More or Less, Circumstances Depending, Weather & Budget Permitting, All Things Considered, etc.)'.

Unnoticed by all, God gave the Archangel-in-Chief a rare see- what-I-still-have-to-deal-with-sometimes look.

"Not quite what You'd call soul-stirring, is it?" Heaven's second-in-command whispered in return.

There was a silence while the two quietly contemplated the less-than-satisfactory scene before them, and all they knew, and the entire universe didn't.

At least not yet. Catching each other's eye, they began to laugh.

"Takes all kinds," the Archangel of All Archangels observed with wry compassion.

Since the cosmos had been God's idea in the first place, the Genuine, Original Supreme Being *Extraordinaire* could only agree. And make a mental note to see that, as soon as possible, the Milky Way Galaxy would enjoy the many benefits of a little private tutoring in what Big D liked to call spiritual cut-and-thrust.

Sometimes the best way to move forward is simply to move.

&.

If Heaven's wide-ranging workforce was professionally inclined to be discreet, the less inhibited residents of Planet Earth, watching from their unexpected vantage point high above the stadium, were anything but.

"We came all this way – with barely a few hours sleep – to cheer for them?!"

"Somebody should have asked for our opinion!"

"A billion stars in our native galaxy – and that's the best rep they can come up with?!"

"Boooooooo!"

Fortunately for Earth's inhabitants, only the most highly attuned of celestial beings could hear them. Though hear them, both clearly could.

"I take it Eve's descendants are not entirely satisfied with things?" the Archangel of All Archangels inquired dryly.

"Then again, they rarely are," God replied.

"Good point."

&.

The grand processional continued to wind its way past the reviewing stand. The Galaxy of Supreme Scholarly Insights, whose central constellation consisted entirely of incomparably well-read (if perennially under-funded) ivory towers serving their surrounding communities, advanced to the leisurely sounds of a languid violin concerto, their forthright academic banner, 'Ever Loquacious (If Sometimes Ad Nauseum) for Love', bobbing and weaving in the breeze.

Moments later, the unrestrained, much-envied team members from the secluded Galaxy of Totally Transformative Thrills raced past in merry circles, hoisting high their orange-and-white flag affirming 'Love is Fun; Fun is Love!' (their appearance, needless to say, getting an extra loud round of applause from Valentina, Tatiana and, seated most appreciatively between them, the peacock-blue Unofficial Ambassador (Plenipotentiary) of Cosmic Hedonism).

The Galaxy of Eternal Wakefulness followed. A little known, even less appreciated world, it was represented by a thousand of its ever-serene citizens who, in lieu of sleep, forever kept a fondly contemplative watch on the universe, sending brief but invaluable reports back to Heaven in code.

Their discreet white-and-gold pennant bore a lone vigilant eye above the single word 'Love', the latter in a tantalizingly ornate hieroglyph which, no matter the viewer's language, was instantly understandable by all.

❦

It all seemed, everyone agreed, a totally unprecedented, uniquely spectacular afternoon. Perfectly organized, perfectly orchestrated, and, so far, at least, almost perfectly carried out.

And also – however strangely – somehow more than slightly anti-climactic. Indeed, by the time the umpteenth, equally impressive galactic team had passed the reviewing stand, it was hard not to have a certain sense of celestial *déjà vu*.

Not that anyone said anything, of course. On one's first visit to Heaven, it seemed not only good manners but also probably a wise precaution (perhaps, even a discreet form of after-life insurance) to appear as unconditionally appreciative as possible.

Nonetheless, it surely wasn't so very surprising – given the recently-returned presence of a power equally able to conjure up everything from microbes to mammoths to anti-matter with the snap of mighty, if invisible fingers – that cosmic citizens everywhere should find themselves secretly wishing for something slightly more, how might they say, extraordinary!

It wasn't that God's creatures great and small were unhappy with everything they'd seen. Far from it. They just wanted more!

ε

As the assertive little Galaxy of X-Ray Vision bowed in passing, their black-and-white banner, 'Love What You Don't See; See What You Don't Love', fluttering in the breeze, the Archangel of All Archangels glanced to his right to find God covertly checking the current intersection of Time and Eternity.

"Don't tell me You're starting to get just a little bored, too?" he ventured with the liberty of long acquaintance.

"Quite the contrary."

The great luminous ball of light looked upwards into the pure blue celestial sky, God's eyesight indisputably better than most.

"I think we can now safely say the real fun is only just beginning!"

ε

The latest in aviator sunglasses shading his far-seeing eyes, his white scarf and even whiter beard streaming behind him, Abracadabra made the deftest of adjustments to his flight controls. Checking his watch and speedometer simultaneously, he whispered into the microphone of his high-frequency head-set, "Estimated time till touch-down ... five minutes!"

ε

Only the most privileged and proven of the Angel of the Golden Hammer and Gong's celestial associates knew that what appeared to be his perfectly fitted ear-plugs were, in fact, also miniature radio receivers. As the enterprising old wizard softly repeated his advance warning, God's favourite percussionist smiled a hugely satisfied smile, flexed his shoulders and wiggled his nimble fingers. Then, almost imperceptibly, he brushed the surface of his two great brass circles, sending out the first, faintest shimmers of sound.

Close by, a pair of seemingly nonchalant globe-shaped angels found their wings vibrating excitedly in tune. The Angel of Unprecedented Opportunities regarded his twin brother with an increasingly excited eye; facing him, the Angel of Hidden Agendas did the same. A moment later, swivelling in unison, they gave a matching pair of reassuring nods to three carefully poised, outwardly unruffled associates.

For their part, the Celestial Aerospace Engineering Angel, the Angel of Celestial Fireworks, and the Angel of Truly Infinite Resources together let out perfectly synchronized sighs of relief, and then began whispering urgently into the tiny microphones carefully hidden up their long alabaster sleeves.

On a little blue-and-white planet parked breathtakingly close to Heaven, increasingly disappointed residents were beginning to wonder what all the celestial fuss was about. The little whirling ball they called home was itself now a long way from home, and not a few aboard were wondering why they'd come. For its part, the Sun, while secretly just as perplexed as the rest, appeared unable to shed any light on this particular puzzle. Nor did its more reflective companion, a now long-faced moon.

As subsequent intergalactic histories record, it was at that precise moment, as the faintest, far-off sounds of the Whole Earth Choir, Orchestra and Marching Band Combo could suddenly be heard, that a small formation of determined little white clouds began rising steadily above the celestial horizon.

On the huge reviewing stand, surrounded by so many familiar angelic faces from over so many aeons, one ageless being of light turned in admiration to another even greater.

God's smile was calm, humble – and proud.

"Somehow I always knew I could rely on her!"

Return to Paradise

"THE APPLE DOES NOT FALL FAR FROM THE TREE."

— Adam

Above All, Courage

&. HUNDREDS OF THOUSANDS, even many million years later, the universe still gratefully celebrates the climactic events of that afternoon.

Thanks to the Heavenly Broadcast Studio's latest, spare-no-expense cameras and highest-resolution lenses, viewers around the cosmos leaned forward in their chairs, the first enchanting images of a V-shaped flight of unstoppable little white clouds growing larger and larger on their screens.

In the crowded rows of the Heavenly Games Stadium itself, visitors from every corner of Creation twisted and turned as they searched for the best possible view; those with the keenest eyesight (or best binoculars) already murmuring excitedly to their companions on either side. In their specially reserved section, the charter members of the Ancient and Honourable Sisterhood of the Interplanetary Dawns of Creation rose together as one, fingers crossed, already murmuring, "You go, girl!"

To one side of the reviewing stand, the Angel of Hidden Agendas and an equally anxious Angel of Unprecedented Opportunities waited a moment longer, just to be sure; then decided they had earned the right to start jumping up and down. Around them countless angelic colleagues who had happily taken Eve's ultimate intentions on faith, burst into enormous smiles and the loudest applause of their long careers.

Close by, Team Earth's distinguished coaches from The Great Beyond beyond the Beyond began shaking hands

"Told ya. Given the right wake-up call, Earthlings are a whole lot tougher than they look!" the tallest of two skeletons exclaimed in eloquent, bare-bones approval.

"Shake, rattle and let 'er roll!" his shorter ivory associate replied, offering a suitably-clattering high five.

"Go, Team, Go!" Aurora yelled in a surprisingly piercing voice, clambering on her seat, fists clenched, punching the air in satisfyingly unladylike fashion.

Scheherazade, her thoughts racing back over all that had come to pass since her first, seemingly-fruitless visit, only weeks before, to one of the universe's most forgotten retirement homes, shook her head in delight.

High above the Heavenly Games Stadium, the fiery centrepiece of a normally far-off solar system took a second amazed look at the emerging scene. Then, swiftly adjusting its beams from floodlight to spot, it focused as precisely as possible on a fast-approaching flight of little white clouds, each with its own exultant sorcerer at the helm.

Close by, on Earth, crowds of people of every karmic complexity pointed as one.

In his control booth high atop the stadium, the stately angel in charge of the Celestial Secretariat for Ceremonial Parades spoke softly into his mouthpiece.

"Over to you," he whispered, the faint tremor in his voice betraying not only delight at being part of so momentous an occasion, but also an insider's irrepressible excitement at the spectacular sound and fabulous fury about to begin.

"Blow the budget – literally!"

❦

His own celebrated expertise notwithstanding, the Angel of Cosmic Fireworks had had no hesitation in asking for help in meeting Eve's sudden, non-negotiable request for the most tremendous mid-afternoon display ever. Even the most daring of fizzing, popping, dazzling midnight spectacles were, by comparison, mere pyrotechnical child's play.

As expected, it had taken wild angelic genius to be able to develop, in a few sleepless hours, a wholly satisfactory daylight star-shell, its initial darkness providing the contrasting background for a sudden ecstatic explosion of sound, light, colour and power.

As musicians from seven hundred and seventy-seven star systems launched into their most rousing version of the Heavenly Games anthem yet, the glowing presence at the centre of the great reviewing stand gazed calmly and expectantly toward a very rapidly-approaching cluster of little white clouds.

Elsewhere, in their carefully-concealed control room, the Angel of Cosmic Fireworks put his hand on the first of two switches marked, respectively, 'Ode to Joy!' and 'To a Trillion Times More Joy!' In the same moment, his equally-illuminating associate, the Angel of Celestial Star-Bursts, reached out to the second.

At an almost imperceptible nod from God, they began to set fire to the sky.

Huge clusters of fire arced across Heaven, exploding into millions of secondary flowers of flame. To the innumerable intergalactic viewers, the whole celestial scene became suddenly ablaze, a now-frenzied Heavenly Games Symphony Orchestra blasting happily away.

At the helm of the leading white cloud, tinged by light from the ever-louder explosions, Abracadabra pointed ahead with his magic wand.

"You want me to go through that?!" he called out mock-gruffly, already beginning to adjust for turbulence as their unorthodox little craft slipped and bounced in the ever-hotter air.

"Got any better ideas?" Eve responded cheerfully, planting her feet and taking a firmer grip on Adam's hand. Neither had forsaken Paradise, endured so much, lasted so long or come so far, only to turn back now.

The old wizard simply grinned in reply, millions of years of intrepid sorcery and occult courage now proving to have been his own far-sighted preparation for this flight of all flights on this day of all days.

Adjusting his goggles, increasing his speed, Abracadabra spoke quickly into his throat-microphone to all the other sorcerers on their own little clouds flying unerringly on either side.

"Tighten your seatbelts … Team Earth's a comin' through!"

Below, the Associate Angel of Celestial Starbursts exultantly re-doubled his efforts, blast following blast without pause.

At first, everyone was completely entranced, awestruck and thrilled as ever more impossibly-flamboyant detonations lit up the skies. Then, as the fleet of little white clouds drew closer, the huge crowd in the Heavenly Games stadium, along with everyone watching throughout the entire universe, began shifting nervously in their seats.

Eyeing the resounding maelstrom, angels of every age and stage of aeronautic expertise crossed their fingers, said their prayers and trusted that, whoever were flying these unlikely arrivals, they knew exactly what they were doing.

Over the aeons, the Office of Emergency Celestial Preparedness had made a near-infinity of plans against seemingly any and all contingencies. The prospect of a hundred little white clouds all crash-landing together in Heaven, however, was one that had definitely not been considered.

ҙ

On a little blue-and-white planet, people suddenly found themselves holding both one another and their collective breath.

Then, just as everyone throughout the cosmos began to get their first perfectly clear, close-up glimpse of the leading little white airship, a smiling, fiercely-determined couple standing proudly at its bow, it vanished suddenly from view, lost among thunderous starbursts. Moments later, all its equally crowded, equally fluffy white airborne companions also disappeared, in line and in turn, amid the mounting smoke and flame.

"This time, Adam and Eve seem to be making a considerably more dramatic entrance," God observed thoughtfully.

"*This* time," the Archangel of All Archangels responded, "they have a considerably larger audience."

"*Touché!*"

ҙ

It only seemed like a long time.

In the skies above the stadium, the unprecedented mid-afternoon fireworks display reached its ultimate crescendo. Throughout the universe, everyone found themselves gripping their seats, anxiously praying for the renewed sight of a daring cluster of little white clouds.

Behind their control panel, the Angels of Cosmic Fireworks and Celestial Starbursts double-checked the last in a long list of precise instructions and crossed their fingers. Then, with both personal and professional abandon, gleefully flipped the inter-linked, inter-locked switches marked: Luminous Grand Finale!

Soaring undaunted through a million starbursts, Abracadabra adjusted the stabilizers, brushed bits of stray soot from his beard, then looked up into the far-seeing eyes of the woman who had made possible both this day and their current, daring jaunt. Moved as never before, he stood, balancing himself against the turbulence, bowed, then kissed Eve's cheek. "I really think that I'm the one who should be saying, 'Thanks for the ride!'" he murmured.

Squeezing his arm in gratitude, Eve glanced back over all the crowded little clouds behind, her thoughts too full to speak.

Abracadabra turned, taking Adam's hand in both of his and shaking it warmly. "Congratulations on a victory that we all know Eve could never have won without you."

"What can I say?" came the proud reply. "She had me at her first hello." He paused, chuckling as modestly as possible given the occasion. "Actually, I like to think of us as the original package deal."

A moment later, back at the controls, ready for the kind of ovation sorcerers only dream of, Abracadabra spoke forcefully into the tiny microphone at his throat. "Resume Heaven-storming formation. Prepare to raise banners!"

As might be expected, God was the first to see them (though in reality, of course, they'd never once been out of the Boss's far larger, longer sight).

As the fireworks ended, a tense new stillness settled over Heaven. An instant later, a small V-shaped flight of crowded little white clouds emerged from the last few flames and drifting smoke, serene, untouched and still unwaveringly on course.

All over the universe, the same cry went up as everyone, everywhere, leapt to their feet. "Eve! Eve! Eve!"

In perfect unison, the resolute little band swooped into a long turn and began their carefully-timed descent.

In their two specially-equipped, extremely fluffy white clouds on either side of Abracadabra's, and only slightly behind, the members of the Whole Earth Choir, Orchestra and Marching Band Combo seized the same moment to break into their very own planetary tribute to so unreservedly grand and glorious a day.

It was a rockabilly, full-volume rendering of a medieval hymn, which now offered up a little planet's hard-won truth to Heaven's welcoming applause: "Courage leads on, and on, and on … but fear forever betrays!"

At the same moment, celestial and solar light glinting together on their new blue-and-white tunics, all the members of Team Earth rose as one, bracing themselves against the sides of their respective airships.

High on the bow of the leading cloud, framed in light, Adam and Eve stood together hand in hand. Immediately behind them, their chosen team leaders from Earth's past and its future – the World's Greatest Gravedigger and its Most Beautiful Astronomer – proudly unfurled, for the first time ever in the history of the entire universe, the bold new banner of a now-resolute new world.

On cue, flag-bearers on every other cloud in the little formation now beginning to circle the vast celestial stadium did the same. In perfect unison, a hundred and one huge blue-and-white flags, all bearing the same now-unretractable vow, began waving fiercely back and forth above Heaven's cheering crowds.

Team Earth
Valiant
For
Love

While Earth might not be the oldest or most knowledgeable planet in Creation, it seemed that a little blue-and-white world that would not be denied was coming to the Heavenly Games of Love after all – and making it clear that, come what may, whatever they might lack in seniority, sophistication or expertise – they would more than make up for in courage.

Without which, no lasting love was possible. Spiritual or otherwise.

&

Timing was everything, especially this time.

As the formation of little white clouds began to slow in front of the great reviewing stand, ecstatic residents from every longitude and latitude on an unexpectedly nearby planet suddenly found themselves waving their own matching blue-and-white pennants.

Thrilled by the scene unfolding below, everyone on Earth began jumping up and down to their new collective rallying cry, the planet itself bouncing in rhythm from their collective weight. It was a slightly unnerving moment until several larger, more muscular members of the solar system quickly whirled in closer, carefully bracing the ecstatic little blue-and-white ball on either side.

Stirred by both spectacle and sound, the entire crowded Heavenly Games Stadium quickly began to pick up the chant.

An instant later, as those images were transmitted throughout the universe courtesy of the Heavenly Broadcast Studio, galaxy after galaxy joined in what was becoming a now universal refrain.

Valiant, Valiant, Valiant for Love!

Forgotten for the moment, God gazed quietly round, a tear in one eye, the oldest of smiles in the other.

"I think everybody's finally starting to get it."

The Archangel of All Archangels nodded slowly, taking his time to adjust to so welcome but unfamiliar a prospect. "I'm profoundly happy for You, of course; but, if I may say so, it sure took them long enough."

"Not entirely their fault," God responded softly. "Remember, it's My first universe, too."

Keynote Speakers

 WHILE EVERYONE IN the Heavenly Games stadium was thrilled by Eve's spectacular return, the exhausted members of the Celestial Coordinating Committee were ecstatic, their cheers unconstrained. For his part, the Angel of Divine Back-Up couldn't resist putting two fingers to his lips, whistling louder than the inner teenager he'd never lost.

In the stands, the official delegates from the Milky Way Galaxy turned awkwardly to their now-grinning colleagues from the perennially bland, terminally risk-avoidant Planet of Exquisitely Diplomatic Doubletalk.

"It's OK," the hitherto well-pressed principals of this now even more ill-suited choice admitted, cheerfully loosening their polyester beige ties. "Actually, we much prefer Eve's approach, too!"

A hundred motionless little white clouds, their work for now complete, momentarily screened the reviewing stand from view.

"My deepest thanks for all your help," God whispered, pinning the newly-created insignia of Honorary Grand Counsellor of Heaven (and very first celestial gold medal of the Games) on Abracadabra's best velvet robe. "Diligent, discreet and, above all, the most dedicated sky-pilot since the Archangel-in-Chief graduated from flight school!"

"It has been a truly enormous pleasure," the oldest, wisest man in the divination business responded softly, shaking his head in boundless professional admiration. "Although it certainly took me a while to figure out Your not-so-very-little celestial *jeu d'esprit*!"

"I always thought you'd welcome the challenge – and the fun," the very best judge of character (visible and invisible) in the universe replied, before murmuring one further request in Abracadabra's willing ear.

❦

If, as is reliably reported, a thousand years in God's sight are but as yesterday, it's not surprising that a minute or two can go by far faster than a neutrino late for a date.

After a series of elegant bows to renewed cheers from every direction, Abracadabra and the rest of his assorted aeronautical wizards flew off in perfect low-level formation to park their unorthodox craft on the far side of the stadium. Meanwhile, Team Earth found itself face to face, for the very first time, with the God not just of their understanding but also, more unnervingly, of an entire universe.

It was an experience at once unforgettable and highly unsettling. While every member of Team Earth had talked with his or her so-called Maker, quietly and carefully, on numerous occasions before (and generally felt much the better for having done so), none among them had had so unusually public an encounter. This time, however, not only was the Heavenly Games stadium completely packed but, thanks to the diligent technicians of the Heavenly Broadcast Studio, the eyes of an entire cosmos were now also upon them.

"Second thoughts?" Adam whispered, standing at Eve's side. Like her, he already knew the answer: one which they both had shared, for better and so often for worse, ever since that long ago day when the great gates of Eden had closed silently behind them, and the mysterious events that might re-open its invisible, encoded lock began.

"Never!"

As Earth's first couple ascended the reviewing stand's steps, Eve suddenly felt herself trembling, her hand tightening against Adam's. So much had happened since that first daunting moment when God had vanished from Heaven, leaving (so it seemed) both the celestial realm and an understandably nervous cosmos in her care.

The great ball of light just back from vacation moved forward, sweeping Eve into an embrace so incandescent that she seemed for an instant to disappear into light itself.

"Well done, My dearest, most reliable rebel," the most sublime of voices whispered with infinite tenderness. "I'm so deeply, deeply proud of you!"

There was a long silence as the only two occupants of the Heavenly Throne ever – one timeless, the other gratefully only temporary – shared a moment of unique communion. Then, turning to her side, she paid tribute where tribute was profoundly due.

"You remember Adam, of course," Eve said teasingly.

"Hmmmnn." God made a deliberate show of scratching a radiantly invisible head. "It's been quite a while since our initial encounter, but I seem to recall him asking Me right away: "What's a ... woman?""

Eve could not resist. "Seems like now you both know!"

❧

The eyes of every star system were fixed on the great silent ball of light at centre stage.

Much could now be revealed. And yet so much more must, inevitably, remain for every cosmic citizen to discover for themselves.

"Given today's events," God began, "I can only confess how grateful I am that My earlier, well-intentioned efforts to house this particular Adam and Eve should have turned out to be, how shall I say, so providentially inadequate."

The glowing smile grew steadily greater, reaching out to embrace the entire cosmos.

"It's profoundly reassuring to discover that one's offspring are not only capable of looking after themselves, but even (given angels, one or two delicate hints and a discreetly well-timed fiery nudge) something so intricate as an entire universe, however experimental and preliminary!"

❧

"Why the look?" Scheherazade asked softly in the stands.

Big D began to rub one of the two spots on his forehead housing the retractable long-range antennae so often mistaken for horns.

"In my far-from-humble experience," he replied, raffishly speculative eyebrow now rising in salute, "my old Boss rarely says anything without considerable, if not complete foreknowledge of the consequences."

"Then let me guess why you're suddenly smiling," said Scheherazade.

"But that's enough by way of a brief prelude. You can hear from Me (whether you like it or not) anytime you choose." With the appreciation of one professional for another, God nodded imperceptibly to the Angel of the Golden Hammer and Gong. Then, as the latest, loudest intergalactic reverberations died away, led Eve forward by the hand.

✿

"That's her!"

Nearly everyone on the little blue-and-white planet suspended un-expectedly high over Heaven stood simultaneously on tip-toe; an act which, while causing Earth to vibrate alarmingly, also served to catch Eve's much-sought attention and brought from her the warmest of reassuringly steadying waves.

"She sees us! She sees us!" Earth's inhabitants cried aloud.

"Never really took her eyes off you for a second," Abracadabra whispered to himself.

✿

To receive the tribute of a prolonged standing ovation from gazillions of creatures from a hundred and one billion galaxies, together with all the permanent residents and temporary guests of Heaven, is a relatively uncommon experience. It is also very loud and very overwhelming.

Eve could only clutch Adam's hand more tightly, and he, just as proudly hers, as they waited for the applause to end. Which, for what seemed a small eternity, it appeared it never would. At her side, God kept perfect time with the crowd, every instant sending out new and ever greater ripples of light.

As the unanimous show of appreciation at last began to slow, Eve found both a moment of stillness and her own true voice.

"Thank you; thank you all – one and all."

Her eyes moved slowly round the stadium, taking in so many teams from so many star systems, each of them bringing their own special gifts (however partial and imperfect) of wisdom, passion and grace.

"Whatever honours you offer now, should more justly be awarded to yourselves." Eve paused, reliving in an instant every step in the long, hard road out of a hushed and empty Eden. "Though God may have provided the inspiration, and somehow chosen me as an instrument, these are, truly, your very own Heavenly Games of Love!"

Gracefully, gratefully, Eve began to applaud her audience in turn, paying her own small tribute to the great, if still uncompleted cosmos from which she sprang; and which, so movingly, even majestically, had answered the call of one of its own.

At her side, Adam joined proudly in her applause. The lump in his throat, far from the first in their long, ever-more-intimate union, was definitely the largest.

ቈ

"You know what this means, of course," declared one of Earth's most inclusive theologians, a suitably sanguine yet light-hearted interpreter of its many often seemingly contradictory divinities.

"Our little-ball-of-flesh-and-fervour is not likely to be the same again?" replied his companion, one of the planet's most honest (and therefore perennially unelected) statesmen. His new blue-and-white pennant was clutched in one hand, a second, more familiar flag of the until now, over-optimistically named United Nations, in the other.

"Obviously – and neither are we!"

"No more time for excuses?"

"We ran out of that long ago."

ቈ

Eve's gaze travelled across the vast reviewing stand, acknowledging one by one the many celestial veterans so clearly thrilled that this day of all days had finally arrived.

"I would especially like to thank today's official Grand Master of Celestial Ceremonies; a tirelessly selfless presence better known as the Archangel of All Archangels. A resolute, decisive and yet (when one gets to know him) eminently delightful acquaintance, he has been a source of infinite encouragement." She gazed affectionately at the imposing figure by her side. "Not to mention a seemingly endless supply of incomparable angels – without whose help this day would never have been possible."

386

As Eve rose on tiptoe to kiss a flushed Archangel-in-Chief on his smooth-shaven cheek, the entire universe yelled, whistled and stamped their feet.

"Three cheers for the angels," Adam called out, quickly adding, in fitting homage to their hitherto less- appreciated, crimson-clad cousins down under, "everywhere!"

As the universe's prolonged applause echoed among the stars, it was the turn of countless members of Heaven's full-time staff to blush with suddenly shy delight, their flushed faces sending a becomingly pink glow off immaculate wings.

ꝫ

As she continued her speech, Eve found her gaze lingering on the special section reserved for the Ancient and Honourable Sisterhood of the Cosmic Dawns of Creation. Surveying her co-founders' timelessly resilient faces, she whispered a quick prayer that she might now speak truly for them as well.

"Shortly before handing me the keys to Heaven," she began, "God cautioned me to think big. And when I asked how big, the answer was the same it has always been since Creation itself was first cherished into form. 'Love', God had replied, 'It is love, and only love, which forever guides us onward.'"

Eve took a deep breath, her outstretched arms embracing so many kindred mothers of Creation. "That same first bold, exploring, ever-more inclusive Love for the universe and one another, in fact, that helped each of us, whatever our galaxy of origin, to leave our first, now-outgrown homes in search of all we had yet to become."

Heaven's first-ever official temporary substitute Supreme Being raised her eyes, speaking directly to the universe at large.

"May you rejoice in the challenges of coming days, always remembering that these Heavenly Games of Love, however wondrous they may be, are but an image of that greater opportunity which still daily awaits us all."

Eve took Adam's hand, raising it in their own personal victory gesture.

"In centuries and millennia to come, you will inevitably discover many harsh yet wondrous things." Eve paused, gazing on Earth's first man – and he on her – as if for the first time once more, eye to far-seeing, equally determined eye. "And this, among them, above all: the successively greater paradises you must build for yourselves … are better by far than those first offered us, untested and unearned."

The voice of the first woman on Earth strengthened with a fierce tenderness. "So, as you go forward, today, tomorrow, an aeon from now, go forward humbly, gratefully, wisely, forever … *Valiant for Love*".

֍

Leaning against the bow of his little white cargo-carrier, Abracadabra gave a prolonged sigh of wizardly fulfilment. "From shy, sheltered and distinctly innocent beginnings," he declared to companion cloud pilots nearby, "that young lady has definitely come a very long way!"

He looked upwards, able, as the greatest sorcerers are, to see the ever-present infinity of stars hidden behind daylight's delicate veil.

"Reminds me of something a dear old philosopher friend once said, now centuries ago, reading his latest revisions by the banks of an endless, swan-lit river: 'We are such stuff as dreams are made on – and our little sleep is rounded with far larger lives.'"

֍

The stylishly exotic visitors from The Great Beyond beyond the Beyond added their own discerning applause. For his part, the small, triangle-headed sage, hoisted on the shoulders of his loftiest crystaline cousin, waved as wildly as his arms would allow. "This is definitely one of those moments when, despite all the hassles and truly stupendous jet-lag, time travel is totally worth it!"

Meanwhile, on a proud little planet called Earth, billions of little blue-and-white prayer flags continued to wave in the celestial winds, its long-divided peoples now celebrating together as the firm new friends – and true cosmic citizens – they had finally become.

"Valiant for Love! Valiant for Love! Valiant for Love!"

As the Archangel of All Archangels slowly surveyed the cheering crowds, monitors ringing the stadium showed footage of enthusiastic viewers around the universe, all on their feet and applauding fiercely, the cosmos resounding with a newly passionate delight in its own ceaseless becoming.

"You're right. I do think they're all really beginning to get it," the Archangel-in-Chief exclaimed softly.

The response came as a judicious nod. "Let's certainly hope so." After a brief moment, God raised an unseen, shimmering hand, the gesture encompassing the entire cosmos. "But, just in case…."

Everything, everywhere, instantly disappeared in light – or, perhaps, finally reappeared as light. And only light.

In the twinkling of a celestial eye, Creator and Creation, God and God's countless guises, revealed themselves as one: eternity forever rejoicing in its own sweet, ceaseless ephemeralities; spirit and form inseparable from one another in an endless creative embrace.

Wave and particle. Particle and wave. Past, passing and yet to come. All in One. One in All.

"I think they'll find that hard to forget," an awed Archangel of All Archangels whispered, as even the glow of numberless stars now seemed tinged with a new tenderness and power.

"It's something I like to think of as My ultimate party trick," God replied modestly, quietly savouring the faces of every being in the entire universe now gazing on one another in mutually translucent recognition and wonder.

"All the same," the genuine, original Supreme Being *Extraordinaire* added, "I suspect this sudden outburst of advanced collective saintliness will probably take some getting used to!"

Second Time Around

❦ AT LONG LAST, God could finally relax and enjoy the show.

As countless cosmic histories happily record, the success of the first-ever Heavenly Games proved far greater than even its congenitally optimistic angelic organizers could have dreamed. Over an eventful two-week period, countless galaxies daily inspired one another to ever-greater triumphs in all the limitless fields of Love. New far-flung friends were made, new lessons learned and shared, new hopes for a better future freely confessed and mutually explored.

Numberless champions were crowned, and (as some guardian angels had confidently predicted, making a little extra loose change in celestial bets on the side) quite a few well-toned competitors from quite a few exceedingly acrobatic star systems quietly came to know quite a few others exceptionally well. After all, as so many hitherto improbable interplanetary couples whispered, what better place for spiritual beings from opposite sides of the cosmos to have a truly Heavenly encounter!

God didn't seem to mind. Quite the opposite, in fact. As the classified files of Heaven's top-secret Eternity Planning and Development Office subsequently revealed, God was elated to see Creation finally beginning to make the most of those transformative energies which (secretly but so successfully) had sustained it from the very beginning.

All in all, God decided, beaming contentedly, things could be worse. Indeed, had been for far too long. It was not quite a cosmic graduation party. That – depending on possibilities God was only just beginning to explore – could come later, but it was definitely a major step forward in everyone's continuing cosmic upbringing.

No small achievement, all things considered, for Someone who had supposedly been away on holiday.

⚘

Standing together with Eve on the reviewing stand, God's extended reverie was interrupted by the return of the Archangel-in-Chief who, after whispering briefly, beckoned to two identical globe-shaped angels.

"Afternoon, Boss," said the Angel of Unprecedented Opportunities, looking very pleased with the afternoon's developments.

"Afternoon, Deputy Boss," the Angel of Hidden Agendas said to his now unemployed supervisor, likewise smiling from ear to ear.

"How lovely to see you again," Eve cried, embracing both angels with outstretched arms. If there were ever a time for giving credit where it was due…, "Thank you for everything."

"Our pleasure," replied the first, taking a deep breath.

"Ditto to the max," said the second, taking a matching one.

While a host of senior members from the Celestial Coordinating Committee hovered discreetly on the borders of earshot, the two globe-shaped figures looked at God intently.

"Given our recent close association, we were wondering," they both began, "if it might now be possible for Eve, and Adam, of course, to make another complete circuit of the Heavenly Games stadium?"

"And not just at the head of the intergalactic teams, but also…."

With a smile of captivating generosity, God completed the query on their behalf. "But also, perhaps, as the leader of a much overdue victory lap featuring all the many angels who, one way or another, have worked so long, hard and lovingly to make Eve's stay in Heaven so memorable?"

"How'd You guess?" they both agreed laughing, looking over their shoulders at all the many bright-winged figures watching intently and, in some cases, waving shyly.

Not for the first time, God and the first woman of a little blue-and-white planet read one another's minds perfectly.

Eve reached out, once more embracing the two look-alike twins. "I thought you'd never ask – and, yes, I'd be honoured!"

It had been a very long time, if ever, that Heaven had heard so many angels cheering so loudly for so long. Then, of one accord, they all rushed off to prepare for a richly deserved circuit of the great stadium.

Serene, subtle and sedate might be eminently suitable on the Sabbath. Right now, however, was a truly rare opportunity demanding nothing less than the angelic fast and flashy.

God leaned over to the Archangel of All Archangels, whispering in his ear. "Under the circumstances, I think it's only right to include...."

"I've already spoken to Big D himself, who assured me that every member of Heaven's secret SWAT Team would be more than happy and honoured to join in." The Archangel-in-Chief paused, eyes twinkling in near-perfect imitation of an imperturbably devilish smile. "He did, however, have one small question in return ... what took You so long?!"

God's laughter that followed, resounding as it did throughout every underworld in Creation, was something the illustrious members of the Interplanetary Senior Devils' Association would treasure for aeons.

As silence returned, God and the universe's pre-eminent celestial *consigliore* contemplated their extraordinarily ancient and ever more satisfying association.

"As you, better than anyone, well know," God began, "I don't always reveal My innermost thoughts. Or often enough, perhaps, My abiding appreciation." Voice breaking with emotion, the great glowing ball of light extended an invisible hand. "Thank you so very, very much!"

"My pleasure," came the wry, infinitely affectionate reply. There was a delicate pause. "But, if You don't mind, next time You suddenly decide to skip town...."

₰

At the announcement that Eve would soon reappear, by extra-special request, to lead a hugely well-deserved procession from the many regional offices of A.S.F. (Angels Without Borders), renewed cheers rang out across the entire cosmos.

On a nearby Earth, billions of people passed the time by linking arms and singing, loudly, renderings of the Whole Earth Choir, Orchestra and Marching Band Combo's inspired new theme song:

> Maybe not silver, prob'ly not gold;
> It don't really matter,' cuz we're goin' for bold!
> Angels and devils, when push comes to shove,
> We're valiant, we're valiant, we're valiant for love!

"Kind words notwithstanding, I did have a lot of help in Your absence." The Archangel-in-Chief hesitated. "Which reminds me. Whereabouts exactly did You go on vacation?"

The surrounding air crackled and flashed, the great radiant ball of light beginning to pulse with barely contained excitement.

"Uh oh!" Heaven's first and foremost spiritual confidant exclaimed, having seen that particular mischievous grin only once before.

"Afraid so," God agreed, looking even more pleased. "A little advance reconnaissance."

The secret source of all subsequent sources studied this oldest of old friends carefully. "Pardon My inevitable curiosity, but what are you doing for the next few billion years?" God leaned in closer, beginning to whisper. "No unalterable plans, I hope?"

"Here we go again," the Archangel-in-Chief murmured, laughing despite himself.

While the occult sciences offer their own esoteric rewards, they usually don't pay very well. It was, accordingly, not all that surprising that (given both location and circumstances) Abracadabra and his sorcererly associates should enjoy the opportunity to make a little unexpected extra cash for the eminently worthy Cosmic Wizards Benevolent Fund.

Visitors from every corner of the universe were thrilled to pay for the privilege of an experience like none other: namely, a comprehensive aerial overview of all the wonders of Heaven, courtesy of a fifteen minute ride on a perfectly-piloted little white cloud; plus, a highly selective but exceedingly well-informed commentary by an accompanying angel, an in-flight taste of one of a selection of Abracadabra's speedily-prepared special elixirs and, last but not least, a miniature (deactivated) version of a genuine magic wand.

This hastily improvised plan proved an enormous success, with a hundred or more little white clouds hurtling to and fro above Heaven's gleaming towers, their ecstatic passengers leaning precariously over the sides, waving to companions below and sending airborne selfies to the folks back home.

"I think you should definitely join Adam and me at the front of the parade," said Eve. "It's only fitting."

"You don't mind?" the Archangel of All Archangels asked, turning toward the infinite radiance on his right.

"*Carpe diem!*" The great ball of light whirled contentedly. "In fact, I rather doubt your inimitable staff would even dream of starting without you."

Blushing once again (twice in one afternoon after how many aeons?) the Archangel-in-Chief still managed to bow as impressively as only he was able; then, excusing himself, he raced off to join his countless celestial friends and associates.

❧

"So…," said Eve, regarding God thoughtfully.

"So…?" God replied just as evenly.

"Everything working out as You'd hoped?" There was a long pause while the temporary and permanent rulers of Heaven read each other's not unrelated minds. "Or should I say, as ever-so-cunningly planned?"

"You guessed?" said God.

"Weeks ago." Eve grinned. "Woman's intuition."

Very quietly, the Genuine Original Supreme Being *Extraordinaire* began to hum a favourite, once wordless tune; one to which one of the best of all possible visionaries had later added the best of all possible lyrics: "All will be well, and all manner of thing will be well…."

Eve shook her head, recalling Scheherazade's so unexpected arrival at the Fountain of Eternal Youth Retirement Home, and those first tentative questions now seemingly so very long ago.

"You set me up!"

"If I remember correctly," God replied quietly, "you applied."

"I was beyond bored," Eve's eyes narrowed with a determination older than time itself. "And besides, I really had no choice. I had, how shall I say, some unfinished personal business to attend to!"

"I know the feeling," God agreed.

The great radiant ball of luminous wisdom and love chuckled softly, at the same time spreading up-turned, invisible hands and shrugging omnisciently. "What can I say? I needed someone I could rely on … absolutely."

Eve's eyes softened with memory, going back across the generations to a vision of standing with Adam, alone on the threshold of choice, time and transcendence.

And now they were here. All in all, they hadn't done badly.

Eyes misting, Earth's first woman suddenly felt a limitless, divine tenderness and understanding envelope her completely.

"On the first occasion – of necessity, of course – you were, how shall I say, conscripted." God began to smile. "This time around, however, I thought it would be far better for everyone concerned – and considerably more enjoyable – if somehow or other you found a way to volunteer!"

The now former substitute Supreme Being *Extraordinaire* raised a mock-accusatory eyebrow.

"This time," Eve admitted, "has been far more fun."

"Felt I owed it to you," God said gruffly.

"Not to worry." Eve winked, humble (barely) even in ultimate victory. "All things considered, I'm more than happy to take the Fall…."

The second grand processional (far less scripted and formal than the first) was announced by the roll of a hundred thousand celestial drums, the graduating students of the Heavenly Golden Hammer and Gong School happily showing off their abilities in a hastily improvised, extended percussive cadence. As the introduction reached its crescendo, advance flights of angels criss-crossed the Heavenly Games stadium, dipping and soaring, showily alternating their speeds between super-slow and supersonic.

Adam and Eve, sitting once more at the front of Abracadabra's little white cloud now whirling happily around the parade route, waved again and again to the crowd. Directly behind them, the Archangel of All Archangels, together with his oldest and most accomplished angelic associates, smiled and waved shyly in turn, their images beamed out to the farthest stars ystems.

Behind them, a cluster of angels of every size, shape and official responsibility exulted in such dazzling, if admittedly well-deserved appreciation.

Two more little white clouds followed, crowded with as many members of the Big Band & Be-Bop Orchestra as could make it on extremely short notice, led by their tall, elegantly top-hatted concert master, the Angel of Tender Yet Terrifying Rhapsodies. His famously classical violin becoming just as easily a fiddle with a free-style flavour all its own, he launched into the finest hand-clappin', toe-tappin' compositions from all the compass points of a rock 'n' rhythmic universe.

Behind the little white clouds, the teams from across the cosmos once more made their appearance – though now no longer in alphabetical order. Mixing happily together, beings with six heads marched arm in arm with those having only two.

To roars of approval, a cast of now even more notorious characters brought up the rear. Dressed in their custom-cut crimson tunics, leaping, dancing, holding their freshly re-sharpened pitchforks high with pride, and led by all the exalted satanic eminences of the Intergalactic Senior Devils' Association, the universe's most multi-talented demons entered the Heavenly Games stadium for the very first time.

Strolling contentedly, even casually, as if this was indeed where they truly belonged, they managed at the same time to keep a stern but encouraging eye on their own very special guests, the well-steamed, near-exhausted but now wholly contrite figures of former enemies of the good, the true and the beautiful.

Chastened, cleansed and now transformed by last night's unsought adventures in the chimerical Fyres of Olde Hell, they now walked humbly side by side with their smiling demonic parole officers, overcome by the unexpectedly reassuring cheers of the crowds and the unsparing brightness of celestial light.

Big D leapt to his feet, fiercely applauding his hot-tempered old friends and their trusty satanic crews, delighted for them at their fittingly warm reception by a universe finally appreciative of their subtle, oft-misinterpreted skills.

"Who knew?" Scheherazade declared, just as pleased for her gallantly unconventional escort.

"You did," Big D answered, reaching out his arm to bring her to his side, joining him in waving proudly back to his own little personal underworld gang of salvation's secret agents. "You most definitely did – all along."

"Mmmnn."

All but two of the members of Team Earth had split up, finding themselves new companions and places in the long, gyrating parade, enjoying every changing moment and chance encounter.

The Whole Earth Choir, Orchestra and Marching Band Combo – honouring their little planet's own not entirely-uncheckered past – joined the ranks of the intergalactic devils' brigade and their fully repentant wards.

Midway along, taking their place somewhere between the very oldest and youngest competitors from some of the most eccentric galaxies in Creation, the co-leaders of Team Earth walked arm in arm, happily enjoying each other enjoying everything. In full view of gazillions of onlookers, at a moment captured by both the Heavenly Broadcast Studio and not a few celestial paparazzi, the World's Greatest Gravedigger suddenly stopped and, sweeping her into his arms, kissed the World's Most Beautiful Astronomer for what (fittingly) seemed like an eternity.

"Very big universe," said the unfinished past to the incomplete future. "So much still to discover."

"And to do," the tall beauty in the starry dress replied, kissing him back.

Most lovers, given time and sufficient lack of inhibition, can find new ways to make the Earth move. It's a rare couple indeed, however, able to help shake up Heaven as well.

&

"So very glad you invited us," the exotic visitors from The Great Beyond beyond the Beyond declared in unison. In their seats in the stands, Marina, Leila, Qingling, Yazmina, Tatiana and Sybilla turned to embrace their happily hodgepodge assortment of time-travelling friends; all of them responding with an affection the greater for coming from beings whose real home lay in a future Scheherazade's associates could only visit. If, perhaps, a little more frequently from now on.

One and all, these distinctly unorthodox advisors had definitely done their best for Team Earth, even if that ultimately only meant encouraging its members to do infinitely more for themselves.

In the meantime, further exposure to all The Great Beyond beyond the Beyond's even more advanced high-tech, higher-trance tricks could safely wait: until, that is, the good citizens of Earth were themselves at last ready to venture beyond all the transient illusions of Time. For the present, it was enough simply to enjoy the day, the great processional of angels, teams and devils combined, and all the grandeur of Heaven.

Their current assignment completed, all the coaches from the Great Beyond beyond the Beyond looked at their respective watches and spoke as one.

"Since it's a holiday, we've probably already missed the last bus back to The Future. If you don't mind, we'd all really like to stay for the party!"

Cosmic Relaunch

ꮥ WHEN, BY NATURE and long habit, One can be everywhere at once, taking shape in only two places at the same time is effortless in the extreme.

"Enjoying yourselves?" a familiar voice inquired. Scheherazade turned, finding herself eye to eye with a small white-and-gold bird perching easily and unconcerned on her left shoulder.

How long ago had it been since the same little emissary had flown through her open window, bringing with it an invitation impossible to refuse. How long ago too, it seemed, since she had first heard that same, now so unmistakeable voice welcoming her to Heaven itself.

Auspicious though the inimitable little bird's reappearance might be, Scheherazade couldn't keep from laughing. "The last time we met, as I recall, You were much bigger and considerably more radiant."

"Still am," eternity's most effervescent astrophysicist confessed, one wing tip gesturing to the reviewing stand where a glowing ball of light was simultaneously enjoying the passing parade. "It's one of the more pleasurable rewards of My position: no matter the occasion, I get to dress as I like, go where I want, anywhere and everywhere simultaneously."

The new arrival ran a gleaming beak over shimmering feathers, clearly luxuriating in an enduring favourite among an infinity of disguises. "Under the circumstances, this particular choice seemed suitably discreet as well as eminently practical. The proverbial bird's eye view, as it were!"

"Afternoon, Boss," said Big D warmly, long hidden halo now elegantly askew.

Given what he liked to call their unique family history, the intrepid

Chairman of the Intergalactic Senior Devils' Association always knew it was only a matter of time before The One And Only made a sudden, perfectly-judged reappearance. Even if (as the universe was beginning better to appreciate) the particular form in which God chose to arrive was usually impossible to guess in advance.

"Good afternoon to you, My stealthy old friend," God replied, looking Big D in the eye and the heart.

"My compliments on such truly magnificent efforts over these past few weeks." The little gold-and-white bird cocked its small head. "Just so you know, I'm very, very proud of you!"

Big D flushed an even more becoming, if rather touching, shade of crimson.

"So am I," Scheherazade echoed, their fingers interlaced.

❦

"So ... it turns out to be true," Scheherazade ventured teasingly.

"What's true?" God replied, happy to go along.

"That You do work in mysterious ways, Your wonders to perform." Scheherazade's eyes widened.

"Seems to suit Me somehow," the little bird answered laconically. "Or so I'm told."

There was a long pause while still more teams continued to pass, and God, Scheherazade and Big D simply savoured one another's company.

"Thanks for inviting me, in Your own inimitable fashion, way back when," the most beautiful secret agent in the universe whispered softly. "Adventures You promised; adventures You definitely provided."

"My pleasure." The little white-and-gold bird inclined its head to the ever-gallant, ever-vigilant gentleman at Scheherazade's side. "Although I shouldn't really take all the credit. In fact, given what I know of Big D's talents, I'm exceedingly tempted to say the devil made Me do it!"

"The pleasure is mine," the current Chairman of the Intergalactic Senior Devils' Association replied with a suitably saintly grin.

"Any plans – after this is all over?" God continued, gesturing to the ongoing wonders of the first-ever Heavenly Games of Love.

"How unsurprising You should ask." Scheherazade's voice was excited and slightly shy. "We were just discussing the possibility of a little, well-deserved getaway. Somewhere private – sun, shade and sea combined."

"A nice little tropical paradise, perhaps?" God inquired blandly. "I may still know of a few. Untouched. Tranquil. Totally discreet."

"Very tempting offer," Big D exclaimed. "And thanks, but no thanks. Remember, I've already got a fairly good idea how these things can turn out. Despite Your best intentions, of course!"

"Sorry." The little bird spread its white-and-gold wings, shrugging winningly. "Force of habit."

There was a well-timed pause.

"Actually...," God smiled, all-seeing eyes holding Scheherazade and Big D gently yet effortlessly. "When you get back from your travels – if, that is, you happen to be interested – I may have a new job opening."

The little bird swept a shimmering wing-tip over the Heavenly Games stadium, the hidden yet ever-encircling stars, and a little blue-and-white planet continuing to wave its bold new banners, its newly-inspired citizens now clearly in no immediate danger of relapse.

"We've known each other for quite some time...."

Big D nodded. It was unquestionably true: so much holy water under so many spiritually wobbly bridges.

"And though it's certainly taken long enough," God continued, pointing to the now even more exuberant march-past, "this particular cosmos finally seems to be getting the hang of it."

"And so?" Big D inquired warily.

When it came to the many celestial subtleties of charm, entice and lure, Creation's pre-eminent devil knew he would forever be outclassed. Not that he really minded, since his own best supporting role looked better the better the leading actor was.

"And so maybe it's time for a change!" Eternity's chief entrepreneur replied, spreading white-and-gold wings. "Time to think even bigger!"

The little bird tilted its head. "Since I happen to own the entire cosmos, I can't very well do a private equity buy-out with Myself." There was a judicious pause. "On the other hand, what would you say if I told you I was thinking of opening ... a brand new universe?!"

Their visitor raised a tiny eyebrow, then continued. "A chance to make up for, how shall I say, some of My earlier, more regrettable design flaws."

Scheherazade did not hesitate. "Such as?"

The little bird blinked ruefully. "Well, take your pick: death, disease, income tax. Just for starters."

There was a long silence, while Big D savoured the pleasure of earlier suspicions confirmed. And Scheherazade the presence of a companion who, despite so many aeons away on foreign service, clearly hadn't lost his old celestial touch.

Before Big D could reply, the little bird added, "And I could certainly use a good devil. Emeritus or otherwise."

"So could I," Scheherazade interposed quickly.

࿐

"Alright, leave it with Me. I'll see what I can do."

The little white-and-gold provocateur gently touched its beak to Scheherazade's cheek, winking affectionately at Big D before preparing to fly off to the huge reviewing stand to rejoin its own larger, more luminously-visible expression of omnipresent divinity. "After all, I…."

"Do believe in love," Scheherazade declared triumphantly, her smile just as capable of making both Heaven and Hell instantly weak at the knees.

"Game, set and, in this case, a perfect match!" the genuine, original Supreme Being *Extraordinaire* replied contentedly, given that everything that had recently happened also just happened to have been God's idea in the first place.

࿐

As the competitors continued their second circuit of the Heavenly Games Stadium, the supporters from vast and various galaxies – all having quickly lost sight of their home sides now happily intermingling – began cheering, instead, for that greater, grander, more glorious combined spiritual force that was Team Universe as a whole.

In the winding parade, beaming angels happily borrowed their nearest colleagues' pitchforks, hoisting them skywards with an ease and agility suggesting that they too had their own well-concealed demonic powers. At the same time, grinning devils hastily snatched up an enormous number of angelic haloes in turn; also finding, as they secretly expected, that they fit (almost) perfectly.

The Archangel of All Archangels, looking on, smiled to himself. It was heartening to see his charges beginning to discover for themselves the subtle wisdom of the greatest saints and sages, most especially that overriding virtue which he himself liked to call spiritual ambidexterity: namely, the hard-won ability to understand one's apparent opposites and adversaries from within, all the better to love and let love.

He looked to his left, and saw Big D looking at him equally shrewdly from the stands, hand in hand with the second most beautiful woman in the universe.

The two old comrades faced one another and bowed.

§**

Where better a place to be, God thought once more, than on so resplendent a throne of light, on such a day, contentedly watching the combined power, pleasure and purpose of Team Universe go by.

There was a sudden tiny tug on an invisible hand. Looking down, God gazed into the troubled, shy but deeply determined, ever-beguiling purple eyes of a small yellow monkey.

"Hello, Aurora."

The little Curator of the Cosmic Museum of Historical *Culs-de-Sac* blinked. "You know my name!"

"Of course I do," God replied softly.

The little visitor tilted her head cautiously, appraisingly. "These Heavenly Games of Love are wonderful!" Aurora ventured slowly. "All sorts of beings from fascinating galaxies I've never heard of. All kinds of exciting possibilities and prospects."

"I'm so glad you like them," God said, then smiled. "But...."

"But...," the small yellow monkey agreed, biting her lip. "I do have a question."

God nodded, waiting serenely.

"A big one." Aurora drew herself up, little chin jutting out, gaze fixed, determined to be brave, whatever the answer. "Tell me everything ... about evolution," she whispered.

The mysterious source of the biggest, loudest bang ever (so far) reached down, gently lifting the little yellow monkey into welcoming arms, an invisible luminous hand smoothing the fine, soft, slightly damp fur of her forehead, soothing the anxious rhythm of a small and trembling heart.

"Once upon a time...", God began tenderly.

"In other words," said a beaming Aurora, "all things are possible!"

"That has generally been My experience," God acknowledged, voice lowered so that only the small yellow monkey could hear. "Offhand, I can think of a least a hundred million constellations, across the whole universe, where…."

Unable to help herself, and knowing that God would most definitely understand, Aurora did a fast somersault. And then two more.

"I feel better already!"

"You must come to tea when all this is over," God mused, thinking far ahead into an increasingly abundant, multi-dimensional future. "I think it's time we had a talk about expanding your resumé."

"I'd like that," Aurora answered. "Very much."

⚜

As the last of the great parade was completing its second turn of the stadium, the Heavenly Games Celestial Coordinating Committee double-checked their watches and the slanting celestial sun.

Bathed in its deepening glow, the Angel of Cosmic Fireworks re-read the little white-and-gold note just handed to him, then began once more to revise his often-rewritten schedule, angling for that precise magical meeting point of night and light.

⚜

The infinitely spectacular opening ceremonies of the Heavenly Games of Love appeared to be almost over and the residents of Earth were in a quandary. Miraculously, they had come trillions of miles in mere moments so as to cheer on Team Earth and, just as importantly, to see up-close and personal that singular woman who was, to them, the most beautiful and talented Eve in the entire universe.

The Sun, however, while it wouldn't have missed this day's celebrations for anything, had belatedly (and most unfortunately) just remembered it had a long-scheduled, if largely routine constellational sub-committee meeting (on the steadily increasing costs of satellite debris collection) early next morning back where it usually belonged.

Under these extraordinary circumstances, it wondered aloud, perhaps something could be arranged…?

The residents of planet Earth, for their part, would have been happy to stay in, or more accurately, fairly near Heaven for eternity (or at least the next few weeks) watching the Games unfold, cheering on every competitor, and waving their little blue-and-white flags with expansive abandon.

On the other hand, however, given the breadth, depth and height of their new-found selflessness, they also didn't want to impose on their own much larger galaxy any more than they already had.

Then again, this was a uniquely special occasion. Who knew what might still happen?

"May we please stay a little while longer – at least till it gets dark?" they asked with one voice.

Homecoming

᪥ GENTLY NUDGING HIS little white cloud once more to rest before the great reviewing stand, Abracadabra helped his passengers to disembark.

Eve, remaining on board a little longer, waved fondly to her sister namesakes in the section reserved for the other founding mothers, then rested her head on Adam's shoulder. Such a long day – after so much longer and eventful a journey.

While the Games of Love, which were to follow the parade, might still be just beginning, her work here, and his, rightly appeared to be coming to an end. While Eve had tried to do her dedicated, fallible best to help the universe onwards, it was with gratitude and relief that she entrusted it once again to infinitely more capable, experienced hands. Even if they happened to be – most of the time, at least – so compellingly invisible.

Outlined in gold by the setting celestial sun, a vanished Eden's paragons turned to one another once more.

"Where next?" Adam asked, taking Eve's hand, the prospect of time, space and all their restrictive, propulsive demands already beginning to open around them once more.

"More of the same, probably," Eve replied, looking at the silent, watching crowds from every corner of Creation, then whispering confidently against his cheek. "Works of faith…."

"And labours of love."

"Wherever they may lead."

There silence while Earth's first couple contemplated the future.

"Don't suppose there's any chance of taking our own small vacation first?" Eve sighed softly. "All in all, it's been a very long day!"

With evident delight, Adam brought from behind his back a pair of white-and-gold tickets. "Care to join me in a leisurely intergalactic cruise – for two? A little farewell present, 'To the ultimate come-back kids, with our deepest admiration and gratitude, from Big D, the Archangel-in-Chief and *tout le gang*.'"

"Glad though I may be that this particular job is ending," Eve replied, "I've got a feeling I'm really going to miss the fringe benefits!"

Showing up long before being invited, answering well in advance of being called, God seemed always to have an inimitable, unfailing way of anticipating events or unconscious demands. Especially when, as in the case of this truly special day, something extra appeared to be required – a celestial finishing touch.

The great radiant ball of light turned, opening invisible arms toward that contingent of too often under-appreciated planetary founding mothers of Creation, standing together with their equally resilient consorts.

"Ladies and gentlemen, esteemed friends, and truly illustrious co-creators: I'd be profoundly honoured if you would join Me now, in the most well-deserved ride of your long and irreplaceable lives!"

At God's side, it was the Archangel-in-Chief's turn not to resist what was, after all, also the ultimate angelic accolade.

"It's ... show-time!"

As a perfectly-timed, perfectly-tinted evening slipped over Heaven's towers, the great radiant ball of light joined Adam and Eve at the front of the first little white cloud, her cosmic sisters and their partners happily packing themselves into the six that followed.

At a signal from Abracadabra, all seven lifted off simultaneously and, to the cheers of the crowd and the delight of countless galaxies across the universe, the original parents of so many planets in so many ever-more remote constellations began to circle the huge Heavenly Games Stadium. The elegantly top-hatted Angel of Tender Yet Terrifying Rhapsodies led the Big Band & Be-Bop Orchestra in a long lost composition now magically re-found: the once plangent, now triumphant Gardens of Eden Waltz.

As the last rays of a celestial sun transformed the little clouds into flaming chariots of pink and purple and gold, the Angel of the Golden Hammer plunged the world into darkness, and a new, vibrant stillness.

An instant later, in an ultimate display of divine *joie de vivre*, that omnipresent energy everywhere known as God disappeared once more into light; flashing outwards in every direction to ignite a trillion newly-beckoning fires on the farthest edges of a universe still in the making.

Everywhere, a still small voice was heard: "Go as far as your heart and soul can see … and then see how far you still can go."

Throughout the universe, angels and devils, coaches and competitors, officials, guests and spectators drew the same, shared breath.

In the morning, as scheduled and promised, the first-ever Heavenly Games of Love would go on. Seen or unseen, God would be there, forever nearer to everyone than they were to themselves.

High above the great stadium of Heaven, Adam and Eve tenderly embraced one another and, together, a now incomparably larger future once again. To one side, on a little blue-and-white planet called Earth, billions of people stared towards the distant beacons of paradises to be found and earned: silently committed to all the universe had yet to do, all it could – and would – one day become.

Apart from Earth's performance in the Heavenly Games, its citizens – so affected by the preparation for the Games – had already dedicated themselves to a challenge worthier by far; valiantly to fight the God-given struggles of each new day, until at last they, their ancestors and their descendants would finally stand at the welcoming gates of a now universal paradise regained, triumphant, humble and proud, having helped to win for a fully-awakened cosmos and for themselves … the promised, final, far-off victory of Love.

Neil Cole wrote this book at his home in Toronto
from Christmas 2006 until Easter 2014, as he expressed it.
He died three days later.

જી.

His manuscript ended with the following quotations:

The fulness of joy is to behold God in everything
— Dame Julian of Norwich, *Meditations*

The first thing God made is love …
The first thing God made is the long journey
— George Seferis, *Stratis Thalassinos Among the Agapanthi*

Be not forgetful to entertain strangers:
For thereby some have entertained angels unawares
— Hebrews 13:2

www.ingramcontent.com/pod-product-compliance
Lightning Source LLC
Chambersburg PA
CBHW020833030726
47496CB00001B/209